Hidden in the Stars

(a Falling Stars novel)

Sadie Grubor

ISBN-13: 978-1514788622
ISBN-10: 1514788624

Dedication:

In remembrance of Dahlias, buckwheat pancakes, and Christmas.
-    FOR G-Ma

Acknowledgements:

Mister Grubor – Thank you for kicking my brain into gear when I can't think of the word I'm thinking of. ☺ Nothing but love for you, baby!

Family – Thanks for supporting me and my crazy efforts.

Monica – You totally get where I'm going and trying to say, and that's not easy when half the time I don't know what the heck I'm doing. ☺

The BETA Babes – If it weren't for you ladies, I wouldn't have the motivation to kick out word counts, chapters, and new ideas for upcoming books. I appreciate your willingness to chat and guide me so much.

Grubor Groupies – You all are amazing supports and great fun! Thank you.

iTunes and YouTube – Again, thank you for the never ending source of music to inspire my moods and ease my soul.

Table of Contents

Blurb

When you're Jackson Shaw, guitarist of The Forgotten, and your heart's been broken, shattered by the deception of a woman you thought was the one. When you can't hide from cameras and millions of fans hanging on every dirty detail printed and posted...

When you swear off love and dull the ache with gorgeous women who look nothing like the girl who tore you apart—a supermodel girlfriend and sexplicit escapades splashed across the tabloids is the ultimate revenge. It's also the perfect way to hide your pain in the media. But when the ache turns to a hollow pit and there isn't enough sex, drugs, or alcohol to fill the emptiness, what do you do?

You cut your losses and head to L.A. to mentor the latest reality talent show. You follow an old friend into a world where the art of the bump and grind was perfected. Where the sound of her voice calls to every primal instinct buried within your body and makes the demand for your attention.

Jackson's an addict and just one taste puts him back in the precarious position of falling in love with a woman who's mastered the art of ensnaring and teasing.

The End of Us
Jackson

It's everywhere. The TV, internet...the fucking tabloids. My fucking girl going into a hotel at three in the fucking morning with a random fucking dude. And just to make it more painful, they plastered fucking GIF images all over the internet. Groping, Kissing, Laney giving just as good as she was getting from the asshole who ended it all.

The fact that she called to confess before the media ran with the story means shit to me. I offered the cheating bitch my heart on a goddamn platinum tray and what did she do? She shit all over it.

All around me, my brothers are getting married, having fucking kids, and starting a new phase in their life. A phase I cannot think about without wanting to vomit. And it's all thanks to a heartless, selfish slut.

She didn't even want to work things out. Just confess and walk away, as if I'm just some guy off the fucking street, not the man she's been practically living with and talked about starting a life together.

Well, fuck her and every douchebag she spreads her legs for. I didn't want some white picket fence fantasy and I sure as fuck don't want to be in love with someone who cares so little.

A jerk of my arm and a flick of my wrist sends my cell crashing into the flat screen TV on the wall. Snorting a humorless laugh, I put the bottle of Captain to my mouth and drain the last of the 1.75 liters.

Slamming the bottle onto the tabloid covered table, I stare at the picture of Laney in dark sunglasses, holding a hand out to cover her face. A blurry male face just over her shoulder makes me wonder if this is her new man—my replacement.

Fuck you, Laney. I can move on from you just as quickly as you have from me.

Chapter One

Jackson Shaw

The Forgotten sitting in a studio working on our next single and upcoming CD feels like fucking déjà vu. Elliott drumming his sticks on the soundboard. Jimmy strumming on his bass in a corner, ignoring the way our lead singer and my step-brother, Christopher, tears into Elliott.

Chris threatens to shove the drumsticks up Elliott's ass, and he responds with a grin, saying, "You know just the way I like it, baby."

Slipping my guitar from my lap, I grab Elliott's sticks out of his hands and set them on the table in front of me.

Pouting, Elliott grabs the iPad from a nearby table and plops down into one of the chairs. Chris rubs his face, releases an annoyance filled sigh, and returns his attention to the soundboard.

It's been fucking months since we've been together like this, which is a goddamn shame. Because the walls surrounding each of us never used to be like this. We used to be together each day and night; working and playing. But life gets in the way and things—people—have a way of destroying the things you once loved most.

"Dude, this guy sucks." Elliott sits with his iPad resting against his legs, his feet now kicked up on the sound table.

"Get your fucking feet down," Chris growls, a scowl marring his face.

"I'm just saying, I could sing better than this douchebag." He brings his feet down, but keeps up the conversation. "Have you listened to these yet?" he asks, looking up from his lap.

I shrug. "Most of them."

"I still can't believe you agreed to this," Jimmy scoffs from his lounged position on the leather couch. "I hate those fucking reality shows."

I shrug again.

"Listen to this one!" Elliott's already chuckling when he turns up the sound.

"Christ, who picked these people?" Chris shakes his head and stands from his chair, walking over to Elliott.

"A board of music professionals chose the hundred online contestants," Elliott says, pointing to the list of names alphabetically displayed.

"Why didn't you get to help choose?" Chris asks, looking over at me for answers.

"I didn't want to."

"Why the hell not?" Chris moves back to his seat.

"I agreed to coach and mentor for ten long ass weeks. I'm sure as fuck not doing anything else with these fame hungry assholes," I answer, wishing this conversation would end. The ring of a cell phone grants my request.

"Hey, baby, what's up?" Elliott grins. "What time?" He nods.

"She can't see you, dipshit," Jimmy says, chuckling.

Elliott scowls and flips his thick middle finger up at him.

"Okay, babe, I'll pick it up on the way home...I love you, too." He ends the call.

"So, back to this contest—"

"No," I growl.

It's bad enough I agreed to do this, hearing about it all the time is beyond annoying. Between my parents, the band, the girls, and the hype this damn show is already getting, I'm over it.

The click of the studio door brings a welcome distraction.

"Mia," Chris croons.

As soon as Mia's within reach, he grabs her hips, pulling her onto his lap.

"Hey, guys," Mia greets, allowing Chris to situate her.

"Hey, guys?" he scoffs. "I'm the important one."

Turning her head, she places her lips on his before pulling back just a bit. Foreheads pressed together, a breath away from each other, she smiles. "Hi."

"That's better." With a large grin on his face and a hand on her thigh, Chris settles back into his chair. "Well, assholes, don't be rude. She said hello."

We all greet Mia in unison, heeding to Chris' demand. I don't have to look around to know I'm not the only one shaking my head. Hush Mentality toured with us almost two years ago during our Soul Abandonment Tour. Mia, their lead singer, had flipped a switch inside of Christopher. She'd brought him to life after years of living in the darkest hells of his own memories. And I swear, the minute he got the engagement ring on her finger, he became more obsessed...no, arrogant...no... *wait, what's the word?* Cocky, obsessed, arrogant bastard—that's it.

With talk of the show over, we go back to working on some new tracks. Mia offers her input, Elliott argues with Jimmy about bass, and Chris keeps *correcting* the knobs when I move them.

In my peripheral, I see everything Chris does to Mia. Palming Mia's breast, slipping a finger into the back of her jeans, kissing the side of her neck, and pulling her down harder onto his lap are just some of the things I wish I hadn't seen. She slaps him away, but he isn't easily deterred.

Maybe ten weeks away from this group wouldn't be so bad. Seeing Mia and Chris only intensifies the hollowness I carry inside. And, hell, seeing Mia makes me think about Laney.

Hushed Mentality hadn't only brought Mia into our fold, but the entire all-girl band. Serena: drummer, older sister to Mia, and now wife to Elliott. Kat, their bassist and all around free spirit in the group. And Laney, Hush's lead rhythm guitarist.

Fucking Laney!

As much as I don't want to admit it, Laney's betrayal still crushes me. The first month after she cheated, I drowned myself in booze. After that, I spent about five months buried balls deep in multiple women, trying to fuck her out of my system. Booze, sex, and the revolving door of female company didn't erase her. Nothing seemed to worked. Whenever I feel like I'm finally over her, the bitch manages to bring me back to my knees.

Like when she started dating the actor used in the last Hush video. It shouldn't have bothered me, but the hurt tore through me like dull razors.

"Hey, Jack, I saw Kristyna's Gucci ad. She looks fantastic." Mia smiles, but she isn't good at hiding how she feels. Her eyes reflect sadness. She always tries to talk to me about my "womanizing and partying" ways, telling me it's not who I am.

"You aren't this guy, Jack. This guy isn't the same one I spent months discussing classic rock and pop songs with," was how Mia ended our last conversation about my life.

It wasn't as bad as she, Chris, and my parents thought. I was just having a good time with fun people.

"On TV or the billboard?" I ask.

"TV." She pulls Chris' hand from between her legs.

"That one is *so hot,*" Elliott purrs. "I just have two questions. How can you stand some other dude having his hands on her tits? And how the fuck do I get that kind of job?"

Mia leans to the side and narrows her eyes on Elliott.

"What?" he shrugs. "I love your sister, but we are talking about a job where you hold boobs."

Mia shakes her head, laughing.

My cell vibrates against my thigh and I lean back, slipping it from my pocket.

"Speaking of Miss Please Hold My Boobs..." Elliott leans over my shoulder as Kristyna's picture flashes on the screen.

When none of my efforts to forget Laney were working, I decided to cut out the multiple women and settle on one who likes to have fun and can handle the crowds. Kristyna Molvic, the fashion world supermodel, is used to publicity, rumors, likes a good party, and welcomes the media attention following our every move. The celebrity bad boy and fashion's sweetheart—our media coverage is frequent and sexplicit. Kristy still has a way of coming across as the sweet girl being corrupted, though. If only they knew the fucking truth.

From the moment Kristyna and I were introduced through a mutual friend, she demanded my attention. Our first night out together, she incorporated other women: bringing other hot girls to grind against me, encouraging sexy socialites to lick different substances from my body...things only she could convince these paparazzi princesses to do. I was a bit put off the first time I watched her snort coke off a girl's bare tit, but Kristyna is ever the seductress with skills rivaling mythological sirens.

The first time cocaine entered my system was in the back of a limo on the way to an award ceremony. I was in a funk knowing I would run into Hush and Laney.

Always needing to be the center of the universe, Kristyna straddled me in the back of a car—designer evening gown pulled to her waist, sans underwear. When her mouth crashed against mine, bitterness invaded. I pushed her back. The shit tasted horrible. She only grinned.

"Trust me, baby. You will feel as fantastic as I do right now." Taking a vial out of her purse, she sprinkled the white powder into her cleavage and leaned forward. "Don't you want to feel good?"

I hesitated still.

"You won't believe how amazing it is to fuck when you're high." She slipped the straps of her thin dress from her shoulders, the material catching on strapless lace cradling her tits. Cupping her breasts, she pushed closer and ground herself against me.

My cock stirred to life in a rush of heat and need. Grabbing her ass firmly, I pulled her against me harder, leaned forward, and buried my nose in her cleavage.

Kristyna's hand grabbed the back of my head, pulling me away to look into my eyes.

"Give me your tongue." She tightened the grip on my hair and my cock pulsed with the mixture of pleasure and pain.

I offered my tongue as a sacrifice to this goddess. Guiding me by my head, she ran my tongue between her breasts to clean the rest of the powder from her soft skin. When she pulled my mouth away, she crushed her lips to mine and sucked my tongue, giving me a preview of what she would do with my dick.

The moment she released my tongue, my head fell back against the seat. The incredible sensations running through my body made me feel like I could rule the world. Nothing else mattered. Only us. When she undid my pants, pulled my aching cock from its confines, and fucked me till we arrived at the award show, I knew I'd found one fucking hot piece of distraction. A distraction Christopher hated more than anyone else.

Hearing it's Kristyna calling, Christopher mumbles something. Knowing how he feels about her, I really don't want to start the same old argument again. He could tell me how I only put up with her because she was the complete opposite of Laney and enables my "out of control behavior" some other time. What a fucking hypocrite.

"What's up?" I answer.

"Hey there, sexy," she hums. "Are we still on for tonight?"

"Of course." I settle back into my chair. "Nine o'clock, right?"

"Yep. Pick me up at my townhouse."

"Will do."

"Bye," she says, making a kissing noise through the phone.

"Later."

"I can't believe you're with that—"

"Christopher," Mia warns.

"What? I can't!" Moving Mia from his lap, he leans toward me. "Why are you fucking around with some dimwitted bitch?"

"Fuck you, Chris." Stuffing my cell back into my pocket, I push away from the sound table and stand. "You don't have to like her, I do."

"You mean a nice fuck buddy, who likes to get as wasted as you," Elliott chimes in.

"You, too?" I round on Elliott and then turn to Jimmy. "What about you? You have something to add?"

Jimmy shakes his head. "Fuck no. At least you're dipping your stick in a hot piece of ass."

Mia's groan pulls my attention toward her.

"I know you don't approve either, so don't act like you're interested in my relationship," I snap, taking out my anger on Mia.

"Hold up, fucker." Chris stands, putting himself between Mia and me. "Don't talk to her like that!"

"Chris." Mia slides a hand over his arm, gently pulling him back toward her.

"Christ!" I push my fingers through my overgrown hair. "Just back the fuck off. I'm having a good time. There's nothing wrong with that, especially after the shit Lane...*she* put me through."

With quick, heavy steps, I make it to the door, ready to leave. Pausing quickly, I turn back to Mia. Her eyes, sadness swimming in them, meet mine.

"I'm sorry, Mia."

She nods, offering a small smile.

"Kristy, you ready to go?" I ask. She's finally brought her high ass back to our VIP area.

"Why?" she asks, breathless from dancing. She sticks out her bottom lip and slips onto the red couch. "Aren't you having a good time?"

"I'd rather go back to your place and have a better time." Tossing a wink at her, I lift the glass to my mouth.

She makes a purring noise and slides across two of her friend's laps, laying her head on my thighs. Her long, thick, blonde hair fans over my legs as she nuzzles my crotch. I drop my head back onto the couch and close my eyes as arousal heats my thighs. Hands caress my chest and damp lips press against my neck.

At first, I don't think about the fact that Kristy's face is still nuzzling, so it can't be her kissing me. When the lips press against my mouth, my eyes shoot open. Instead of Kristy's dark brown, I'm looking into summer-sky blue.

This wouldn't be the first time a third joined us—hell, a fourth—but my arousal instantly flees. I shove the girl away and she squeaks in protest.

"What's wrong?" Kristy asks, popping out of my lap.

"I'm not in the mood." Bringing my tumbler glass back to my

lips, I drain the last of my watered-down drink.

"Not in the mood?" Kristy straightens, eyeing me suspiciously. "Since when, are you not in the mood to be fucked by two women?"

With I shrug, I sniff and set my glass on the low table in front of us. My buzz is wearing off. "Just not."

"Fine," she huffs. Slipping from the couch, she puts a hand out to her friend and pulls her up from the sofa. Her angry eyes shoot back to me. "I'll just find someone who won't turn the two of us down."

"You know I don't share, Kristy." Narrowing my eyes on her, she tosses a haughty look over her shoulder before moving into the crowd. "Kristy?!"

Fuck, she's crazy. Why do I put up with this shit? My head spins. *Christ, I need a bump.*

Growling, I stand from the couch and blend into the gyrating crowd in search of her.

Bodies grinding, sliding, sweating...the atmosphere once held appeal. The VIP treatment, celebrities, music, girls, drugs and drinks—this place was so locked down, you could get away with almost anything in here. And Kristy was the one who showed me the way. It had been exactly what I thought I needed and wanted. To get lost in numbness. To feel without fear. I used to get that here. But now? Fuck. Now I was dealing with a six-foot blonde woman known for her tantrum throwing tendencies. I swear, holding her breath and stamping her foot was not out of the question.

"Kristy?!" She and her friend are grinding against some young pretty boy who has his hands in all the wrong places. Wrong, because she's here with me and while we may dabble with other women in our bed, there are no other men involved.

The look she gives me is pure defiance and the hand she slips to his crotch is done to taunt me. "Don't you think it's hot to watch me with another guy?" Extending her tongue from her mouth, she leans forward and licks the kid's neck. His head drops back and his mouth parts, his visible hand high on her bare thigh.

"You know I don't," I growl, and step closer, pulling her off the pretty boy.

"Don't grab at me!" She pulls away from me, her arm quickly slipping free. "You know, I let you have other women and don't say a thing."

"It was your idea for the threesomes and you chose the girls," I argue back.

"If I let you choose the girl, can I choose a boy? We could pick a couple to—"

"No," I growl. Her eyes narrow.

"Fuck you, Jackson! You don't own me. I could find ten other guys who would love to share me." Crossing her arms over her chest, she stands defensively.

"So, this is how it's going to go now." It's not a question. "You want to be treated like a whore, be my guest. But you won't be my whore." Turning, I leave her on the dance floor, still fuming.

"Jackson!" she screeches, her voice actually louder than the thumping music. "Jackson Shaw, do you know what you are giving up?!"

Without turning around, I give a wave over my head. This trip to L.A. couldn't come at a better time. I'll gladly put up with tone-deaf and uncharismatic wannabes if it means getting away from this shit.

Apparently, no woman in my life can be happy with me. Hopefully, Randall can hook me up with a few rails of the good shit. This shit she brought isn't doing a damn thing.

Chapter Two
Jackson

Walking through LAX, I try to stay incognito—black beanie hat, dark glasses, my *NSYNC t-shirt, just for laughs, and jeans. However, at almost seven feet tall, it's virtually impossible not to stand out.

The cameramen move in, fans try to slip next to me for pictures and autographs. Even with the bodyguard assigned to me during this trip, they still push and shove. It doesn't bother me. In fact, it's pretty flattering. But when the paps start with the questions, I want to slam the cameras into their faces.

"Jackson, is it true you are in town to meet up with Laney?" one overweight pap calls out.

"No comment," I growl. *Of course, she's fucking here.*

"Are you here to stop her from marrying Hollywood's golden boy?"

"No comm—"

She's getting married?

"Were you invited to their secret ceremony?" another pap shouts.

"No, I wasn't." Gritting my teeth, it takes everything in me not to lash out.

"Is there anything you want to say to Laney and Chanse on their special day?" This time, it's an attractive man with a video camera following him. He looks familiar and it only takes a minute to recognize the well-known web-based gossip show host.

"Best wishes," I call out, and slip into my waiting car.

Settling back into the leather seat, the divider window lowers.

"You okay, boss?" The bodyguard-slash-driver, who

identified himself as Sam, twists in the front seat to look over.

"Call me Jackson. I'm cool."

With a nod, he turns to the steering wheel, starts the car, and pulls out.

Just as I lay my head back, my phone rings. *Fuck.*

"What, Chris?" I sigh.

"It's Mia."

"Why are you calling me on Chris' phone?" There's no hiding the annoyance I feel.

"I knew you wouldn't ignore him." She forces a laugh. "No matter what, you guys are always there for each other. It's why he loves you so much."

"Mia, if this is about the argument before I left, you should know it's all good."

"Oh, I know. It's just...well, bloggers work fast."

I growl and drop my chin to my chest, using the pad of my thumb and index finger to rub my eyes. "They got that broadcasted quick enough."

"She's not, you know?"

"Why would I care?"

"Jack, come on. I know you still care. I just want you to know she's not."

"Is she in L.A.?"

Silence. It's the only response I need.

"So, she's here and she's with this Chanse guy." Not a question.

"Jack, she's—"

"Give me my phone!" Chris yells in the background.

"Stop it!" Mia yells back.

"Hey, man," Chris says, gaining control of his phone. "Fuck that whore."

"Christopher..." Mia's warning is muffled.

"Baby, this is between Jack and me. Listen, don't think or worry about her. L.A. is huge and you won't see each other."

What do I say? What am I supposed to say? That part of me wishes I would see her? Granted, it's the sick, masochistic side, but it still wants the very thing I shouldn't.

"You still there?" Chris barks.

"Yeah, I'm here. Are you done now?"

"Did you get in touch with Xavier?"

"Yeah, before the flight. We're going to meet up at the hotel. He wants to visit some club Redman's thinking about investing in."

Xavier Stone was the drummer for Corrosive Velocity, which was not only the first band we went on tour with, but the first where we were the opening act. Xavier had taken Chris under his wing early on in the tour. He was only a few years older than us, but had been on the tour circuit five times—he knew the ropes. We learned good things that first year, and some bad—Redman, their road manager, kept us in line and protected from too much trouble with Nicholas, though. The last time we'd all been together was for their lead singer's funeral five years ago.

Ethan Crowne had ignored his headaches and vision problems until it was too late. The best doctors tried chemotherapy and experimental treatments, but nothing worked against the brain tumor. When Ethan opted for surgery, everyone knew the risk was too great. Hell, finding a doctor to perform the surgery took forever. Corbin, Ethan's twin brother and fellow band mate, almost had him talked out of it. One hour into the surgery, Ethan was gone. Corrosive Velocity fell apart and each member went on to do solo projects.

Xavier now co-owns a small studio with his best friend, Randy, who was also the bassist for the band.

"Tell him I may be out that way while you're staying there. We'll have to get together."

"You going to introduce him to Mia?" A small smile creeps up the corner of my mouth.

"Fuck no. Lord knows he will use her to mess with me," Christopher scoffs.

My small smile blows up to a full, tooth-revealing grin. Chris and Xavier always messed with each other's women, until Xavier got married. But even then, Chris messed with his now ex-wife,

Maria, just to piss around. Nothing ever happened between them, but Chris would flirt a little too much just to rile him up. Thank God Maria was a good sport.

"True, he would, especially now that he's divorced."

"Exactly. Well, tell Red and Xavier they still owe me a drink."

"Okay, but I need a favor.

"Like?"

"Like keep an eye on my mom and Nic. I'm still not sure what's going on with them."

Their behavior is still causing concern. The worry often lining Nic's eyes, the quiet looks they would share when I last visited, and the way their happiness seemed false. Shit was off and they weren't sharing what the fuck is wrong with them.

"Me either, but I'll keep watch."

"Thanks."

"Just stay away from that bitch." Chris ends the call without a goodbye. *Typical.*

Sitting back into the seat, I close my eyes and tried not to think about Laney or Kristy. *"Are you here for the wedding?" How do I get that out of my mind? And why do I care so much?* Kristy was supposed to make all of it go away. Instead, I find myself easily leaving her behind without a second thought. Yet, Laney—fucking Laney—still knows how to rip me back open.

My cell blares from the seat next to me just as Sam announces our arrival to the hotel. Glancing at my phone, I see *her* number. It takes everything not to hit the decline button and send her ass to voicemail, but I've had enough.

"Quit fucking calling me," I greet.

The catch of her breath tugs at feelings I wish would die already.

"It's over, Laney, your choices are made and I'm not going to be best fucking friends with you."

"I just..." she hiccups.

"I don't care what 'you just'. In fact, I fucking hate hearing your voice, seeing your number show up, and...fuck, if I hear you say you're sorry one more time, I'm going to stab guitar picks in my ears," I say, my rant starting strong, but ending on a desperate plea.

Her sob goes straight to the unwanted feels in my chest. Fisting the material of my shirt just above my heart, I regroup and focus on my anger.

"We aren't going to be friends. Leave me the fuck alone."

"I know you can't forgive me, but I hate to lose the—"

"You know what? I hear a lot of I's from you. You're such a selfish bitch," I bark the last word. "Hate is all we have and loss is all that's left. Don't call me again, Laney. Just leave me the fuck alone."

I press the end button, not allowing her to make any further attempts.

The back door opens and with a deep breath, I climb out of the car, shoving my cell into my pocket. *Why would she call? Did she see the footage the gossip site put up? Fuck, I can't get to my room fast enough.*

I'm thankful for my dark sunglasses as I look up at the Bel-Air hotel. The sun has come out in full, eye-burning force and I'm still feeling the effects of partying withdrawal. Sam clears his throat, a noise made to get me moving. The sounds of camera shutters and murmurs of the gossip leeches finally force me into the hotel.

I step into the lobby, the cameras and questions silenced with the shutting of the glass doors. A small crowd turns to watch the commotion of my arrival while others carry an air of being too important to worry about me.

"G-good afternoon, Mr. Shaw." A small, round-faced girl with dark black hair done up like a 1950's pinup appears next to me, her right hand outstretched, her left holding a black leather portfolio. "I-I'm Julia, your personal assistant."

"I don't remember asking for an assistant." I keep my hands at my sides.

Her face drains of color and she drops her hand.

"T-the sh-show provides—"

Jesus, I'm making the girl a nervous wreck.

"Hey, sorry. I'm a dick." Putting my hand out, I wait for her to take it.

"I would never call you—"

"You might not, but you should," I laugh.

A tentative smile forms on her lips. She takes my hand and shakes firmly.

"So, what's the plan?" I slip my arm over her shoulders and walk toward the concierge waiting near the elevators. The nervous look on his face and the way his eyes watch me are the first clues he's waiting for me.

"Well, sir—"

"Listen, Julia, first things first, it's Jackson or Jack, not sir. Got it?" I wink.

"Okay, Jackson." She smiles. "This is William." She motions to the concierge. "He'll be taking us up to your suite."

"Great." I pull my arm from Julia's and clap my hands together, rubbing them. "Let's get going."

"Welcome to the Hotel Bel-Air, Mr. Shaw." William nods. "If you would, please follow me." He motions to the open elevator door behind him.

We step into the elevator and my cell phone vibrates in my pocket. *The last thing I need is a voicemail from her.*

"Julia," I say her name a bit abruptly, causing her to jolt in surprise. "What's on the schedule?"

"Tonight, you have plans to meet with Mr. Stone. I've arranged for a car to retrieve him and be here by eight to pick you up."

The surprise on my face stops her.

"Is there a problem?" Julia chews on her lip.

"How did you know about my plans tonight?" Furrowing my brow, I try to think of how she might have found out.

"It's my job to know." She winks.

I laugh. I like this girl.

Eliza Campbell

"Liza, you should've let me enter you," Sid whines without looking at me. Her eyes stay on the iPad as she goes through the contestants in the latest reality music show sweeping the internet: *Hidden Talent*. "Some of these people suck. I mean, they must have their whole hillbilly, redneck, mountaintop-wood-mutant family members voting for them." Her head pops up. "Huh, I didn't think you could get the internet in those backwoods areas."

"I've got enough to deal with without the reality show drama." Shaking my head, I continue hanging up today's clean clothes on a fifteen dollar clothing rack between my son and younger brother's rooms.

"You could win, I know it." Sid appears next to me, grabbing my son's clothes from a basket and taking them into his room. "There are so many shitty voices that are going to get to the next level. I swear, I don't know what people are thinking."

"I'm sure you made your feelings known," I laugh.

"Of course I did—on my blog, Twitter, Facebook, their site, and a few other necessary locations." She stands in the bedroom doorway with a look of self-satisfaction before leaning down, grabbing my brother's clothes, and walking into his room.

Sid, my wonderfully outspoken cousin, was visiting me in L.A. when an internet site began taking submissions from singers who wanted a chance at stardom. The catch? You have to sign on for public criticism, fan voting, and six weeks of live taping if you're chosen into the final twenty, which would be unveiled to the public for the final judging. And all of this while living with a group of competitors and being mentored by people from the music industry.

"Of course you did." I pick up the empty basket and walk down the small hallway, stopping at the bathroom where I find the damp towels left on the floor by the boys this morning. "Looks like it will be one more load today."

The worn couch, which also folds out to become my bed, sags under my weight.

"You need a washer and dryer." Sid sits next to me.

"Where do you suggest I put them?" I laugh, thinking about the size of my small two bedroom apartment. I'm surprised Sid fits when she visits.

"True," she giggles. "Your place is way too small."

Blunt as always, but I still love her.

"You need a new place." She looks at me with narrow eyes. "If you would've let me enter you, you could be on your way to fame and fortune right now."

"Yeah, okay." Kicking my feet up on the second-hand coffee table, I take a look at the small open space doubling as the living room and my bedroom. "It's not that bad." I shrug.

"Liza, why the hell don't you come back to Pittsburgh with me?" Sid turns on the couch, facing me. "Mom would help you out until we found you—"

"Your mom has done enough," I argue, giving her a frown. "She's the only one who cared when I was pregnant. I'll never be able to repay her for everything she did."

"Your poor excuse for parents should've been there for you," Sid grumbles. "But, anyhow, I hate seeing you struggle."

"I'm not struggling." Sighing, I lay my head back on the cushion and roll it to face her. "My apartment may be small, I may not have a washer and dryer, and it may not be glamorous, but I don't struggle."

"You know what I mean," Sid whines. "You have a voice that could open so many opportunities, but you work at a run-down burlesque club in East L.A. instead."

"Hey, you like coming to Lux Hedonica."

"Yes, but I still think you are better than the club," she huffs. "Besides the fact that Miss Jazzmin takes center stage, yet you could out sing her any day of the week."

"She's been the lead for years." Turning my head, I look up at the ceiling. We have this discussion every time she visits.

"And she'll stay that way now that she's married to your boss," Sid growls.

The couch cushions shift as Sid stands up, walking toward the kitchen. Since the only thing separating the rooms is a breakfast bar with seating for two, I see her pull out the last of the cheap wine.

"But you'll still be there tonight and you know it." I walk to the breakfast bar just in time for her to set a half-full glass of wine on the counter in front of me.

"It's my last night here, obviously I'm going to come watch you." She rolls her eyes and sips at the blackberry merlot.

"Then shut up, you hypocrite." Grinning, I take a sip of my own wine.

"I never said I made sense, but I am always right." She gives me her largest smile.

I shake my head and laugh.

"I'm going to miss you," I admit, sobering at the thought of her leaving again.

"Well, you will have to come visit me. You need to come see my new apartment once I move in," she says, forcing a smile. While I know she's excited about the new apartment she found, she, too, hates leaving.

When I found out I was pregnant with Lucas at fifteen, it was her mother, my aunt, who took me in after being kicked out by my parents. A debt I could never, ever pay back, not that Aunt Charlene would expect it.

Sid and I have always been close, but it was during my teenage pregnancy when we grew to be more like sisters more than cousins. She was like a second mother to Lucas, giving up high school dances to babysit while I waitressed at a local restaurant.

"I'll try." It's my standard response. I haven't been back to Pennsylvania since I was eighteen and old enough to pack Lucas and me on a bus to California.

Being a young mother made me grow up a lot, but I still held onto my youthful dreams of fame—making a name for myself as a singer and becoming a star. Then I'd be able to take care of Lucas and my aunt. Unfortunately, like most young girls in Hollywood, I learned too soon it wasn't like the movies.

I was rejected at most auditions, only landing a couple to find they would cut me later. Having a toddler with me also cost some opportunities, but my son always comes first.

At eighteen, I didn't have a lot of options. Not comfortable with stripping, I ended up waiting tables at a strip club. The hours were late and the crowd crude, but the tips were good. It was also easy to find a high school age girl in my building to sleep at my apartment with Lucas.

After waitressing for a little over a year, a co-worker, Anna, mentioned an opening at Lux Hedonica. Not fully understanding what burlesque and cabaret was at the time, I figured it was another strip club. I tagged along one afternoon when she applied and watched the girls practicing on stage. At that moment, I fell in love with the costumes, songs, and dancing. I inquired about being on stage and was referred to Thom, the owner. After singing and being shown a few dance moves to repeat, I was hired as a backup. So, I would waitress at the strip club and during the afternoons, rehearse with the dancers at Lux. When one of the girls quit, I got to take her spot. For six years, I've been an active entertainer at Lux.

"Yeah, yeah, yeah, that's what you always say." She gives me a knowing smile. "How are things with Kelvin?" She leans forward, placing her elbows on the counter.

"He's eighteen. How do you think they are going?" I snort, and take another drink from my glass.

My brother, Kelvin, came to live with me four years ago after my mother and father were killed in a car accident. Aunt Charlene tried to convince him to stay with her, but after his second attempt to run away to California, she let him have his way.

Lucas and I welcomed Kel with open arms, but I was definitely afraid of having a five-year-old and fourteen-year-old boy under my care. It's not like I made a bunch of money. Thankfully, my social worker found this two bedroom apartment, available to the housing authority, and was also able to help with assistance.

"So, he's still adamant about going to work full-time instead of college?" Sid asks with a sigh.

"Unfortunately. He thinks he needs to 'earn his keep' around here." I shake my head. "I wish he would take the tuition assistance we can get and go to college. He's too smart to get stuck washing dishes and bussing tables." I drain the last of my wine and place the empty glass on the counter.

"Time to finish the laundry?" Sid's lip curls in disgust.

"Yep." I nod.

"I hate the creepy basement laundry room." She shivers, emphasizing her statement.

"It's better than the laundromats around here." I raise my brow.

"Good point." She grabs the basket of clothes and walks toward the door. "Cross your fingers that Mick the Dick isn't down there," she calls over her shoulder, reaching for the doorknob and peeking out.

Laughing at the nickname she's given my creepy, perverted, but harmless neighbor, I exit the apartment with laundry soap and dryer sheets in hand.

"Though, he is the only guy who's hit on me the entire time I've been here," Sid mumbles.

"Stop it," I say, cutting off the conversation before she can even get started.

Sid may be bold and outspoken, but she holds an underlying insecurity: her weight. Being five-foot-four and roughly one hundred and seventy-five pounds—not that she would ever tell me her exact weight—she considered herself short and fat. Fact is, Sid's a curvy girl. But what she fails to see is the way men and women both eye her curves. Her rounded hips and butt draw almost as much attention as her double D chest. At least fifteen pounds alone was due to her cup size. She is a short, old school Hollywood starlet reincarnated as a computer and graphic art nerd.

"What? It's true. Your creepy neighbor is the only one who has hit on me," she snorts. "With you around, I can't get any attention."

"Didn't I tell you to stop?" I shove the laundry soap into the middle of her back.

"Ow, that hurt. I could've fallen down the steps." She sticks her bottom lip out.

"We aren't even to the stairs yet, drama queen," I laugh.

"Close enough." She shrugs, raising her chin.

We reach the stairs and descend to the laundry room level. As if we're on a spying mission, Sid tiptoes into the room, practically pressing her back against the wall.

"It's clear," she shouts, dropping the basket in front of an empty washer.

Stepping forward, I start loading the machine.

"Will tonight's show be the same? Or will it be something different?"

"Tonight will be different since it's Friday night. We'll go more modern, rather than the old school burlesque route. Next weekend will be old school stuff. It switches back and forth." With the last towel in the wash, I push in the coin tray and turn the washer knob to start the cycle.

Sid starts mumbling something under her breath.

"What now?" I jump up to sit on the washer.

"Oh, nothing. It's just a luck chant an old college roommate taught me." She shrugs.

"A chant?"

"Yeah, a chant. Too bad I don't have a curse for Jizzswallow." Her grin is mischievous and infectious. Soon, I'm smiling with her.

"Leave Jazzmin be, she's not so bad." Shaking my head, I jump off the washer. "Come on." I motion for Sid to follow. "I'll come back down in twenty to throw this stuff in the dryer. Lucas will be home soon."

"Is it that late already?" Sid asks, looking at her bare wrist. "I do need to spend some more time with him before we leave for the club."

"He'll love it."

Chapter Three
Jackson

After going over my schedule for the next week, Julia informs me of a package left by a guy named Randall and motions to a table near the entryway. Quickly, I make an excuse to retreat to the bathroom, snatching up the paper wrapped package along the way. Once in there, alone with my thoughts, I dig through my black carry-on bag until I reach my brown vial. Taking it out, I refill the little bottle and scoop some up before stashing the package back into my black leather bag. Two bumps later, I'm in a steaming shower, feeling remarkable.

When the car arrives at the hotel, just as Julia said it would, my mood is lighter and carefree. Coming face-to-face with Xavier brings back a ton of memories. I can't fight the smile taking over my face.

"My man." Xavier grasps me by the forearm. "Fuck, it's been too long." He pulls me in for the one arm bro-hug.

Flashes of light surround us, causing us both to slip quickly into the car. *Damn reporters!*

"Well, you let your hair grow, even tried to cover your face, but the beard doesn't hide that you're still ugly as fuck." Laughing, I settle into the backseat of the limo.

"Look here, you overgrown bastard." He flips his middle finger up, the smiley face tattoo complimenting the smile on his face.

"I don't fuck on the first date. Oh, wait, how old are your daughters?" I grin.

He scowls.

"Their only thirteen, you fucking pedophile."

I put my palms up between us. "Okay, so I've got five years."

"More like only if I'm dead, you little fucker."

"Little?" I raise my brow. "Have you seen the size of me?" I gesture to my crotch.

"Christ, you haven't changed a bit, have you?" His scowl melts into a grin.

"I'm a bit wiser." Shrugging, I see the look on his face. I know exactly where he's going to go and I'm powerless to stop it.

"Listen, man, I'm sorry about that Laney shit. You don't need that bitch. She didn't deserve you." He shakes his head, furrowing his brow.

"No big deal." My voice cracks unintentionally, but I shrug it off.

"Yeah, sure. Besides, you just have to get over that whore, ya know?"

I snort.

"What?" He gives me a curious look.

"Nothin'." With a shake of my head, the conversation changes.

We talk for the next forty minutes about old times on tour and I don't miss the edge of sadness in his voice. He clearly misses the band. Instead of opening up old wounds, I change the subject by asking where the hell Red has us going tonight.

Xavier grasps the subject change like a fucking lifeline. He tells me Redman will meet us at the club and is really serious about taking over the ownership. He also discloses that this is the first time he's asked anyone to come check the place out.

We pull up to a rundown brick building in East L.A. Stepping out of the car, I hear and feel the music coming from inside. Above two black doors, an arched red and purple neon sign flashes the words Lux Hedonica with a neon-lit pinup girl kicking a leg next to the name. Xavier and I look over to each other at the same moment.

"This is really it?" I raise one brow.

"Yep," he sighs, looking back toward the building. "It looks like a rundown strip club."

"I was thinking the same thing."

"The kind with cracked out, flabby strippers?" He catches my eyes again.

"Remember that one in Idaho?" I crack a smile.

"When we had that stripper with the C-section scar give Chris a lap dance?" He starts chuckling.

"That's the one," I laugh.

The poor girl tried to cover the scar with a poorly done tattoo, and it had clearly not been long after she'd received either of the marks. *Christ, we'd been some major assholes then.*

Walking through the doors, we're greeted by two large men dressed in black. They eye us both before allowing us to walk by. Next, we come to a wisp of a man in a top hat and a sleeveless red tuxedo.

"Welcome to Lux Hedonica. This evening you will be thoroughly entertained by our lovely display." Everything about this man is over the top, but it works.

"We're supposed to meet a friend. Redman." Xavier takes a small step forward.

"Ah, yes. He is expecting you in the VIP booth." With the removal of his hat and a grand bow, he extends an arm out, directing us to continue. As we pass, I notice the intricate dragon tattoo wrapped around his bald head.

"They have a VIP booth?" As I ask the question, my eyes soak up the velvet-lined walls. There are pictures of different dancers—some wearing feathers, others lace, and some with thin straps of material and tassels. The women are attractive, not strung out and withered. *I'm getting a better feeling about this place.*

"Well, fuck me," Xavier exclaims, pulling my attention forward.

Before us is a large room laid out with lush red, purple, pink, and gold. Red and pink velvet couches, lined with black leather, fill the area five feet from the stage. Black tables and chairs covered in gold lace rest around the stage and just outside the couch area. A large gold and crystal chandelier hangs in the center of the room. Along dark purple velvet-lined walls, are plush red booths with round, black tables at the center of the booth, a gold lantern light hanging from above each one. Large antique, gilded mirrors sit behind each of the booths.

My eyes land on Redman, just as Xavier announces he sees him. We walk toward the largest booth in the room. It has a direct view of the stage and sits on an elevated platform.

As we move closer to the table, the bar comes into view. Shiny black and gold detail wrap around the curved bar. Red velvet stools line it. Two men and one woman, all dressed in black vests with gold chains, tend to the patrons who've arrived.

"Hidden little gem, isn't she?" Redman exclaims once we reach the table.

"Jesus, man, I thought this was going to be some shithole, but...well...fuck. How did you find this place?" Xavier slides into the booth.

"Fucked a girl who tried to get a job here and came to check it out one night." Redman beams. "I couldn't believe this place."

"So, you just asked the owner to sell it to you?" I ask, sliding in on the other side of the booth.

"Jack, how the hell are you, man?" I clasp his offered hand and release. "Actually, I became a regular and got to know the owner. When he mentioned selling, I jumped on that shit."

"You definitely wouldn't know this was inside," I chuckle.

"It needs some work, but mostly it just needs some PR." Redman waves a hand in the air and a girl in tight black pants and a purple satin corset appears.

"You want another, doll?" She smiles, bright white teeth flashing from behind burgundy lips.

"Definitely. What do you guys want?"

"I'll have beer, whatever is on tap," Xavier responds, but his eyes stay on the girl's chest, which is pushed up tight and bulging.

"Same here," I say, finally finding my voice. *Fuck she's hot.*

"You guys like that, just wait till you see the show. No super skinny, over inflated tits on these girls." He shakes his head and smiles. "These are real women with curves for days. Thom is brilliant in his recruitment."

"When does the show start?" I ask, looking around at the

barely filled tables.

"In about twenty." Redman licks his lips. "The place will fill up. It always does on Friday and Saturday nights, but I think it could do better."

Silence lingers for a moment, just before Redman goes straight into the topic I hate most.

"Hey, Jack, heard what the bitch did. She supposed to be with some dude in Hollywood now, right?"

I shrug and furrow my brow. *Why is this topic always up for discussion?*

"I know it sucks, but trust me, you'll get over it. Hell, you have that hot little model chick, right? And this place will—"

"Laney was the one, Red. How do you replace that? How do you move on? That's right, you don't." Slouching back into the red velvet booth, I toss back the last of my drink. "What you do, is find something or someone bearable enough to focus on. Unfortunately, in my case, I wasn't enough for her either."

"Sorry, man, I didn't mean—"

"Let's just change the fucking subject. I'm okay if we just don't talk about the...about her."

"Yeah, sure."

For the next ten minutes, Redman discusses his ideas and plans for this club and we barely notice the increasing crowd.

When the music changes to an old fashion bump and grind, my eyes land on a small band off to the side of the stage. The lights dim and a hush falls over the patrons. A stocky man approaches our table.

"Thom," Redman motions for the man to sit, "these are two friends of mine. This is Xavier, an old bandmate, and this is Jackson, a longtime friend of ours. Guys, this is Thom, the current owner."

"Good evening, gentlemen. I hope you will enjoy the show. I'm afraid we've had to make a bit of change up tonight."

"A change?" Redman sat up straight. "Why?"

"Well, I'm afraid my wife has become ill and cannot perform. I've asked a couple of the girls to step in for the night." Thom smiles, but the twitch in his cheek gives away his nervousness.

"Your wife?" Xavier asks.

"Thom's wife is Jazzmin, the lead performer. She's pretty amazing." Redman furrows his brow. "Who is going on instead?"

"Well," Thom clears his throat, "we've had to make a change to the format so the girls are more comfortable with the songs. Miz Liz will start off the evening, but I know you also enjoy Bette. She will come on for a solo as well. Since this is the modern weekend, I'm confident they can handle this."

"Miz Liz and Bette, huh?" Redman nods. "Bethany's good, but Liza is amazing! She's probably your best singer. No offense, Thom."

"No offense at all," Thom says, looking more relaxed now that Redman is too.

"Wait till you hear Miz Liz." Redman wears a huge grin. "This girl sounds like she swallowed a Baptist choir," he laughs, taking a drink from his beer.

The music changes and the room goes dark. Heavy beats drum through the air. Gold lights fade in on girls dressed in white corsets and thigh-high outfits strutting onto the stage in exaggerated motions of hips, legs, and arms.

The first raspy words fill the room with the appearance of one stiletto wearing leg from behind a black curtain. She steps into the bright white light like a sexy, dirty porcelain doll with curly white ringlets flowing down her back and over one shoulder. A black, lace corset wraps around her, pressing her tits high and round, and a black garter holds up red, lace thigh-highs.

The backup girls sing and dance around her, running their hands over her body. Miz Liz runs a hand up her tiny corseted waist, over the bulging mounds on her chest and the side of her face, pulling on a lace mask as she sings, "This is what you came for." Tossing the lace away, she gyrates and slides against the other dancers, making her way to the front of the stage.

She continues to sing about what they came for, taking more, thrilling her, and I can only stare at her red-stained lips. The stark color against her paleness is shocking and sexy as fuck.

At the edge of the stage, she sits and spreads her legs.

Running her hands over the inside of her thighs, she flips the snap of one garter belt.

This one action causes a tightening in my jeans. Shifting in the booth, I seek relief, but quickly forget all about my efforts when two of the backups set themselves so Miz Liz can lay over them. Her back arches and another dancer pulls down one lace stocking, only removing the stiletto long enough to get the material off.

The removal is so riveting, I don't notice the dancers untying her corset until Miz Liz starts to sit up while repeating the chorus. Still singing, she holds the piece of clothing to her chest.

Rolling herself, one hand on her chest, one red stocking on, she crawls ever so slowly across the front of the stage. With every arm reaching forward, the audience is given a hint of creamy, plump, white skin.

As the song comes to an end, she is at the edge of stage left. Miz Liz slides flat to her stomach as backups crawl over her and pull away her clothing. In the end, she lies stomach down, in nothing but sheer black panties.

The room goes dark once more and when the lights fade back up, the stage is clear.

The audience explodes in accolades.

"Damn, she's good," Redman says, breaking the silence at our table.

I can only nod in response.

She's captivating. Her stage presence commanding, charisma off the charts, and her heart shaped ass made my whole body rise to attention. Her voice is like a siren's call, a snake charmer's song. By the end of the performance, my chest rises and falls in heavy breaths, sweat dampening my forehead. I'm surprised I didn't blow in my pants like a teenage boy.

When the sounds of another song begin to play, I turn my whole body in anticipation. But this time, it's a brunette with short hair wearing a bunch of balloons. The audience near the stage is prepared and begins popping the balloons as she walks to a slinky beat at the edge of the stage. She playfully scolds them as they do and the crowd eats the shit up.

"This is a small performance, allowing time to set up the next. As I said, we had to do some last minute changes," Thom says in a rush.

"No, this is good for audience interaction." Redman nods to Thom.

Thom relaxes at the positive response.

Glancing to Redman, the smile he wears proves he meant it.

The moment the words, "Come here big boy," purr through the air, I know it's her. A spotlight casts a silvery glow around her. She sits backward in a chair, singing and moving provocatively. Slowly, she removes a military inspired short jacket and gloves. When the stage lights go up, I can't focus on the backups. Her voice is a spell casting over my mind and body.

Suddenly, she shoves the chair to the floor and walks off the stage, into the crowd. A bump and grind plays while she moves around the crowd, flirting with both men and women.

She sashays her gorgeous ass toward us and begins singing again. She removes more items of clothing until she stands in a camo bra-like top and high-waist camo underwear.

At our table, she puts her finger on the edge and drags it over before reaching out and taking my half-filled glass. She tosses it back and slams it on the table, growling about dirty boys. With that, she crawls onto the table, standing center before stepping over Redman's head onto a small black stage I hadn't noticed. Against the large gilded mirror, she slides up and down the surface asking...no, begging, for a spanking. In those damn pants leaving half her ass cheeks on display, my palm burns to comply. But the mirror flips and she disappears.

Swallowing hard, I reach for my glass to ease my dry mouth and cool my rising temperature. Then I remember she drained it. Reaching over, I take Xavier's beer and chug it.

"Hey, fucker! I was drinking that," he complains.

"Get another," I gasp, and close my eyes, trying to mentally will my dick to stand down.

The familiar sound of Jeff Beck's guitar riffs fill the air and the words "I put a spell on you" wrap around my neck, slide down my chest, and stroke my cock to life again.

Opening my eyes, I find her at the mirror behind Redman once more. This time, in a simple, slinky black dress with a hip-high slit and long, white gloves.

Slipping down, she sits on the small stage next to Redman and caresses his head. Turning his face to hers, she runs one satin covered finger across his face.

A fire roars to life inside me, wanting to rip her fucking hands off him. *What the fuck?*

The shock from the jealousy and possessiveness boiling inside of me replaces the lust. I sit, scowling, when she lies on the little stage and slips off to the floor behind me. Passing by me as if I'm not right here, she stops to kiss Thom on the forehead before moving to the big stage for her finish. The urge to slap the crimson lip stains from Thom's face sends another wave of shock through me.

Jesus, I'm acting like...like a...fuck, I'm acting like Christopher.

Back on stage, she unzips the back of her dress to the top of her ass. *Jesus, I want to sink my teeth into her ass. I could spend days with that ass. And that voice. Christ, she hardens my dick and nipples in one note.*

As she lets the dress drop, she pulls the corner of a velvet curtain around her body. Singing the final lust inducing note, she drops the curtain with her back to us and twists at the waist, only revealing her ass and a little side boob. Surprisingly, it's more intoxicating than any full frontal nudity has ever been. This is a woman who holds power, enough to own me—cock, heart, and soul.

The thought clears my lust induced haze. *There's no way another fucking woman is going to own my heart and soul. Not again. I'm not some fool who will let the same shit happen to me twice.*

Grabbing my refreshed drink, I chug.

"Amazing, right?" Redman practically bounces in excitement. "This place is going to be a fucking gold mine. I'm right,

right?" He looks to Xavier for reassurance.

"I wish I'd found the place first." Xavier chugs his replacement beer.

"I'm glad you liked the show." Thom stands from the booth. "Redman, we will talk later, yes?"

"Definitely," Redman puts his hand out and they shake. "I am one hundred percent in on this, my man." Satisfaction pours off him in waves.

"I'm relieved to hear it." Thom sighs in relief.

"Why relieved?" Red scrunches up his face.

"Well, when we had to change everything, I thought maybe you would be turned off—"

"Fuck no. Don't get me wrong, Thom, Jazzmin is great, but I doubt she'll stay on very long after you sell. It's a relief to see the show will be just as amazing without her." Redman grins. "As a matter of fact, let's just get this worked out now."

"I should get going," Xavier says, sliding from the booth. "My mom is bringing the girls to my place tomorrow for a few days."

"Yeah, and I've got one hell of a day coming up with this singing show bullshit." I stand.

Redman slips out last and gives Xavier a one-armed hug.

"I'll talk to you later. Tell the girls Uncle Red says hello." Releasing Xavier, Redman pulls me in for a hug as well. "Don't be a stranger, man. Give me a call. We can hit this place again while you're in town. The show changes weekly, but I also have some ideas and I'd like to run them by you guys."

"Sure thing." I pat his back.

Stepping back from each other, I catch sight of some of the performers mingling with the crowd. My eyes suddenly have a mind of their own, scanning for her. Then I drop my gaze lower, looking for her ass. *My heart and soul are off limits, but she can own my cock for a night.*

Redman leaves us to see about his business and Xavier bumps me with his elbow.

"Yeah?" My eyes never stop searching.

"You ready or...what the fuck are you looking for?"

"Nothing." I shrug, but keep looking. "Just checking the place out."

"Yeah, okay. Well, I'm outta here."

I nod and mean to follow him, but I stay in my spot, searching instead. I shake off the weird need to search her out and looking around for Xavier. Realizing he's nowhere to be found, I send a text to my driver and stop by the bar for one more drink before I head for the exit.

Outside, my car sits at the curb, the driver waiting as I sign some autographs. While taking some pictures with fans, two women walking by catch my attention.

"Did you even realize who was at that table?" The one with long, dark, wavy hair laughs. "I mean, let's just for a minute acknowledge that you just sang to two of the members from Corrosive Velocity and Jackson Shaw! Like, from The Forgotten, Jackson Shaw."

"Sid, keep it down." The other hisses so low, I'm almost unable to hear her.

Realizing this is my snake charmer, I slip into autopilot with the gathering fans: nod, smile, and sign.

"You've got to be more excited. I mean, the man is seven feet of lickable body graffiti. Whew! I'd climb his beanstalk any day."

I cover my laugh with a cough, not wanting to give away my eavesdropping. This Sid girl is fucking hilarious.

"You're awful." My snake charmer laughs.

"No, I'm horny. With the lack of horizontal action in my life, I'm worked up from watching you and the girls. Then for the fates to put rock star hotness just a few feet away and not one of them attainable...it's just not fair," she sighs heavily. "I don't know how you could slink around their table and not be a big, sloppy, wet mess."

"Eww, gross, Sid." Her voice rises and the musical quality of the laugh following her words stirs my body to life.

Deciding it's time to formally introduce myself, I try to step around the fans. But they cram in tight and a bus rolls to a stop in front of them.

Fuck!

"What I wouldn't give to have your body!" the brunette exclaims, stepping onto the bus.

The comment brings my attention to her figure. *Huh, there's nothing wrong with her. She's got amazing curves. Hell, she's Xavier's wet dream. It would be pure testosterone driven desire.*

The blonde steps up behind her, scolding her for the comment. I continue weaving through the crowd, but by the time I get close enough, the bus is already down the street.

Sam, my driver, appears, moving in next to me. He herds the crowd and gives me a questioning look before motioning toward the car. Nodding, I let him guide me into the anonymity of the dark backseat.

Tonight, I'd go back to the hotel, but this wasn't the end of things. My snake charmer needs a lesson on how to sing my name while on her back beneath me.

Liza

"I'm serious, Sid, stop being so self-deprecating. There is nothing wrong with your body."

Sid snorts. "Please, tell me another one."

"I'm not spending our last night arguing with you." Sighing, I put my head back against the bus window.

"Okay, okay." Sid raises her hands in surrender.

The apartment is dark when we arrive, as it should be at this time in the morning. While I check on Lucas and Kelvin, Sid gets ready for bed. She's leaving in the morning for the airport, and all I want is for her stay.

"Goodbye, Aunt Sid!" Lucas calls out as the taxi pulls away from the curb. Kelvin and I stand behind him, waving until the car rounds a bend and out of sight.

"Alright, we need to get a move on the day." Placing my hand on Lucas' shoulder, he turns and looks up at me.

"Do I have to clean my room right now? Brandon and Sean are biking over to the park. Can't I go with them instead?" he pleads as we walk into the apartment building.

I grab yesterday's mail from our box before we climb the stairs to the second floor.

"You can go after you've cleaned up the disaster." I narrow my eyes and purse my lips. "Do you know I found what I think used to be pizza in your dirty laundry bag?"

"Did you leave it there?" he asks over his shoulder, entering our apartment.

"Of course not!" *He really thinks I'd leave that nastiness in his room?*

"Then it's cleaned up already. Can I go to the park?"

Kelvin laughs from behind me.

Turning toward Kelvin, who's leaning against the breakfast bar, I glare. "Don't encourage him." Then I twist back to my too-smart-for-his-own-good son. "Lucas, get your butt in your room and clean it."

"Fine," he growls, stomping off.

"I want all the cups and plates out of there and washed," I call after him.

His door slams.

"I'm going to beat his ass." Grumbling, I walk into the small kitchen, toss the mail onto the counter, and begin washing the breakfast dishes.

"You always say that." Kelvin hops up onto the breakfast bar, watching me at the sink.

"I know, but one of these days I am going to let him have it."

"Leave him alone. He's a good kid, acting like a kid."

Sighing, I drop my shoulders and turn to look at my brother.

"I wish you would act like a kid instead of trying to grow up so fast."

"Don't start again." He slides from his seat on the counter. "I already have a couple interviews lined up for better jobs and I'm going to take the test required by the city to try to get a job with them."

"Kel—"

"Liza, that's enough!" He turns to me with hard eyes. "You've taken care of me, of everything, for long enough. I want to take care of myself. I want you to be able to worry less and get a job better than walking around a stage naked."

Though I know he didn't mean it to, that hurt. I don't hate what I do. Performing is something I enjoy—love, even. I hadn't planned to do burlesque or cabaret style performances.

Having seen me flinch from his comment, Kelvin closes the distance between us in two large steps. He wraps me up in his arms, holding me tight, his chin resting on my head. It's hard to believe he's so much taller than me now that he's an adult.

"I didn't mean it like that, sis. I'm sorry." He rocks us. "You know I didn't mean it like that, don't you?" Pulling out of the embrace, he looks down, worry creasing his forehead.

I pat his side. "I know. I just get a little defensive about it. I don't hate what I do and it's better than a lot of other jobs I could be doing."

"Liza, you're so much better than that club. I wish you would realize it and do something about it." He gives another firm squeeze before ultimately releasing me. "I'm going to go clean up my room before you threaten to beat my ass next."

"Ha-ha." I shake my head.

"If you ever get the chance for more, just promise me you'll take it." He grins, retreating to his bedroom.

Shrugging, I go back to the sink, wash the dishes, wipe down counters, and fold the pullout bed back into a couch. Then, the real cleaning begins. I have a lot to get done before this afternoon.

With the apartment in better order and Lucas finally finished scrubbing some sticky brown substance from his bedroom carpet, he's dressed for soccer practice and slipping on tennis shoes while he waits impatiently by the door.

"If I'm late again, Coach is going to make me run laps." *Jesus, he's only nine and I want to slap the teen out of his mouth.*

"Hey, you're the reason you were late last week, not me," I remind him. "When I say go straight to practice, that doesn't mean stop by Sean's house and wait for him so you guys can be late together."

Lucas opens the door, we step into the hallway, and I lock the door behind us.

"We didn't plan on being late," he argues, his voice lowering. "He couldn't find any socks, so I ran back here and got him some of mine."

Before he could push the button for the elevator, I grab him and pull him into a hug. "You're amazing, you know that?"

Lucas' best friend since Kindergarten, Sean, lives with his disabled grandmother, Mrs. Johnson. She tries her best, but can barely take care of herself. His father is just as MIA as Lucas', but Sean doesn't have a mom. Well, he does, technically, but she only shows up to collect her monthly check, get Sean's hopes up that she is sticking around this time, and get whatever she can from her ill mother. So, when Lucas says Sean couldn't find clean socks, that probably means the only pairs he has are now lost or beyond dirty.

"I'm going to be late." He pulls away. "And don't hug and kiss me when we get to the field." His scowl would be more convincing if there wasn't a hint of a smile on his lips.

"We should invite Sean to stay over," I say as we step into the elevator.

"Cool." Lucas shrugs, a gleam of excitement in his eyes.

We didn't exactly have a lot, but both Kelvin and I try to help Sean out as much as we can. And since it's getting closer to the end of the month, I'm sure Mrs. Johnson is struggling. I'd have to make sure Lucas helps him pack most of his clothes—dirty and clean, so I can wash them while he's distracted with video games.

Cutting it close, we run the final block to the park and make it just in time.

"See," I gasp for air, "just in time."

Before he can reply, I grab his head between both my hands

and kiss his forehead. He swats at me.

"Mom," he whines. "What did I say about the kissing?!" Pulling away, he runs across the field, his green duffle bag bouncing against his back.

"Uncle Kelvin will be here by the end of practice," I shout after him.

Turning and jogging backward, he gives me two thumbs up.

His coach catches my attention with a wave, so I wave back. Coach Stan and his wife—the team mom—keep an excellent eye on the kids during practices. Knowing most of them come from this neighborhood of poor parenting and/or families who sometimes have two jobs just to cover expenses, they do their best to keep the boys all accounted for.

With a deep breath, I rush for the bus stop to run my afternoon errands and check in on Mrs. Johnson. When I finally arrive back home, I start dinner.

Chapter Four
Jackson

The ringing phone interrupts my velvety lace dreams of my snake charmer. Then comes voices combined with a knock on the bedroom door. I guess the day is starting whether I want it to or not.

"What?" Groaning, I sit up on the side of the bed.

"Jackson," Julia's voice is muffled by the closed door, "we need to get moving to the arena."

"What?" I mumble from the bed.

She begins talking through the door—again.

"Julia, open the damn door."

Julia enters the room. "Jacks—"

Having stood to stretch, I twist to see why she stopped speaking.

Julia's eyes travel up and down my body twice, her mouth hanging open.

I look down my body to make sure everything is in order. I'm wearing a pair of shorts, sans morning wood, so all is good. Turning back toward Julia, she holds a hand over her face, her cheeks flush.

"Christ, girl, I'm not naked." Chuckling, I shake my head.

"Sorry." She reddens further.

"No reason to be sorry." Scratching at the overgrown hair on my head, I walk toward her. "What's going on today?"

Julia doesn't speak until I pass by and stand at a breakfast cart.

"Yes, today, the schedule." She finally collects herself. "You need to be at the arena this morning. The Morning Show will be there to interview the judges."

Nodding my acknowledgment, I sit down at the breakfast

bar and start in on egg whites, pancakes, and hash browns covered in ketchup.

"Then you have a meeting at the studio to listen through some of the contestants who have qualified for the next stage. From there, you have lunch with the judges, as well as a radio and a local TV show appearance "

"Departure time?" I ask around a mouthful of eggs.

"We need to be downstairs in an hour." Julia moves to my side as she answers.

I shovel in the last of my food and push away from the table to stand, needing to get dressed for the day.

At the bedroom door, I turn back to Julia. Her eyes lock on me, an eager, ready-to-please expression on her face. I smile.

"I need a table at the same burlesque club I was at last night. Can you make that happen?"

She nods and begins typing away on her iPad.

Closing the door behind me, I dig through the closet and pull out my standard attire: dark jeans, white t-shirt, and black leather belt with my favorite oversized buckle with "Cock Fight" in bold silver. Slipping into black boots, I walk into the bathroom and wet my hair to gain some control over the mess.

"Fuck, I need to get my hair cut."

My eyes catch on my black leather bag. Licking my lips, I reach over and take out the brown paper package. Lining up a couple rails, I take care of second breakfast and wash any remnants from my face.

Shaking water out of my hair, I stride back out into the main area of the suite. Julia jumps to attention.

"I made arrangements with a Thom for your table at the club tonight." She grins in satisfaction. "He's pleased you will be joining them again and wants you to let him know if you have any requests before you arrive."

She looks at me expectantly.

"Oh, I have a request alright, but I don't think he can lay her out on the table for me." I grin down at Julia and her eyes widen. "But," I continue, "if he can arrange for the snake charmer spread out, I'll take it."

"Umm..." Julia stands completely still, even as I make my way to the door of the hotel suite.

"Julia?"

She looks up when I call her.

"Don't worry about it, sweetheart. I'm just being an ass." Smirking, I pull open the door to the room. "Come on, doll, we gotta get moving."

With a deep breath and a nod, she moves into gear.

And when Julia kicks into gear, she talks a mile a minute. From the itinerary for each meeting, interview, and meal, to assuring me she made the subject the interviewers weren't allowed to address clear. *She's definitely thorough.*

Inside the L.A. Memorial Sports Arena, an assistant shows us to a large waiting room. There is only one co-judge I know personally.

"Gemma," I exclaim.

Her bright, neon red head turns toward me, a large grin spread across her porcelain face.

"Jackson Shaw." Gemma excuses herself from the group, approaching me with open arms.

She wraps her arms around me and I lift her off of her high-heel clad feet, spinning her in a circle.

"Put me down, you beast," she laughs. "I think I'm getting a fucking nosebleed."

Smiling, I put her back on her heels. She grabs my arm and pulls me over to a couch.

To look at tiny little Gemma, with her neon red hair, black pin-up girl eyeliner, and bright red lips, you would think she's a member of Hush. But hidden beneath the wild hair, elaborate make-up, and a multitude of tattoos currently hidden by her clothes, is the latest operatic sensation. The voice of this girl is unbelievable. Her range is out of this world.

"How you been, gorgeous?" I sit on the couch next to her.

"Good." She shrugs. "Still can't believe I'm doing this type of show."

"How *did* you end up doing this?" I settle into the plush leather, Julia flittering around the room with production assistants catching my attention briefly before I turn back to Gem.

"I'm about to star in a rock opera." She leans back into the cushion beside me, laying her head on it. "This is supposed to help bring it to the attention of the masses." Always one to talk with her hands, her arms stretch out at the end of her sentence.

"Well, I guess it will be pretty good publicity." I nod.

"What about you? How'd you get roped into this?" Her head, still resting on the cushion, rolls in my direction.

"Unanimous vote by band and management sentencing me to weeks of ear piercing headaches."

"Maybe it won't be that bad."

We stare at each other for a moment before bursting into laughter.

"Okay, so maybe at first it will be..."

"Excruciating?" I finish for her.

Laughing louder, we draw the attention of the other judges. As they begin gathering around, Gem and I stand from the couch, and introductions are finally made.

I know of these judges, but this is my first time meeting them in person. Melody Waymen: a tall, curvy, young, golden-blonde, who can't be mistaken for anything but a country girl. She has dominated the country music charts for the past four years and recently found some pop chart success. Gideon Thorne: an average-sized man with a broad nose and dark hair, who's produced some of the greatest artists at Bel Suono Studios—the sponsor of the show. Kamden "Big Kam" Miller hit the rap scene nine years ago, built an empire around his name, and has discovered at least five major rap artists. And Cheyenne Post: the most hard ass music critic around. To this day, I think even Chris gets nervous about her reviews in HITS magazine. Hell, the whole band's balls shrivel up when she's involved.

After the last introduction, I do a count.

"Someone missing?" I ask anyone who has the answer.

"Zar—"

Just as Cheyenne is about to answer, a tall, wide-shouldered man enters. He stands a foot shorter than me, his dark hair just brushing his shoulders.

"Cheyenne, you talking about me already?" With a broad grin, he winks at her.

She blushes. *Holy shit, he just made the hard ass blush! I may love him, too.*

"Hey, man." He steps toward me first, his hand out.

We clamp hands tightly and shake. The sleeve of his shirt pulls back, revealing some nice ink around his wrist disappearing beneath the fabric.

"Hey." I give a nod. "Jackson Sh—"

"No need to introduce." He releases my hand. "I'm honored to be in the room with you." His grin grows larger. "I'm Zarek Sisko, singer for Vehicle of Destruction."

"Fuck, man. I'm sorry." *I'm such an ass.* "Best New Artists 2013." I smile. Finally recognizing him, I feel like an ass cheek.

"No apologies necessary." Zarek turns to the rest of the group, greeting them. When he comes to Gemma, he pauses for a second and scowls.

"You," she growls from beside me.

"That's right, sweetheart. Me." A smirk tips the corner of his mouth.

"Are you stalking me now? And don't call me sweetheart!"

They step toward each other, facing off. The rest of us take a step back—a step way back.

"Don't flatter yourself, *sweetheart*." Zarek's nostrils flare. "You aren't worth the effort to stalk." He crosses his arms over his chest.

"You self-absorbed, arrogant jackass!" Gemma closes the distance, clenching her fists at her sides.

Zarek leans close to her face. His lips move, but no one could hear. Except Gemma—she hears him. Her face reddens and she starts shaking. Her hand snaps back and across his face so fast, if you blinked, you missed it.

He grabs her wrist and yanks her against his chest. I step

toward them.

"Okay, you guys don't like each other. We get it." Putting my arm around Gemma, Zarek's eyes go to my hand before they meet my face, anger flashing. "Let go, man."

For the briefest second, I think he might attack me. I don't know what the hell went on with these two, but I don't want any part of it.

"Calm down and let go. Don't do something stupid." I keep my voice calm and level.

He takes a deep breath, exhales, and turns to Gemma with a smirk. "This isn't over." Abruptly, he releases her and walks to the other side of the room.

"What the hell was that?" I look down at a flustered Gem.

"Nothing," she mumbles, pulling herself free of my arm.

"It didn't look, or sound, like nothing."

"It's nothing, okay?" she snaps.

Putting my hands up in surrender, I walk away. *As I said, I don't want any part of it.*

"Jackson, I'm sorry," she calls after me.

I just lift my hand in a loose wave. *I don't need this shit. Women are fucking crazy.*

Sitting down next to Julia, I bury my head in my hands.

"When can I get the fuck out of here?"

"Good morning, everyone. Thank you for joining us today." I look up from my hands at the sound of a man's voice. "If you will all follow me, I will get you set up with your microphones."

He waits as we file out the door. I motion for Julia to exit before me and scowl at the man as he checks out her ass. When he sees he's busted, his eyes drop to the floor. *Yeah, fucker, how do you know she ain't with me? You don't.*

In a large, open space with multiple cameras and crew members, our interviewer, Meriwether Shay, sits, flipping through oversized index cards. We sit to the left of Meriwether in assigned director chairs. Crew members flit about, wiring us up and having each of us test the small mics. The gleam in Meriwether's eyes when they land on me tell me she's not going to hold back. So much for topics not to be discussed. This bitch is going to bleed me for everything she can get. With shaking hands, I feel around my pockets for the little brown vial of numbness and think of a reason to escape to the bathroom.

Liza

My bag for work is packed and the chicken macaroni bake is in the oven. Sitting at the breakfast bar, which is already set for three, I'm finally sorting through mail.

Junk mail, cable bill, phone bill, a manila envelope undoubtedly containing documents my case worker told me to expect, and a thick, white envelope. The junk mail goes unopened into the trash. *Last time I checked, I am not old enough for AARP and I don't need a preapproved credit card.* Groaning, I open each bill and mark the due dates in my Dollar Store purchased monthly planner. Slipping from the stool, I put the bills in the wall organizer near the phone.

Already knowing the manila envelope contains papers I have to complete every year and return to our social worker, I pick up the white envelope.

I tear open the side and slide the papers halfway out as the oven timer goes off. Placing the papers on the counter, I silence the timer and retrieve dinner before it burns.

I burn my finger through the worn potholder and curse just in time for Luke to hear me.

"Ah, you kiss your baby boy with that mouth?" He chuckles.

Kel's laughter follows.

"Ha-ha, smart-butt." I set the hot dish onto the counter and grab a serving spoon.

"You've got to admit, it was pretty good." Kelvin slides onto the stool next to Luke, both of them facing the small kitchen.

"No, I don't." I dish out chicken macaroni onto each plate, trying not to laugh while Kelvin serves the salad.

"What's this?" Kel picks up the papers I have yet to look over.

Pushing the dish off to the side, I shrug. "I haven't been able to read them yet."

He unfolds the papers, then folds them back up quickly. The look he shares with Luke doesn't go unnoticed.

"Hand them over," I speak around a mouthful of food, my arm stretched over the spread before us.

"They can wait." He shrugs, pushing the papers off to the side.

Standing, I walk around the breakfast bar, grab the papers from the far corner Kel shoved them to, and move back to my seat. Before I can sit, I freeze, reading the words on the paper.

CONGRATULATIONS!
You have progressed to the next round in Hidden Talent! Enclosed are necessary documents needing your review and signature.

"What the hell did she do?" Falling back onto my stool, I keep flipping through the papers, not actually seeing anything but a blur of congratulatory remarks, signature lines, dates, times, addresses, and that damn logo.

"Who?" Luke chokes out, just as Kel asks, "What's wrong?"

I look up at them, my eyes still wide with shock.

"Sid! She entered me into that Hidden Talent competition

somehow!" Standing quickly, I move straight to my bag by the door, dig around, and pull out my cell phone.

"What are you doing?" Luke jumps down from his seat, hurrying to my side.

"I'm going to give your Aunt Sid the biggest earful!" Scrolling to her name, I touch the screen to initiate the call.

"Mom, wait!" Luke protests, reaching for my phone.

"Go finish eating. I'm going to go cuss her out in Kel's room." I step to walk away, but Kelvin stands in front of me.

"Miss me already?" Sid's voice chirps.

"What are you doing?" I ask Kelvin.

"Um, working on designing the website I told you about," Sid answers in confusion.

"Not you," I speak to Sid, then angle the phone away from my mouth. "Move."

"No." Kel shakes his head. "We have something to tell you."

"We?" I ask.

Kel reaches out and pulls Luke to his side.

"What the hell is going on?" Sid asks, my phone still to my ear.

"I wish I knew. Sid, I'll call you back."

"No way, sister. Put me on speaker!"

"Well, what is it?" I look between the both of them expectantly.

Kel nudges Luke and he drops his head.

"Remember when we went to the carnival fundraiser?" He peeks from under his lashes. I nod. Clearing his throat, he continues, "And how they had those booths to record yourself singing?"

"You didn't," I gasp.

His head pops up, determination on his face.

"Mom, you are sooooooo good! All my friends thought so, too, when they heard you sing at the carnival. You deserve to be famous, to be a star."

"Holy Shit, did he do what I think he did?" Sid whispers through the phone.

"Yes, he did." I take a deep breath and exhale.

"YES!" Sid's scream makes me pull the phone from my ear. "I love that boy, I tell you! He is just like me. I might cry." She fakes a sniff.

"Sid, I'll call you back." Before she can protest again, I end the call. Turning my attention to Kal, I ask, "You knew?"

He gives a nod. "He needed help filling out the forms."

I shove the phone into my back pocket. "Back to the table and finish dinner."

I ignore the vibration from my phone; Sid apparently trying to call me back.

My words are weak. I'm still attempting to process what my son and brother have done. It's not a bad thing. He did it with all the best intentions possible, but he also illegally forged my application.

Neither of them argues with me. We sit silently, none of us touching our food.

"Luke..."

"I know I shouldn't have filled the application out without telling you. But, Mom..." he pauses, and I focus on his face, "you deserve better than working all night at that club."

My heart aches. Lucas isn't stupid and I don't hide my job from him, but I've never provided details either. However, by the time he was old enough to visit friend's houses, he was also old enough to overhear parental gossip. I knew there had been gossip about me when the news spread around. It was never a big issue, nor did anyone approach me about it—mostly because no one wanted to admit how they knew I worked at the club.

"I'm sorry I...I do what I do. I know it can be embarrassing for a boy—"

"You think I'm embarrassed by you?" he cuts me off with a hard worded question, matching the scowl on his boyish face.

"I'm sure it can be—"

"You're totally not understanding me," he cut me off, again. "I'm not embarrassed. I'm proud you are my mom. Look at Sean, Mom. His mother runs off with all the money and lets him go without food or clothes. I've never lived like that, and it's because of you."

Unexpected tears fall from my eyes.

"I didn't mean to make you cry." Luke drops his head.

"I don't think she's sad, buddy." Kel wraps an arm around his shoulders.

"No, I'm not sad." I wipe the wet streaks from my cheeks. "I love you, Lucas, and you just made your mother cry happy mommy tears."

He smiles. "Then you won't be mad about the papers?"

His hopeful expression tugs at my heart.

"You know that forging information is not something you should do, right?"

He nods. "Yes. I just knew you wouldn't do it. I *had* to do it."

"Finish your dinner before it gets cold." I start reading over the papers again.

"So, you'll do it?" Kel asks.

I look up from the papers. "After I read through this and see what's involved."

By the time we finish eating, we're having a new debate.

"But Aunt Char would stay with us!" Luke argues as I slip on my jacket to leave for the club.

"Your great-aunt doesn't need to fly across the country to take care of my responsibilities. She's done enough for us."

"What about Sid? She'd come, too." Luke tries another tactic.

"She was just here for a week. I'm not going to ask her to take time out of her life to spend weeks here with you two so I can go lose a reality show." Sliding my bag strap over my head and into place on my shoulder, I palm both sides of Luke's face and plant a big kiss on his forehead. "Don't give Uncle Kel a hard time when he tells you to go to bed, okay?"

"Uncle Kel could take care of us while you go on the show." His eyes light up.

"You both have school and he has work. Listen, baby, it just doesn't seem like it's going to work out. Thank you for believing in me, though." I kiss him again and turn to the door.

"Night, Kel," I call over my shoulder, leaving for a crazy night at Lux.

Jackson

"Jesus, man, you look like shit."

It's only been a day, but Xavier looks like someone chewed him up and shit him out. Sitting, once again, at Lux Hedonica, we wait for Red to show up. He was more than happy to accommodate my request to visit again tonight as well as receive a proper introduction to the staff. Most importantly, one particular snake charmer.

"Yeah. I feel it, too." He rubs at the back of his neck.

"What's going on? You sick?" Leaning my forearms on the table, I shift most of my upper body weight forward, allowing the table to support me.

"No, I'm not." He chokes up a bit, something I wasn't prepared to come from the cocky bastard. "Maria's sick." His hands run through his hair.

"Sick how?"

His bloodshot eyes meet my blue ones. "She has heart problems."

"How serious?" I press.

"Serious enough she's being hospitalized for surgery, but apparently not severe enough to fucking tell me about these issues until a week before the surgery," he growls.

They may have split up, but they worked hard at being close. At first, it was for the twins, but over time, you could tell while a marriage didn't work, their friendship was intact.

"Her husband called me because he didn't think it was right for me not to know!" He snorts. "Her new husband told me, but she hasn't. You believe that shit?"

I shook my head. Honestly, I wasn't sure what I would do in that situation.

"They haven't told the girls about the operation or anything. They know she's been sick sometimes, but Maria hides the seriousness. She's just going to send them for their week with me and slip into the hospital." Shaking his head, he tosses back the last of his drink.

"Why don't we get out of here?" I slide to the end of the booth and tilt my head toward the exit.

He shakes his head. "No, you stay. I thought this would get me out of my mood, but I don't think it's going to work."

I go to stand with him, but he motions for me to stay seated.

"Why don't you just call and talk to her? You guys are still close. Just yell at each other and then talk it out."

"Oh, I'll yell alright." He gives a mean laugh.

"Hey, man, just remember, she's probably scared out of her mind and though this may not be the best way to handle everything, she's more than likely having a really, really hard time processing all of this, too."

Xavier's shoulders relax just a bit and he nods.

"You're right, but she should've told me."

I nod. "Yeah, I know."

"Tell Red I'm sorry." Then, Xavier is gone, lost in the sea of bodies that filled the club during our conversation.

The waitress stops by the table two more times before Red finally shows. He's wearing the same shitty grin he was yesterday.

"Where's Xavier?" Red asks, sliding into the booth.

"He just took off. Got some shit to take care of," I say, keeping it short. That story ain't mine to tell.

"His loss." Red motions to a waitress, who eagerly comes at his call. As the curvy, dark haired girl scurries off to the bar, Red settles into the leather. "So, it's all set. The transfer of the club should happen next month."

"Congrats, man."

"Thom's letting them know about the official ownership

change before the show. Afterward, we'll head back so I can formally introduce myself."

"You haven't met the girls yet?" I raise one brow.

"As a customer, not as the new owner. I want them to be assured their jobs are safe. I mean, I have a few ideas for this place, but I'm not going to do an overhaul. Mostly, I want to get some better PR and curb appeal. I'm also going to see about some celebrity guests and shit." He shrugs.

"Sounds like a good start." I nod.

The waitress returns with drinks and takes my empty glasses.

"You think Mia or Hush would be interested?"

My eyes shoot to Red's face to make sure he's serious. I can't hold back my laughter.

"What?" he asks around his beer bottle.

"You think Chris is going to let Mia on that stage in lingerie?" I laugh, slapping the table.

"Who says I'm asking Chris?" Red lifts one shoulder with a mischievous grin.

Taking deep breaths, I calm my laughter.

"Just be prepared for him to charge the stage and carry her off. That's all I'm saying." I take a pull from the long neck bottle.

"Could be worth the publicity," Red states just before the lights dim and music fills the air.

"This is new," Red says to my back, but I'm already captivated.

Her voice already has me by the balls.

"I know you want me," she half sings, half purrs at center stage.

She's naked, except for black, silk, bandage-like straps around her chest and black, silk panties. Sheer panels sway around the platform she stands on. Backups sing "erotic" repetitively from large, silk-covered platforms around the stage.

Wrapping her body in a sheer panel, the bandage-like strips fall away, giving a barely visible view of her body. She moans and I press my palm to my crotch to ease the pressure.

Again, she sings, "I know you want me."

Fuck yes, I want her. This show can't end quickly enough.

Chapter Five
Liza

"Jesus, girl, you were on fire tonight!" Bethany, or Miz Bette to the audience, sits at the cluttered dressing table next to mine.

Still catching my breath from the last performance, I only nod.

Bethany, Jazzmin, and I share the dressing room. It's the largest of the four private backstage rooms. We all do quick touch ups and changes in the common area, but for the most part, we each have our own dressing table. But with the news from Thom this evening, Jazzmin's table would probably be empty soon.

"Do you think this guy is really going to be good for the club like Thom says?" Bethany asks, stripping the layers of stage makeup from her face.

"I don't know."

With a shrug, I sit up, take out a makeup removal wipe, and follow Bethany's lead.

"Ladies, can I please have you out in the main area?" Thom calls from outside our door.

In all the years I've worked in the club, not once has Thom walked in without knocking and waiting for a response.

Dropping the wipe, I stand, tying my robe tighter.

"How do I look?" Bethany asks, her hand grabbing my arm and pulling.

Turning to her, I see where she started removing her eyelash and tried to get it back on.

"Lean forward." I wave her toward me.

She does as I ask and I use my fingernails to put her lash back into proper place. Reaching over to my table, I grab a tissue and wipe around her eyes to even out the leftover makeup.

"There, all good." I smile to reassure.

She tightens her robe and we exit to the common area.

The rest of the girls and stage crew have already formed a circle in the common area. Bethany pushes her way through to the front, pulling me along behind. When she stops short, I bump into her.

"Beth," I hiss.

Stepping to the left and pulling me to her right side, I see why she stopped.

Center of the circle is Thom, Jazzmin at his side. And with them is the new owner of Lux.

"Thank you, everyone, for gathering so quickly. I know you all want to get out of here, but I feel it's important for you to formally meet the new owner." Thom motions to the wide-shouldered, tattoo-covered man with a shaved head, but it's the giant, lickable body art next to him capturing my attention. Jackson Shaw. And Jackson Shaw is looking right at me. Our eyes meet and a small twitch of his lip sends my heart into erratic palpitation. Thom speaks again and it's a physical effort to look away from Jackson.

"This is Steven Redman. Mr. Redman will officially own the club next month. However, you will see him for the next few weeks backstage, in the offices, behind the bar, so forth. Please be sure to treat him as you would me...well, perhaps a bit more boss-like." Thom smiles. "Mr. Redman, do you have anything you would like to add?"

The wide, thick wall of man takes one step forward. I fight to keep my attention on my new boss, instead of the man I can still *feel* looking at me.

"First of all, call me Red. No, mister or other shit. Second, I don't want any of you worrying about jobs. I'm not here to overhaul. I have some ideas, but none of them involve getting rid of staff. If you do your job and do it well, you've got nothing to worry about. You got me?" He looks around the room. "I said, you got me?"

Yesses come from all around the group.

"Christ, people, relax. No one's going to bite." His eyes shift toward where Beth and I stand. "Unless you want me to." He winks.

I blink at the comment. Beth giggles and I can't help but smile.

Subconsciously, my eyes move to Jackson. He's scowling at Red.

"Okay, with that out of the way, as Thom here mentioned, I'll be around, so don't be surprised if I ask you some questions. You guys are the experts back here, so I'm looking to learn from you. By the way, great show, everyone." Red turns and stops halfway.

"Oh, I forgot. This tall fucker is Jackson Shaw." Red throws a thumb in his direction. "Don't be surprised if you see him or other singers and bands around. I've been in the industry for a while, so I know some people." He winks, giving another smile.

Red turns to Thom and begins talking privately. The group takes this as the time to break up and go about our close up routines.

"If this place is going to fill up with celebrities, I'm going to fall off the stage," Beth whines. "I'll be a hot mess."

"You'll be fine." I loop my arm in hers.

"Beth, Liza," Thom calls.

We turn as he approaches with Red and—God help me—Jackson Shaw. I force my eyes to stay on Thom and not the tall, lean, billboard of naughty sin.

"Ladies, great job tonight." He smiles.

"Thank you," we reply in unison.

"This is Bethany and Liza, or Miz Bette and Miz Liz." Thom motions to each of us.

"It's a pleasure to meet you." Red extends his hand toward us.

Bethany takes it first, squeaking when he pulls her forward to kiss her hand.

Thom frowns for a second, but clears the look before stepping between Red and Beth, and reaching for a clipboard I know he doesn't really need.

"You both did fantastic tonight," Red praises.

"I'm glad you enjoyed the performance," I respond.

"Girl, you have a voice many singers would kill for." He smiles.

"Thanks." The heat climbing into my cheeks makes me uncomfortable.

"She was on fire tonight," Beth adds, wrapping an arm around my waist.

"It did get pretty hot." The drawl of Jackson's words sets off a flurry of butterflies in my stomach. Our eyes meet and the room fades away around us.

"Thom, we have a problem with the control board for the mirror stages." A crew member appears, breaking the moment.

Jesus, Liza. I shake my head. *Quit acting like a twit who's never seen a boy before.*

"Okay, I'll be right there." Thom nods.

"No, let's go now," Red insists, then turns to Jackson. "You good for a minute?"

As hard as I try not to, I look right at Jackson.

"Yep," he answers, keeping his eyes on me.

How can one word, one simple everyday slang word, melt my insides?

"Oh my," Beth whispers next to me.

At least I'm not the only one acting like a star-struck teenage girl.

Thom and Red walk away to examine the control board and Jackson Shaw takes one step...then two. I unknowingly back up, pressing myself against the wall beside the dressing room door.

His body is flush against mine, blue eyes boring into mine, trapping me in a lusty trance.

"Tell me, Liza, where do you go after you've seduced every person in the audience?"

I open my mouth, but nothing comes out. My throat is so dry, I pant like an idiot.

From the corner of my eye, his long, inked fingers capture my hair, twirling it until it's wound tight and pulling. For a moment, I fear the extension will fall out into his hand.

"Home," I blurt, grabbing the strand of hair from his fingers.

"Home," he repeats.

Finally, his eyes release mine and search my face. While he does this, I inspect the intricate lines and swirls of ink on his neck, until his art-covered limbs raise and trap me against the wall. His forearms on both sides of my head bring his face closer to mine. I press back, trying to create more space. My lips are so dry, but I resist the urge to lick them.

"What about breakfast?" His warm breath wafts across my lips, a touch of beer scenting his question.

Unable to fight my chapping lips any longer, I wet them. His eyes drop to my mouth and I quickly pull my tongue back inside.

"What about it?" The question comes out as a whisper of sound.

One side of his mouth lifts and I bite my tongue, fighting the urge to lick his half-grin.

"Have breakfast with me." It's not a question.

The slight pull tells me he's playing with my real hair, the carefully created curls slipping through his fingers. When his fingertips touch my scalp, I swallow a whimper. The act is so simple, but affectionate. And intended or not, it's been so long since I've received an affectionate gesture from a man.

"I really need—"

One of his fingers touches my cheek, tracing an invisible line to my bottom lip, surprising me.

"It's just breakfast," he says, watching his finger move over my chin and down my neck.

I grab his wrist.

"I really need to go home."

He looks from my hold on his wrist to my eyes and grins. Dropping his other arm from the wall, he places a hand on my waist. I tense.

"I'll have you home after breakfast." His body moves closer. "I promise."

"Th-th-thanks," I stutter, "but I can't—"

"Have breakfast with me, Liza."

The way he says my name makes my insides melt to goo.

This is Jackson fucking Shaw and he wants to take me out for breakfast...or eat me for breakfast. I'm not sure which is the real offer, but I'm pretty sure I'm hoping for the latter.

The fingers of his right hand are back, twirling my extensions again.

"You know I don't look like this outside of the club, right?" I keep my eyes on his fingers, mesmerized by the way they move through the hair.

"I would hope you don't go out dressed in a robe," he chuckles.

"No, I mean, the costumes, the makeup, the hair."

His fingers untangle from the extensions and grip my chin. Bringing my face to his, he leans in closer.

"It's not the costume I want..." my breath catches, "to eat breakfast with," he finishes, a sly smile on his lips.

Suddenly, I feel like Little Red Riding Hood being seduced by the Big Bad Wolf. A seduction I'm falling into head first. A seduction I should turn from and never look back.

He licks his bottom lip and the heat of his tongue radiates against my bottom lip.

I nod. "Okay."

He leans forward, his body pressing against mine, his lips a breath from mine.

"How long do you need?"

I want to gulp down the words passing over my skin.

"Thirty—"

He pushes away before I even finish. My body arches, following his retreat, causing him to smile wide. Walking backward, his eyes never leave mine.

"I'll meet you out front in thirty minutes."

"You know I won't be wearing the corset, right?"

"This time," he responds, sucking on his lip ring before disappearing.

Closing my eyes, I lean back against the wall. Every part of my body pulses, some more so than others.

I just sold my soul...well, my body, all because his tongue almost touched my lip.

"Oh. My. God." Jennifer's voice causes me to open my eyes.

Groaning, I realize the audience we've had the whole time.

"I don't know how you held out as long as you did," Beth sighs from the door of our dressing room.

"I thought he would just fuck you against the wall." Nikki stands, wide-eyed and fanning herself.

I groan again and slip past Beth into our dressing room.

What am I doing? This is so stupid.

"Girl, what are you going to wear?" Beth is right on my heels. I can hear the smile in her voice.

"I don't know." I throw myself into my chair and look into the mirror. "What the hell am I thinking?" I ask the painted reflection.

"You're thinking he's Jackson Shaw and you have been thoroughly seduced." Jennifer, or Madame J, as she's known on stage, appears to the left of my mirror.

"I can't do this." I shake my head.

"He's waiting right outside for you," Beth states, pointing toward the door.

"There's no way he's letting you get away." Nikki, also known as Lady Nikle, adds, entering the room with clothes over her arm. "We all saw the determination in that man."

"What are those for?" I furrow my brow at the clothes.

"You can't meet him in the leggings and tunic you wore to work today."

"She's right," Beth agrees with a nod.

"I'll just sneak out the back and find a cab tonight." I turn in my chair, looking at the three of them.

"What will you do when he comes back to the club looking for you?" Beth asks.

"And, the most important question, why would you pass this up?" Jennifer looks at me as if I'm crazy.

"I have to get home to Lucas and Kel," I state matter-of-factly. "I don't have time to be a one night stand."

"They're in bed," Jennifer says.

"Kel's eighteen," Nikki adds.

"How long has it been since you've acted your age?" Beth sits in her seat next to me.

"Have you been talking to Sid?" I narrow my eyes.

"No, but maybe I should." Her response is sharp. "Go out to breakfast. You don't have to sleep with him."

They all start laughing, full on belly laughs. I roll my eyes.

"You so have to sleep with him," Jennifer snorts. "And I want details."

"Look," Beth gets my full attention by placing her hand on my arm, "go have breakfast. If you don't want anything more than breakfast, then don't do anything else. You get up from the table, say thank you, and leave the restaurant." She shrugs. "Though, you would be crazy not to. I mean, he's probably only in town for a short time. You do him, then lose him. It's perfect."

"Do him and lose him?" I ask, trying not to laugh.

She grins, grabbing a makeup wipe and bringing it to my face.

"We're running out of time."

The three of them swoop in to clean away the stage makeup and put everyday makeup in its place. They swiftly remove the extensions and let my real hair fall, touching up the curls with a wand.

When they finish, I'm wearing a pair of dark blue skinny jeans, light blue tank top, and a dark navy military style jacket. Slipping my feet into some nude wedges, I grab my messenger bag, slip it over my head, and reach for my work bag.

"I'll drop it off at your place." Beth grabs the bag and pulls it away.

"No, you'll wake up the boys." I reach around to snatch the bag back.

Lifting the strap to my shoulder, I reach out with my other hand and grab a hair tie, slipping it on my wrist.

"You look like a beautiful homeless woman," Jennifer sneers.

"Leave the bag," Beth whines.

I shake my head. "I need this bag and you know it."

"We don't work tomorrow," Beth adds. "I'll bring it to you tomorrow."

I'm prepared to argue, but she cuts me off before I can start.

"We can say you forgot the bag in my car since we are going out for breakfast together this morning. See, I just gave you an alibi." She smiles, proud of her quick thinking.

"Fine." I sigh and drop the bag to the floor.

Pulling out my cell, I send Kel a quick message with my alibi. *Dear God, I need a damn excuse. This is a bad idea. I'm just going to go out there and tell him I changed my mind.*

With a deep breath, I take one last look in the mirror, glance at the girls, who give me a thumbs up, and exit the dressing room. Eyes of the other backups who witnessed the-great-Jackson-seduction follow me all the way to the door. I pause for a moment, taking one more breath before pushing the door open.

Jackson

The whiskey isn't doing anything to ease my anxiety. After thirty-five minutes, I'm ready to go back and drag her out the door. *Christ. I've never been so aggressive in my pursuit, but I can't let her just walk away.*

Tossing back the last of my drink, I stand straight and turn. A petite, curly blonde exits the stage door and turns toward me. She stops. Her hair is shorter—just past her shoulders, but the same color and curled. She takes a visible breath and begins walking in my direction.

Pushing off the bar, I let her come to me. As much as I want to carry her out the front door to my waiting car, I need her to make this choice.

She stops about four feet away from me, trying to keep distance between us.

"Hey." She grabs the strap of her bag with both hands, nervously moving from her left to right foot.

Closing the distance, I step into her personal space. She stiffens when I brush the curls off her left shoulder and cup the side of her neck, my thumb rubbing her jaw. I can feel her body start to melt into mine.

"Ready?"

"Yeah," she breathes.

I want to make her completely melt. I want to devour her on the spot, but I show restraint.

"Come on, snake charmer," I say, grabbing one hand away from the bag and pulling her behind me toward the exit.

"What?" She stumbles at first, but quickly matches my stride.

"Hmm?" I pull her through the door and toward the waiting car, trying to be quick. I don't want fans or cameras getting involved.

"What did you call me?" She pulls her hand from mine as we reach the car.

Sam stands with the door open. I turn, motioning for her to climb in.

"It's just a nickname." Grabbing her arm, I urge her to get into the car.

"But, why did you—"

"If you don't want to be on the front of a gossip rag or website, I suggest you get in the car."

She glances around, eyes wide, and then hurries inside the back of the car. I follow, my eyes on her perfect ass.

Liza sits, looking out the window as the car pulls away from the curb. While she's distracted, I take in the off-stage version of my snake charmer. Instead of sky-high stilettos, she wears a thick-soled shoe in a skin color. In place of lingerie is skin tight cotton and denim. Where she's usually clad in only satin, silk, and lace, there's now cotton covering her skin. It's surprisingly enticing.

Knowing the curves lying beneath these everyday materials, I'm eager to unwrap the gift of her heart-shaped ass and plump tits.

I wonder if she's cotton underneath her ordinary girl clothes or if hints of the naughty snake charmer hide close to her skin.

"Where are we going?" Her voice draws my attention from the curve where her ass meets her thigh.

"To have breakfast." I shift closer.

"But where?" Her brow slightly wrinkles.

"I'm surprised it took you so long to ask." I deter from answering, not wanting to give her the opportunity to back out.

Slipping my arm over the back of the seat, I settle into the leather. My legs, as long as they are, relax to the side. Our thighs touch. She shifts, a fruitless attempt for space. I've made sure there isn't any.

"Where are we going, Jackson?"

The stern sound of my name coming out of her mouth sends a shot through my chest. Closing my eyes, I drop my head back, hoping she'll say it again if I ignore her.

"Jackson?" she presses.

I start to harden. *Her voice is like a fucking spell on my dick.*

Rolling my head in her direction, I open my eyes.

"I'm just guessing, but I think you would prefer not having cameras and reporters following our every move, right?"

She nods.

"Okay." Closing my eyes, I roll my head back. "I'm taking us to a place where I can control the exposure."

"Oh," she whispers.

Five minutes pass and she relaxes. Her thigh is no longer tense. Her head rests back in the seat.

My fingers move of their own accord, wrapping curls around them. The action is soothing for some reason and when I caress Liza's scalp, she shivers. Lifting my head, I turn and watch, testing the action again. She tries to fight it, but a small shudder gives her away. Before I can further explore this reaction, the car goes completely dark.

We're here.

Chapter Six
Liza

The minute I realize we're in a parking garage of a hotel, I tense. By the time the adrenaline kicks in, Jackson has my hand in a vice-like grip, pulling me onto an elevator. The way we move through back hallways, staff entrances, and elevators, feels like we're criminals. We reach a hotel room door. He swipes the key card and opens it with practiced movements.

Inside, he releases my hand when we reach the sitting area of the hotel suite. The room is muted colors with dark wooden accents, large windows with gauzy sheers draping from decorative wrought iron bars, and plush, oversized furniture. Finally catching my breath, I focus on Jackson.

"Well, that was...interesting." I flex my numb fingers, speaking to his back, which is turned toward me.

Jackson stays silent, slipping his t-shirt over his head and tossing it onto one of the beige chairs. In a white tank top thin enough to see the designs covering his skin, he turns, locking his eyes with mine.

Is he going to take everything off? Does he expect me to strip down and get to business? I'm such a slut. I making this way too easy.

Keeping his eyes on mine, he fists the white cotton at his stomach and pulls it free from the waist of his jeans.

I wonder if his tattoos go all the way down to...

With quick movements, he grabs his belt, undoes the buckle, and slides it through the denim loops.

Inhaling sharply, I watch as he drops the belt to the floor, the thud of the thick silver buckle startling me.

"Breathe, Liza." There's a velvety edge to the way he says

my name.

I exhale at the sound of a knock.

Jackson strides by to answer the door, certain to brush his bare arm against me.

A young man in a hotel uniform pushes a black cart into the room. Keeping his head down, he delivers the cart and exits without a word or even hesitating for a tip.

"Breakfast, as promised." Jackson lifts silver lids from dishes, throwing me a grin over his toned shoulder.

With his head, he motions me over.

Pushing aside my lusty urges, I make my way to him.

"Here." Jackson shoves a tray of scrambled egg whites and bacon into my hands. "Can you get this, too?" He holds out a second plate with five pancakes stacked.

The food smells amazing and my stomach rumbles.

Oh my God, please let me just die right now.

Redistributing the weight of the eggs, I take the pancakes. Jackson hooks something on one long finger, lifts a tray of muffins and bagels on one arm, and wraps his free arm around a covered basket.

"Come on." With a nod of his head, he leads the way back to where we started.

Heat prickles under my skin thinking of the way he provided me my own personal striptease.

Using his foot, he clears items off the coffee table. I can't hold back the giggle escaping me.

"Just put them here." He starts putting his items down, so I do the same.

He toes off his black boots and kicks them to the side before sitting on the couch. Patting the couch cushion next to him, he looks expectant.

"Relax. Take off your jacket and stay a while."

There's a mischievous twitch to his lip.

I know he's proud of himself for getting me back to his hotel room, the arrogant, cocky, sexy, gorgeous man, but I'm not making this any easier than I already have. In fact, I should just say thanks and take my leave right now.

"Liza, you've got to be a woman once in a while..." I hear Sid's voice in my head, *"not just a mother and provider. Let loose."*

Slipping my jacket off, I lay it on the arm of one chair across the table from him. The same chair I choose to sit in.

Grinning, he leans forward, elbows on his knees.

"Is that how you're gonna play it?"

"I didn't realize we were playing something?" I raise one brow.

He grins and points to the spread between us.

"Help yourself."

Grabbing a piece of bacon, he sits back onto the couch cushions. Wrapping his lips around the bacon, he bites and chews slowly.

I sit forward and pick up a bagel. Grabbing a container of peanut butter and a knife, I sit back. His eyes feel like invisible hands running over my skin—touching, undressing.

Avoiding his gaze, I nervously slather half the bagel in peanut butter, getting it all over the fingers of my right hand. I put a finger in my mouth and suck, placing the bagel onto the table.

His groan draws my attention away from my hand. He unfolds his long, lean body from the couch, stepping over the coffee table between us.

I drop my finger from my mouth and press back into the chair. Mouth open, I stare up his towering form.

"What's—?"

The hot and gripping hold he takes on my knees silences me. We lock eyes as he jerks my legs apart. Licking his lips, he kneels between them.

Clamping his long fingers around my wrist, he holds my right hand between us and leans forward. His tongue snakes out and around the peanut butter covered digits before sucking them into his mouth. His eyes drift closed and he moans. With each sweep of his tongue, my body rises higher, pressing closer until my nipples tingle with every breath he takes.

Releasing my wrist, his hands slide to my hips, gripping hard.

I moan and pull my fingers from between his lips, replacing them with my mouth. His lip ring digs into my flesh enticingly. It's intoxicating. Our tongues twist and slide, urging me on. Pushing my body flush against his, I run my saliva dampened fingers through his hair and grip tightly, sucking his tongue deeper. The sharp bite of his lip ring makes my thighs tingle. Jackson growls low and deep, yanking me to the edge of the chair by my hips.

Forgetting the play-harder-to-get idea, the I-should-really-just-go thoughts, and shoving away the feeling of stupidity for following him tonight, I embrace my one night with hot as fuck rock star Jackson Shaw.

Wrapping my left arm over his shoulder, I bunch the cotton material on his back in my hand.

He grinds a deliciously frustrating rhythm between my legs, but I need more. Tilting my hips, I slip from the chair into his lap.

Jackson's arms move around my back, one hand flattening, the tips of his fingers dipping inside the waistband of my jeans. With the other, he shoves at the unmoving chair. His mouth breaks from mine to release an irritated snarl. Keeping my arms around him, I drop my head back and take a moment to catch my breath.

What am I doing? This is going to end—

The chair flips onto its side and his mouth captures the skin between my neck and shoulder as both his arms wrap around me. Settling me onto the thick carpeted floor, his hips resume their incredible, torturous rhythm.

His hands are everywhere all at once: my hips, waist, pulling my thighs higher, tracing my sides, skirting around my breasts. Arching my back, I want to be closer. I want more. I need everything.

I claw my way down his body, fisting and bunching his shirt until I feel bare skin. At my touch, he rises above me, sitting on his heels and staring down. Keeping eye contact, he pulls the thin, white shirt over his head and tosses it away.

I'm tempted to look away, to take in his heavily inked skin, but he keeps me prisoner in his burning gaze. His long fingers curl into the front of my jeans and work the button and zipper like a professional de-pantser.

Lowering his body, he peels back the front of my pants. Air enters my lungs, but I can't catch my breath. My clit pulses, wanting everything he's silently promising.

His lip ring is cool against my hot skin as his lips touch above the lace band of my panties.

"Lace," he whispers, his breath scorching against my flesh.

"Wh—?"

The heat from his tongue against my skin makes speaking impossible. When he dips his tongue beneath the lace, all thoughts disappear.

The denim pinches my skin as he grips the material at my hips and tugs. With each tug, my pussy throbs. Tug at hips, throb. Tug at thighs, throb. Tingles prickle across my skin when he bows down to touch his lips inside of my thigh. Tug at my knees, throb.

Legs free, I squeak in surprise as he pulls me across the carpet. My lace-covered ass meets his denim-covered knees and long, determined fingers twist into my tank top, yanking the offensive clothing over my head.

He leans forward, his hands in the carpet above my head, and hovers over me. Staring down, he puts one hand around my throat and sucks his bottom lip into his mouth. His fingers on my throat twitch, and I tense.

"Relax." Lightly rubbing his thumb along my jaw, he lowers his face close to mine. "Tell me what you want, Liza."

My brow furrows.

"Tell me you want me," his words heat my lips, "please."

I flatten my hands on his chest, feeling his muscles tighten beneath my touch. He's frozen, unsure of what I'm going to do. His breaths across my face intensify and I open my mouth, inhaling deeply, savoring.

Slipping my hands down over his ribs till I reach his stomach, I grip the front of his jeans and slip the button free. His eyes close tight. Instead of unzipping, I grasp each side and yank. The sound of the protesting zipper fills the room.

Jackson's eyes snap open. Pupils dilated, they gleam like

volcanic rock.

"Fuck, Liza," he groans.

I feel bold.

"That's exactly what I want you to do, Jackson."

His hand around my throat flexes, but not painfully. Reclaiming my mouth with punishing force, our teeth clink. My hands move in a flurry of desire and need, shoving the denim down his hips.

The hand on my throat slides over my collarbone and chest, pulling the lacey cup of my bra aside. Long fingers tease and pinch my aching nipple before cupping the mound as an offering to his talented mouth.

"Oh, fuck, Jackson." I bring my hand to his head and fist his hair.

He sucks harder and I arch my back, pushing myself closer.

I lift my knees higher to his sides and hook my big toes into his jeans, pushing them further down.

Releasing my nipple, Jackson pushes up. Kneeling above me, his eyes travel over my body, watching my chest rise and fall. The savage inner fire within them heats the chill he left behind.

He reaches back into the pockets of the jeans hanging off his body. While he's distracted, I take the moment to enjoy the unobstructed view of his art-covered chest. The wings of an Egyptian lion cover each pectoral, the words *Strength in Loyalty* scrawled across his collar in elegant script, a bird on each shoulder, and holstered black pistols on each rib are the largest of the ink. The rest are small designs, intricate swirls, and what I think is ivy on his hip. *Seven feet of lickable graffiti* pops into mind and my thoughts randomly jump to the flavored wallpaper in *Willy Wonka*.

I wonder if he tastes like snozberries.

Closing my eyes, I force myself to stop thinking about snozberries. The crinkle and rip of a wrapper bring my attention back to Jackson.

Eyes raking boldly over me, he spits a piece of the silver foil away from us. The heat from the back of his hands warms the inside of my thighs as he frees himself from his underwear.

My eyes drift down to watch as he puts the condom on, but his words stop me.

"Strip for me, Liza."

He gazes at me expectantly again.

Raising my brow, I slide my hands over my stomach, up to my breasts, and finger the bunched lace beneath them.

"I'm not a stripper, Jackson," I retort in challenge.

I don't know what it is about him that makes me so bold.

He grins wide, beautiful. Warmth aches in my chest. I push it away to revel in the tingles of lust instead.

"No, you're a snake charmer." His voice is husky, gravely.

Done with his task, he scans my body. I eye his, taking in the latex covered length of him. My clit pulses impatiently, knowing what it wants. I tighten my pussy muscles, seeking something to relieve the ache.

Jackson flattens his hand on my chest, dragging it down between my breasts, over my stomach and hip. Tingles flare into aches. I actually twitch, anxious for him. And he knows it. With a cocky grin, he repeats the act with his other hand. This time, my hips raise from the floor, a final invitation to fuck me.

His hands tighten on my hips, fingers gripping the lace there. The tips dig into my skin as he pulls the lace as far as he can with his body still between my legs.

Releasing the lace, he palms the back of my knees and pushes them high. A moment of self-consciousness causes me to pull away, just a bit. But he notices.

"Don't you dare move," he says, his eyes locking onto mine. The command stills me.

Keeping eye contact, he slides the panties up and over my feet and tosses them away before pushing himself back between my thighs.

With his bare hips flush against my thighs, I squirm, pressing to get closer.

"Do you want me to fuck you, Liza? Is that what you want?"

Rocking his hips, the long length of his cock brushes against my thigh—hot, hard, and ready.

I close my eyes and bite my lip.

"Tell me, Charmer."

He angles forward, bringing his length against my swollen lips. The shudder of his body gives away the effect his teasing has on him.

"Yes," I growl, raising onto my left elbow. Grabbing his hip with my right hand, I pull him against me.

"Christ," he pants, sliding his hand between my legs. He slips one finger against my clit and I drop my head back. Pressing down harder, he earns a gasp. Sliding through my wetness, his long finger enters me in a smooth invasion before a second joins.

Unable to hold back any longer, I buck my hips and fuck myself against his hand, needing more. He gives it. One more long finger fills me, stretching me.

"You're so fucking hot," he rasps, watching his digit move in and out of me while his hand stays motionless. I close my eyes, reveling in the feel of his palm rubbing my clit with each downward motion of my hips. "There's no going slow, Liza."

His finger disappears and my eyes open, meeting his. The connection between us like summer lightning.

"I won't apologize for wanting you hard and rough," he grounds out, entering me in one long, rigid thrust. "Fuck, Liza!"

"Oh God," I gasp, falling to the flat of my back and digging my nails into the carpet.

"Look at me," he demands.

Not realizing I'd closed them, I open my eyes. The moment my eyes connect with his, a storm engulfs us.

Still above me, he reaches out with his right hand, fists the lace between my breasts, and starts thrusting. Each drive jostles my body. His left arm snakes under my right thigh to find purchase and hold me in place.

Electrical currents zap through my veins. All of it charging between my legs. Each thrust flipping another switch. The pleasure builds, bubbles, arching my back and neck.

"Jackson," I moan, loudly. "Don't stop."

Clawing at the plush carpet, I wonder for a moment if I'll

tear it. It's been so long, too long, since I've had a man-induced orgasm. And this man...fuck, this man knew exactly how to induce.

"Oh yes, yes, yes, Jackson." I sing so much praise, it's practically blasphemy.

"That's it, Charmer, sing for me." His words come with harder pumping hips.

The electrical charge hits a crescendo and I cry out. Jackson rides the waves of my climax hard and nasty. His hand on my thigh digs into my flesh, the lace of my bra protests his grip, and he shouts.

"Fuck."

Jerking forward once, twice, and a final time, he comes just as hard as he rode me.

Jackson releases his grip on my thigh and bra. Collapsing forward, he presses his forehead to my stomach. We lie silent, satisfied, and panting for breath in the middle of his hotel room.

Jackson

Lifting myself off Liza, I look over a body built for sin wearing the evidence of the hottest fuck I can remember. Deep red and purple sucker bites on her breasts, the reddened skin where the lace rubbed, and my sweat on the inside of her thighs. For a moment, the regret of wearing a condom flashes through my mind, wishing it was a mixture of our sweat and cum between her legs.

What the fuck am I thinking?

The shift of her body distracts my crazy thoughts. Looking at her face, her eyes are closed and breathing steady. Asleep. I grin, knowing she sang my name and passed out from my cock. She shivers and goose bumps form on her skin.

I slip from her body and bite back a moan. My legs wobble on the way to toss the used condom in the trash. The wall mirror catches my attention and I stare at myself holding my jeans up, cock tucked back into my underwear.

"You haven't touched that shit tonight, you know that?" I whisper to my reflection.

Liza groans and I return back to my little snake charmer, who's curled onto her side. I slip my hand beneath her body and lift her into my arms. She doesn't wake. Taking her to my bed, I lay her on the mattress. Before covering her, I unhook and slip the bra from her body. She curls onto her side once more.

I shove my jeans down my body, step out of them, and crawl over her sleeping form. Settling in beside her, I wait almost a whole goddamn minute before wrapping her in my arms and bringing her to my chest.

"Ow, shit."

A hushed cry wakes me.

"What are you doing?" I ask, my voice clogged with sleep.

"Sorry," she whispers. "Bathroom?"

"Other way," I mumble and then yawn.

The click of the door lets me know she found it. Rolling to my side, I rub my face and watch the bathroom door with heavy lids.

The door opens, casting a heavenly glow around naked Liza. Her right arm flails out to the side and the room darkens.

"Sorry," she whispers.

I hear the embarrassment in her voice. *I wonder if she blushes all the way to her delicious nipples.*

When I don't feel movement on the bed, I glance around the darkened room.

"Liza?" I call out.

No answer.

I climb out of bed and walk to the sitting room.

Bent at the waist, Liza picks up clothes from the floor. The light from the large window puts her pale, heart-shaped ass on display.

"What are you doing?"

She startles, straightening and turning to face me. Holding her jeans to cover her body, her eyes dart to the door and then back to me.

Well, that won't fucking do.

"It's really late. I should get—"

I reach out, take the jeans from her, and throw them off to the side. She watches where they fall and even in the dim light, I can see she's nervous.

"I should get going." Her eyes return to my face.

"Why?" I ask, arms over my chest.

"It's late."

"We still haven't had breakfast."

I drop my arms.

"Um, we, uh..."

Her discomfort is almost funny, but she's standing less than a foot away from me completely naked and I'm hard as fuck for her.

Bending, I lift her over my shoulder.

"Put me down." Her giggle kills the demanding effect she's going for.

"Okay."

I drop her onto my bed and she bounces to the middle, pushing her I've-been-fucked-by-Jackson-Shaw hair from her face.

"What do you plan to do with me now?"

She leans back on her hands, straightening her legs and crossing them at the ankle.

Fuck if I don't love the little challenges she likes to pose.

"My plan," I place my hands onto the mattress, "is very straightforward." I crawl toward her.

Her eyes widen and she sucks her bottom lip into her mouth.

At her ankles, I hesitate, grasping one in each hand.

"It's to spread your creamy, smooth, sexy as fuck legs..." I pull her legs apart and she doesn't resist.

"And then what?" she asks, her question breathy.

Crawling between her open legs, I use my palms to push her

thighs wide apart and lower my body. The muscles under my hands tighten in anticipation.

"Then," I make sure to speak with heavy, hot breaths over her exposed flesh, "breakfast."

I drop my open mouth to her spread pussy. Her fingers slip through my hair and fist the strands. My dick throbs, wanting release. He remembers how tight she is, how hot and wet she was for us. And at this moment, my dick hates my tongue as I delve deep inside to fuck her with it.

"You taste like heaven," I say, my wet mouth sliding against her lips.

"Less talk," she groans, pressing her hips into my face.

Pushing closer, I use my shoulders to hold her thighs wide and high, leaving my fingers free to explore. I lick up her slit and suck her swollen clit into my mouth, plunging my middle finger deep inside her. The mixture of her arousal, my saliva, and the way she holds my head in place makes me thrust into the mattress, searching for some kind of relief.

I add another finger and the heel of her foot presses between my shoulder blades. It's hot as fuck how she goes from nervous and awkward to teasing, demanding, and greedy. *I could fuck this girl for days.*

"Yes. Right. There." Her body trembles.

Pulling my fingers out, I kiss her clit one last time and pull away.

"No," she whines, gripping my hair tighter, making the tip of my dick prickle.

Chuckling, I reach up and untangle her fingers. She allows me, but wears an adorable pout on her face.

On hands and knees, I crawl to the edge of the bed. The soft touch of her hands caress my thighs and slide up over my ass. *Fuck, I should've taken off my underwear.*

At the waistband, she curls her fingers beneath the fabric. The scratch of her nails against my skin sends a shot of pleasure straight to my poor, neglected dick. I don't think he can take much more. She pulls, slowly stripping me. My cock springs forth, hard and ready.

I reach over the edge of the bed, my stomach pressing against her tits. The hard pebbles rub and I clench my teeth against the tug in my balls. Her hands slip up my back, dipping into the valley of my spine, gripping softly.

Unable to find the handle for the bedside drawer, I grab from beneath and pull. It crashes to the floor and her hands still.

"Are you okay?"

Her body shifts, pressing flush against mine as she tries to get up.

"Fine. Don't move," I bite out, my cock throbbing with every shift of her skin.

Putting more of my weight on her, I keep her in place and grab the foil wrappers.

Condoms in hand, I return to hover on hand and knees above her body. Our eyes meet. *Damn, I love that naughty glint in her eye.*

"Shit," I groan, closing my eyes.

Her hand moves around and over my rigid cock. Instinctively, I press forward and fuck her soft, little palm. When her thumb swipes over the head, she inhales sharply.

I open my eyes and grin down at her, knowing she just found my piercing. I drop to my forearms, still thrusting into her hand, and bring my mouth an inch from hers.

"Don't worry, baby. You loved it last time." Slipping my tongue from between my lips, I lick her mouth. She moans, squirming beneath me.

Liza's free hand slides up my ribs, over my shoulder, and down my arm. Reaching my hand, her fingers work their way into my fist. Keeping eye contact, she frees one foil package, brings the packet between her white teeth, and tears it open.

I lick my lips, our faces so close I can practically taste the latex on my tongue.

She slips the condom over my steel hard cock using both hands. Her thumb swipes once more over the tip, causing a reflexive jerk of my hips.

She leans up slowly and presses her mouth to mine. With one hand against my chest, she pushes. *There is no fucking way I'm moving off of her right now.*

She pushes again, harder.

"Please," she says against my lips.

Fuck me if I don't push up onto my arms.

Sliding around beneath me, she manages to sit up and manipulate me into sitting on my legs.

Frowning, I move forward, but she puts a hand out. I narrow my eyes, waiting.

She crawls over and straddles my thighs. Instinctively, I palm her ass. *Jesus Christ, her ass is made for my hands.*

One small arm wraps around my shoulder as the other snakes between us, gripping the base of my cock. I groan and bury my face in her neck, sucking on her skin. She positions me at her entrance and drops down hard, taking all of me in one motion. I press my teeth against her flesh and she moans.

Her arms wrap around my shoulders as she rises and falls in rapid succession. My fingers curl into her bare ass, digging deeply into her porcelain skin and spreading her cheeks. *There will be marks.* I grip harder, ensuring it, and guide her against me.

The slap of sweaty skin and panting fills the room. The scent of latex, arousal, and pussy surrounds me. Every pint of blood in my body rushes to my dick. Sharp aching tightens my balls.

Releasing one perfect globe, I grip her hip and pull her against me harder.

"Oh, fuck." Her moans grow louder and dirtier. "Fuck. Your dick is amazing."

Sliding my hand inward, I find her clit with my thumb and rub.

"Jesus. Christ. Don't stop," she screams, her thighs tightening on my ribs. Her hips pump faster, seeking orgasmic bliss.

Her dirty mouth makes it nearly impossible to hold back. My dick throbs painfully, the tip aches to release, and my balls may never drop again.

"Jackson." My name sounds like a fucking prayer.

Liza fists the hair at the back of my head with one hand and pulls my face from her neck.

Fuck, if she makes me look in her eyes, see that naughty gleam, I'm gonna explode. I focus on her parted lips and the flush of her damp skin. She pulls on my head again.

Our eyes lock.

"Come with me, Jackson."

I release a breath I didn't realize I was holding.

"Come with me...now."

Releasing my hair, her head drops back and she screams out for the heavenly father before calling out to me like the charmer she is. My cock pulses hard at the sound of my name and for a moment, my mind goes blank. Then, in a violent combination of clarity and ecstasy, all the energy in my body explodes into hers.

I drop my forehead to her chest, my heavy breaths washing over her tits. I want to cup one and roll the hard tip in my fingers, but I'm completely fucking spent.

She squirms, an attempt to move, and my sensitive cock can't take it. I grip her hips and quickly pull her off. A shudder rolls up my spine and I stare down at my softening cock, removing the condom.

What kind of fucking shit is this? Is it broken?

Liza rolls from her back to her stomach, the movement catching my eye. She's still trying to catch her breath, but inching to the edge of the bed.

"Where are you going?"

She looks back over her shoulder. The picture she creates is one a fucking artist would love to paint or sculpt. Her naked skin a blank porcelain slate: flawless. That ass: something to be worshiped. The curve of her hip: the perfect place to kiss, lick, bite.

"To get my clothes?" It sounds like a question.

Knotting the condom opening, I drop it next to the bed and move to her.

She stiffens, but doesn't try to run. It wouldn't matter. I'd catch her.

I grab her by the knees and pull her back to the middle of

the bed. The contrast of my inked skin against her clear perfection causes a pang in my chest.

Ignoring the feeling, I angle my body on the bed so I can lay the back of my head on her thigh, right where it meets her ass.

"Are you hungry?" I slip one hand underneath her knee, holding.

"No," she answers, and then yawns.

"Tired." It's my turn to yawn.

"A bit." She giggles out the response.

"Sorry, if I bore you to sleep."

Turning my head, I rest my cheek against her skin. I'm a sick fuck, 'cause the smell of sex, of us, coming from between her legs is oddly satisfying.

"You'll just have to make it up to me." I can hear the smile in her voice.

I release her knee and roll to my stomach. Leaving my cheek against her thigh, I bring one hand to the right cheek of her ass.

"How long have you worked at the club?"

My question catches her by surprise. The muscles beneath my cheek and hand tense.

"A few years."

I don't like how guarded she sounds.

"Are you from here?"

I brush my thumb over her skin, feeling the muscles relax a little.

"No."

"Where are you from?"

"Pennsylvania."

"You aren't comfortable with questions." It's not a question.

"Why are you in L.A.?" she asks, turning the tables.

I shrug.

"Promotion. Music stuff." It's not a total lie, but part of my contract with the show is keeping my identity as a judge a secret.

"So, you'll be heading back home soon." This isn't a question.

"Tell me about you, Liza." I trace invisible patterns on her skin.

"Not much to tell." I feel her shrug and then she sighs. "I came to L.A. thinking I would be famous. Turns out, a lot of people have the same idea." She laughs quietly.

"How did you find the club? To be honest, I wouldn't have given that fucking place a second glance from how it looks on the outside."

"Waitressed with a girl who told me about auditions. I went to check it out and the rest is history."

The room falls silent, but it's not an uncomfortable silence. It's too fucking comfortable.

"Do you often go back to hotels with people who come to watch the show?"

It's a shitty question and I know it, but being with her is too easy. Time with my snake charmer is up.

Her body stiffens.

"Why would you say that?"

"I didn't *say* anything. I asked a question."

"You know exactly what you're saying." Her body disappears and my head hits the bed. I immediately miss her presence.

"Don't get pissy. It's just a fucking question." Rolling onto my back, I rub my face. I want to jump up and drag her back to me.

"Fuck you, Jackson. You got what you wanted from me, don't be an asshole about it now."

The bed shifts and I angle my head, watching her walk toward the bedroom door. Without thinking about why I need her to leave, I roll from the bed and catch her around the waist. She squeals as I lift her into my arms.

"What the hell are you doing?" she asks, more confused than mad.

"I didn't say you could leave."

Kneeling on the bed, I lay us both down onto the mattress.

"I don't take orders from you. I'm not a whore or whatever you want to believe I am."

I pull the rumpled blanket over our naked bodies, tucking the white cotton around her.

"What are you doing?" she asks, her voice exasperated. "I was leaving, just like you wanted me to."

Mid-tuck, I freeze. She figured my shit out.

"I'm not stupid," she whispers.

"No." I settle in and wrap my arm around her, making sure she doesn't get up. "You're worse."

She exhales loudly and I know she's going to speak, curse me, and do what I need her to do, but I won't let her leave. I can't.

I cup her cheek, bring her face to mine, and press my mouth to hers, ending the conversation before it starts. Something inside me shatters. My chest burns and I deepen the kiss.

This kiss is different—sensual, soft, explorative. It's goddamn meaningful. Holding her face, I bring my body flush to her side, but it's not close enough. I wrap one leg around hers, pulling her into me.

Breaking away from each other, I drop back to the pillow and hold her head to my collarbone. We breathe heavily into the silence.

And if I wasn't fucked before, I am now.

Chapter Seven

Liza

A sound wakes me. Disoriented, I look around, remembering where I am and who's next to me. I lift onto an elbow and look over at the bright white numbers on the bedside clock.

3:12 A.M.

Twisting my body, I peek at Jackson. He's stomach down, facing away from me. The butterflies in my stomach settle a little. With the practiced movements of a one-time mother of an infant, I ninja my way out of the covers and stand by the bed.

Jackson lays with a white sheet low enough, I can see the beginning slope of his ass. Part of me wishes he'd wake and stop me like before, but the smart, common-sense part knows I need to get home.

I close my eyes and inhale the scent of him, sex...us. Saving it to memory, I turn for the door. Every muscle in my body aches deliciously with the memory he left on my body. At the door, I risk one last look at him before quietly pulling it closed and collecting my things.

Slipping from the hotel room—without the bra I couldn't find—I make sure the door closes soundlessly. I look down both sides of the corridor and take a breath when I find it empty. I start toward the elevators and my skin prickles, uneasiness and the feeling of being watched shoving at my back. I glance over my shoulder and find the corridor still empty. Reaching the elevators, I press the call button more times than necessary. The moment the elevator arrives, I dart inside, pressing the *close door* button repeatedly.

Paranoid much? Jesus, one-night stands with rock stars are horrible for the nerves.

The doors slide open to the lobby and no one gives a second glance as I swiftly step toward the rotating door. Keeping my head down, I exit the hotel and use my peripheral vision to find a cab to drive me away from my one night with hot as fuck, way-too-easy-to-fall-for, Jackson Shaw.

"He should come with a warning label," I mumble into the backseat of the yellow taxi.

"Someone got in late." Kel's voice pulls me from my restless sleep on the couch.

Having gotten in so late, I didn't want to wake them by messing with the squeaky pullout. I groan and rub my eyes.

"What time is it?" I ask in a half-yawn.

"Almost nine-thirty."

I open my eyes to find my brother looking down at me with concern.

"What's wrong?"

Unease lining his face, he sits on the coffee table.

"What happened last night, Liza?"

Pushing up to sit, I face him.

"Nothing. I went out with Beth and—"

"Did you get hurt?" His brow raises.

"What? No." Scrunching my face in confusion, I ask, "Why would you think that?"

"Then what happened to your lip." He points.

Bringing my hand to my mouth, I fight a wince. *Shit, shit, shit.* I jump to my feet and hurry to the bathroom.

"Mom, where are my—?"

The closing of the bathroom door cuts off Lucas' question. Guilt stabs at my chest, but I focus on my reflection in the mirror.

So caught up in the moment, I didn't even feel how hard our

mouths met, but the evidence is staring me right in the face. I explore the swollen red mark on my bottom lip with my tongue. The taste and smell of Jackson assaults my senses. Shaking my head, I flip on the faucet and splash water on my face.

"Liza?" Kel knocks on the door. "Are you okay?"

"Yeah," I blurt, reaching for the hand towel. Patting my face dry, I pull open the door.

Kel and Lucas stare at me with concern in their eyes.

"Guys."

I tilt my head and toss the towel next to the sink. Stepping forward, I take them both in my arms.

"I'm fine. Bethany kept me out later than I planned. I'm just tired."

"Do you wanna skip my game so you can get some sleep?" Lucas asks.

I lean down and kiss the top of his head.

"I wouldn't miss your game for anything. Now, go finish getting ready." Releasing both of them, I step back. "Your shin guards are hanging in your closet." I ruffle his hair.

"How'd you know what I was looking for?" he asks, but turns into his room before I can respond.

"What's going on?" Kel frowns.

I place my hand on his face and smile.

"Beth accidentally bumped me in the mouth last night while changing. It's nothing," I say, cringing internally at the lie.

"Yeah, okay," he offers, and walks down the hall.

I close the bathroom door again, turn on the shower, and wait for the water to heat. The scent of Jackson wafts off my clothes as I strip and my body reacts, thinking it can still have him. Taking a deep breath, I turn for the shower and catch my reflection in the mirror.

I gasp at the dark purple and red sucker bites peppering my left breast. *Clearly, he has a favorite.* Lifting my hair, I take in more evidence of my night. Light bruising on my ass confirms his hands had spent time there. Carpet burn mars a spot on my lower back. Angry red marks show where my bra rubbed last night.

"You almost done?" Kel's voice and the knock on the door startles me. Without thinking, my arms shoot out, covering my body like he can see through the door.

"Almost," I respond, jumping into the shower.

After taking the quickest shower ever—part of me mourning the idea of washing Jackson away—I wrap a towel around my body, another over my shoulders for complete coverage, and step into the hallway.

I rummage through the storage drawers beneath my clothing rack and grab a pair of black workout capris, matching sports bra, and a loose yellow t-shirt before hurrying back into the bathroom to dress.

I situate my shirt, making sure the V-neck doesn't expose any of my Jackson reminders, tear a brush through my hair, and apply tinted moisturizer, eyeliner, and mascara. After years of wearing elaborate, sexy pin-up makeup, going out without something makes me feel exposed.

"Mom, the game is in thirty-five minutes," Lucas yells down the hall.

Running some frizz reducing hair serum through my hair, I twist and wrap the length into a loose bun and tie a yellow bird print bandana around my head to complete the look.

"I'm coming," I call, walking down the hall and meeting them at the door.

Lucas stands in his uniform, soccer bag slung over his shoulder.

Kel holds his messenger bag close and opens the door.

Sliding my feet into flip flops, I grab my bag, slip on a thin black jacket, and we're out the door.

"So, what made you decide to go out last night?" Kel asks, holding the stairwell door open.

I shrug. "Celebrating."

We begin descending to the main floor.

"Celebrating what?" he presses.

"Still having a job," I blurt.

Kel and Lucas both stop, looking at me.

"What happened to your job?" Lucas sounds worried.

"Hey, nothing happened." Stepping close, I smooth my hand over his head.

"Then what do you mean, Liza?" Kel asks, his question laced in annoyance.

"Thom sold the club." I look from Lucas' relieved face to Kel's suspicious one. "There had been talk, even from Thom, but last night was the first night we got to meet the new owner. He basically assured us our jobs were safe and he's not overhauling the place, but there will be some changes."

Kel's face relaxes a little.

"Now, let's get moving or we'll be late."

With a gentle shove from me, Lucas starts walking down the last flight of stairs.

"So, do you like the new owner?"

"Kel, please stop worrying so much."

Stepping off the last step, I dig through my bag for sunglasses and slip them on.

"I'm just asking," he grumbles.

I sigh and slip my arm around his, guiding him out of the apartment building.

"I guess. He seems good. He'll definitely bring in new people and the celebrities are going to be—"

"Celebrities?" Kel tugs my arm, stopping us.

"Come on!" Lucas shouts from twenty paces ahead.

"Keep walking," I say, pulling on his arm. "The new owner is Steven Redman. He's from—"

"Corrosive Velocity," Kel finishes. "Holy shit, Liza. They're amazing! He's your new boss?"

The excitement in his voice makes me laugh.

"Yep. He's already brought one of the other group members and a...another guest to the club." Memories of Jackson flash through my mind. His long, skilled fingers curling into my skin and inside me.

"You cold?" Kel's question confuses me.

"No, why?"

"You shivered," he responds with a shrug. "Please tell me you can get me an autograph."

"I can probably do better than that." I squeeze his arm. "I'll see if I can introduce you. Then you can ask for one yourself."

Kel's arm slips out of mine to wrap around my shoulders. I curl my arm around his back.

"You're the best." His lips press against the side of my head.

"This is almost too precious to interrupt."

My heart begins to race, palms sweat, and stomach flutters from the sound of his voice, a mixture of panic and thrill rushing through me.

Kel turns to face Jackson at the same time I do.

"You're—"

"Don't mean to interrupt your moment, but you forgot this."

Jackson's hand disappears behind him only to return with my lace bra in his hand.

"You must not have been able to find it in the dark light of early morning. Thought you might want it back."

With a flick of his wrist, the lace lands against my chest.

Reflexively, I grip the bra to my chest, ball up the material, and shove it in my bag. My eyes burn with tears I fight not to shed.

How in the hell am I going to explain this to Kel?

"What's your problem?" Kel's angry question surprises me.

"Kel—"

"I don't have a problem," Jackson sneers. "She's your problem, my man."

"Mom," Lucas yells, running to my side, "we're going to miss the bus."

"Are you for fucking real, Liza?" Jackson throws an arm out toward Lucas. "Seriously, you're a goddamn mom, too? Wow. I bet he's so proud."

A whimper escapes my throat when he nods to Lucas.

"Don't talk to my mom like that!"

Lucas moves, standing between Jackson and me.

Putting both hands up in surrender, Jackson backs away.

"Don't worry. Your mom gave me all I needed from her."

His words are as sharp as a dagger and he throws a look, confirming his intent to hurt me before turning and walking away.

"Mom?" Lucas looks up at me, his brow furrowed.

"Let's go. We don't want to be any later than we are," I say, putting an arm around his shoulders and leaving the scene behind us.

We arrive at the field at the end of warm-ups. After apologizing to Lucas' coach, I sit next to Kel on a set of bleachers. The silence between us is uncomfortable and the longer I think about what happened, the angrier I get.

"That was Jackson Shaw, right?" Kel asks in a hush.

"Yes."

"You know, after the game I'm gonna take Luke over to check in on Sean."

He slips his arm around my shoulders, pulling me to his side.

"Okay." I nod. "I have some things for you to take to his grandmother."

Kel gives a squeeze.

"You know, by then, it will be about noon in Pennsylvania."

A tear slides over my cheek. My brother knows who I need. My best friend, the closest person I have to a sister, Sid.

Jackson

She's just like the rest of them. Quick to fuck a celebrity and forget all about what she has at home. Fucking whores.

Julia jumps at the sound of the hotel room door smacking the wall.

"Jackson," her voice is a mixture of relief and nerves, "I've been trying to call you—"

Slipping my hand into my coat, I pull out my newly cracked

cell and hold it out to her.

"Oh." She takes the phone as I walk by her. "I'll have another sent within the hour."

"Jackson, I need to—" she starts, following behind me.

I shove open my bedroom door, wanting to hear anything but perky Julia.

"Hey, baby." The sickly sweet tone of her voice grates on my nerves.

Another fucking whore. I guess I'm a magnet for them.

Stopping just inside the door, I cross my arms over my chest and take a deep breath. "Why are you here?"

"Is that any way to greet me?" she pouts from her perched position at the edge of the bed.

"Sorry. I was trying to warn you," Julia whispers from behind me.

Uncrossing my arms, I reach back and close the door in her face. I know I'm being a dick and I'll have to apologize to her later, but right now, I have a tall, blonde egomaniac to handle.

"Again, why are you here?"

I walk the edge of the room, avoiding her.

"Don't look at me like that." Kristy stands from the bed wearing nothing but an open hotel robe.

"Desperation doesn't look good on you," I sneer.

"You think I'm desperate?" One perfectly manicured nail presses into her chest. "I came here for you." Her arms cross over her chest, making sure to push her breasts up.

At one time, this did it for me, *she* did it for me, but now— nothing.

"I didn't ask you to come here." I turn, giving her my back, and walk into the bathroom, shutting the door behind me.

"You can be a real dick, you know that?" she yells from the other side of the door. "You seem to forget who was there for you after that bitch fucked you over."

Leaning, palms onto the counter, I look at myself in the mirror. Isn't this just typical? She's going to throw Laney into this shit.

"I'm honest about everything with you, I'm open to you, and now you want to condemn me for it?"

The door doesn't muffle her bitching enough.

First Laney pulls her cheating bullshit, now this bitch wants points for *allowing* me an open relationship—one she pushed and schemed to get—and the nail in my fucking coffin is Liza. *Fucking Liza*. The seduction and first fuck, I controlled. Then she turned the tables, making me want more from her. More of what, I don't even want to fucking think too much about.

Grunting, I push up from the counter and grab my black leather bag, finding the brown package inside.

You didn't use this shit the other night. You didn't even want it, think about that.

With a shake of my head, I set up enough lines to snort it all away.

My nose and lips tingle, the numbness spreading like a warm blanket.

Reentering the bedroom, Kristy twists away from a window. I run my tongue over my teeth. *Fuck, their so smooth. Just like Liza's thighs.*

"What are you grinning at?" Kristy's eyes narrow.

Dropping to my back on the bed, I close my eyes and laugh. *Didn't even know I was grinning.*

"Did you get high without me, baby?" Kristy's hands travel up my thighs, warming them. Her hands work my belt and jeans with a practiced touch. Before I can say stop, the warmth of her hand surrounds me.

"Are you going to let me make you come, baby? I know how much you love it when you're high."

The warmth of her mouth touches my tip. Sitting up, I push her off me and look down. *Not even fucking hard. And what I love is the way I come inside of Liza. That place where clarity meets ecstasy.*

"What the hell, Jackson?"

"Not in the mood." Rubbing my hands over my eyes, I force myself to stand and button up my jeans.

"Not in the mood," Kristy repeats. "Not in the mood?" Her question is incredulous.

"Nope." Licking my mouth, I stagger to the door.

"Don't walk away from me, Jackson," she demands, the tone of her voice a threat.

"It's over, Kristy. Go find someone else to play with."

I pull open the door and step back into the sitting area.

"No one leaves me, Jackson Shaw!"

Slamming the door shut behind me, I grin at Julia.

"Sorry about all that."

Her eyes follow my staggered movements.

"Are you okay?" Julia asks.

"Yep." Reaching her, I put my arm around her shoulders for support.

Christ, Randall actually came through. This shit is excellent.

"Where do I need to be, dearest Julia?"

"Umm..." Her brow furrows and she looks down at her iPad. "You have an hour before you need to meet with the judges."

"What for?" I whine, pulling her closer.

"The contestants were notified of moving to the next stage. You're supposed to listen to them and discuss mentoring plans and such."

She slips away from me, staring into my eyes.

"Jackson, are you drunk?"

Laughter bursts from my mouth so hard, my stomach hurts.

"Are you a total idiot?" Kristy's insult doesn't stop my hysterics. "He's as high as the fucking Space Station."

Julia's mouth drops open, causing another round of laughter out of me. Kristy walks by in perfect catwalk fashion before disappearing out of the hotel room.

"You know, I used to think her ass was beyond this world." I sigh, rubbing my bottom lip.

"I'll get you some coffee," Julia mumbles, sounding disappointed. Why, I'm not sure.

"But she's way too skinny," I continue. "Now, Liza, that girl has got an ass you can hold onto." To accentuate my point, I bring my hands up and curl them.

"And food. Hopefully, it will sober you up." Julia leaves me holding the invisible ass of the woman who's turned me from being the guy cheated on to the other guy.

Way to bring me full fucking circle, snake charmer. Bravo.

Liza

"Okay," Sid clears her throat, "just to recap, Thom sold the club to a member of Corrosive Velocity. The one who looks like a shorter, flesh tone, inked hulk. Not the tatted lumbersexual."

Gotta appreciate the way Sid breaks it down.

"You met Hulktoo and Jackson Shaw, agreed to breakfast with the latter, but ended up being the grand slam breakfast to his Denny's."

"Do you really have to call it—?"

"Don't interrupt. I'm not finished," she scolds. "By the way, I am so getting more details than you gave me, but for now, let's continue. Then, Tall, Tatted, and Talented acts like an asshole in front of Kel and Lucas. Right?"

"Yes," I breathe out, heat warming my chest.

"First, you're a dirty, dirty, whore, Eliza Mae Campbell." Sid's laughter takes the sting out of the insult.

"Sid! Focus!"

"Sorry, sorry." She sighs wistfully. "Is he tattooed *all over*? I gotta know, does his pen have ink, Liza?"

"Really?" Annoyance drips from my question.

"Fine," she grumbles. "Let's be all serious and suck the fun out of me vicariously living through your sex life."

"Great, let's do that." I nod, though she can't see it.

"Okay, what's your biggest concern right now? Kel knowing you were playing hide the celebrity salami or Lucas being there this morning? 'Cause I think he only witnessed some guy being a douchebag to his mother."

"Kel doesn't think he really knows what's going on," I confirm.

"Alright. Well, Kel seems to be acting like a grown up about this and I don't think he really has a say in your sex life."

"I know. I'm so embarrassed for him." I cover half my face with my hand.

"So, what is it then? Is it Jackson's girlfriend or that you don't know why he showed up the next morning?"

I drop my hand, planting it in the worn couch cushion.

"What?" I choke out the question.

"You said you don't know why he—"

"No, not that. The girlfriend thing. I thought he split up with his girlfriend?"

"Hmm, maybe. Is that what he said?" The familiar click of Sid's keyboard comes through the phone.

"He didn't say anything." I raise my voice. "But I saw they split a few months back all over the magazine stands. It was like a national tragedy."

"Oh, that was Laney. They've been broken up for a while."

I relax and breathe deeply.

"I'm talking about the model."

"He has a girlfriend." It's not a question.

"The internet talks about some conflicts, but I don't see anything officially breaking them up."

"Oh my God." Face meet palm once more.

"Hey, listen, that doesn't mean they are together. Shit happens and the media doesn't know. Maybe it just hasn't hit the news yet."

"Oh my God."

"Don't start hyperventilating. I'm not there to smack you out of it."

"I'm an idiot." Groaning, I slouch back into the cushions.

"Well, yeah, but..."

"But?" I press. "But what, Sid?"

"Does his pen have ink?"

Chapter Eight
Jackson

"Jackson." The rattle of the door handle accompanies my name.

Ha-ha, I locked that shit last night. I don't need any more Kristy visits.

"Damn."

Pound.

"It."

Pound.

"Jackson!"

Pound.

Well, Julia's pushy this morning.

"You have forty-five minutes to be at the arena!" she yells through the door.

"Alright!" I yell back, dragging my naked ass out of bed and to the bathroom.

Showered and dressed, I emerge from the bedroom.

"Here." Julia shoves a paper bag into my chest.

"What, no good morning kiss?" I pucker.

Julia's blush is the only thing revealing her embarrassment. Latching her tiny hand onto my arm, she pulls me behind her and through the hotel like a disobedient child. As we step out of the hotel, I'm blinded by the California sun.

"Fuck, I need to get my—"

She shoves black Ray-Bans on my face and my body into a limo. Climbing in after me, Julia collapses back into the seat as the driver closes the door.

"Rough morning?"

My smirk is met by her glare.

"You are a massive pain in the ass," she grumbles, motioning to the paper bag still clenched in my hand. "Eat," she orders. "I'm sure you need it."

Opening the bag, I find hash browns, a breakfast sandwich, and orange juice.

Grinning, I look up from the bag.

"I might have to marry you, Julia." Pulling the sandwich out of the bag, I take a large bite.

"And I might have to break your heart with a big fat no, Jackson." She forces a grin before looking down at her iPad.

I clench my chest with my free hand, feigning hurt.

Shaking her head, she fights a smile.

The girl finally shows some claws.

"I'm glad you could finally join us, Mr. Shaw," Mrs. Pierson, the show's producer, says, welcoming my late entrance.

I bow before taking a seat next to Gemma.

"As I was saying, the online semi-finalists have been contacted. We have a few still being confirmed, but by next week, we should have new song submissions. You each have a binder with some contestant information—training, current profession, but minimal personal information, and no pictures. They will be identified by contestant numbers for the time being. You'll need to start going through them now to get an idea of each person's tone, style, and sound. Figure out how you want to mentor and critique. And, if you look at the final section, you will see our guest performers and those who will also mentor."

Flipping through the pages, I stop on Hushed Mentality. Mrs. Pierson continues to speak, but all I can think about is my and Laney's first publicized appearance together.

"Are there any questions?" The producer's voice pulls me from my anxious thoughts.

Without waiting more than thirty seconds, she excuses herself from the room. The production assistant arrives moments later, leading us to a soundproof area to listen through contestants.

"God help me." I rub my eyes.

"You look as if you need Jesus," Gemma comments from my left.

"What's that supposed to mean?" I raise a brow.

"You're pale, eyes bloodshot, and if you sniff one more time in my ear, I'm going to shove a marker up your nose." Gemma's faint smile holds a touch of sadness.

"I must be getting sick." I shrug, relaxing back into the chair.

"Yeah," she says, disbelieving, "that must be it."

Shaking her head, she turns her chair to face me.

"I know you've dealt with a lot of shit lately, Jack. Really, I get it. And I'm the last person to lecture someone for having a good time, but you worry me."

"You don't have anything to worry about," I assure with a smile. "I was out too late last night with some friends and got carried away."

"Oh, really? What friends?" Leaning on the armrest of her chair, she purses her lips.

"Jack D and Captain," I answer.

Gemma shakes her head again.

"Don't get lost, Jackson," she says, her voice barely above a whisper.

"Get lost?" I ask, but she's already facing the table again.

"How many more do we need to get through tonight?" she asks the table.

"As many as it takes, sweetheart." Zarek slips into an empty chair on the other side of her. "You could be stuck with me...I mean, us, all night long." He wiggles his brows.

"I swear to God." Gemma's voice is tight, jaw clenched, and hands balled into fists on the table.

Zarek slides his chair closer, leaning into her side. Whatever he whispers results in Gemma's water bottle being dumped over his head.

"Babe, you don't have to get me all wet to see me strip." Standing, he pulls the soaked T-shirt over his head.

"Will you just shut up?" she yells, her face reddening—

though, I'm not sure whether it's from anger or his stripping.

"Okay, you two, let's separate and get this done." Grabbing Gemma's chair, I slide her over and put myself between the two of them.

Christ, this can't end soon enough. Patting my pocket, I find the small brown vial and relax.

Days of half-listening to the initial submissions have me on edge.

Liza

"You submitted the papers on Monday, right?" Sid questions.

"Yes. I took them in when I recorded the next song for submission," I answer, stepping onto the bus and finding a seat.

"Did you stick with the song we picked?"

"Yes, I did," I answer with a giggle.

"Awesome! I love the way you sing *I Knew You Were Trouble*," Sid sighs dramatically. "It's also entirely fitting."

"Let's not rehash the subject."

"No further word from him, huh?"

"Nope and let's hope it stays that way," I say, but even I'm not convinced.

"Uh huh." Sid isn't convinced either. "How many times have you thought about that night?"

"Not that many." I sound like a little kid.

"Okay," she laughs out the word. "And you don't think about him at all? Not the way he got all up in your face, seducing you and getting you back to his hotel, all so he could have his dirty way with you?"

"Shut up," I grumble.

Heat flushes my skin. The memory of him is still fresh and

alive in every cell of my body.

"That's what I thought," she says. "So, how horny are you now that I brought it up?"

"I hate you," I groan.

"You love me so much. I'm like the girl you would totally get with if we weren't related."

"You're sick. And I'm almost to the club, so I gotta go." I end the call, and stand, following two other passengers to the steps.

As soon as I'm inside the club, Red gathers us backstage for an announcement.

Standing between Nikki and Jennifer, I can feel them watch me out of the corner of their eyes. They want details from my breakfast with Jackson. Swallowing down the anxiety, I focus on Red.

"I'd like to try something new. This weekend we will have our first guest performer. She's going to rehearse with Bethany for a couple days before the show. What I would like to do is open up with a small number and then bring out our guest. From there, we will continue on with our show." He scans the room, looking at everyone.

I take the moment to look for Bethany and find her standing behind Red.

"Now, with the recent interest in Dominant and sub relationships, like with *Fifty Shades*, I'd like to design the show this weekend around the theme. Play on the popular idea. Any ideas? Song suggestions?"

"We could perform *Erotica*," Bethany suggests. "Most of us know the song and the choreography."

Red nods in agreement.

"What about the guest? What is she performing?" Nikki asks.

"Good question." Red points a finger in her direction. "Kristy will be singing *Hanky Panky*."

I almost groan out loud. *Really? Could you be more literal?*

"Got something to say, Liza?" Red eyes me, amusement on

his face.

Glancing over his shoulder, I focus on Bethany covering her mouth.

Fuck, I groaned out loud.

"I just think maybe we should do something not so literal. Instead, take some songs and interpret them to the theme. There's a lot we could do." I shrug, shrinking back a bit into the crowd.

"I like it. Let's throw out some songs. Even if you don't know them, we can work on that part." Red starts walking around the open space we're circling.

"*Wicked Game*," Jennifer suggests.

"*Tainted Love* or *Evidence*," I offer.

"Good." Red claps his hands together, turning to face me. "Liza, pull together some songs and go over them with Nikki, Jennifer, and Bethany. Ladies, I want you guys to put your sets together. Then we will work on staging, choreography, and build this show."

I fully expect a fist pump when he's done. Instead, he claps once and loud. The girls are on me the minute we're dispersed.

"So?" Nikki follows close behind into my dressing room.

"So, what?" I delay answering.

"Don't play stupid, Liza." Jennifer enters with Bethany at her side.

"Well, she definitely made an impression on him." Bethany smiles, sitting down in her chair next to mine.

"Spill it." Nikki plops down on the loveseat in the far side of the room.

"We have a set to put together." I shove my bag under my table. "He isn't giving us much time to pull this off."

"Don't change the subject." Jennifer leans against the faded wallpaper next to my table.

I cover my face with my hands.

"We ate breakfast and I went home."

Flashes of inked fingers on my thighs, soft lips on my neck, and penis jewelry enter my mind.

"Yeah, okay. That's the reason he called Red to get your

information the next day?" Bethany purses her lips.

"What?" I snap my head to her.

The teasing look fades from her face.

"He called Red asking where you lived."

"But Red wouldn't know my address unless he was here and those are private employee records. He can't just give—"

Bethany's hands come up, stopping me.

"No, no. I gave him the information." Her eyes widen at the look on my face.

"You what?" I screech.

"He said you forgot something and he wanted to return it. I didn't think—"

"No. You didn't think, Bethany." Angry and needing to get away, I stand and leave the room.

Bethany and Nikki call after me, but I ignore them and don't stop until I'm up in the control room going through songs.

By Friday, I'm feeling anxious, edgy, and stressed. Kel's informed me how sick Sean's grandmother really is, Hidden Star called and confirmed my information, and I'm not too sure the show is going to go smoothly. My stomach is in a knot when I step off the bus and see photographers. Keeping my head down, I slip by them and into the club.

"What's with the photographers?" I ask, stepping into the dressing room.

"Our guest performer draws attention," Bethany answers flatly.

"I never did ask what she's famous for." Settling into my chair, I start pulling out the sponges and brushes. Bethany stays quiet.

"You okay?" I set down the applicators, twisting to face her.

"Oh, are you speaking to me now?" She presses a hand to

her chest.

And the Oscar goes to Bethany Hall for dramatic performance.

"Look, I was pissed, okay? You really have no idea what happened and that's not your fault. I'm sorry for the silent treatment. It really wasn't all about that, either."

Turning back to my table, I start twisting my hair into curlers.

Bethany sighs heavily beside me.

"I'm sorry if you didn't want him to know where you live. I really didn't think it through further than Jackson Shaw wanted your address."

Out of the corner of my eye, I see her smile.

"I'm sorry."

Twisting hair around the pink, bendable curler, I meet her gaze in the mirror.

"It's over now. Let's just forget about it." Giving a smile, I reassure our reconciliation.

But my mind does anything but forget. My hand pulses, remembering the silky hardness of him fucking my hand. Tingles prickle my fingertips recalling the cool steel of his piercing.

"Liza?" Nikki says, her tone telling me this isn't the first time she's said my name.

"Yeah?" I blurt.

"Geez, girl, where were you?" She laughs and shakes her head. "Never mind. Guess who's here to see you tonight?"

Wrapping the last of my hair, I turn away from the mirror to face her.

"I have no—" *Oh, yes, I do have an idea.*

"You figured it out," she sings the words.

"Excuse me." Annoyance laces the sickly sweet female voice.

Stepping aside, Nikki allows the tall, willowy blonde entrance. Kristyna Molvic: Gucci spokesperson, supermodel, and Jackson Shaw's girlfriend.

I face my mirror, keeping my eyes on my makeup.

Why does karma strike so quick?

"Thanks, sweetie," she coos, obviously insincere.

"Yeah, sure." Nikki turns her nose up, leaving the room.

"Red said I could use this dressing room." She bats her long, fake lashes at Bethany and me.

"Yeah, that table is free. It used to be Jazzmin's." Bethany points to the empty table.

"Oh," Kristyna pouts. "I thought I'd have the entire room to myself."

"Sorry, not in this place," Bethany quips, turning back to her mirror.

A small huff sounds from behind us, but I need to put all my focus on my makeup.

"Is there a makeup artist?" The sound of her voice sends a sharp twinge of guilt through me.

"We do our own, but I can give you a hand if you'd like," Bethany offers, pushing up from her chair.

"Would you?" The chair creaks under the pressure of Kristyna's weight. "I'd really appreciate it."

"Sure." Bethany moves to assist our special guest performer, the real reason Jackson is here to watch the show tonight. After mistaking Kel for something other than my brother, the sick bastard must love this.

Chapter Nine
Jackson

Before Red called to invite me to a "special night" at Lux, I'd resolved not to return. But the moment his name popped up on my phone, I knew I was a fucking liar.

"What the hell?" Leaning toward the tinted window, I take in the crowd of paps surrounding the club entrance. I groan as the car pulls to the curb, preparing to exit.

The flashes, already annoying, intensify from the amount of cocaine surging through my system.

"Hey, Jackson, how are you tonight?" one calls.

"Jackson, give us a shot," another demands.

Keeping my head down, I slip my hands into my pockets so I won't flip them off or punch someone. *Fucking leeches.*

A slow, steady beat fills the air of the extremely packed club.

"Jack!" Red's call pulls my attention to the VIP table.

I sit in the booth and one of the busty servers sets a drink on the table.

"Thanks." Grasping the cold glass, I bring it to my lips.

"You feeling okay?" Red examines me through narrow eyes.

I nod, setting the glass down on the table.

"What's with all the commotion tonight?" I ask, lounging into the booth and stretching an arm over the back.

"It's time to publicize this place." He grins. "I have a guest performer tonight that will draw some buzz."

"A guest, already?"

Completely unlike Red, he stays silent, a mischievous smile on his face.

The lights dim and a man's deep voice fills the room.

"Tonight, ladies and gentlemen, let's give tribute to rope, paddles, chains, blindfolds, and handcuffs. Please welcome special guest, Kristyna Molvic, for your viewing pleasure."

My lips part, chest tightens, and anger boils my stomach. *What is this bitch up to now?*

The flirty music fills the room, curtains part, and Kristy steps forward, asking to be spanked and for hanky-panky. She doesn't really sing, it's more of a rhythmic talking.

She's got nothing on the other girls and sure as fuck, not my snake charmer.

Kristy's eyes lock on to me. Sitting straighter, a flash registers from near the bar.

Damn, paps!

In a silky, pink corset, short shorts, white fishnets, and other accessories, Kristy struts off the stage through the crowd. She reaches our table and hops up, leaning back on the black lacquered surface. Pulling herself up to end the song, she spins and lands into my lap. Her big finish is straddling and kissing me.

Instinctively, my hands clasp her hips, but I feel the urge to toss her off. Another flash from a camera stops me. *I don't need any more damn press involved in my life.* Going lax, I let her finish the act.

She pulls back, her look telling me she's pissed by my lack of reaction. Another camera flashes and she's quick to put her practiced smile in place. Slipping off my lap, she soaks in the applause and accolades from the audience as she returns to the stage, disappearing stage left.

"You're one lucky fucker," Red boasts.

"You think?" I narrow my eyes at him, my mouth tight.

"What, man? I thought you two were together. She wanted to surprise you," he explains.

"Ah." I nod, now understanding. "She's a psycho, man. I've tried to drop the bitch twice now, but I can't get rid of her."

"Why would you get rid of someone so ready to ride you?" His eyebrow quirks in curiosity.

I close my eyes and rub my face, fighting not to say the three words that will make it perfectly clear. So, instead of "she's not Liza", I say, "She's like single-white-female meets Jigsaw."

Red's brow furrows in confusion.

"She'll do whatever it takes to get where she wants to be and her games are fucking twisted and bloody."

Before he can react to my explanation, every light goes out, including the ones over the tables. The lights flicker in synchronization to the beat of *Tainted Love*, until her voice deliberately ear fucks everyone with the first verse.

In a black and gray striped corset, lace bottoms, sheer black thigh-highs with fuck-me-now bows, and black stilettos, she slinks to the edge of the stage. A large, black pole in her hand, she stabs it into the stage, singing and grinding. Her blood red lips push the words out to the audience. This version is harder, edgier, like Manson's but slowed to a sexier tempo.

Stepping to the extended runway part of the stage, she struts, dragging the pole behind her. Two backups dressed in red follow. Once she stabs the pole into the stage floor again, they dance around it.

Leaving the dancers with the pole, she enters the crowd. Moving like a panther on the prowl, her body curls around the tightly packed bodies.

I rub my sweaty palms on my jeans, my cock painfully hard. It knows exactly how slick and hot she feels, and he wants more.

Chest rising and falling, I inhale hard as Liza puts a foot on some asshole's chair between his legs. She unclasps one thigh-high before swaying her torso forward, pushing the sheer stocking down.

Gripping the table, I hold myself in place. She fucking transforms on stage, giving the audience a glimpse at the naughty charmer I know intimately.

No one else should see this. It's mine, damn it!

With a small shake of my head, I remove the thought like shaking a fucking Etch-A-Sketch.

It's not mine. She's not mine. She belongs to another fucking guy.

She pushes away from the guy, giving him her back, and

shimmies, releasing the clasp on the other leg. The douchebag reaches his hand out.

I start to stand, but Red puts a hand on my arm, and mouths, "You don't want to leave now." Grinning, he points to Liza.

I look back, seeing she's tied the asshole's hands behind his back with a napkin before walking away. Smiling, I start relaxing until she pulls another guy from the crowd onto the stage.

The backups quickly strap the guy to the pole and Liza plucks at the fingertips of her gloves before shoving one in his mouth. The man bites and she pull her hand from the glove.

After repeating the action with the other glove, she kicks away her heels. The backups remove her stockings and then Liza practically crawls up the guy's body. When the dancers start loosening her corset strings, the whooshing sound of my heart ricochets in my ears.

The corset hangs loose, her hand holding it to her chest, and bare back against the dickhead I plan to track down later and kill. She finishes the song almost on a whimper, begging for him to take her tears and lets the corset drop. My heart stops, starting again when the backups move their heads in the way before anyone actually sees anything but black X pasties.

Darkness falls around us again. The roar of applause is deafening. She's brought every man and woman to their knees, or possibly to orgasm.

My fucking snake charmer. One night was supposed to be enough. I'm not supposed to care about you flirting with the audience, revealing the seductress I'm intimately acquainted with, or...fuck, I'm not supposed to care at all, to want you the way I do.

The lights in the booths and on the tables fade back to dim.

"I fucking love that girl," Red boasts, proud and impressed.

I grunt. If I speak, not only will I lose my shit on Red, I'll find those douchebags out in the audience and show them what a spanking with a fist feels like.

"Don't worry. I'm not making a play for her," Red laughs.

My eyes meet his.

"I thought you were just looking for a distraction, but it

looks like she may have gotten to you, huh?" He puts his beer bottle to his mouth.

"Nah," I shake my head, "she was just a distraction."

I reach for my glass and toss back the watered down JD. Red's boisterous laugh draws other people's attention.

"Dude, you were ready to go Captain Caveman when she was performing." His big hand slaps the table.

"I was not." I lie my fucking ass off. "In fact, she's just like the rest who have someone at home, but still fuck around."

The server appears with fresh drinks, clears the old, and disappears.

"That girl is good." I point to the retreating server but look at Red.

He nods, taking a pull from his new beer.

"Liza's got an old man?" Red's question annoys and amuses me.

"Old man? Really?" Furrowing my brow, I'm a little surprised by the label he chose.

"Yes, really, fucker," Red responds. "Anyhow, I swear Bethany said she's single. Lives with her sons, or brothers...or something. Fuck, I'm not sure. She was naked and I got sidetracked." He shakes his head.

"Well, that didn't take you long," I taunt, changing the topic to him.

"Actually, she took a couple weeks to break down. Even then, I had to be pretty persuasive since I'm the new boss. She was all worried about fucking her boss and how it would look," he snorts.

"She has a point." Raising my brows, I sip my drink.

"No, she doesn't. I'm not fucking everyone who works for me. And I wanted her long before I bought the place. Though, she doesn't seem to like when I call her my little signing bonus."

The lights dim again while we're laughing. A spotlight pierces the dark stage. Liza stands center in a pair of golden silk underwear, gold mesh belt, and a thin, gold, chain metal top. The top clings to the curve of her breasts, hanging exquisitely from the peaks of her nipples.

I lick my lips, the memory of her taunting my taste buds.

The beat of the song is familiar. One of the first I heard her perform, but tonight, it's darker...dirtier, somehow. She opens her mouth, and sings, "If I let you in, let you deep inside."

I've been inside and somehow you got deep in me. What the fuck did you do to me?

An ache fills my chest, while warning bells resonate in my head. And, just because he doesn't like to be excluded, my cock presses painfully against my zipper.

Without a word, I leave for the bathroom, patting my pocket for the small vial.

Liza

"Jesus, Liza, I haven't seen you go so deep into Miz Liz in a while." Jennifer stands in the open dressing room door, watching as I slip my red robe over my bare torso. The silky material is much more comfortable than the rough mesh top.

"Really?" I play it off, hanging the chain metal top in its place and cleaning up my vanity. The last thing they need to know is seeing Kristyna all over Jackson, in front of the crowd and cameras, hurt.

It shouldn't hurt. I dip two lip brushes into cleaner and scrub with a paper towel. *He's not mine. It was one night.* Placing the brushes in their case, I move onto the foundation brushes. *I'm jealous over something I could never have. Why did I watch Kristyna's performance? You said you'd stay in the dressing room, but no, you just had to see how she would do.* I snort.

"Liza?" Bethany asks in a small voice.

"Yeah?" I respond, keeping my attention on the brushes.

"Are you okay?"

Taking a deep breath, I look up at her.

"Yes, I'm fine. Just tired and ready to get out of here." I force a smile.

She nods, but there's a look of pity in her eyes. A look I don't want.

"Tonight was amazing. Thank you so much for all your help." Kristy breezes into the room, "I'll just get my things. Jackson's waiting."

"Jackson?" Bethany asks, spinning around in her chair.

"Yeah," Kristyna's reply is quick, obviously in a hurry.

I look up from under my lashes, catching Kristy's smile reflected in my mirror. Before she catches the scowl I now wear on my face, I drop my gaze.

Damn karma. Damn. Damn. Damn.

Closing my eyes, I breathe deep and fight a shudder.

"Well..." She pauses. "Thanks again."

The click of her heels silences behind the closing of the door.

I dip my chin to chest, my hair falling around me like the stage curtain, and release the breath, swallowing the emotions clogging my throat.

"Liza, I—" Bethany starts.

Putting one hand up, I silence her.

"I just want to go home," I say, my words a broken whisper.

"Sure," she replies, resignation in her tone.

I allow myself one more moment to marinate on things before raising my head. The reflection of the painted face in the mirror stares back with raw hurt glittering in her eyes.

Get over it. You saw trouble written all over him from the start. Grow a vagina and move on.

"Can you help me with the laces?" Bethany's question pulls me away from the mirror.

I straighten from my chair, pushing down my unreasonable feelings.

"Yep." I reach out and slip my fingers through the silky strings, loosening them enough for her to shimmy out of the corset.

"Are you sure you're okay?" She doesn't allow me to answer before continuing. "If this is about...if it's about him, Liza, you didn't know. And even if you did, just forget about it."

I turn my head and open my mouth with the intentions of telling her I'm good, but I burst out laughing instead.

"Beth, can you put the girls away? They're pointing at me," I snort, covering my eyes.

We've obviously all seen each other naked. In our line of work and quick changes, it happens. However, being eye level with her hard nipples and trying to talk is just too much. Her arm comes around her chest.

"Sorry," she apologizes on a laugh.

The dressing room door slams against the wall and Bethany screams, rushing to cover her nudity with a robe. Spinning around in the chair, all air leaves my lungs.

His predatory gaze sends my heart racing. I stand, straightening my shoulders.

The fluid prowl of his body knocks all defiant strength out of me. I retreat. One step, two, bumping into Bethany's chair.

"What the hell do you think you're doing?" Bethany yells, tightening the belt of her robe. "You can't just burst in here because you feel like it," she says, continuing the lecture. The screech of a chair pulls my attention back to him. He's shoved my chair over.

Damn it, Bethany. Your distraction cost me.

He's gaining. Pushing on the chair behind my legs, I put it between the predator and me.

His eyes narrow on mine. The left side of his mouth twitches devilishly. My hands tighten on the chair just before it disappears, slamming to the floor next to Bethany. She shrieks, hurrying out of the room.

Long, too familiar arms wrap around my waist. He lifts, carrying and pressing me against the wall.

"Jac—"

One arm untangles, his hand cupping my chin and thumb pressing against my lips, silencing me.

I grab his wrist.

"I don't care about him." Jackson's voice is thick and unsteady.

"Kristyna," I say the words in a muffle against his thumb.

"I sure as fuck don't care about her," he sneers.

The pad of his thumb presses and swipes my bottom lip before his mouth crushes mine.

Squeezing my eyes shut, my left hand tight on his wrist, I fist my right hand at my side.

Don't give in. Fight against it.

All my senses fill with Jackson—the sound, scent, and feel of him. His lip ring pinches my unresponsive lips.

Christ, I want him.

He pulls back and his fingers slip into the hair at the back of my head, fisting. My head tilts in response and lips open on a gasp. He captures my mouth, plunging his tongue inside. The arm around me loosens enough so his hand can slip over my ass and squeeze—hard.

The sound of my heart beats between my ears. The rapid rise and fall of my chest against his through the silk robe hardens my nipples. I moan, sliding my tongue against his. A salty, chemical taste hits my taste buds.

What the hell?

The flavor isn't Jackson. It's wrong. Slipping my hands between our bodies, I place my palms against him and push. He doesn't move, so I push again, harder, and turn my head away from him. The pull of my hair stings my scalp.

"Stop," I pant.

"Never." His mouth moves against my cheek and over my jaw.

Pushing even harder, I bring a leg up and dig my knee into his thigh, separating us.

"Stop, Jackson," I growl.

Hands fisted at his sides, chest heaving, his eyes grow hard.

"Now you care?" His brows raise in amazement.

"You don't know what you're talking about," I blurt. "But I know Kristyna is here for you, with you, or whatever. Pretty hypocritical, aren't you?" I only hope he doesn't hear the tremor in my voice.

Pressing forward again, he traps me against the wall with an arm on either side of me. He leans in, his face coming to the side of my head.

"I don't give a shit about Kristy." The husky words warm my ear. "And if you gave a shit about *him*, we never would've happened. Yet, you let my tongue and cock between your legs." A shiver runs down my spine. "So, I don't give a fuck about anything else. I've had you."

I jump when his fingers touch my bare thigh.

"And now, I have a taste for you."

His hand slips under my robe.

I squeeze my eyes shut tight. My body surrenders, but my head spins. His "taste for me" comment hurts, like an insult. His touch moves higher up my thigh, burning my skin. Flames lick their way between my legs, my need for him becoming consuming. But not like this. Something is wrong. Bringing my hands up, I press against his chest again.

"I fucking want you, Liza."

Jackson's head dips, his mouth claiming the skin of my neck.

"What the fuck, man?" The boisterous question snaps me from the lust-filled cocoon Jackson's created. "Get off of her!"

I stiffen and press on his chest.

Jackson sighs against my neck. Without moving away, he looks over his shoulder.

"Christ, Jackson, you can't just barge into the dressing rooms." Red's lecture comes from directly behind Jackson. "Look, man, you gotta go."

His muscles tense against me.

"Don't give me that look. You're the one who created this goddamn problem. Bethany is freaking out and Kristy isn't going to be distracted by those cameras for much longer."

It's my turn to tense. *Kristy. He had a taste for her once.*

With Jackson focused on Red, I duck under his arm and out of his trap. Red's eyes look me over before meeting mine with unspoken concern. Jackson stands to his full height, watching our exchange before locking eyes with me.

"You should go," I say, my voice low and more composed than I thought possible in this moment. I turn away from them and move toward my dressing table, giving both of them my back.

"Come with me," Jackson states.

"Can't." Sitting, I pull my bags out from under the table.

"Come with me," he says, his voice deeper, harder, demanding.

"Jackson, you—" About to tell him he has the wrong idea about Kel, drama enters the room.

"Baby, I've been waiting for you." Kristy sounds contemptuous. "The car is here to take us back to our hotel. I want to celebrate."

Silence, densely thick, fills the room.

"Kristy?" Jackson's voice slices through like the edge of a sword.

"Yeah, babe?" Her tone perks.

"We. Are. Not. Together." He punctuates each word, his tone ruthless. "And you knew that before you came to L.A."

Onlookers gasp.

He didn't. What a dick move.

Kristy sputters for a moment. I don't care for her, but I can't help but empathize with her.

"I told you that shit before I flew down here. Don't act like it's a big fucking surprise," he says, contempt now in his voice.

"You fucking bastard. I will fucking ruin you." Her threat is calm, almost too calm. Without further prompting, Kristy turns on her heels and walks out.

"Alright, everyone," Red breaks the uncomfortable silence, "let's close up and get out of here. It's been a long fucking night." He sounds exhausted.

"He needs to go," Bethany stresses from the doorway.

"Jack, come on." Red motions for him to follow.

Jackson's eyes stay on me—watching, searching.

He has a taste for you. When the craving goes, you'll be another Kristy.

"You heard him." Bethany steps in the room, pointing to the

door.

"I don't give a fuck about him, Liza." Jackson takes three strides to stand over me.

I tilt my head back to meet his eyes.

Leaning down, his hands grip the armrests. His face stops inches from mine.

"When I want something, I can be very persistent."

My eyes drop to his lips. He stands, smiling with satisfaction, a promise in his eyes.

"Jackson," Red says, his irritation evident.

"I'll be outside, snake charmer." Licking his bottom lip, he turns, leaving the room.

Exhaling, I slouch in the chair.

I have to find a way out of here without him seeing me.

"I don't know whether I should be scared for you or jealous." Bethany rights her chair before sitting.

"Scared," I respond. "Definitely scared."

Chapter Ten
Jackson

Over an hour. I've waited for over a fucking hour.

"Hey, we're closed." The flamboyant doorman tries to stop me. One look and he stays back.

Striding into the empty club, I make my way to the hidden door at the side of the stage. It swings open, causing me to jump back.

"Jackson?" Red's brow furrows, a combination of annoyance and confusion on his face.

"He's here?" Bethany squeaks, pushing by him to narrow her eyes at me.

"Where's Liza?"

Red opens his mouth, but Bethany moves in front of him.

"She's gone." She smirks. "She went home, Jackson, where she should be. The last thing she needs is another night with a lying asshole."

She snuck out the fucking back? She avoided me.

"Babe." Red's large hand clasps her shoulder.

"I'm the liar?" I snort in disbelief.

"You're also an asshole," she adds, shaking Red's hand off. "Liza's a good person. Quit fucking with her." Her arms cross over her chest.

"Mind your own fucking business," I growl, turning away.

"Leave her alone. Liza and the boys don't need your kind of shit." She throws the words at my back.

"Boys?" I spin around, anger and hurt stabbing my chest. She fucking snuck out to get away from me, to get to him, leaving me standing on a fucking curb. "Maybe the fact that he's a *boy* is why she spent the night with me. Ever think of that?"

Her mouth opens, and then closes. Brows furrowed, she looks over her shoulder to Red and back to me.

"What the hell are you talking about?" She drops her arms.

"Nothing," I snap, done with it all. "Tell her she can fucking have him. I get it and I'm nobody's bitch."

Turning, I take quick steps toward the exit.

"What are you talking about?" Bethany asks my back.

I don't stop or look back.

"Red, what's he talking about?"

The heavy metal door slams shut behind me, cutting off her grating voice. I approach the car and Sam stands from the driver's seat. Putting up a hand, I stop him.

"I've got it," I say, grabbing the handle and letting myself into the car. "Just get me the fuck out of here."

Reaching a hand into my pocket, I pull out the vial and open it. Empty.

"Fuck!" I toss it at the seat across from me.

Rubbing my face, I fight the urge to shout until the windows shatter. My cell vibrates against my leg, distracting me from the craving—the need.

I lift it up, reading Red's name flashing on the screen.

Yeah, just what I need. His bitch probably has him banning me from the club or some shit.

Ignoring the call, I drop the phone into the seat next to me. It vibrates again—this time, a text.

Red: We need to talk

Swiping the screen, I touch delete and rest my head back for the remainder of the ride.

I push open my hotel room door, my stash in the bathroom the only thing on my mind. Kristy's form in the dark doorway of my bedroom halts my steps.

"Are you fucking serious?" Running my shaky hands through my hair, I lick my dry lips.

"I'm willing to forgive you for tonight, but I won't forget how you embarrassed me." She steps into the light, naked. "You're going to have a lot of making up to do, though."

What did I ever find attractive about her?

She raises a fist and uncurls her fingers, a brown vial laying center palm.

"I know what you want, Jackson."

Her long fingers uncap the vial and sprinkle it over her chest.

"You just have to say you're sorry." Licking her finger, she runs it across the white powder before rubbing it on her gums. "Tell me you're sorry and I can give you what you need, baby."

She steps forward, the powder trickling between her breasts.

I rub my hands on my jeans, but can't get them dry. I take deep breaths, but can't get enough oxygen.

Charging forward, she flinches back a little, but holds her ground.

I bury my face between her breasts and inhale before licking up to her neck.

"That's it, baby. Take what you need," she coos, her hand in my hair.

Reaching out, I grab the vial from her hand, shove her away, and leave her in the sitting room by herself.

I lock myself inside the bathroom and get three rails into my system.

"You're pathetic!" Kristy bangs on the door. "You fucking junkie!" Something smashes against the door.

One more bump and I slide down to the cool floor tile. Closing my eyes, I revel in the numbness.

Fuck Kristy and her screaming ass. To hell with Liza and her clueless man. Screw. Them. All.

Silence finally fills the air. Leaning against the sink, I reach up to the counter, grasp the vial, and bring it to me. Another hit and the shower stall slants. My face meets the cold tile with a slap. Shifting to my back, I let the numbness take possession.

"Jackson!"

Doesn't she ever go the fuck away?

"Open the door, Jackson!"

"Fuck off," I groan, pulling the blanket to my chest.

"Oh, thank God." She sounds way too relieved. *Didn't she want to kill me last night?* "Can you please open the door before hotel management gets here?" she pleads.

I bury my face in the blanket and inhale, a musty smell filling my nostrils. Shoving the blanket away, I open my eyes to the sterile, white tile bathroom. Rolling to my back, I rub my hands over my face.

"What the fuck?"

"The manager is going to be here soon," Julia pleads from the other side of the door.

Shifting my jaw, I grab the counter and pull myself up. Every muscle protests and my bones crack.

"Jackson, please—!" Opening the door silences her yell.

"Quit yelling." Yawning, I stumble by her and face plant into the bed. The smell of chemically clean linens assaults my nostrils. *Fuck, I shouldn't have let them wash away the scent of her.*

"You want me to quit yelling?" she asks, incensed.

"Yeah, that'd be great." The mattress muffles my response.

"How about don't lock yourself in the bathroom with a bag full of...of whatever that is!"

"I'm out now," I mumble. "You can go tell the manager not to bother me. I'm going to take a nap."

I jolt up from a sharp pain in my shoulder blade before a decorative statue thumps to the mattress. My scowl doesn't intimidate Julia.

"You have a schedule to keep and it's my job to make sure you do. Now, get your ass out of bed, in the shower, and meet me in the sitting room for breakfast." She turns and takes three giant steps before spinning back. Pointing a finger at me, she narrows her eyes. "And stay sober." Her voice is low, threatening. "You need to get to the sound studio for meetings, listening sessions, and promo shots."

She slams the door and I wince at the sound. I roll my head to work out the stiffness and make my way to the shower.

Thirty minutes and two hits later, a still angry Julia escorts me to the studio in silence. Even when we arrive and Sam opens the door, she exits without a peep. The silence from her, a usually chatty girl, grates my nerves.

"Are you going to give me the silent treatment for—?"

"We need to go to studio room C." She keeps her eyes on her iPad.

"Julia, look—"

"We're going to be late." She steps from me and into the studio.

My eyes land on Sam, who wears a grim look. Sighing, I follow after the pissed off little pin-up.

She stops at the door and stands aside.

"Do you need anything?" she asks, her voice flat.

I stop before entering the door.

"I'm sorry about this morning."

She gives a nod and I exhale heavily before stepping into the room.

"I don't need anything," I call over my shoulder, not looking back.

Who the fuck is she to judge me? I don't need shit from her too.

"You look like hell," Gemma greets, her nose wrinkled.

"The more you deny your attraction to me, the more I know you want me." I drop into a chair beside her.

She groans. "Please, if I hear one more pathetic flirty comment, I'm going to blow chunks all over this table."

"Zarek?" I raise a brow.

"Of course," she mumbles, her eyes moving to where he sits

at the other end of the table.

Not wanting to be part of that shit, I stay quiet.

"You need to take a break from the shit," Gemma whispers, her face closer than before.

"Okay, Mom." My words are a bit more bitchy than intended.

"Jackson, we're friends and you're looking worse for wear." Her hand slips over my bicep, bringing my attention to her.

She's closer than I realized, our heads only a few inches apart. Giving her a smile, I cover her small hand with mine.

"I'm fine. You have nothing to worry about."

"Maybe we should get started." Zarek's voice booms so loud, I jerk my head in his direction.

His eyes burn into Gemma and me—especially where our hands touch.

He's got it bad. Poor fucker. I know all too well how you're feeling.

Gemma and I put space between us and begin today's listening session.

The new submissions are better since they were recorded in a professional studio. We get through a fourth of the contestants— listening, discussing, critiquing, listening again, and putting together comments—before a show executive enters the room. She tells us about the upcoming processes and how we will actually be listening to live recordings next week for contestants who are able to come to this studio and another one across town. For others, we will be patched into some different studios via a live feed. We will need to break up into groups to cover them all, but will all hear the final recorded tracks eventually. This just allows us to offer immediate mentoring and feedback as they record.

Gemma and I team up to take the local studio and live feed from the Seattle Mack Productions Studio. We've both worked with Leo Mackey and his wife, Chloe, in the past. The others team up and get their assignments before we are ushered to promo shots and interviews.

Today's entertainment reporter, Perry Flores, is well known for his attempts to shock and incense his targets.

"Why the hell are they using this guy?" I grumble.

"Because they want publicity," Cheyenne states. "He has a huge following, and if you haven't noticed, this show isn't exactly taking off the way the producers had hoped."

"Really?" I'm not shocked, but surprised I hadn't already heard this news.

"Perhaps you should keep your head up instead of face down on smooth surfaces," she quips, brushing her finger under her nose.

"Excuse me?" I growl, gripping the arms of the director's chair tight.

She only snorts.

"So, who would like to begin?" Perry leans his chin into his palm, scanning us. Before any of us have a chance to respond, he continues, "I know. Gemma, let's start with you." He gives her a sleazy smile.

Fuck, this is going to be bloody.

"Okay." Gemma smooths her black polka-dot skirt.

"So, tell me about your relationship with fellow judge Zarek." He bats his eyes.

Tension pours off Gemma. In my peripheral, I see Zarek stiffen.

"Well..." she clears her throat, "aside from our work together at the music awards and now as co-judges, we really don't know each other."

"Really?" He draws out the one word with disbelief.

She nods. "Yes."

"My sources tell me you two had an altercation backstage at the music awards. Is that true?"

You can actually see the glee in his eye at causing discomfort.

"It was a simple misunderstanding. Not by any means an altercation." Gemma laughs, but it sounds forced.

"So, you didn't hit him?"

"I, uh..." she stutters.

"Like she said, it was a misunderstanding," Zarek chimes in, drawing Perry's attention. "I wasn't exactly kind when we met, which was a misunderstanding on my part. It resulted in me getting something I deserved." He shrugs.

"How sweet. So quick to defend her." Perry's grin widens.

"I'm not defending anyone. I just want to make sure it's clear that—"

"Tell me, Zarek, my sources say you and Ms. Harper were seen entering a hotel room together. Is this true?"

Gemma gasps.

"Look, buddy, I don't know what this shit is, but I thought we were here to talk about the show?" I bark, pulling the slime ball's attention and instantly regretting it.

"We'll come back to that." His grin widens. "Jackson Shaw. This has been quite a hard year for you." A forced pout forms on his face.

"I've done okay." I narrow my eyes at him, hoping he gets the hint to leave it alone.

"I, for one, am glad to see you looking so well after the whole cheating debacle." He nods, looking positively sincere. "Now, with the medical concerns you're dealing—"

I laugh. "I don't have any medical concerns."

"Oh, I know. I'm referring to your poor mother. All those doctors and tests."

My chest constricts, breathing becoming impossible.

"Can you share with us whether she is doing alright?"

I try to swallow, but choke. Coughing, I see Perry's mouth and pen moving, but can't hear anything.

Mom? Doctors? Tests? What the fuck is...how can he....what if...?

A glass of water appears in my face and I reach for it, but it slips through my fingers, crashing to the floor. Standing from the chair, I rip the mic wire from my chest and toss it to the floor before exiting the room.

"Jackson," Julia's voice is filled with concern, "I didn't know he was going to—"

"I need to leave." I turn on her, grabbing her shoulders. "Get the fucking car, Julia!"

Her eyes widen as she steps back, bringing her phone to her ear.

Seeing her phone makes me reach for my own. Scrolling, I tap *Mom* with more force than necessary.

Julia grabs my elbow, pulling me down the halls toward the exit.

No answer. I call again.

Outside, Sam stands, holding the door open. I throw myself into the car and disconnect the unanswered call. Julia slips in behind me.

I scroll again, this time calling Christopher.

"Yeah," he answers on the first ring.

"What the fuck is going on with Mom, Chris?" I shout.

His sigh is heavy.

"I don't fucking know, man. Neither of them will answer my calls. I'm on my way over there now."

"So, you knew she was seeing doctors? Why wouldn't you fucking tell me?"

"I didn't fucking know until today," he snaps. "Mia got cornered in the airport by a reporter. She called me right before she got on the plane."

"She won't answer me," I say, my voice breaking.

"I'm on it, Jack," Chris assures. "As soon as I get to them, you are the first person I'm calling. I'll fucking put you on speaker."

I shake my head and take a deep breath.

"I'm taking the first flight out of here."

"Jack, I know you want to, but wait. Let me find out what's going on."

"I can't wait for that. This is my mom." A sob escapes.

"You don't need to travel right now, brother." Christopher's voice is low. "Get a drink and let me do this. I can get answers before you can fly out. Don't be on a plane where I can't reach you.

Okay?"

I hate that he makes sense.

"Fine," I snap, "but you better fucking call me as soon as you get there! I'm dead fucking serious, Christopher."

There's a long silence and I'm about to rage at him once more.

"Jackson, you're my brother." He pauses, and I know this shit is hard for Chris. "Gwen is my mother, too. There's nothing I wouldn't do for the two of you."

Tears clog my throat, the fear of the unknown and the rawest response I've ever experienced from Christopher fucking with my emotions.

I nod even though he can't see me.

"Hang in your hotel room. Grab a drink and the book you write your poetry shit."

My eyes widen and mouth pops open.

"Yeah, fucker, I know you still write that shit." Chris' tone is back to normal. "You should probably consider writing some lyrics instead of exhausting my brilliance all the fucking time."

A laugh breaks through the emotional clog in my throat.

"You're an arrogant bastard," I state in a strained laugh.

"You'll do what I ask, yeah?"

"Yeah," I sigh, dropping my head back on the seat.

"Good. Talk soon." He hangs up. *Typical Christopher.*

The sound of my cell phone shocks me from the Jack Daniels and cocaine stupor. I twist to grab my phone from the side table. The motion knocks an empty bottle onto the floor.

Rubbing my eyes, I try to focus on the screen.

"Fuck!" I growl to the empty room, seeing a text from Red and not the call from Chris I'm expecting.

I do a quick dial to Christopher and it goes straight to

voicemail. Sniffing, I drop the phone and rub my face. Wrapping my fingers around the neck of the JD bottle beside me, I lean back against the headboard and uncap the bottle, draining the last drops. I close my eyes, letting the liquid burn in my chest.

Picking the vial up off the bed, I put two bumps into my system before returning to Rod's text. Anything to distract me. I swipe the screen.

Red: Since you won't return my messages. Kel's Liza's lil' bro. She doesn't have a man.

Her brother? He's her fucking brother?

"He's her fucking brother." Saying the words out loud somehow makes it humorous. Laughter erupts from my chest.

Chest warm and body numbing, I stagger off the bed. She's let me believe she's with someone. It's time to find out why.

Liza

"So, he didn't show up tonight?" Sid asks, sounding a bit distracted.

"No, thank God," I sigh, readjusting myself in the bus seat. "I was sure he'd confront me for ducking out."

"Not gonna lie, I'm kind of disappointed he didn't show."

"Gee, thanks." I roll my eyes, not that she can see me.

"What can I say? I live vicariously through your romantic interludes," she says, her voice a wistful sigh.

"I don't think I'd call them romantic interludes," I snort.

"True. More like lust-crazed, hard-on directed stalking," she retorts, her voice growly. "Whew, it's enough to get me worked up just talking about it."

"You have problems," I laugh.

"*You* say this like it's a surprise," she responds. "So, why are you calling me if there aren't any gritty, dirty, rocker tales to spin?"

"Oh, I'm sorry, does my regular life bore you?"

"I wasn't going to say anything, but after all the excitement lately, I don't know if I can go back to the mundane of these late night calls."

"Bitch."

"Flatterer." Sid's voice is sickly sweet.

"I'm calling because we had an employee meeting before the show tonight."

"And?" she presses.

"And Red is implementing compensation packages."

"He's what?" Now I have her full attention.

"Yeah. I'm actually getting a raise, health benefits options, and there are fringe benefits as well."

"What kind of fringe benefits?" Sid perks. "Like access to hot, dirty, tattooed rocker boys?"

"You're such a slut," I giggle. "No, not the rocker boys. However, we will have consultations with a dermatologist, full access to a local spa, and a gym membership benefit."

"Wow." Sid follows the word with a whistle. "This is good, right?"

"Yes and no."

I rub my forehead.

"I think this is going to really mess with the assistance I receive," I admit, dropping my voice. Not because I'm embarrassed, but because not everyone on the late night bus needs to know my business. "Don't get me wrong. I'm all for supporting us on my own."

"But?" she pushes.

"Well, just mentally calculating my finances, this new compensation plan will probably mean I'll lose the HUD funding and have to find a new place to live. It will also cut off medical assistance for Kel and Lucas."

I take a deep breath.

"Sid, this puts me in a bracket that should be great, but what it really does is make me more financially strapped. A new place means moving expenses. And one I'll be able to afford may result in moving away from a neighborhood I feel good having Lucas in. It could put him in a new school district and be crappier than where we live now. And call me crazy, but what about Sean? He's staying with us until his grandma gets out of the hospital. What if she doesn't get better? How am I supposed to walk away from him?"

"Don't get too worked up yet. Let's sit down and go over everything. Get all your budget information out, have your comp plan ready tomorrow, and give me a call. I'll do a quick search for some apartments to get average costs and utilities. We'll work this out. But, Liza, Sean is a different story. I'm not trying to sound like an asshole, but you don't have any legal rights to the kid. There's nothing you can do there."

"You sure you want to deal with all this?" Guilt wrinkles my forehead. I haven't told her about Mrs. Jackson's request to sign over guardianship to me. "It's not really something you have to—"

"Don't finish whatever you're about to say," Sid says, her words laced with anger. "I love you. You're more like a sister than a cousin. I'll always be there for you, so stop being stupid. Hell, maybe I'll just move out there with you. I haven't signed the lease on the apartment here yet."

"I'm not letting you give up your apartment. I know how much you love it. Plus, your work is there." I lean my head on the cool window and close my eyes.

"I'm an online based business, Liza. I can do it anywhere, and I'm pretty sure I could pick up clients in a city like L.A."

"Sid, thank you, but you have your own life. I won't let you change it to accommodate mine." Taking a deep breath, I decide to stop the conversation before she argues with me further. "I'm almost to my stop. I'll get everything together and call you tomorrow. Okay?"

Sid huffs. "Fine, good night."

"Night." I hang up, knowing it's not the last I've heard from Sid.

With a folder full of my financial future and the guardianship information on the counter for tomorrow, I change into a pair of yoga capris and one of Sid's famous t-shirt gifts. This one with the silhouette of two tap dancers on each side of the words *I'd Tap That*. Sid loves a good t-shirt and wearing it keeps her close. I settle onto the pullout bed, startling at a thud on my door.

Who the hell would be here this late at—?

The next thud is louder, harder.

Hurrying from the bed, I rush to the door and pull till the chain catches.

"Tell me who he is, snake charmer." His words are loud and slurred.

"What are you doing here?" I whisper.

"Tell me," he demands, his voice louder. He presses on the door and the chain creaks in protest.

"Shh!" I scowl through the small opening. "Stop, you'll break the chain."

Jackson's forehead thumps against the wood.

"Tell me." His plea is muffled.

"Kel's my brother," I say, my voice hushed, not wanting to cause a bigger scene.

"Your brother," he laughs loudly, pushing away from the door. "He's your fucking brother!"

I shut the door and unhook the chain. Pulling it back open, I'm met by Jackson's chest. I blink and step back.

"Why did you let me think he was your man?" There's sorrow in his eyes and I'm not sure why.

"You made the assumption and turned into an asshole." I cross my arms over my chest. "And aside from the fact that you really haven't given me much of a chance to correct you, it's not like you deserve an explanation."

"Let me in." He sways to the left and reaches up, steadying himself with the frame.

"You need to be quiet and go, Jackson. Lucas has a soccer game in the morning and I don't want him woken up."

"Please," he slurs, his body slumping into the doorframe.

Reflexively, I reach out to steady him. My hands grip his

biceps.

"Come on," I whisper, guiding him into my apartment.

He wraps his arms around me, pressing our chests together. The warmth of his cheek flattens on the top of my head.

"Is your car downstairs?" I ask, moving him so I can shut my door with a foot.

"No. I took a taxi." His hands skim down my back until he grips my ass with both hands. "Fuck, you feel so good."

A shiver runs along the base of my spine and my pussy throbs. *Goddamn him.*

I reach around, pull his hands off my ass, and step back from him.

"You took a taxi?" I try to scold the stupidity of his actions, but the grin on his face makes it difficult. "That was dumb."

"Probably." He shrugs and sways once again.

"You're drunk," I sigh. "Come over here."

Taking his wrist, he quickly slides his hand into mine, and I lead him to the pullout couch.

"Sit down. I'll see if I have some instant coffee left."

He sits, but pulls me down on top of him. Long, familiar arms encase me, holding me against his chest.

"Jackson," I warn on a whisper.

One hand slips up my spine to the back of my head. He pulls my face to him, taking my mouth in an all-consuming kiss. His mouth is warm, tongue strong and determined, but the taste is wrong. Pushing on his chest, I free my mouth.

"Let go." I shove a little harder.

"I don't think I can, snake charmer," he sighs before going lax.

I push once more and his arms slip away to the old mattress.

Standing by the bed, I look at his prone form. His overgrown ass will never fit on the pullout bed, even if I try to move him. I grin and pull a throw blanket over him.

Locking the apartment door, I press my head to the wood.

What the hell am I going to do with him?

I lift my head and look over my shoulder.

With everything else, the last thing I need is to be a rockstar's fling. It was supposed to be one night. Only one night.

With a deep breath, I move away from the door toward Lucas' room. I peek in, finding Lucas and Sean still sound asleep. I let out a sigh of relief, go back to the pullout, and climb over Jackson. Finding a spot on the other side, I lay down and try to get some sleep.

I'll just have to make sure I'm up before Lucas, Sean, and Kel. He's got to be out of here before they wake up.

The squeeze of my left breast jolts me awake.

"This is the best fucking way to wake up." Jackson's warm breath fans my cheek.

Relaxing just a bit, I pull his hand out of my shirt and sit up.

"You need to get going." I rub my neck, trying to work out the stiffness.

"Jesus, you don't sugar coat, do you?" Chuckling, he rolls to his back and groans. "Christ, do you sleep on this thing every night?"

"Not all of us live out of five star hotels." The words are sharper than intended, but I'm tired and stressed. "Look, you need to go before Lucas comes out here and finds you."

"Why?" He sits on the edge of the bed, rolling his neck till it cracks.

"Why?" I ask, exasperated.

"Yeah, why?" He stands, stretching his arms over his head. His fucking fingertips touch my ceiling.

"Because he doesn't need to see you waking up here." I step into the bed and walk across it, intending to show him the door.

"Where's your bathroom?" He starts down the hall and finds it on his own.

I groan and step into the small kitchen, filling my kettle with water before setting it on a burner.

Jackson strides back down the hall, hair in disarray, clothes rumpled, and a half-grin on his face. My nipples, heart, and pussy join forces in the great fuck-him-now campaign. I swallow hard, fighting the urges.

His eyes meet mine, holding them while he sits on a stool at the breakfast bar.

"You need to leave." Even I can hear how weak it sounds.

The half-grin on his face widens to a full smile.

"Have breakfast with me." Mischief glints in his eyes.

"Funny," I blurt, still battling the urge to lay across the bar and let him have whatever he wants.

He licks his bottom lip in a slow motion. I hold in a whimper and walk away.

"I need to use the bathroom."

"Uh huh." His chuckle follows.

After relieving myself, I wash my hands and splash cold water on my face before exiting the bathroom.

In the kitchen, Jackson opens and closes cabinets.

"What are you doing?" I keep my voice down, not wanting to wake anyone else.

"Looking for mugs." He opens the right cabinet. "Ha, found them."

Taking two out, he places them on the counter.

"Do you have coffee?" He raises a pierced brow.

"I don't know if there's any left. I have tea bags up there." I point to the small cabinet above the stove. "If you move, I'll get the stool and—"

"Stool? Really?" His look is incredulous.

Raising one arm, he opens the cabinet and pulls down the tea bag box.

"Yeah, well, I have to use the stool," I mumble.

He snorts.

"If you'd like, I can lift you up?" Wiggling his brow, he sticks his tongue out.

"You're such a comedian in the morning."

Taking the box, I move the mugs to the bar and put a teabag in each one. Jackson returns to his stool with the kettle and pours the water. I grab the sugar and a spoon. When we both finish doctoring our tea, he pulls the folder I left out in front of him.

"Hey." I slide it away from him.

"I already looked at it." He puts the mug to his mouth and blows.

Heat flushes my chest and neck.

"It amazes me how you can get on stage the way you do, but blush like this in person. It's intriguing." He sips.

"You didn't have the right to look at my personal things." Head down, I keep my hand pressed on the folder.

"I know," he responds without regret. "So, Red is doing well by his staff, but you're worried."

Surprised by his assessment, I look up and meet his eyes.

"What makes you say—?"

"Your previous budget," he responds, still no regret or shame.

I drop my face again, feeling the heat rise.

Damn it, what am I going to do? If he can eyeball the problems with a short glance, I am right to be so worried.

"Hey," his finger slides under my chin and lifts. Our eyes meet. "You don't have to be embarrassed. My mom and I lived on state—"

"I'm not embarrassed because I get help." I pull my face away from his fingers. "I mean, no, it's not something I bring up in everyday conversation, but I'm not embarrassed. I'm not one of those sit at home and leech money off the government types."

His hands come up, palms out.

"I know. I'm sorry. I didn't mean anything. Just saying I didn't always have money." He shrugs. "Sure, I've spent more time with money than without, but it wasn't always like that."

"I didn't mean to get defensive. I'm just stressed."

Why the hell am I talking about this with him?

"Anyhow, it's not something we need to talk about." I sip at my tea and look at the wall behind him.

"Where's Lucas' dad?" Jackson puts his forearms onto the bar, leaning forward.

"He's not around."

"But where is he?" he presses. "Why isn't he around?"

Setting my mug on the bar a bit too hard, I place both palms on the countertop.

"It's not any of your business." I narrow my eyes.

"No, but I made a mistake about your brother and that cost me time with you, so I'm going to make damn sure I know what's up." His eyes don't leave mine. "Plus, I'm curious."

"It's not an unusual tale. Pregnant at fifteen, he just turned eighteen. I thought he loved me. He didn't. End of story." Straightening, I pick my mug back up.

"I think there's more to it."

"He didn't know how young I was," I say around the mug.

"You told him you were older," he says, but there's no judgment in his voice.

"I had a fake ID to get into a bar to watch a local band. Met him in the crowd. He drove me and Sid home. From there, I saw him for almost six months. I got pregnant and he confessed about the girlfriend he was planning to propose to." I shrug.

"Sid?" Jackson's brows raise.

"My cousin."

"He knows about Lucas?"

"He knew I was pregnant. And about four years ago, I paid a lawyer friend to help find him and have him sign away his rights to my son."

Our eyes lock. His hold a little surprise.

"It wasn't cheap, but I don't want him popping up in Lucas' life, or mine."

"How's Lucas with it all?"

"So far, he's okay. I've told him about everything. I don't hide it from him."

"What about your parents?" He sits up, folding his arms over his chest.

"Will there be a blood test to go along with this life history?" I raise a brow.

"I'm just curious about you, Liza. You fascinate me and I want to get this right."

His answer is not what I expected.

"Don't look so surprised." He grins, dropping his arms. "I plan to know everything about you." The smile turns devilish.

"Mom, who are you talking—?" Lucas stops at the end of the hallway.

I straighten and put my mug on the counter before walking around the bar.

"What's that asshole doing here?" Lucas snarls.

"Lucas," I scold.

"It's okay." Jackson stands from the stool.

"No, it's not." I keep my eyes on Lucas. "You aren't allowed to talk like that. Jerk, Butthead, or something is fine. Heck, I might have even been okay with douchebag."

"Gee, thanks," Jackson mumbles.

I ignore him.

"What are you doing here?" Lucas narrows hard, angry eyes on Jackson.

"Your mom was nice enough to give me a place to stay last night."

Lucas jerks his head in my direction.

"He stayed with you?" A grimace curls his lip. "After the way he treated you?"

"Lucas Campbell, watch your tone." Stepping to him, I put my arms around his shoulders. "He needed a place to sleep, so I let him stay here. Nothing else."

Lucas leans around my body to land a scowl on Jackson, and growls, "You should've told him to buzz off."

"Oh. My. God." Sean's voice takes my attention. He stands frozen a foot behind Lucas. "You...you're..." He points at Jackson, eyes wide and mouth in a large 'O'.

"What's your problem?" Lucas escapes my arms and stares at his star-struck friend.

"My problem?" Sean points to himself. "Don't you know who that is?" His voice hitches higher in excitement.

"What the hell is going on?" Kel stumbles out of his room, rubbing his left eye with his palm, his blond hair in disarray.

I cover my face with my hand.

"That's Jackson Shaw!" Sean shouts. "You have the lead guitarist for The Forgotten in your kitchen, Luke."

Lucas turns his head and examines Jackson through narrow eyes.

"Are you sure?" Lucas asks Sean.

"I can show you my ID," Jackson offers with a chuckle.

"Holy crap!" Sean bolts back into Lucas' room, returning in less than a minute with a CD case, magazine, and a school folder. "You've gotta sign these for me. Please!"

Lucas grabs the magazine from his hand, looking over the cover and back up at Jackson. Recognition slowly dawns on his face.

"You have a pen?" Jackson asks.

Sean pulls a black marker out and holds it up.

"Bring it over here." Jackson sits back down, taking the items from Sean and signing them.

Lucas walks over and tosses the magazine on the counter. Jackson looks up and their eyes meet.

"You say one mean thing to my mom again and you'll regret it."

Jackson stays silent, but gives him a nod and draws an invisible cross over his heart.

"Wow, little Luke is kind of badass, huh?" Kel whispers in my ear.

I fight a giggle and smack his arm.

"Don't worry," I interrupt their staring contest, "Jackson is getting ready to leave."

"Is the rest of the band here?" Sean asks, sitting on the stool next to him.

"Nah, but they'll be coming to town in a couple weeks." He finishes signing and hands the treasures back to Sean. "Hush will be here too if you're a fan—"

Oh, no. Here we go.

"Hushed Mentality?" It's Lucas' turn to go fanboy.

"Yeah." Jackson nods, sipping from his mug.

"Mia Ryder will be in town?" he asks, a wistful look in my little boy's eyes.

Jackson laughs. "Yeah, man, she will. But be careful, Chris is a little jealous."

Lucas blushes.

"I'll see if I can set you up to meet with them, okay?"

"Really?"

"If their schedule is flexible enough, I'll see what I can make happen."

"Cool." Lucas grins, but quickly gets serious again. "This doesn't change anything. Be nice to her." He points to me.

"He gets it, Lucas." I grab his finger, pull him to me, and ruffle his hair. "Now, you two need to eat. You have a game today."

"Okay," they reply in unison, moving into the kitchen to gather bowls, cereal, and milk.

Jackson moves so they can sit. I go into the living room and fold the bed back into the couch. It gets stuck, which is not uncommon. Two inked arms appear on each side of me, helping to shove. When it collapses into the couch, Jackson lies over my back, his groin just above my ass.

He straightens, his hands coming to my hips and face dipping to my ear.

"If there weren't impressionable young minds over there, you would still be bent over the couch, but screaming my name." His tongue flicks my ear before he pulls away.

I fight the shiver and focus on putting the cushions back on the couch.

"I don't know how you sleep on that every night." He shakes his head.

I shrug. "Used to it."

Clearing my throat, I move to step around him. His hand grasps my arm, stopping me.

"I want to see you," he says, his voice level.

"Jackson, I know I spent a night with you." I keep my voice low and watch the boys to ensure they aren't listening. "And I gave you that impression, but I'm not that girl."

"No, you're not. And I don't want that girl," he responds. "I want the woman who laid claim to my body and then let me stay in her bed because I'm the man who doesn't want to give you up."

Oh my God.

"I'm not interested," I say, my lie a broken whisper.

"You and I both know that's a lie." The caress of this thumb against my skin sends shots of need through me.

Damn him,

His phone rings and he's quick to answer.

Saved by the cell.

"Yeah." He pauses. "Shit." His eyes come to mine. "The press is all over this place, is there a back way out of this building?"

"The fire escape," Kel suggests, sitting down on the couch.

"Where is it?" He turns to Kel.

"Tell him to park a street over. I'll get you out of here." Kel stands. "Just let me grab my shoes."

Jackson relays the message into the phone and hangs up.

"Tonight?" he presses.

I shake my head. "I have things to do with the boys and plans this evening."

A flicker of something dark flashes in his eyes.

"You ready?" Kel calls from the door.

"Yeah," Jackson calls over his shoulder, his eyes never leaving mine. "I'm not giving up."

Before I can respond, he cups the back of my head and crushes his mouth to mine.

Releasing me, he turns and follows Kel out the door.

"Dude, Jackson Shaw just kissed your mom. That's so cool," Sean crows.

I cover my mouth with my hand and close my eyes.

What am I supposed to do with that? I don't have time for this game he wants to play. Not right now.

Chapter Eleven
Jackson

Liza's brother stays silent, leading me down the fire escape, around the back of the building, through an alley, and behind another building. The familiar black car waits at the far end of the next alley. Sam flashes the headlights.

"It's Sam," I confirm, taking the lead toward the car.

A few feet from the car, Sam climbs from behind the driver's seat, his large form more imposing in the shadows of the alley. He rounds the car in practiced movement, opening the back door.

Before coming around to the door to get in the car, I turn to Kel.

"Thanks for helping me out, man."

"Anything to get you away from my sister." His eyes level on me with an unexpected fury.

"Ah, not a fan, huh?" I cross my arms over my chest.

"Of The Forgotten? Sure." He nods with a shrug. "Of you imposing on my sister and using her? No, man. I'm. Not. A. Fan." Mimicking, his arms cross over his chest.

"I'm sorry for the way I treated your sister. I apologized to her and I'm going to make that shit up to *her*." I straighten to my fullest height, knowing my size intimidates. He doesn't flinch or back down. *Impressive.* "Let's get one thing straight. I'm not using her."

He snorts. "Oh, really?"

"Yes, really." I step closer, insult slowly boiling to anger.

"Look, I get it. You're in town for celebrity stuff." He puts his hands out, palms forward. "You wanna have a good time and see my sister in character on stage. Liza has a lot of shit going on and doesn't need any more baggage than what Lucas, Sean, and I cause her." I furrow my brow at this knowledge. I know about her financial concern, but what else is going on? *And how the fuck does the Sean kid play a part?*

"She's not Miz Liz, Jackson. She's so much more. Much more than the on-the-side or while-I'm-in-town piece of ass. She's too good for you " he finishes

Anger flares, swelling my chest and surging into my limbs. Snatching him by the T-shirt, I shove him against the brick building on our right.

"I'm one person you don't have to tell that she's too good for me." Pressing forward, I hold him against the building with my forearm across his chest. "And, Kel, your sister is Miz Liz. You may not want see it, but it's a part of her, of who she is." He tenses, ready to fight back. "And I, for one, fucking love it." His chest muscles relax a little. I release him from the wall, taking a step back. "No, she isn't Miz Liz. Liza is a mixture of many things and each one she shows me is more amazing than next."

Kel rubs his chest. "You barely know her."

"I plan on fixing that shit as soon as she allows me."

"And when you're done here, then what?" One brow raises over his light blue eye.

"I don't know if I'll ever be done." I level him with a look, and he stiffens in response.

"Don't break her, Jackson. Liza is everything to us. I don't care who you are. If you hurt her..." Kel closes his eyes, breathing deeply.

"Huh, and here I am afraid she's going to break me." Turning, I step around Sam and climb into the car.

Kel's hand stops Sam from closing the door. He grabs the boy's shoulder to move him away from the car. "Step back, son," Sam orders.

"It's okay." I half pull myself out of the car. Sam eyes Kel before going to the driver's side and climbing inside.

"You mean that, don't you?" His brow furrows, causing deep lines for such a young face.

"Mean what?" I glance away for a moment, pretending not

to know what he's asking.

"You do," he says on a breath. Then, on a laugh, he says, "You really are scared she'll break you."

Rubbing the back of my neck, I ask, "Are we done here?"

Kel nods, finally returning to his more sober self. "There's a park four blocks that way." He points over his shoulder.

Confusion twists my face.

"She'll be there most of the afternoon for Lucas and Sean's soccer game." Shaking his head, he walks backward. "Jackson Shaw has a thing for my sister."

I narrow my eyes, not enjoying the amusement he's getting on my behalf. He grins wide, gives a salute, and runs off in the direction we arrived.

I slide back into the car and pull the door shut. *Cocky little fucker.* Sitting back into the leather seat, I grin. *I think I like that kid.* I put my head back on the seat, close my eyes, and pound on the ceiling. Sam backs out of the alley and away from a place I'd much rather stay.

My cell beeps, causing reality to crash down on me.
Mom.

I pull the cell out of my pocket, seeing missed messages from Chris. Tapping the voicemail notification, I realize the beep is because the phone is dying. The screen darkens and I get the damn white apple before it goes black.

"Fuck," I growl, throwing the cell on the floor.

"Is there anything I can help you with?" Sam offers from the driver's seat.

"Yeah, do you have Julia's number on your phone?"

"Of course." Lifting his phone from the seat, he taps the screen. "Call Julia."

"Thanks," I say, taking the phone he offers back to me.

"Sam, if he's giving you a hard time, you have my permission to—"

"Hey, now." I stop her tirade.

"Tell me you're in the car and Sam's okay." The panic in her voice is evident.

"Yes and yes. I need you to call my brother for me."

"He's already called."

"When?" Sitting straight, I grip the cell a bit too tight.

"Last night and this morning. He said, and I quote, 'didn't I fucking tell your stupid ass to stay at the hotel', end quote."

"That's all he said?" I rub my face with my free hand and take a deep breath.

"He also said to turn your cell phone up so you can hear his call, along with a few other insults."

"Great." *Bastard couldn't leave a message about my mom, but left detailed insults.*

"Jackson, tell Sam to bring the car into the garage. You need to come in through the staff entrance." The seriousness in her voice spikes my curiosity.

"Why?"

"The press is all over the place. You're..." she pauses.

"Perry already put that shit out there, didn't he?" I can't keep the disgust out of my voice.

"Yeah, but that's not all, Jackson."

"What else could—?"

"He's teasing an upcoming interview with Kristy about your split." Discomfort changes the pitch of her voice.

"That bitch."

I shove the hotel room door open a bit too hard when I enter. Julia jumps and twists in a chair, focusing her wide eyes on me. Kristy's voice comes from the television and Julia lifts the remote to the screen.

"Don't," I snarl.

Walking by her and grabbing the remote, I sit on the coffee table for a front row view.

"Thank you for joining us, Kristy."

"It's a pleasure." She plays the demure girl so well.

Perry gives the camera a sleazy smile, tilts his head, and addresses the viewers.

"Stay tuned for an exclusive interview with Kristyna Molvic, fashion's leading lady, and until recently, the star in Jackson Shaw's life. What separated the happy couple? You'll find out on Perry Exclusive."

The screen cuts to a commercial.

"What the fuck is she up to now?" I growl, tossing the remote to the couch.

"Una wants you to call her," Julia speaks to my back.

"Yeah, later." Reaching into my pocket, I pull out my dead cell. "Can you charge this for me?" I toss the phone to an unprepared Julia. It hits her leg and bounces to the floor. "Sorry."

"Sure." She purses her lips, picking up the phone.

"I believe Una wants to talk about this Kristy situation. She wasn't aware your relationship had ended." Julia studies me.

"It ended before I came here, so wipe that look off your face."

"I don't have a look," she denies.

"You sure as fuck do have a look. It's the 'you cheated on your girlfriend' look. Which, I didn't, so get that shit out of your head. Kristy doesn't know how to take no, go away, or it's over as responses." Crossing my arms over my chest, I match her glare.

"Well, with your current behavior, it wouldn't be so unexpected would it?" She plops back down into her chair.

I open my mouth, but Perry quiets me.

"Welcome back, my lovelies. We have a very Perry Exclusive for you today. And while we are honored to have Kristy with us, we are shocked and devastated to hear of the demise of her relationship with Jackson Shaw."

The camera pans to Kristyna. Her glassy eyes are an act I know too goddamn well.

"Thank you for letting me stop by, Perry. I am such a fan." She bats her lashes.

"The lying bitch!" I exclaim. "She fucking hates this guy." I turn to Julia. "She called him a vial, drama-sucking leech under her breath when we were around him."

Perry starts discussing her Gucci campaign and the upcoming launch of her perfume before getting down to business.

"Kristy. Kristyna. Tell me how you're doing." He wears the most sympathetic expression, but the gleam in his eye gives away his thirst for the dirt. "You can tell your friend Perry." His hand comes to her knee and pats gently.

"Well, it's a private matter, so while I will confirm we have split, I would really appreciate if everyone would allow me the time to heal from the event."

"Allow you to heal? But not him? So, he ended it?" Perry presses.

"Oh, it was just a turn of phrase. I meant, so we can heal." Kristy plays her role well. If I didn't know her, I would believe she's sincere.

"Of course, we'll give the two of you time to heal, but personally, girl, I wouldn't protect a man who's treated you like he has." Perry rolls his head, pursing his lips.

"It's just been a conflict of time apart and going different directions, really," Kristy feigns.

"And what about these pictures that surfaced last night?"

My heart clenches and stomach drops. A picture of me in a club with two women, one's face in my lap and the other's tongue in my mouth. Bottles of liquor, full and empty, fill the table, along with white powder lines.

The audience gasps and groans.

A sob rips from Kristy.

"You don't have to tell us anything. These pictures tell your story for you, honey." Patting her knee with one hand, he pushes tissues toward her with the other.

She grabs two and holds them to her face.

"Those are the girls she picked out!" I cry, standing.

"What do you mean 'she picked out'?" Julia questions, her tone filled with disgust.

Turning toward her, I narrow my eyes.

"She liked to take people home with us. Men, women, one, two, or three—she didn't care. The more, the merrier."

Julia's mouth forms a small 'o', but she stays silent.

Kristy's newest sob gets my attention.

"It's so hard, Perry. I was never enough. He needed the attention and the partying. If he didn't..." She buries her face in tissues.

"Didn't what, my dear?" he asks, his hand resting on her knee.

She is fucking insane.

Kristy shakes her head, hiccupping and sniffling.

"It's okay, sweetheart. We all see what you've been dealing with." He turns to the audience. "Don't we?"

A chorus of "yes!" and "you don't need him, girl!" sounds out from the audience.

"I don't believe this," I groan.

Collapsing back down to the coffee table, I hold my head in my hands. Cell phones ring out behind me.

"He. He just. Needed. Them," she hiccups. "And. Without them. He would get angry," Kristy finishes, touching a tissue to her still perfect makeup. Funny how the tears don't ruin her face.

"You're better off without someone like him. Someone who is so hard on women." Perry pulls Kristy into an embrace.

"This is so ridiculous." I throw my hands out at the screen.

"Jackson, Una's on the phone." Julia holds her bright purple phone out for me to take.

With a heavy sigh, I grab it.

"This is complete bullshit, Una," I answer.

"Jackson, tell me everything now," she demands in typical Una fashion.

"We invited others back to bed with us sometimes. That's it," I bark.

"That's it? You think that's it, Jackson?" Una doesn't scream; she's perfected the scolding tone of calmness. Like when your parents would just say they were disappointed in you, instead of yelling.

"Jackson, she has pictures of you partying in a VIP area with two half-dressed girls, which I hope to Jesus Christ are of age, surrounded by liquor and drugs. So, what else do I need to know? Because I need to know it all right goddamn now if I'm going to help you."

"Okay, yeah we partied a bit, but that's it," I lie, the craving having taken its hold the moment my phone died in the car. "We invited other women into our bed, which was her idea, by the way, we drank and did some coke. It was nothing more than that," I continue the lie.

Julia snorts from behind me. Twisting around, my glare silences her.

Una sighs, heavily. "Jackson, I pray to God she doesn't have anything else, but something tells me she isn't done. What does she want?"

"Me."

"You? That's it?"

"No. Now she wants revenge, too."

"For what?" Una's voice hitches.

"For dumping her and rejecting her attempts to get back together. There may also have been one occasion where I publicly embarrassed her."

A thump and then three more come from the other end of the phone.

"Una?"

"You're killing me, Jackson. We'll talk later." She hangs up.

I hand Julia her phone and she holds up her iPad for me to look. The online community is already running rampant with the story and picture. Women are coming out of the woodwork claiming to be one of the many. Photoshopped images of me with another woman popping up.

"Christ!" I groan and stride to the bathroom, slamming the door.

Leaning on the counter, my eyes land on the small, black leather bag. Licking my lips, I dig into my stash and line up a couple rails.

Satisfied with the numbness, I climb in the shower and let the hot water slide over my skin.

Fucking Kristy. What the fuck am I going to do? What if Liza sees this shit?

I raise my head and narrow my eyes on the white tile. I'm not sticking around this hotel all day.

Liza

"Sid, slow down, I can't understand what you're—"

"It's all over the place, Liza. Kristy, Jackson's ex, is saying they split because of him cheating and partying," Sid rushes out.

"But...wait, so why would she still be trying to impress him at the club? That doesn't make sense." Slipping off the bleacher seats to get away from the eavesdroppers around me, I point to my bag. Kel nods, understanding it means to keep an eye on it.

"I don't know," Sid sighs. "Maybe she's crazy, but that picture wasn't. Do you want me to send it?" A mischievous tone enters her voice. "It's kind of hot."

I walk the dirt path toward the parking area.

"No, thanks," I say, hoping she doesn't hear the catch in my voice.

Hornets buzz around in my stomach. *What do you expect from a rock star surrounded by groupies?*

"Hey, you okay?"

"Mmhmm. I'm fine," I hastily mutter.

"Liza, I'm sorry."

"You didn't do anything," I say, the words coming out calmer than I feel inside.

"I've told you before, you can't believe everything online. Or TV, for that matter. And from what you told me about this girl, she really may be crazy. I'm sure the longevity of starvation to her body has eaten away at her brain."

The tension breaks and I snort. Soon, we're both laughing.

"I swear, I miss you more every time you leave after visiting," I say between catching breaths.

"Ditto that, babe," she agrees. "So, do you think your

caseworker will be able to help with Sean?"

"I'm not sure. She isn't his caseworker, so it's not as easy as her handling paperwork." Shrugging, I stop a few feet from the end of the path and start walking back to the benches. "His grandmother already completed a guardianship form, but they still have to review my living arrangements and situation."

Looking up from the dirt, I realize instead of going back to the benches, I'd turned and walked back to the lot. *Great, I'm pacing.* Pacing being a nervous habit of mine, this only means my stress levels have hit maximum.

"We should just move in together," Sid states flippantly.

"Um, I'm not moving back to Pennsylvania, and you have a job and life there. I don't see how that's going to work." I glance out to the field, watching the boys run and kick the soccer ball. Guilt sets in. "Listen, I need to get back to Lucas' game."

"Shit, that's right. Sorry. We're still talking later tonight?"

"Yeah, we are."

A tingling sensation makes me look to the left. A figure approaches in the distance. I can't tear my eyes away.

"Okay, call me when you're settled in tonight. We'll get things figured out then. At least...as far as we can, alright?"

I nod, even though she can't see me.

"Liza?" Sid presses.

"Huh?" I return, distracted.

"Are you okay?" she asks, worry rushing the question.

Opening my mouth, I prepare to reassure her, but all the breath leaves my body. Heat flushes my chest and neck, climbing into my cheeks. I blink twice and swallow my response.

"Eliza, what the hell is going on?"

The dark beanie and aviator sunglasses don't hide the half-grin on his lips.

"I'll call the police in three...two..."

"I'm fine," I blurt. "But I've gotta go."

"What's going on?"

At his arrival, I tilt my head back and look at him. His driver, large enough to be security, stops a couple feet away.

"Jackson?"

"Jackson?" Sid echoes.

"What are you doing here?"

"Oh shit, this is about to get good," Sid says, drawing out the last word. "I want details. Dirty, hot, ink filled pen details, you hear me!" she whispers.

Shaking my head, I pull the phone away and hit end.

"What are you—?"

"My afternoon's free. I'm here to watch some soccer." With a broad grin and a shrug, he steps around me, walking toward the bench seats.

I reach out and grab his arm. He stops, turning halfway back toward me.

"If you think the sunglasses and hat will hide you..." I shake my head, starting to slide my hand away.

His long, inked fingers slip over my hand, stopping my retreat.

"I've been doing this for a while. It'll be fine."

Warmth surrounds my hand as he picks it up from his arm, transferring it into his. Lacing our fingers, he pulls me back to the bleachers.

I scan the crowd of game watchers, finding only a couple people lingering on Jackson a bit longer than necessary. I swallow down the riot of bees wanting an escape from my stomach. Instead of the swarm of fans I expect, they turn back to the kid's game.

Jackson stops next to Kel. His eyes, amused and watchful, stay riveted on Jackson. With a quick nod, Jackson steps one bleacher up, releases my hand, and sits down.

Hesitantly, I lick the nervous dryness on my lips and move to retake my seat by Kel. Large hands grip my hips, twisting and situating me so I'm sitting between Jackson's long, sprawled out legs. When he attempts to pull me back against him, I resist.

Too much, too fast. Too close and I will want to climb up his body.

A small shake of my head clears the naughty thoughts and I focus on the game.

"Where are the boys?" Jackson asks, the fingers of his right-hand twirling in my hair.

"Sean just came out, so he's on the bench," Kel answers, pointing out his position. "Lucas is the left forward."

I change my focus from Sean to Lucas. He's standing on the side closest to us, his body tense and ready for the game to start. He snaps into action the moment the ball is in play.

My attention is pulled away from the game when I feel Jackson's closeness. His arms come to rest on his knees, which are on either side of me, at shoulder level. My body tingles and I fight a shiver when he leans against my back. His right thumb grazes my bicep, causing goose bumps to form on my skin.

"You're going to have to help me out." He purposely draws lazy circles with his thumb. "I'm not familiar with soccer."

"Sure," Kel answers, as if we don't have a famous rock star sitting behind us. Like said rock star isn't sending my body into a riot of tingles and pulsing need.

"Hey." His voice is low and close enough to warm my ear.

"Yeah?" My voice cracks.

Jackson sweeps my hair off my neck and over my left shoulder. The brush of his fingertips causes my muscles to tense.

"Stop worrying," he whispers.

"'Kay." My response is unnaturally high pitched.

He chuckles against my back.

"No one gives a shit about who I am, Liza. It's all good." He buries his face into my neck.

My body melts and I close my eyes, inhaling Jackson.

Cheers from the crowd pull me from the lusty cocoon he so easily wraps around me.

Sitting straighter, I focus on the field.

"What did I miss?"

"Our goalie had a pretty awesome save." Kel's answer is laced with amusement.

Turning my head, I narrow my eyes on him. He ignores me, keeping his attention on the field.

"Excuse me?" someone asks from Kel's side of the benches.

Assuming it's someone being polite about walking in front of another, I watch Lucas.

Lucas gets his feet on the ball, maneuvering toward their opponent's net. I stand, hands clasped, waiting for the kick. Instead, Lucas passes the ball to the striker and she puts it in the net.

My shout is accompanied by the rest of the crowd on our bleachers. Kel stands, clapping, and I hop on my toes. The movement causes my balance to waiver. Jackson's hands grip my hips, steadying me. Turning at the touch, I grin down at him before looking back to the field.

My baby just assisted with a goal!

"Nice teamwork!" Kel yells over the crowd.

Lucas looks into the stands and smiles.

"Um, excuse me?" This time it's louder, closer.

Looking to my left, two young girls stand, biting on their lips with curiosity in their eyes—which are dead set on Jackson.

"What?" Kel asks, retaking his seat.

They look around Kel.

"Are you Jackson Shaw?" Hope fills the girl's question, matching the excitement in her eyes.

"Yeah," he answers, nonchalant.

I sink back down to my seat and his hands slide up my sides. Ignoring the way my body responds to his touch, my wide eyes watch his reaction to being found out.

"Ohmygod!" she yells. "Isoknewitwasyou. Oh. My. God. You're Jackson Shaw." Her grin is wide and she grips her friend's arm tightly.

The other girl stands with her mouth open. For a moment, I'm sure she'll cry.

"It's nice to meet you." He smiles, giving them a quick nod.

"Will you sign my shirt, please?" she begs, digging in a bag and pulling out a pen.

"Sure." He shrugs.

Removing his hands from my sides, he takes the pen and leans over so he can reach where she stands.

The girl blurts something I can't make out before pulling her shirt over her head and setting it on the bench.

"This is a kid's game," one parent scolds.

"Calm down, I'm wearing a sports bra. It's just like a tank top," she snottily replies.

I wrinkle my nose at her attitude and realize my brother's eyes are fixated on the half-naked girl.

"Ow," he shouts after I smack his arm.

"Stop staring," I scold in a whisper.

Jackson signs the shirt quickly and hands it back.

"You better get this back on."

"Are you crazy?" she gushes, clutching the shirt to her chest. "I can't wear or wash it ever again."

"Can I get a picture with you?" The star-struck mute girl finally speaks.

"Uh, how about after the game?" Jackson offers. "I don't want to interrupt. Plus, I came here to watch a buddy of mine."

"You know someone on this team?" Snotty, half-dressed girl scrunches her face.

"Yeah," Jackson answers with an is-there-a-problem tone.

"Oh, okay." She perks up once she realizes his annoyance.

"Great. Catch me after the game."

Sitting back up, he pulls me between his legs and wraps an arm around my shoulders.

"This could get out of control," he whispers.

"I won't say I told you so," I mumble.

My chin disappears into his hand. Cupping it, he pulls my head back to look up at him. With a half-grin on his face, he says, "Sassy little mouth you have there."

I try to pull my face away, but he holds it still. Dropping his voice, he whispers, "You're lucky I enjoy the fuck out of your sassy little mouth."

The half-grin grows full and painstakingly beautiful.

The blow of a whistle pulls us away from the moment.

The game is over and the teams are lining up.

"Lucas' team won." Kel leans toward me. "Figured you'd want to know since you were a bit busy."

"Shut up," I growl, crossing my arms over my chest.

Jackson chuckles, loudly.

After three cell phone pictures with the two girls, they are finally on their way.

"I told you it's him." Sean's voice rings out from behind me.

Turning, I take in most of Lucas and Sean's team.

"You thought we were lying," Sean scoffs, wrapping his arm around Lucas' shoulders. "We told you Jackson is his mom's boyfriend."

My eyes widen and heat burns my cheeks and nose.

"It's really him." Scotty, one of the kids on the team, steps forward. "You're really him, ain't you?"

Jackson walks to the group of boys, pulling the sunglass on the top of his head.

"Sure am," he confirms, causing a murmur of excitement.

"You're really his mom's boyfriend?" Another teammate takes a step forward.

"I never said he was my mom's boyfriend," Lucas growls, pushing to the front of the group. "They're just friends." His eyes narrow on Jackson.

"Friends don't kiss," Sean scoffs.

Lucas turns his narrow eyes to glare at Sean.

"What?" He shrugs. "He kissed your mom. And," Sean continues, "he was hugging her in the stands." He motions to the bleachers.

Dear God, please let this end.

"Alright, what's going on here?" Their coach steps forward.

"Coach, this is Jackson Shaw from The Forgotten. He's famous!" A girl teammate exclaims.

"Famous, huh?" The coach studies Jackson. You can actually see the realization smooth out the curiosity wrinkling his face.

Soon, a crowd of kids, coaches, and parents circle Jackson. He's asked to sign soccer balls, bags, jerseys, hats, and one mother even asked for him to sign her chest. Luckily, it was near her collarbone, not her breast.

"Can we go?" Lucas sighs, impatient and unimpressed.

"Yeah. We'll go."

Standing, I move through the remaining crowd toward Jackson. Our eyes meet and calmness settles into his.

When I'm close, he reaches out and pulls me to him.

"We're going to go I, um...I want to thank you for coming to his game." Even I hear the discomfort in my words.

"I'll have Sam take us to your place." Jackson releases me, motions for Sam, and turns to the crowd.

"Us?" I furrow my brow.

"Thanks, everyone, for making me feel welcome at the game today. I really appreciate it. Unfortunately, I have a prior engagement." His arm wraps around my waist. "So, I need to get going." He puts his free hand up, waving to the crowd.

A mixture of "thank you", "you're awesome", and "I love you" comes from the group.

Sam's presence is felt before his hand comes to my arm. Gently, he guides me away from the crowd. Jackson breaks free from last second autographs and strides to my side. Sam releases my arm, allowing Jackson to take his place.

"I need to get the boys." I dig my feet into the ground, looking back to where I left them.

My heart drops into my stomach. They're gone.

"They are already in the car," Sam informs.

The panic ebbs.

In the car, Kel is lecturing the boys about playing with buttons.

"Guys," I sigh, sliding into the back seat, "behave."

"Okay," they grumble in unison.

"Push whatever you want." Jackson settles in next to me. "Just leave the windows up."

"Why?" Lucas wrinkles his face in confusion.

"Because people will try to get pictures and stuff. Duh," Sean answers.

"That's part of it," Jackson confirms. "People throw stuff at the cars, too. I don't want anyone getting hit with something."

"What kind of stuff?" Lucas studies him.

"Um..." Jackson hesitates. "Clothes, rocks, stuffed animals, flowers...and other stuff."

"Rocks?" Sean asks, disbelief in his voice.

"Yeah, they'll wrap notes around them sometimes." Jackson shrugs.

"Just don't push any buttons." I give both boys the I-have-spoken look.

"Okay," Lucas responds.

"Yes, ma'am," Sean answers.

"Damn," Jackson mutters under his breath.

Arriving at my building, part of me expects him to leave us on the curb. The more irrational girly side of me does backflips when he climbs out and follows us upstairs.

"Lucas, don't drop your bag in the middle of the floor," I order before the door is even closed. "Sean, change and shower."

I flip the lock on the door.

"Are we still doing pizza?" Kel unloads the mini cooler on the counter.

I nod and grab the coupons from the drawer of my small desk. Sorting through them, I begin to feel self-conscious. I've forgotten Jackson. He's currently witnessing the routine of our life.

Looking up from under my lashes, I find him sitting on a stool at the breakfast bar, watching me. He grins. I force a smile through the semi-embarrassment of couponing in front of Jackson Shaw and quickly divert my eyes back to my task.

"Do we still have the one that includes the 2-liter?" Kel asks, bent into the fridge. "If not, I'll run down to the corner." He straightens and shuts the door.

"I don't see it. Didn't we use it when Sid was here?" I wrinkle my brow, walking toward the breakfast bar.

Laying the coupons out, Kel and I go through them again.

Jackson grabs a coupon. Both Kel and I follow the action and study his reaction. He sets it on the bar and pulls out his cell phone.

"What are you doing?" My body instinctively shifts toward

him.

"I invited myself, so I'll get the pizza." He touches the screen of his cell.

"You don't have to—"

"Does this place have beer?" Jackson looks to Kel.

Kel's eyes shift to me briefly before he gives Jackson a shake of his head.

"I can run out and get some," he offers.

"No, you can't," I scoff. "You're only eighteen."

Kel shrugs. "I have connections."

"I don't want to know." I shake my head.

"Hey, yeah, man, I need..." Jackson pauses, giving me an expectant look, "a large pepperoni and a 2-liter."

"What about your—"

"We're good," I cut Kel off.

"Sorry, just give me a minute," Jackson speaks on his phone before handing it to Kel. "Order whatever you usually get, but add a large pizza with pepperoni, sausage, mushroom, and olives."

Kel takes the phone and relays the order. This time, he includes my Sicilian style pizza and Caesar salad. After the address is provided, he hands the phone back to Jackson.

Putting my bag on top of the bar, I rummage through and pull out my wallet.

"I don't think so." Jackson grabs the worn leather, shoving it back into my bag.

"Jackson, I can pay for food." A bit of insult and embarrassment sharpen my tongue.

"I know you can." He stands from the stool, reaching into his pocket. "But I said I'd get the pizza since I'm a self-invite."

Sighing, I give a resigned, "Fine."

Leaving my bag on the bar, I take my irrational embarrassment and anger with me to make sure the boys are cleaning up.

Showers complete, Lucas, Sean, and Kel convince Jackson to join them for video gaming. I'm thankful for the moment away from his little touches, seductive looks, and that damn mouth of his. My mind is almost cleared when Sid calls.

Of course, she's more interested in the fact that Jackson is in my apartment. And keeping her on topic regarding my budget is practically impossible.

"You do realize you have Jackson Shaw, guitarist of The Forgotten, playing domestic daddy in your apartment, right?"

"Sid," I use my warning tone, "it's not like that, and stop referring to him by his full name and job description. It's creepy."

"It's not creepy, Liza. It is panty melting, nipple tightening, hot as fucking hot can get. The fact that you don't realize this concerns me. Is your vagina working properly?"

"Stop it," I laugh.

"Perhaps you should have him check under your hood. And when I say hood, I mean clitoral hood," she deadpans.

"Oh my God, stop it!" I cry out in laughter.

"Should I be jealous?" His voice, next to my unoccupied ear, ensures my vagina is working just fine.

"Sweet Lord of penises, his voice is sexy," Sid sighs over the phone.

"Jealous of what?" I pull the phone away from my mouth and tilt my head.

"I only want to hear 'oh my God' when it's followed by my name and you coming around my cock." His tongue flicks the lobe of my ear.

I shiver and tighten my crossed legs.

"That's it. I'm ruined," Sid cries dramatically. "No man will ever live up to this."

"Both of you stop." My words are breathy and it takes all my strength to lean away from his mouth.

"Pizza!" Lucas shouts, running toward the buzz of the intercom.

Jackson straightens and steps back from me. Taking a deep breath, I move to stand, but his hand on my shoulder stops me. Instead, he walks over to the door, pulling cash out of his back pocket.

"Damn cock blockers," Sid grumbles.

"Sid!" I scold, but smile.

"Well, damn, the kid just killed the ear porn I was getting," she whines.

"Don't you have enough porn already?"

"You can never have enough," she snorts. "Besides, this was real life rock star ear porn. Girl, I need to freshen up after that."

"Okay, TMI, Sid."

"Like you aren't used to it," she counters.

Pizza boxes slide onto the counter next to me. Kel sets out paper plates and plastic cups. I stare at the old mismatched cups and feel embarrassment creeping back to the forefront of my emotions.

Oh my God! I have nothing to be embarrassed about. They are clean. Just because Jackson is in my home doesn't mean everything is now worth shit.

Suppressing the shame, I redirect Sid to our conversation about my budget. I try to keep my voice low, but Jackson decides to sit next to me instead of with the boys in the living room.

"I think living together is ideal," Sid presses the issue again.

"I'm not moving back to Pennsylvania," I counter. "And you just found an apartment you love. Didn't you sign the lease?"

"Not yet and I don't have to. Plus, I didn't mean you move back here. I told you before I can move out there," she says, her tone serious.

"I'm not asking you to change your life so you can come out here for me."

"I miss you," she mutters.

"I miss you, too," I sigh.

"No final decisions, just think about it. We can find a four bedroom place and share the expenses."

"Sid..."

"It's a thought," she cuts in. "Did you hear anything else about Sean today?"

"No, same as before. His social worker has the guardianship papers from his grandmother, but I haven't heard anything."

"What about his mom? Won't she try to swoop back in?" Sid, knowing Sean's family life, is right to worry about her.

"Apparently, since she lost custody of Sean to her mother, there's really nothing she can do. However, they did reach out to her. I guess she didn't realize her mother's house had a reverse mortgage. So, if Mrs. Jackson doesn't return to the house, it goes to the bank. His mom wasn't happy to find out she wouldn't be getting the house and I guess that's all she cared about."

"What a cunt." Jackson's voice surprises me.

I stare at him.

"I second what he said," Sid chimes in.

"What?" He shrugs. "She is."

"Stop eavesdropping on my call." I give him a flat look, but the grin he returns ruins my attempt at annoyance.

"You know, even when he's saying cunt with a negative connotation, I get hot. That's goddamn talent. Ask if he does 900 number work?"

Laughter bursts out of my mouth and tears pool in my eyes.

"What?" Jackson asks, one brow raising over his eye.

I shake my head. "Nothing," I choke out between laughs.

"It wasn't that funny," Sid states, laughing at my reaction.

She's right. It wasn't that funny, but it was just one of those moments and now I'm stuck in a giggle fit.

Jackson watches, studying me, with amusement in his eyes and that damn half-grin on his face.

Taking a deep breath, I force my eyes back to the financial papers and documents from my social worker.

"So, back to the budget," I redirect, purposely keeping my eyes off Jackson. His presence is enough distraction, causing tingles, pulsating parts, and goose bumps. "You think I'm playing it too safe with the rent budget?"

"Of course you are." Sid exhales dramatically. "You always play it like that, but I understand why. You could probably pad that with a couple hundred, though."

I purse my lips, hesitating to change the number on the paper.

"You're not going to change it," Sid states. "We already know you won't. Just know you could, okay?" Understanding laces her words.

I nod even though she can't see me.

"Okay," I breathe out.

The boys enter the little kitchen, dumping their dishes and garbage.

"You coming?"

I look up at Sean's question. It was for Jackson.

"We're going to play guitar hero. You should be able to dominate." Sean grins.

Jackson chuckles. "There is a big difference between the buttons on the game guitar and Wifey."

"You have a wifey?" Lucas screws up his face.

"Don't throw me out just yet." Jackson leans his elbows on the top of the bar. "It's what I named my guitar."

"You named your guitar Wifey?" It's Kel turn to look confused.

"Yep. We take care of each other, but there are also days we hate the fu—"

"Ahem." I shift my eyes between him and the boys.

"I mean, days we don't like each other much." The hint of a smile plays at the edge of his mouth.

I want to lick it. Suck his lip into my mouth until I capture the ring adorning it. Giving myself a small shake, I focus back on the papers.

"Aw, come on!" Sean begs.

"Okay." Jackson gives in. "I'll meet you in there."

The boys, including Kel, hurry back to Lucas' room.

From the corner of my eye, I watch Jackson twist on the stool and slide his body from the chair until his chest practically touches my arm. I can feel and see his head move close to my head.

"Just so you know, I am going to find out what you were just thinking about."

"Nothing." I lift my right shoulder, trying to play it off.

"I saw the naughty glint in your eye," he whispers.

Reflexively, I turn my head to him. He grins, bringing his face a breath from mine.

"Now, you know how much your naughty little snake charming side gets me turned on."

"I—" His mouth captures the denial I'm about to speak.

"Liza?" Sid asks in my ear.

Jackson slips a hand behind my neck, preventing my attempt to pull away. His tongue slips into my mouth, intruding and laying claim.

My cell phone clacks to the counter after slipping from my fingers. With both hands, I fist his shirt, holding him close. The warmth of his hands settles on my thighs, trying to part them.

"Jack?" Lucas shouts.

I push him back, wipe my mouth with my hand, and turn toward the hall. I release a breath of relief when I don't see any of the boys standing there. Grabbing my phone, I put it back to my ear.

"Sid?" I blurt.

"Well, that was quick. My fantasies totally have him lasting longer than that."

"Shut up," I grumble and look up at Jackson.

He smiles his little half-grin.

"What are you smiling at?" I purse my lips.

"Fucking perfection, that's what I'm smiling at. Fucking perfection." In a flash, both his hands grab my face. He plants a full lip kiss on my mouth, releases my face, and walks away.

"I don't think we can be friends anymore." Sid shatters the shock of his words with her declaration.

"Wh-what?" I shake my head.

"I can't be friends with you," she sighs heavily.

"What are you talking about? We're related. You can't get rid of me," I tease.

"Crap," she groans. "Well, then, you are going to have to just accept that I will be living vicariously through your situation."

"My situation?"

"Yep. You being the object of adoration and lust for a hot as hell rock star."

"Shut up," I giggle.

"Just as long as you are okay with me fantasizing about your man, we should be good."

"He's not my man," I clarify, shoving the documents and papers into my folder. Clearly this conversation will never get back on track.

"Yeah, keep telling yourself that. Just be careful, I don't wanna go to jail for having to kill someone and I really don't want to be all over TV for killing a celebrity. They always find the most random, jacked up photos. I know they'll go straight to that picture from eleventh grade when I thought blonde would be more fun. Do you remember the rash I had on the side of my face from the bleach? God, they're going to use that photo."

"Sid," my voice is stern, "I appreciate the concern, but I'm pretty sure there won't be any jail time. He'll be gone in a couple weeks and you know how that will go," I snort.

"Why don't you tell me how that's going to go?" Jackson doesn't sound amused in the slightest.

"On that note, you're on your own. I tried to tell you, but you won't listen. Peace out, baby doll." Sid disconnects.

I'm too frozen by the tone of his voice to respond. Setting the phone on the counter, I slowly turn to face my inked giant.

"Hey," I try to play it off, "I thought you were playing video games."

His arms cross over his chest and brow furrows.

"Why don't you tell me how things are going to go, Liza? You seem to have it all figured out," he presses.

"Jackson," I sigh out his name, "we both...we live..." I pause, searching for the right words. "We live different lives, in different places. You won't be around forever." I shrug.

The deep wrinkle in his brow softens just a touch. He opens his mouth, but the ring of his cell interrupts. Pulling the phone from his back pocket, he looks at the screen, eyes wide. Urgency takes over his movements as he touches the screen and jams the phone to his ear.

"Why the fuck haven't you called me back?" he barks in greeting. "I don't give a shit what you thought was best, Christopher!"

I straighten my spine, realizing he's talking to his brother.

"What?" His voice cracks and sadness draws his features downward.

Instinctively, I move to his side.

"How long has she known?" He chokes on the question.

I place a hand on his arm.

"She didn't think I should—"

Flexing my fingers, I grip his arm, but he pulls away from my touch.

I know I should be more understanding, but rejection swirls through my body. Taking steps away from him, I lean against the counter and stare at the floor.

"That's bullshit and you know it," he shouts. "They've known for months and said nothing. She's my mother for fuck sake!"

My eyes come back to him at the mention of his mother. The pain in his eyes and the tension in his body makes my heart ache.

"I'll be home in the morning," he says, his words clipped, angry.

"NO!" he shouts.

Movement in the hallway catches my eye. Kel, Lucas, and Sean stand in the bedroom doorway, confusion on their faces. Kel's eyes come to mine. I shake my head and he pulls the boys back into the room, closing the door behind them.

"You expect me to just stay in L.A., pretend like she isn't sick, and act like she didn't lie to me all this time? You are out of your goddamn—"

His face goes from angry to sheet white.

"Mom," he chokes on her name, "why wouldn't you—?"

His shoulders sag, head drops, and body looks like it's going to collapse.

Sucking up my hurt feelings, I move back to his side and wrap my arm around his back. I guide him to the couch and he lets me sit him down.

"You should've told me." Sitting next to him, I hear the tears in his voice.

His long fingers grip into the denim at his knees.

"I'm coming home." He sniffs. "No, I'm leaving tonight."

Releasing the denim, he rubs his face.

"Damn it, Mom, I can't stay here when you—"

His shoulders tense.

"Fine," he growls. "I'm sorry for cursing."

I fight not to smile.

"I'll be home before the weekend. You can't stop me from leaving after I take care of things for the show."

Show?

"I'm going to talk to the producers and tell them I have a family emergency."

Producers?

"I don't care about the stupid Hidden Talent sh—crap. They can replace me or make accommodations."

Oh. My. God. He's here for the show, THE show, and I'm a contestant. Shit, shit.

"I'll do what I have to tomorrow, but after that, I'll be on a plane. I love you, but you aren't stopping me." He ends his call, dropping the phone on the floor between his feet.

My body aches from the tension in my muscles. *I have to tell him.* I glance at him from the corner of my eyes. He's bent, knees to elbows, with his head in his hands. *I can't tell him right now.*

I open my mouth, but close it.

Suddenly, he stands, stalking down the hallway to the bathroom.

When the door closes, I mimic his previous pose. Holding my head in my hands, I take deep breaths and try to figure out how and when to tell him about the show.

He returns as quickly as he left.

"I'm sorry about—"

Standing, I shake my head. "You don't have anything to apologize for."

He sniffs and rubs under his nose. A white dot·sits on his lip and my eyes can't look away. Not even when his body stiffens and he licks his lip.

My brow furrows.

"I should go," he blurts.

Finally moving my gaze away from his lip, I meet his eyes.

"Are you okay?"

"No," he responds honestly, rubbing his nose again.

"I don't know what all is going on, but I'm sorry you're going through it."

"Yeah, thanks." He bends at the waist and picks his phone up off the floor.

When he moves to straighten, a miniature brown bottle falls out of his pocket. Reflexively, I pick it up. I know exactly what it is and what the nose rubbing is about.

Drugs. My heart drops into my stomach. *Probably coke.* I'd seen too many young girls—waitresses, backup dancers—fall victim to cocaine and other drugs.

Locking my eyes to his, I hold my hand out, palm up.

His eyes shift from the vial in my palm to my eyes and back before he takes it from me.

"I just—"

"You just brought an illegal substance into my home and around my son," I finish for him, shaking my head. "Why?" I furrow my brow.

"Why what?"

"Why would you waste your time and life with that crap?" I motion to the hand fisting the drugs. "I thought you'd be smarter than this."

His face turns to stone, any light in his eyes dies.

"I don't need a mother," he sneers. "Besides, you have enough kids to take care of, don't you think?" His head jerks in the direction of Lucas' room.

I bite my lip and fight tears welling up in my eyes.

"You thought you had this all figured out, didn't you?"

"No, I didn't." I shake my head as the tears threaten to spill.

"Whatever, Liza. Based on what you said to your cousin, you've been planning my exit." Shoving the vial in his pocket, he pulls out his cell before turning toward the door.

The tears escape, falling over my warm cheek.

Grabbing his knit hat and sunglasses from my small desk, he pauses at the closed door. His shoulder's sag and he turns around. I stare at a spot on the wall to the left of him.

"Just go," I say, my voice cracking.

"I—"

"Don't need a mother," I remind him with a whisper before meeting his sad eyes. "And I have enough children, so go throw your tantrum somewhere else." Crossing my arms over my chest, I press my mouth closed tight and clench my teeth.

The sadness dissolves back to anger. Spinning around, he yanks open my apartment door and storms out. No matter how prepared I am for the slam, the noise still makes me jump. A swirl of emotion breaks loose inside me.

"Mom?" Lucas calls quietly from the hall.

"Yeah?" I try to sound as reasonable as possible.

"Is everything okay?" he asks, his voice closer.

"Everything is..." I breathe through my nose, exhaling the urge to burst into tears. Swallowing my feelings, I turn to my son. "Everything's fine."

"Where did Jackson go?" His eyes narrow, suspicious.

"He has things he needs to deal with." It's vague, but honest.

Lucas stands completely still, a look of apprehension on his face.

"It's fine, Lucas. Go finish your game. It will be time to turn it off soon." I force a smile and turn, walking to the kitchen.

I begin rinsing out cups and downsizing the pizza boxes for the trash. When I finish with the small tasks, I look over my shoulder and find Lucas gone. With a deep breath, I lock the apartment door on the way to the bathroom.

In the shower, I break, hiding my tears and quiet sobs under the warm spray.

Chapter Twelve
Jackson

The heavy knock on the door is followed by the familiar bellow of Julia.

"Jackson, we have to be out of this hotel in twenty minutes." She knocks three more times.

Letting the hot water rinse away the alcohol seeping from my pores, I close my eyes. Behind my lids, all I see is Liza. Her blue eyes swimming in hurt. A hurt I put there—again.

"Jackson, come on," Julia pleads, followed by one muted thud.

Rubbing my face beneath the spray, I groan.

"Give me ten," I shout in irritation, pressing my palms against the white tiles.

Christ, I fucked up, but it's all so much. Too much.

I waited days for Chris to let me know what the fuck is going on and the moment he says breast cancer, I lose my shit.

"Mom has breast cancer," I say, testing the words out loud. My tongue wants to choke on them. "Fuck," I shout and turn off the water. Pushing off the wall, I slam my back against the tile instead.

Mom has cancer and kept that shit to herself for almost a month before even telling Nicholas. Then they decide not to tell anyone until more tests and a course of treatment is selected.

I snort, resting my head back against the shower wall. *Fuck them!*

I jerk away from the wall, climb out, and wrap a towel around my waist. Catching a glimpse of the remnant lines I snorted last night, I secure the cloth before lining up a few to get me going this morning.

"I'm going to need it just to get through this talent show

bullshit." The justification sounds weak to my own ears. The shaking in my hands, something I ignore.

Rubbing away the residue from my nose and lip, I enter the bedroom to get dressed.

Julia immediately turns, giving me her back.

"Sorry, I didn't know you were coming out."

"You can look," I tease, feeling much better than a few minutes ago. "I know you want to."

"I'm good," she mumbles, making her way to leave.

"Hey," I call out, stopping her. "I'm only teasing."

"Yeah." Keeping her head down, she walks out.

I close the door behind her, agitation lessening my high. *Who the fuck is she to give me attitude? Everyone thinks they have shit figured out.*

My thoughts travel to Liza. Guilt and anger rage a battle for top emotion.

Releasing the towel to the floor, I slip into my clothes. Securing my "Cock Fight" belt buckle in place, I retreat back into the bathroom to snort away everyone's bullshit attitude and assumptions about me.

The drive to the studio is delayed by Monday morning traffic. Julia is anxious and providing updates to the producers regarding our arrival while I feel fucking fantastic, sprawled in the back of the limo, head back on the seat.

"Are you actually happy or just higher than the Hollywood sign?" Julia asks, her question saturated in criticism.

"You're cute when you're all worked up," I respond without lifting my head or opening my eyes. *Fuck, I feel so goddamn good.*

She huffs, but it doesn't kill my mood.

Upon arrival, she ushers me around from the lobby to the conference room. From there, we are escorted to our secret booth.

It's all kinds of James Bond, so I decide to act the part.

Folding my hands together and stretching out my pointer fingers, I slide against the wall, singing the *Goldfinger* theme song.

"What are you doing?" Julia hisses, eyes wide and face red.

"Come on." I drop my hands to the sides of my body. "*Goldfinger* is by far the best Bond movie. You have to know the song."

She stands, mouth agape.

Raising my brow, I give her my best come-on look. Her lips twitch before a smile splits her mouth, showing her teeth.

"Come on," she giggles.

Taking my arm, she pulls me down the hall to where our escort awaits.

Showing us into the room, my eyes settle on Gemma.

"So glad you could join me," she says, her irritation evident.

"There was traffic." I shrug, dropping into the chair next to hers.

"Look at me," she orders, setting a pen and notepad down hard on the edge of the sound table.

"Why?" I take a notepad Julia hands out for me, keeping my eyes off Gemma.

"Goddamn it," she growls. "How high is he?"

"Your guess is as good as mine," Julia snaps back. "It's enough for him to play James Bond in the hallway."

"Hey," I spin in the chair and raise my arms, "that was our special thing."

Julia rolls her eyes, taking a seat on a chair in the far corner of the room.

"Christ, Jackson," Gemma mumbles.

"We have work to do." I spin back around toward the table. "You can pray to me later."

She gives a half snort, half laugh.

"Bring lots of coffee. When he crashes, it ain't gonna be pretty," Gemma says to someone, probably Julia.

I feign a gasp, and follow with, "I'm always pretty."

"Your eyes are bloodshot, face flushed red, dark circles, and your nose looks like Christmas." Gemma purses her lips, raising one brow.

"Christmas?" I furrow my brow.

"Red as Rudolph and covered in snow," she quips before picking her notepad back up. "We're on contestant number five, in case you're interested."

Annoyed with the lectures and attitude, my anger levels spike.

"Don't act like this shit matters so much to you," I sneer.

"It does matter, Jackson," Gemma counters. "This is my fucking job. It. Matters. And what I don't need is to be partnered up with someone who's too fucking high to get shit done."

"Fuck you," I growl. "You don't know what I have going on."

"You aren't the only one to ever get dumped or cheated on, Jack!" Gemma slams her notebook down. "Grow a fucking pair and get over the little tramp. Why ruin yourself for someone who didn't care enough not to jump on someone else's dick the moment you guys were apart? Huh?"

I flinch from her words. They're harsh, painful to hear, and partly right. But this isn't about fucking Laney.

"I don't give a shit about her," I admit out loud. The truth behind the words surprises me into silence.

"Then what's your problem? The model bitch causing problems with your extracurricular activities? Boo-fucking-hoo." She crosses her arms over her chest, staring at me over her black-rimmed glasses.

"My fucking mom has cancer," I shout, and watch Gemma's face relax. "She's known for months, but didn't think she needed to share that shit. Instead, I find out last night, after all her tests and the decision for a double mastectomy had been made."

"Jackson," Gemma's voice softens, "I'm so sorry."

She places her hand on my arm, but I pull away from the sentiment.

"I am sorry," she says, her words a bit harder, "but it's still not worth it. Your mom would kick your ass if she knew you were—"

"Why should I tell her shit?" I raise a brow in challenge. "She didn't think I should know about her being sick," I shrug, "she doesn't need to know about my harmless fun."

"It's not harmless. You're not the same." Gemma's voice is quiet and sad.

I'd be lying if I said it didn't affect me, but I hit the mic button, blowing the conversation off.

"Who's next?" I ask the studio producer working with us today.

"Contestant number six just arrived," he informs.

"Jackson?" Gemma tries once more.

"We have a job to do," I turn hard eyes on her, "and I don't want to be the reason you don't get your fucking job done."

My attention back on the soundboard, I wait for the first of many headache-inducing performances to begin.

I'm right about the headache. By number twenty-four, I'm on my second dose of ibuprofen and fifth cup of coffee. Not all of them are horrible, not all are even bad—hell, some are pretty fucking good—it's the constant music, the replaying of the same bad songs, and the lack of reception to our coaching grinding my last nerve.

Julia sets a bottle of red liquid on the table next to me and walks away.

"Gatorade?" I ask her back.

"The electrolytes will help with the headache." She sits back into her chair, iPad in her lap.

"Thanks," I say.

She gives a small nod, not looking at me.

"I don't think she knows what to say to you," Gemma offers. "Sort of the way I don't right now."

I take a deep breath and exhale, turning to Gemma.

"Just forget about it and let's get this shit done. I need to talk to the producers and arrange travel back home."

Gemma stops my hand before I press the mic button.

"You're leaving?" Her eyes search my face.

"I'm going home to see my mom face-to-face. If they can't make arrangements around this, then I'm out of the show." I shrug.

She nods, pressing the mic button and asking for the next contestant.

Uncapping the bottle of red liquid, I drink greedily in hopes of easing the ache in my skull. Julia and Gemma both watch my every move, a transparent attempt to keep me sober.

What I wouldn't give for a hit right now...

I close my eyes and sigh at the thought as the stripped down sound of *Toxic* fills the room. Then the voice fills the room, reaching deep inside me. Her voice is unmistakable, husky, sexy, and hypnotic.

"Fuck, this girl is good," Gemma says, writing notes on her pad.

Her voice feels like familiar fingers dancing over my skin.

"Are you okay?" Gemma asks, but I can't focus on anything.

My chest rises and falls, my heart beats erratically, and my dick hardens uncomfortably.

Snake Charmer.

Skull pounding, dick hard, heart pounding an angry beat against my ribs, I shove out the chair. Julia squeals and Gemma curses at my sudden movement.

"What the hell, Jack?" Gemma snarls, standing from her chair.

She's a contestant. Liza is a fucking...did she already know I'd be on the show?

I stride to the studio room door, the hinges protesting when I yank it open.

"Jack—" The door slamming into the wall cuts Julia off.

"It's her," I growl.

"Stop him!" Gemma calls as I exit the room.

How could she know I was a judge? It was kept secret. Our interviewers weren't even allowed to mention it without fear of a lawsuit.

Digging my fingers into my hair, I storm through the hallway, my steps sounding like angry echoes.

She couldn't have known. It's impossible.

The tightness in my chest eases for just a moment.

Grabbing the first door handle, I shove it open. Empty.

"Jackson!" Julia and Gemma yell in unison.

"You can't just—"

I shove the next door open, silencing Julia.

"What the fuck?" One of two sound techs turns toward me. "You can't just barge in here! We're in the middle of recording."

Ignoring him, I step in and look through the glass. Not her.

Moving on, I reenter the hallway and run into Julia, a man in all black standing next to her.

"Jackson, what's wrong?" She attempts concern.

It's fucking patronizing.

Stepping around her, I continue to hunt her down.

Red. The thought stops me cold. *Fucking Red knew. He'd tell that girl he's fucking in a heartbeat. And she's loyal to Liza. Loyal enough to give her the inside scoop for this show.*

Heat rises from my stomach and over my chest, choking my throat. Gulping down a breath, I charge forward on my mission.

"Miss, I have to stop him." A deep voice comes from behind me.

I move quicker, reaching the next door before security reaches me.

Gripping the handle, I shove. Locked.

I raise my fist and large, heavy hands wrap around my forearm, pulling me away from the door.

"Get off me," I protest, shoving the man off.

The force is enough for him to release my arm and smack the wall across from me.

"Don't you fucking touch me," I warn.

A door opens and voices carry out, catching my attention.

My eyes lock onto Liza. Her eyes widen and lips part.

A storm of lust, need, and want rages within me just from the sight of her.

Her mouth opens to speak, but my approach silences her.

The way I want her, need her, knowing she possibly used me

for the show, morphs my anger to rage. I hate it. I hate the way she makes me need her.

Fucking snake charmer.

Pushing into her personal space has her stepping back against a wall.

"Hey, man," the security guy calls out.

"Is this how you play your game?" I ask, narrowing my eyes.

She tries to move, but I trap her with my arms on both sides of her body. Surprise whitens her face.

"Jackson," she starts, her voice a worried whisper, "back up."

"Is it, Liza?" I press, bringing my face closer to hers.

Sweat forms on my upper lip, a combination of heavy breathing and sobering.

"What game?" Her eyes boldly meet mine.

I snort.

"Don't play stupid." Taking my left hand from the wall, I trace her cheek with my finger.

"I'm not. There's no game, Jackson." Defiance tightens her jaw.

"Who told you about me, Red or that bitch he's fucking?"

"You're high, aren't you?" she scoffs, shoving my hand away from her.

I immediately miss touching her. This just pisses me off more.

"Quit fucking evading the question," I sneer.

"No one *told* me about *you*!" she snaps. "I wish someone had." Her voice drops to a whisper and she closes her eyes, pain creasing her face.

"So, you thought you'd fuck your way to the finals or winner's circle?" The poisonous question leaves my lips.

Her eyes snap open. Pain, hurt—*fuck, again with the hurt*—and then fire.

"Move," she commands.

"Your game is good." Grabbing her thigh, I squeeze to emphasize "good". "Maybe if you fuck all the judges they'll be just

181

as infatuated with you."

My head snaps left from the force of her hand.

"You're a bastard," she says, the contemptuous words filled with pure venom.

Keeping my eyes on the wall to the left, I seethe.

"You want to know who told me about you, Jackson?"

I clench my jaw. *I fucking knew it.*

"*You* did!" Her temper flares.

I snap my head back, meeting her angry eyes.

"When you mentioned it on the phone last night." She shakes her head. "That's when I found out and I didn't think it was a great time to mention it."

My anger lowers to a nervous simmer.

"I guess I was wrong. I should've told you then. I mean...fuck it, I should just add it to the other shit you have going on." Her voice is hard, cold.

I hate it.

Guilt rises like a flurry of hornets in my stomach. I raise my hand to cup her face.

This time, the rejection is hers to deliver. She slaps my arm down.

"Don't. Fucking. Touch. Me," she seethes, accentuating every word. Every one of them like a knife stabbing my soul.

What have I done?

"Liza—"

"Don't." She shoves my chest, causing me to stumble back. "I don't want this."

Breathing becomes painful, restricted.

"Keep your drama and your baggage." She waves a hand in the air, motioning over me. "You need to deal with your shit." Closing her eyes, she shakes her head. "I can't do this back and forth with you."

I step forward and her eyes snap open. She puts a hand up, stopping me.

"You're like a razorblade, Jackson. And I'm not thick-skinned enough to survive you." Tears rest at the corners of her eyes.

Fuck!

"I'm sorry," I blurt. The words are simple, but I've never meant anything more in my entire fucking life.

"Sorry is just a word." She shrugs and the movement jars one tear loose. "It's like a band-aid with you."

My eyes track the tear trailing over her smooth, porcelain cheek, until it drips from her jaw. My vision blurs.

"Take care of yourself."

I blink, clearing the blur when tears escape.

Two steps forward is as far as I get before she stops me with a look and turns, pushing by onlookers.

Of its own accord, my body propels forward, needing to go after her.

Four hands press against my chest. I refocus on my surroundings, finding Gemma and Julia pushing against me.

"Let her go," Gemma says softly.

"I don't think I can." A humorless laugh escapes me.

"She needs space, Jack." Gemma wraps an arm around mine, leading me back to the sound studio.

I take a deep breath and pull my arm from hers.

"Where are you going?" Julia asks, her question riddled with panic.

"Restroom," I answer without looking back.

Locking the multi-stall room, my shaky hands retrieve the last of my coke from my back pocket. I line it up on the counter, catching a glimpse of myself before leaning over and snorting the rails. Straightening, I keep my eyes closed, not wanting to risk seeing the truth of what I've become.

I pull out my cell phone and scroll until I find his name.

"Yeah," his familiar voice answers.

"Randall, it's Jack. I need a package." I turn, leaning back against the sink. The drugs are taking longer to feel the effect.

"Christ, already?" He laughs. "You're a machine, but don't worry, I got some killer shit in yesterday. I'll personally deliver and we can party at your place."

"Sounds like a plan." Closing my eyes, I savor the numbness

of my mouth.

Liza

"Sid, call me back. Please," I beg, leaving my third voicemail.

"Still no luck?" Bethany slouches in her dressing table chair.

I shake my head.

"I'm not Sid, but if you need to talk, Liza," her body turns toward me, "I'm here."

Looking up from my phone, I force a smile.

"Thanks. I appreciate that," I say, and I mean it, but I haven't been able to get past my confrontation with Jackson.

Damn him for being an asshole. And damn me for allowing myself to care enough to be this hurt.

I swallow down the lump of tears in my throat. A knock on the door pulls our attention.

"Come in," Bethany calls.

Red's wide body slips inside the room.

"Can I talk to Liza for a minute?" Red asks, his question directed at Bethany.

Her eyes come to me, waiting for my okay. I nod and she turns back to Red.

"Sure." Standing, she shrugs and walks to the door.

Before she can exit, he wraps an arm around her waist. Pulling her to him, he kisses her quick and hard. When he releases her, she tries to look annoyed, but even I can see her fighting a smile.

The minute the door closes behind her, Red steps further into the room, taking a seat on a small, worn loveseat. He bounces and presses his hand to the cushion.

"This thing is shit." He bounces once more. "I need to replace this."

His eyes come to mine. I give my second forced smile since I left stage rehearsal.

"That's not what I want to talk to you about." He clears his throat. "You aren't yourself tonight, Liza. Everything okay?"

Red's never given off the vibe of a jerk, but the tenderness in his question surprises me. He's usually loud, boisterous, and funny. In this moment, I see why Bethany likes him so much.

"Just a rough day." I shrug and sigh.

"I'm not one of the girls," he motions around the dressing room, "but you can come to me with shit."

The total guy attempt to be there makes me giggle.

"I'm serious." His brow wrinkles.

"I'm sorry." My giggle grows. "I don't mean to laugh."

I take a deep breath, getting myself under control.

"I really appreciate you checking on me. And I really appreciate you making me smile for real tonight, even if it was unintentional."

He grins, satisfied with himself.

"I need to talk to you about something else." His face grows more serious.

Worry assaults me for no real good reason.

"Don't look so panicked." He puts his hands up. "I think this is a good thing. I want to make you a featured performer."

I raise one brow, confused.

"I'm not sure I understand," I say, voicing said confusion.

"Liza, you're an amazing performer. Not just because of your voice," he rushes to clarify. "When you step onto the stage, you become another person. You know how to play off the crowd. Fuck, you make them play off you."

The compliments feel a bit uncomfortable, but a pleasant warmness fills my belly.

"Instead of you becoming what they want, you make them want what you give them. That's fucking talent." He rubs the back of his neck. "I want to do a photo shoot, and the leads—like Bethany and you—will have solo shots, but..." he pauses, getting serious, "basically, you are getting top billing. You're going to be the *feature* everyone comes to see."

I open my mouth to protest.

"I know who my best players are, Liza." Red stops me before I can get a word out. "Bethany and Jennifer will still do their solos and we may even bring in some new singers. But I've thought long and hard about this, I've watched the crowd and all of you. You're going to be the spotlight."

This time, I don't know what to say at all.

"Which means your photoshoot is going to be a bit more intense. Once I find the right photographer—"

"My cousin," I blurt.

"What?" It's Red's turn to be confused.

"My cousin, Sid, is a great photographer. I can get her portfolio or the online site she keeps."

"Her?"

"Yeah, it's short for Sidra. She hates it and goes by Sid," I explain. "She went to college for graphic design and online marketing, but she's studied photography since she was in high school."

Opening the browser app on my phone, I scroll through my favorites, knowing I have her Deviant Art account favorited. I adore the photos she posts there.

"Well, yeah, I mean, I really want to take these pictures to an edgy, sexy place. I was thinking of contacting some of the photographers I've worked with for Corrosive Velocity, but if you have her send some pictures, I guess I can take a look at—"

Shoving my phone in his face silences him.

Red's eyes widen and his chin drops a bit. He takes my phone.

"Just swipe left to see more." I sit back in my chair.

His finger moves across my screen a few times before he looks up from the series of pictures titled *TitsAnAss Collection*.

The photos range from woman wearing latex, pushing the material to its limits, to some shots of us from the club. You wouldn't know it's us since Sid focuses on the curve of a lace covered hip or the bone lining of the corset. Her photos are what I like to call sneaky sexy.

"Do you think she'd be willing to do this?" His eyes drop back to the phone, scrolling.

"I can ask," I answer, and shrug. "But I'm pretty sure she'd love to do it."

Red continues swiping the screen. Since he's taken the time to tell me his plans for me in the club, I feel the need to tell him about my involvement with Hidden Talent.

"There's something I need to tell you, too."

Red's eyes lift from the phone.

"Yeah?" he says, his business-like tone in place.

"I'm currently participating in Hidden Talent." Nervousness swirls in my stomach.

His eyes widen. "Does Jackson know?"

I blink, not expecting that to be the first question. I clear my throat.

"He does...now."

He nods.

"That what tonight's about?" Both brows lift over his brown eyes.

I give a noncommittal nod. "And some other things."

"I'm not thrilled at the idea of you winning that shit and leaving this place." He inhales deep, holds it for a moment, and then exhales. "But it could be decent publicity for the club."

"So, you're okay with it?"

Red stands, handing my phone back to me.

"Like I said, I don't want to lose you to some reality show shit, but it's cool. I'm surprised you signed up for it, though."

"I didn't. My son and brother did."

"Ahh..." He nods his head. "Well, just try not to win." He grins largely. "I've got plans for you in this place."

The statement warms me, while also making me wish I'd never agreed to Hidden Talent. Where I belong has never been clearer.

"I'll do my best to suck." I smile.

"No, don't suck. I want people to like you enough to follow you here." He smirks before going to the door.

"I don't know how the hell I'm supposed to be good while trying not to win."

"You better figure it out," he responds, pulling open the door.

Bethany stands right on the other side.

"Really?" he deadpans.

Bethany faux-pouts. "I wanted to make sure she wasn't upset about being the feature."

I blink in surprise, not expecting her to already know.

"She's okay." He pats Bethany on the head before turning back to me. "Get me your cousin's information. I want to talk to her."

I nod my silent okay while focusing on Bethany giving me two thumbs up behind his back. He turns, catching her. Shaking his head, he walks by her.

"What am I going to do with you?" he asks, not expecting a response.

Bethany steps into the dressing room, closing the door behind her.

"He loves me." She smirks, wiggling her brows.

Still no answer or response from Sid, I have too much time to replay every Jackson moment in my life during the bus ride home. Each moment is painfully beautiful, agonizingly raw, or both. My head knows I've done the right thing by walking away. He has too much going on and I refuse to be his whipping boy, but deep down, I feel the ache of separation. Somehow, my heart got caught up in this mess.

I catch the inside of my bottom lip between my teeth, fighting the wobble of my chin. I close my eyes against the pressure of unshed tears, only opening them when the bus comes to a stop. On autopilot, I step down from the bus and walk the small distance to my apartment. Every nerve ending feels raw, exposed.

The soft glow of light from under my apartment door becomes the distraction I need.

They should be in bed.

I allow the annoyance of the boys being up so late to swallow the emotions I don't want to admit I feel.

Opening the door, I search for Kel, Lucas, or Sean, ready to lecture them. Instead, a wave of relief washes over me.

"I'm sorry," Sid blurts. "I meant to surprise you, but my flight had an unexpected layover because of engine problems. My phone was off for a while because of the flights and then I had to rearrange my second flight to get here."

In hurried movements and explanation, she slips off a barstool and walks toward me.

"I saw your calls but didn't want to ruin my surprise. I should've fucking answered."

Her arms wrap around my shoulders and the embrace is my undoing. My bottled up emotions pour from my eyes in salty, wet trails over my face. They erupt from my throat in a combination of sobs and hiccups.

"It's okay. Shh..." Sid holds me tighter.

"He told me to fuck all the judges," I sob out before covering my mouth to quiet the ridiculous reaction.

Sid releases me and steps back.

"You go change. I'll pour the wine. Then we'll eat crappy food, drink cheap wine, and plot our revenge against the oversized, walking-coloring-book asshole."

With the mischievous gleam in her eye, I know she's already done the plotting. And her insult makes me laugh.

"I love you." It's my turn to hug her.

"Of course you do," she responds. "What isn't to love?"

"Now, go change." She steps away, swatting my ass.

"Ow!" I rub the stinging cheek.

"You liked it," she says without looking back.

Almost two bottles of wine, a can of spray cheese, and a box of crackers later, Sid is laying next to me on the pullout bed.

"What if—"

"Sid," I laugh her name, "I don't think I can take any more of your plotting."

I shove a cracker in my mouth.

"No, wait," she slurs, "this is the best. Just—" she hiccups, "just listen."

I nod, drinking the last drop of wine from my glass.

"Okay...what if I hack his twitter feed? You know I can do it." Sid licks her lips, always excited about hacking something.

"You already plotted that about twenty ideas ago," I remind her. "Right after your plan for me to revenge fuck his brother. Like that would even be possible."

The warm tingly sensation from the wine makes snuggling into the pullout bed actually feel good.

"Yes," she shouts, "but this time, we are going to change all his profile pictures to penises and kittens."

I bury my face in a pillow, smothering the laughter bubbling out of me. With a deep breath, I look up from the pillow.

"Penises and kittens?"

She nods, excitement in her eyes.

"Why kittens?"

Sid's face twists into an are-you-really-asking-me-that look.

"Um, wouldn't you question a dude posting penises and fluffy kittens?"

I open my mouth, but close it. She has a point.

"I'll get my laptop."

She starts to crawl over me.

"No."

I grab her leg, keeping her in the bed.

"Sid, stop. You aren't really doing it." I try to sound serious, but can't help laughing.

"Oh, yes I am."

She gets free, slipping from the bed onto the floor.

"And just for the fucking hell of it, I'm going to post gay porn all through his feed. You know I have a membership to plenty of porn."

I cover my mouth to hold in the burst of laughter threatening to wake up the boys.

Rolling to my side, I look down at a half-passed-out Sid.

"Sid?"

I reach down and push on her shoulder. No response.

"Sid?" I try again.

"Yeah," she quietly slurs.

"Get back in bed." My words are followed by a yawn.

"Okay," she sighs.

Rolling to face the bed, she raises an arm and grabs the mattress with her hand, but that's as far as she gets. Her arm falls to the floor.

"It's too far away," she mumbles.

I reach behind me, grab her blanket, and throw it down to her.

"Thanks." She snuggles into the blanket.

My lids grow heavy and my body goes lax.

Every muscle tenses and my eyes pop open at the loud pounding on my door.

"What the hell?" Sid growls, flipping onto her back.

"Liza!" More pounding follows his call.

"Is that—?" She props up onto her elbows.

"LIZA, please!"

With his volume increasing, I jump out of bed and trip over Sid.

"Ow, fuck," she curses, my foot hitting her side.

"Sorry." I look down to make sure she's okay. "You alright?"

"Yeah," she responds in a breath. "Hurry and shut loud mouth up before he wakes the building."

As if on cue, he shouts louder and bangs harder.

Going as fast as my tipsy body will allow, I reach the door, unlock it, and pull it open.

"Liza," he coos my name, his trademark half-grin in place.

He steps into my apartment and I take a step back.

"What are you doing here?" I ask, my voice quiet, yet harsh.

His arms stretch toward me and catch me around my back, pulling me to him.

"I'm so sorry," he says, his words slurred.

"You need to leave." My words are stronger than I feel inside.

My body wants to melt into him; the effort of staying statue-like is exhausting.

"I need you to forgive me, Liza." He releases his hold on me, his large hands palming each side of my face. "I need you."

"Yeah, to forgive you."

I wrap my hands around his wrists, trying to pull out of his hands, but he won't allow it. Dropping my arms, I give up on a sigh.

"Okay, fine, I forgive you," I say, but the words are insincere and he can tell.

"No, you don't." His body sways and I reach out to help steady him.

A small smile forms on his face. "I want you, Liza."

His thumb rubs awkwardly against my cheek. In slow motion, his lips come closer. Letting go of his sides, I cover his mouth with my hands. The heat of his skin is concerning. He's burning up.

"Jackson, what did you take tonight?"

With my hands still over his mouth, I feel his lips move, but can't understand what he's saying. I pull them away.

"What?"

"I need you. I want you. Forgive me."

His forehead rests against mine, the heat and slickness of his skin uncomfortable.

"Well, he's super high, isn't he?"

Sid's question distracts Jackson enough for me to get free of him. As soon as I have space between us, he turns his attention back to me. A frown mars his face.

"How much did you do tonight?" I cross my arms over my chest.

"Liza, fuck, can't you just—"

"How much, Jackson?"

"Randall brought me something new. It's the best I've felt all day." The sloppy grin on his face makes my stomach turn.

"Great."

"I feel incredible," he slurs.

Inhaling deep, I step forward and take his cell phone from his pocket.

His eyes snap open and land on me. The unfocused look saddens me.

Scrolling through his phone, I find Sam.

"What are you doing?" He grins.

"Calling your ride," I inform, waiting, hoping Sam answers.

"You know, I'm going to post penises, kittens, and gay porn all over your twitter feed."

My eyes snap to Sid. Standing only a few feet from Jackson, she has his full attention.

"What?" His face wrinkles in confusion.

"You heard me ash-hole," she taunts, her words slurred, but not nearly as bad as Jackson.

"Who the fuck are you?" he growls, narrowing his eyes on her.

"Your worst nightmare, Jolly-Cokehead-Giant." She crosses her arms over her chest, not backing down when he glares.

"Yes, sir?" Sam's deep voice finally breaks the ringing.

"Um, Sam, this is Liza. I'm not sure if you remember—"

"Yes, miss, I remember you. Did he pass out in your apartment?"

"You brought him here?" I ask, hopeful.

"Yes, miss. He was adamant and I'd rather not risk another taxi ride incident."

"He's not passed out, but he needs to go."

"And he's not willing?" Sam sighs.

"I'll get him downstairs, but be ready."

"Of course."

"Oh, and, Sam?"

"Yes?"

"I'm not sure what he used tonight, but he's on fire.

Someone needs to keep an eye on him."

"I'll call Julia. She's his personal assistant and should be able to make arrangements."

"Okay. We'll be down in a couple minutes."

"I'll be here."

Ending the call, I look up to see Jackson and Sid staring each other down.

"As a matter of fact, I'll also hack all your personal accounts, shut down all your credit cards, and post your cell number to the masses," Sid adds to the end of their heated discussion.

"Jackson?"

His head slowly turns toward me, causing his body to waver.

"Come on." I put my hand out and he studies it for a moment.

"Come on. I'll walk you down to your car."

When Jackson doesn't move, I start to drop my hand with a sigh. He quickly reaches out for it, but misses my hand and stumbles into me.

"I don't want to leave you."

He lays his cheek on the top of my head, embracing me.

Slipping one arm around his waist, I start guiding him to the door.

"Don't make me go."

"Sam's waiting," is my response.

"I don't want Sam." His hands slide down my sides, stalling our progress to the door.

As if he hadn't shredded me like tissue paper earlier today, my body reacts. Fighting the lust, I push forward, unsure whether it's his touch or fever causing the heat between us.

Finally, he starts moving toward the door.

Sam tries to take Jackson's weight off me, but he won't let go.

"I have to go back inside."

I place my hands against his stomach, trying to push him away.

"You...don't...come...mine." He grows more incoherent.

"He's getting worse." Fear grips my chest, restricting my breaths.

"Julia is making some calls," Sam informs.

I feel a tremor run through Jackson's body and my fear turns to panic.

"Something's wrong." I shake my head.

"He's just high," Sam says, disgust dripping in his tone. "From what Julia says, he's been partying hard all evening with his dealer and what she assumes are hookers."

Nausea cramps my stomach, but Jackson's the one who throws up between Sam and me.

"Fuck," Sam growls, yanking harder on Jackson and pulling him toward the waiting car. Jackson's head lolls to the left.

Something's wrong. I can feel it, see it.

"Wait!" I catch up, taking part of the weight.

"Miss, I can get him back to the hotel," Sam states, shoving Jackson roughly into the back of the car.

I look back at my building, glancing up to my apartment window. Then I turn to Jackson, sprawled in the backseat.

What the fuck am I doing?

I climb into the car, closing the door behind me.

Taking Jackson's phone once again, I send Sid a text, letting her know what I'm doing. I'm too much of a coward to call. The car pulls away from the curb and Jackson's body starts to slip from the seat.

Resituating our positions, I slip under his head, placing it on my lap.

Putting my elbow against the door, I rest my head in my hand.

"Snake charmer." I ignore the murmur, but movement draws my attention.

Jackson pulls himself up, digging in his jacket. He takes out a small, clear vial, trying to twist the little cap off.

Anger rolls from the pit of my stomach to my throat.

"Are you fucking kidding me?" I yell, snatching the vial away from him.

"Come on, I'll share." He grins. "Have you ever fucked when high? It's amazing."

He leans, pressing his body against me.

"Yeah, I'm sure with all the shit in your system you could perform real well." I don't hide my sarcasm or anger.

Pressing the window button, I roll it down and toss the vial out.

"What the fuck?" he snarls, reaching for the window. "That's all I have on me."

He turns hard eyes on me.

"But you have more at the hotel?" I ask, meeting his glare with one of my own.

"I don't want to fight with you." His eyes soften. "I'm sorry."

His eyes roll into his head, causing panic to well inside my chest. He goes limp, landing in my lap. The shaking of his body is not a good sign. I wrap my arms around him and yell, "Sam!"

The divider window comes down.

"He's shaking." Looking up from Jackson's body, I meet Sam's eyes in the rearview mirror. "We need to take him to the hospital."

With a nod, he puts his phone to his ear.

Turning my attention back to Jackson, I make sure he stays breathing. I don't hear much of what Sam is saying on the phone, so when we pull into the garage of the hotel, I'm pissed.

"I said he needs the hospital."

Sam ignores me, climbing out of the car. The back door jerks open and Sam reaches in for Jackson. Pulling him out of the car, he throws Jackson's body over his shoulder.

"Why didn't you take him to the hospital?" I follow Sam inside the hotel and onto the staff elevator.

"If he goes to the hospital, it will be public news and gossip. Julia has a doctor on the way."

"News and gossip?" I scoff. "That's better than dead or in a coma!"

The elevator reaches Jackson's floor and Sam exits without

another word.

"I can't believe you would risk his life because of the press." My disgust is obvious in my declaration.

"You don't know how this business works." A small girl with dark hair stands next to the hotel room.

Sam enters, carrying Jackson.

"I know how life and death work. An overdose isn't something to fuck around with," I growl, narrowing my eyes on her.

"You're no longer needed." She gives a nod and follows Sam.

Before the door closes, I shove my arm against it and enter behind her.

Her eyes widen, watching as I step past her and into the bedroom.

"Take him to the bathtub," I instruct just as Sam is about to put Jackson on the bed.

He looks to Julia for confirmation.

"Don't look at her," I snap. "I told you to put him in the bathtub."

"The doctor is on his way—"

"And when he gets here, you can show him in." I narrow my eyes, daring her to challenge me again.

"The bathtub, Sam!"

Closing my eyes, I inhale deep, trying to remember what Bethany did with a girl who OD'd back stage once.

With Jackson in the bathtub, I move Sam out of my way and start removing his shoes and clothes.

"If you aren't going to help, you can get out."

I groan from the exertion it takes to get Jackson's jeans off his legs. Heat radiates from his skin. In all my years of Lucas' colds, flus, and teething, I've never felt a fever this hot.

Finally, Sam leans down and helps me. With all of his clothes off, I grab a towel, throw it over his waist, turn the water to cold, and start the shower.

Jackson jerks, bringing his arms over his chest, but he doesn't wake up.

"Do we know what he took? Was it just coke? Did he

swallow any pills?" I look at Sam while I climb into the tub behind Jackson.

"I'm not sure." He starts looking around the bathroom before exiting to conduct a search.

"Come on, Jackson. Wake up," I urge.

Slipping behind his body, I prop him up into spray. The water is freezing, but his body is on fire.

"What can I do?" Julia's voice surprises me.

"Put the stopper in the tub and get some ice. His temperature needs to come down and we can't give him anything."

She nods, stepping forward to flip the metal piece before exiting quickly.

Cold water slowly creeps up the sides of our bodies. Unable to take the temperature any longer, I slip out and lay him back against the porcelain.

"I've got the ice." Julia returns with two buckets of ice and we dump them into the tub.

Jackson begins to shake, but I can still feel the heat radiating off him. Grabbing a washcloth, I dip it into the water and place it on his forehead.

"We aren't sure of everything he took, but definitely coke, alcohol, and a lot of it." Sam's voice carries from the bedroom.

An average sized man in jeans and a long sleeve t-shirt enters the bathroom. His eyes settle on Jackson, Julia, and me.

"Let me see what we're dealing with." He pushes between Julia and me.

His hands work over Jackson's body: pulse points, forehead, pulling his eyes open. The doctor reaches back, pulls a red canvas bag to his side, and grabs a syringe. He turns Jackson's arm and presses on his skin a few times before jabbing the needle into his vein. It fills with blood and he takes the needle from his arm.

Setting it to the side, he digs through his bag again, and pulls out another syringe and a small bottle. He repeats the same actions as before, but this time, plunges a clear fluid into Jackson's veins.

"Who put him in the ice bath?" he asks, keeping his eyes on

Jackson.

The doctor places a thermometer in Jackson's ear.

"She did," Sam says, quick to call me out.

"Good job." The doctor looks at the temperature reading and shakes his head. "His temperature was at dangerous levels. It's still not good."

"Will he be alright?" Julia asks.

"I think so, but I can't be sure what damage he's caused himself." The doctor stands, facing us. "We can get him out of the bath now. I gave him something to assist with the fever."

Sam and I go to work, getting Jackson out of the bath and into the hotel bed. The doctor stands, speaking with Julia.

"I should have the test results back in a couple hours, but he needs more medical attention. I placed a call to the hospital and they are sending a nurse with an IV. Chances are he's extremely dehydrated. The fluids will help, but he needs to come to the hospital for full testing."

Julia nods, tears filling her eyes.

"Liza?" Jackson calls for me through chattering lips.

I step to his side and brush the hair from his face. "Yeah?"

"I'm s...s...s...sorry," he chatters.

"I know." Leaning down, I kiss his forehead.

"You can expect paranoia, depression, and guilt when he wakes," the doctor says, his eyes on me. "When the fluids start, he's going to start showing withdrawal symptoms as well. Depending on the regularity of his using, the symptoms can be minimal or severe enough to need medical assistance."

I nod.

"He's lucky we aren't dealing with cardiac arrest tonight," he adds before leaving the room.

I sit down on the bed next to Jackson and bury my face in my hands.

"I called his family," Julia whispers.

Without looking, I nod.

"They should arrive in a few hours," she continues.

The silence becomes long and tense.

"I'm sorry for not listening to you earlier and for being a bitch." The bed shifts when she sits next to me, placing a large, white robe around my shoulders.

"It's okay." Exhaustion starts to take over.

"No, I was mad at him for the way he acted tonight," she hiccups. "I could've caused him..." she trails off, soft whimpers escaping her.

I can't tell her she's wrong. Things could've been worse, but it's obvious she never meant for him to get hurt.

"It's okay now. I'll get a taxi and get out of the way."

Julia puts a hand on my leg before I can stand.

"You're exhausted. Get out of the damp clothes and get some sleep. I'll let you know when they arrive and make sure a car is ready." She pats my leg twice before standing and leaving the room.

I stand from the bed, slip out of my clothes, lay them over a chair to dry, and secure the large robe around me. Back in bed, I stare down on him. Tears fill my eyes, leaking over my cheeks.

"Why do you do this to yourself?" My question is a quiet sob, a plea to understand.

I stare at Jackson's sleeping form until my lids are too heavy to keep open.

Chapter Thirteen
Liza

"Where is he?" A woman's voice stirs me from sleep.

I try to stretch, but my body is held down by Jackson. At some point, he rolled over, pinning me underneath his body.

"I don't care if he's still sleeping." The woman's voice is followed by the door bursting open.

Peeking over Jackson's arm, my eyes take in a lovely caramel-haired woman with a classic Hollywood glamor about her. Behind her stands an older, extremely attractive, gentleman, and two recognizable faces: the lead singers of The Forgotten and Hushed Mentality.

"Well, isn't this like fucking twisted déjà vu?"

"Chris," Mia Ryder hisses.

"What?" His face screws up in confused annoyance. "It is." He waves toward Jackson and me. "Like the time Nic found us in bed together on the bus."

Embarrassment creeps in a heated flush over my skin. I shove Jackson, rolling him off me, and stand from the bed.

"Give me a moment, please," the woman says, her eyes on me.

"But—" Mia grabs Christopher and drags him out before he can finish.

"I'll be just outside the door if you need me." The handsome gentleman kisses her cheek and exits the room, closing the door behind him.

"I'll get out of your way," I blurt, feeling nervous.

"Julia told me what you did for him." She approaches, leaving only a foot of space between us. "I want to thank you for taking care of my son."

"Of course." Stepping to the side, I move out of her way.

Her soft hand comes to my face, cupping my cheek.

"Thank you so much," she says, tears forming in her eyes.

Being a mother to a son, I can empathize with her. My eyes grow watery.

"You're welcome." I choke on the words.

"It's Liza, correct?" Her warm eyes study me.

I nod and she drops her hand from my face.

"Liza, this person..." She glances to Jackson's prone form, "this isn't Jackson."

Looking back into my eyes, I see determination.

"But I hope he's still in there."

Before I can stop myself, I blurt, "He is."

I watch as relief softens the deep lines of sorrow on her face.

"Good." Her shoulders relax and she stands straighter.

"I'll just get out of your way," I mumble, moving to collect my clothes from the chair so I can dress in the bathroom.

"You don't have to rush off because of me."

I don't look back or think before I respond.

"I have to get home to my son."

Before she has time to react to my admission, I close myself in the hotel bathroom.

Slipping into my clothes, I realize I came here wearing pajamas. Thankfully, I chose to wear cotton shorts and a t-shirt. However, I hadn't worn a bra and my shirt is white. In the morning light, it would be very noticeable.

I look around the bathroom and see Jackson's discarded clothes on the floor. Grabbing his long-sleeved dark tee, I pull it over my head. The shirt is too big, so I roll the sleeves and tie the hem in a knot.

I pull open the bathroom door, trying to stay as quiet as possible. Five sets of eyes turn toward me. Gwen, the older gentleman, which I assume is her husband, Nicholas, Christopher, Mia, and the doctor stare silently. Nervousness prickles across my skin.

"I'll show myself out." My nerves are evident in the pitch of my voice.

"Like I said, Liza, you don't have to go." I glance at Gwen when she speaks. "But I understand why you need to go." Her warm smile makes me instantly like her.

How Jackson could do this to his mother is beyond me. If only my mom had been like her. Mentally shaking my head, I quickly return the smile and exit the bedroom.

My hope to sneak out without any further notice is squashed when nine more sets of eyes turn to me.

"What the hell are you doing here?" Her voice is familiar and my hair stands on end.

"Kristy, I suggest you shut the fuck up." This voice is unfamiliar, but her trademark blonde and black hair gives her away. Kat Conway, lead guitarist for Hushed Mentality.

Kristy ignores Kat and stands from a chair, the same chair Jackson shoved out of the way so he could—

"I asked you a question." Kristy is barely a foot away from me.

"Obviously, she was here for Jackson." This voice is also unfamiliar, but it belongs to Laney Trimball, Jackson's ex, and bassist for Hush.

"No one asked you, slut." Kristy tosses over her shoulder.

Laney jumps up and moves to attack. The thick arm of Elliott Brockman stops her, pulling her down on his lap.

"Calm down, Fast Lane. She's just pissed because Jackson has apparently moved on..." his eyes roam over my body, "to curvier and better things." He grins for a moment before shouting in pain. "Christ, baby, that hurt." He rubs where his wife, Serena, just pinched him.

"Can you stop flirting for, oh, I don't know, at least five minutes?" Serena glares.

"I'm just honest," he pouts.

"Keep your honesty to a minimum," she scolds.

"Are you jealous?" He smirks.

She narrows her eyes at him.

"Baby, you've got nothing to be jealous about. You know you're the only girl for me." He smiles wide.

"Oh, I'm so lucky," she feigns excitement.

"I know, right!" He sits back on the couch, putting his hands behind his head. "I'm a fucking catch."

Serena's face twists and she grabs her swollen stomach.

"What's wrong?" Elliott pushes Laney from his lap, reaching for Serena.

"Nothing." She sits back, stretching her body out. "He's got his feet in my ribs again."

Elliott winces, but stays on high alert.

"What can I get you?"

"A new husband." She grins.

"Not fucking funny, babe," he pouts again, and I have to fight not to laugh.

"This is all so pathetically cute, but I asked this whore a question." Kristy steps closer and I step back, wanting to keep space between us.

"Leave her alone." Laney gets involved once more. "Apparently, Jackson wanted her here, not you."

"Stay out of this, you cheating slut." Kristy spins, facing Laney. "If it weren't for you spreading your legs to whoever will climb between them, Jackson wouldn't be in this state, would he?" She crosses her arms over her chest.

"Did that Ethiopian white girl just say that shit in front of us?" Kat looks to Serena, who nods.

"Yeah, she did."

I glance over my shoulder, seeing this came from Mia.

"Bitch, are you crazy or just hungry? You know Laney's our sister, right?" Kat leans forward, hands on her knees.

"I don't give a shit about your—"

"Serena, hold my phone. I'm gonna kill this trick." Kat stands, only to be stopped by the final member of The Forgotten.

"Don't go to jail." Jimmy Thompson holds tightly to her forearm. "I don't have enough on me for bail."

"I suggest you leave." Mia's voice comes from right behind

me.

I tense, unsure whether she's talking to Kristy or me.

"I'm his girlfriend," Kristy counters.

"Ex-girlfriend," Laney corrects, causing Kristy's face to redden.

"We all saw your interview," Kat adds, satisfaction all over her face.

"Yes, bravo by the way." Mia accentuates her sarcasm with slow claps.

"You don't know anything," Kristy hisses. "She's damn proof of the way he's treated me." She points a long, manicured finger in my face. "He's a cheating bastard."

Lack of sleep, stress, and the current situation causes something inside me to snap. I slap her hand out of my face, causing her to gasp.

"Then why are you here?" I ask, my voice cold and lashing. I step forward and she retreats, stumbling on her heels.

"If he is so awful and things were so terrible, why are you even here?"

"I...I love him," she responds, too quickly.

I snort.

"You love yourself and the attention. He broke it off and you don't like losing a toy before you're ready to toss it aside."

Her mouth parts, but my head is swimming and exhaustion washes over me.

"I'm so over this." I put my hands up, palms out, turn from Kristy, and walk to the room door. Reaching for the handle, I look back and lock eyes with Mia. "Take care of him."

Then, I leave. Every step to the elevator feels like a knife in my heart.

I focus my thoughts on Lucas, Kel, and Sean. And then I figure out what the hell I'm going to tell Sid when I get home.

Jackson

"Liz-ah?" My throat is so dry, my voice cracks.

Swallowing burns. I grab my neck.

"She's gone."

My mother's voice pulls me completely out of sleep and into a sitting position.

"Careful." She puts out a hand. "You'll rip out the IV."

She sits in a chair next to the bed. Following her eyes, I see the tube attached to the back of my hand.

"What—"

"Happened?" My mother finishes my question.

I look back to her face.

"You almost killed yourself," she says, her face a mixture of sadness and angry.

"Mom, I didn't—"

"Yes, Jackson, you did." She stands from the chair, looking down at me. "What is this?" She waves her hands over me and across my destroyed hotel bedroom.

Shit. Randall and those fucking people he brought with him.

"Mom, listen, it's nothing, really." I scoot back, leaning against the headboard.

"Nothing?" she repeats, her voice almost shrieking. I flinch.

I haven't heard her this mad since the time I went to jail for a bar fight while on tour.

"Is that your goal, to be nothing?"

"What the fu...uh...heck are you talking about?"

"You almost ended up as nothing." She drops back into the chair, desperation on her face. "The doctors found cocaine, ecstasy, and traces of LSD in your system. And let's not forget the amount of alcohol in your blood."

I open my mouth, but she puts her hand up, stopping me.

"You had a fever of one-hundred and six, Jackson. And that

was after the doctor found you in an ice bath." Large tears trail over her cheeks. "If it weren't for Liza, you would've probably had a stroke or heart attack. You could be in a coma right now!" Her shriek makes me wince, but it's her tears that hurt most. "You could still have permanent damage to your heart or kidneys. Do you realize that? You still have to go get more tests to make sure you don't."

I bring my hand to my chest, trying to rub the ache away. Tears burn behind my eyes. *I've fucked up so much. The drugs, lies...Liza. Fuck, where is Liza?*

"You aren't my son."

I stiffen, a tear escaping the corner of my eye.

"You aren't my Jackson," she hiccups. "You're a rock star cliché and it's pathetic," she says, the last word spoken with pure disgust.

"Why, Jackson?" Her question is a plea to understand.

"Why did you hide your illness?" My voice is sharp in defense.

Her body tenses, just a bit, before a heavy sigh leaves her.

"I already explained this to you," she says, her voice quiet, tired.

"Because you're selfish." Even I hear the spoiled child in my tone.

"If that's how you see it, then fine, I'm selfish. I found out I have breast cancer. The doctors ran through the tests, treatments, possible outcomes, and all the variables surrounding *my life*."

"You're a part of my life, too." Tears well in my eyes, blurring my vision.

"I'm sorry it hurt you. That was never my intention." She takes a deep breath, capturing my hand with both of hers. "Jackson, my treatment and surgery will take so much from me. I know it's hard for you to understand, but, as a woman, to have my breasts taken because of this..." She sniffs, and I squeeze her hand. "No matter the choice I made, it is life altering, but the decision I've made now feels like a loss of my femininity, my identity."

She pauses once more, taking stuttering breaths.

"The mastectomy will remove a part of my body, but it's also a part that defines me as a woman. The chemo will ravage the inside of my body, including the parts that make me a woman. Obviously, I wasn't planning on more children and my body already started the process of taking away that possibility, but for it to be taken like this..." she hiccups. "This feels cruel and unfair. I needed to take my diagnosis on without sympathy and fear from others. I hope you can someday understand, but even if you don't, Jackson, I wouldn't change my actions if I could."

The silence isn't uncomfortable. In fact, my thoughts are anything but silent. My mom is going through something I couldn't possibly understand—not completely. I would never know what it's like to be a woman or to have pieces of that stripped away so severely.

"Why would you do this to yourself?" Mom breaks the silence and my thoughts.

"I..." I try to think of an answer. First, one that will satisfy her. Second, the truthful one. All I can come up with is: "It hurt too much. I needed to escape."

She sighs heavily.

"Relationships end. It's not a reason to do this." Her hand slips into mine and grips tight. "You're too smart for this."

Tears flow over both our cheeks.

"It got out of hand," I choke out.

"I know, baby."

She moves from the chair to the bed and embraces me like she did when I was young, her arms tightening around my shoulders.

"I've fucked up."

"Language," she scolds quietly.

"You sure as hell did," Christopher says, announcing his presence.

Mom releases me and sits back, staying next to me, her hand back in mine.

"Go ahead, Chris, get your *I told you so* out of the way." I drop my head back against the wall above the headboard. Closing my eyes, I take a deep breath and wait.

"Are you done with this shit?" His simple question brings my head up and our eyes meet.

He stands at the foot of the bed, arms over his chest, and a serious expression on his face.

"What shit?" I sneer.

My mother tenses, in part from our cursing and because she knows how we fight.

"Don't give me your fucking attitude. I'm not the asshole who almost killed himself because he needed to get high. I'm not the asshole who scared off the one woman who is probably truly it for him."

Clenching my jaw, I glare at him.

"You don't know a fucking thing about Liza and—"

"I know." He cuts me off with two words, retrieving my worn, folded up notebook from his back pocket. He throws it on the bed. "I fucking know, Jackson."

"Stop going through my shit," I sneer.

"Then start talking to me," Chris demands. "You haven't written like this since...Christ, Jackson, I've never seen you write like this." He points to the notebook.

"We don't talk," I scoff.

"That's bullshit and you know it!" He rounds the bed, standing on my right. "We don't chat over tea and fucking cookies, but our music is our conversation. You and me in the studio, that's our talking."

Dropping my head, I focus on the fibers in the blanket covering my lap.

He's right.

"You haven't really been in there with me for over a year. Even before you and Laney split."

I close my eyes and bite my tongue in an attempt to stop the sob wanting free.

"So, are you done with this shit?" The plea in his question surprises me.

Looking up, I see the watery glaze of his eyes.

"Yeah," I respond, feeling my mom squeeze my hand.

Christopher's shoulders relax.

"The drugs?" he pushes.

"Done," I whisper.

"You'll get help," my mother interjects, and I nod.

"We talk?" Chris continues.

"Yeah." My eyes meet his.

Chris gives a hard nod.

"Good." He inhales deep before releasing the large puff of breath. "Now, we've got to talk about Kristy."

My eyes narrow. "Is she here?"

"She was, but after the girls, and Liza," he gives a pointed look, "got ahold of her, she left making a lot of threats."

"I'll take care of Kristy." Una steps into the room. "She won't be posting or talking about Jackson anytime soon."

"Are you sure about that?" Chris turns the pointed look on her.

"Christopher, can I just tell you how much your confidence in me over the past couple years makes me feel warm and fuzzy?" Una tilts her head.

Mom muffles a quiet snort.

"It should," Chris states, turning back to me. "I'll be sitting in for you at Hidden Talent."

"What?" I furrow my brow.

"You are going straight into rehab. You will need at least a week to detox," Una informs me.

"I have things to take care of," I protest.

"You need to give her time." Laney's voice is the last thing I want to hear.

"Great, Laney, you really think you're the best person to come in here?" Chris snaps.

"Christopher," Mom warns.

She releases my hand, slips from the bed, and walks toward the door.

"I believe these two need to talk." Mom takes Chris' arm.

"No, we don't," I state, causing everyone to look at me.

"Jackson—"

I stop Laney before she can say anything else.

"There isn't anything left to say." I shrug.

"Come on." Mom pulls Chris out of the room and Una follows them, closing the door behind her.

Dropping my head back against the wall, I close my eyes and sigh.

"I'm so sorry," she says, her emotions already affecting her speech.

"Don't, Laney."

"I didn't know it would become this." A sob escapes her. "It's my fault and I'm so sorry."

Sorry is just a word. Liza's words come back to me. *Liza. She's the one I want here with me. I need to make her see how sorry I am, but 'sorry' is just a word.*

Epiphanies happen and this time, it feels like a slap to the forehead with a brick. I need to fix my shit and show her she means more than I ever planned.

Laney's sobbing pulls my attention back to her.

"Laney, stop crying."

She hiccups, wiping her face and watching me.

"This isn't your fault." I shake my head. "Yeah, you broke us, but you aren't responsible for breaking me."

Her eyes widen.

"I made my choices. Even before we split, I thought everything was perfect. Chris had a baby and got engaged. Elliott is fucking married, adopted Ryan, and has a baby on the way. Fuck, even Jimmy got married. I thought it was next for us, but I didn't take the time to think about what was *right* for us."

Laney sits in the chair my mom previously occupied.

"I never meant to hurt you," she whispers.

"I know." I nod. "But you did."

"I know," she mimics.

"And it's okay."

Our eyes meet. Hers are unsure and apprehensive.

"I never would've found Liza if you hadn't." I smile.

The worry lines melt from Laney's face.

"She's the one, huh?" Her question is a mix of happiness for me and sorrow for what we lost.

"Yeah, she is." I grin wide.

"Well, she has Kat's approval after the way she handled Kristy." Laney laughs, wiping tears from her face.

"I think I need to hear more about this." I reach a hand out to her.

She leans forward and takes it, careful not to touch the IV.

"Then, dude, sit back and let me tell you about the catfight you missed." Elliott pushes through the door, striding right to the bed and plopping on the end.

Slowly, Serena waddles in, with the rest of the group in tow. My chest warms, surrounded by my family. There's only one thing missing.

Liza.

Liza

Without Julia arranging my ride back to the apartment, I don't know how I would've managed. Having left my cell phone, bag, and shoes behind, I don't think any taxi driver would've let me in their car without verification of funds.

Taking a deep breath, I knock on my own apartment door. It flings open and Sid stands in her black, *I Make Boys Cry* t-shirt and cotton capris.

Our eyes meet and my chin wobbles.

"Come here," she orders without giving me time to move. She reaches out, pulling me into her arms. We stand, embracing, for a few very long moments. It feels nice, but not as great as it usually does.

"You okay?" she asks in a whisper.

I begin to nod, but realizing the lie, I shake my head and

bury my face in her shoulder.

One hand rubs my back while the other releases me to close the open door before guiding me to the fold-out bed. She sits us on the edge and I lay my head on hers.

"Is he okay?"

"I think so." My voice is low, matching hers.

"What do you need me to do?" she asks. I lift my head, looking at her in confusion.

"There isn't anything to be done." I shrug. "He's got some serious problems to handle." Sniffing, I rub my tingling nose.

"You're right. He does," she agrees, letting her arm fall away. "And you can't fix his problems either."

"I didn't say I could." Defensiveness sharpens my words.

"But you're thinking it." She raises her brows and continues before I can say anything else. "I know you. You're a fixer. You've been trying to fix my shit for years, but each person has things no one else can fix."

I straighten my spine, square my shoulders, and open my mouth, but close it, knowing she's right. I've spent years trying to make Sid realize she's better than she treats herself. She's better than her hump-him and dump-him one-nighters, a habit she's created to avoid being hurt again.

"No one could tell you what to do when you had your mind set to move out here with a toddler. You can't make him straighten his shit out. No matter how much you want him to."

I let my shoulders sag. I've gotten too attached.

"I know," I say weakly, my voice having lost its edge.

"He's lost, Liza."

My eyes meet Sid's once more.

"He's famous, known, and...Christ, the size of him alone makes him hard to miss, but..."

"But what?" My throat tightens and my eyes burn with unshed tears.

"He's lost himself in the sea of celebrities, drugs, alcohol, and fame. It's up to him to find himself and get his shit together." Reaching out, she takes my face between her hands. "You can't fix him."

I nod and she releases my face.

"Okay?"

With a deep breath, I nod in agreement.

"I'm gonna need to hear you say the words," Sid presses.

"Okay. I can't fix him." The verbal confirmation satisfies her, but a deep finalization and fear resonates within me. I honest to God understand there isn't anything I can do to fix Jackson, but what if I've just been a part of the high?

What else do you think you are? This isn't a damn movie. Time to let it go and walk away. He has family to help him.

"Everything okay?" Kel's voice surprises me.

"Yeah." I wipe my face.

"Is he alright?" Kel's question panics me.

He knows. What if Lucas saw what happened?

"Calm down," he soothes. "I woke up when you guys were trying to get him out the door. I checked on Lucas and Sean. They were out cold and don't know anything about it."

"Know about what?" Lucas yawns the question.

"That we are going out to breakfast!" Sid jumps up and flails her arms over her head. "So, go get your buddy up and let's hit IHOP. Aunt Sid's got a need to stuff her face with pancakes and pig."

Kel's face lights up and he rushes off to get dressed.

"Thank you." I stand and touch her shoulder.

"Don't thank me yet. You're paying." She grins. "And you better hope they have the never-ending pancake deal. Big girls like to eat."

I roll my eyes at her self-deprecation but finally smile. It's not a complete smile, though. The accepting of this loss is still too raw.

Chapter Fourteen
Liza

"So, what's the song plan for this week?" Sid asks, fiddling with the neon rainbow photography portfolio on her lap. Before I can answer, she complains, "I hate carrying this thing. Tell me again why I couldn't just bring my Surface to go through the pictures?"

"The song is chosen and I'm all ready to record it tomorrow. As for the portfolio," I adjust a corner from poking my leg, "he wasn't specific on what he wanted to see, so it's best to have them both. He may prefer physical photographs to digital." I shrug.

With a heavy sigh, she sits back in the uncomfortable bus seat.

"What song did you choose?" she asks, brushing lint away from a black tee with *Got Milk?* in bold, white lettering across her double Ds.

"*Shape of My Heart*," I respond.

"By Sting?" She studies my face.

I nod.

"I hate how sad you are." Her lips purse and brow furrows.

"I'm fine." I give a small but sincere smile.

"Mmhmm." Keeping the pursed lips, she cocks one brow, disbelievingly.

"Look, it's our stop," I announce, changing the subject.

Her attention turns once more to the portfolio she put together on my apartment floor after a trip to Kinkos and a supply store. Taking a deep breath, I do my best not to wonder how he is.

Inside the club, the space is well lit in typical rehearsal day fashion.

I look around for Red, since his usual front row table is

unoccupied, and find him standing at the bar with a vaguely familiar man. Two young, middle-school-aged girls sit near them at a booth.

"Do they both have the new iPhone and the iPad Air?" Sid asks enviously.

Red looks up from his guest and does a double-take, realizing we're standing a few feet away. He says something to the man before walking toward us, causing the visitor to look in our direction.

"Good afternoon, ladies," Red greets.

"Ladies?" Sid looks behind her and then back to him. "Well, hell, I haven't been called that in like...ever."

Red laughs, loudly.

"Liza said you were funny." He nods. "So," his face turns all business-like, "are those for me?" He motions to the portfolio and tablet in her hands.

Sid goes to respond but stops, standing with her mouth parted.

"Sid?" I ask, following her line of sight.

The semi-familiar visitor walks to Red's side. Christ, he doesn't really walk—he prowls, and it makes me think of the way Jackson moves.

The man is shorter than Jackson...though, most people are. The visitor looks a bit over six feet tall with a wide muscular build bulging beneath the thin, white t-shirt stating *Without Ballet, Life Would be Pointless* across his chest. His head is shaved except for the thick, golden blond strands at the top of his head, which reach his shoulders. Tattoos swirl the shaved area, but his loose hair makes it difficult to see the images. He looks about the same age as Red—late thirties to early forties—but the beard could be adding a couple years.

Giving her some elbow encouragement, it's enough to shake her from mute ogling.

"Uh, yeah, here." Blinking rapidly, she holds out the neon rainbow portfolio.

"Didn't they have anything more obnoxious to choose?" the visitor asks as Red takes it from her, his golden brown eyes boring into her.

Knowing Sid, I try to stop whatever unfiltered madness will spew from her lips.

"Do you have a problem with rainbows?" Her arms come over her chest.

Damn it. Not quick enough.

His eyes narrow in curiosity.

"I'm sure he doesn't—" I attempt.

"Nah," he crosses his arms, mimicking her stance, "my girls love rainbows." With a twitch of his head, he nods toward the young girls.

Sid leans sideways, looking around Tall, Tatted, and Beard, before looking back to him.

"They're a little young to be working here, don't you think? Or are you just starting them early in their career?" She tilts her head, a picture of fake innocence on her face.

The smile he wears slips from his face. Hard lines emboss the sides of his eyes.

"Those are my daughters," he growls.

"Ah...so it's just bad parenting?" she presses.

"Who the hell are you to tell me what to do with my kids?" He drops his arms from his broad chest. Fists clenched, he continues, "I stopped by to bring Red something and there isn't a fucking thing they can't see going on."

"Aw, Dad, you cursed," one little angel-faced girl announces. Having heard his raised voice, she looks over her tablet.

"You know what that means?" the other girl, with the same face, adds.

Twins. I smile.

"Christ," he grumbles, pulling out his wallet.

I put my hand over my face and silently pray the roof collapses and ends this verbal sparring match.

Red's laughter makes me pull my hand from my face.

"Ladies, this is Xavier Stone. We go way back." Red motions toward the golden-red-haired tatted man. The man pulling twenties out of a silver money clip and scowling at Sid.

"Xave, this is Liza and Sidra." Red motions between us.

Xavier stays focused on Sid.

"Call me Sid," she corrects, keeping her eyes on the sixty dollars Xavier pulls out.

"Are you giving them sixty dollars?" Sid brings her wide eyes to meet his scowl.

"Yeah, because *you* made me cuss." He slips the remainder of his money into his back pocket.

Out of nowhere, a little hand appears, and he places the money in it.

"Wait," Sid holds up a hand, "you mean to tell me they get sixty bucks every time you curse?"

"No," the angel-faced girl says, drawing our attention. "We get twenty for each cursing occurrence."

Sid opens her mouth, but is silenced by the identical sister's arrival.

"Each time there's an instance when Dad curses, we each get twenty, unless only one of us is around. However, if it's the F word, we get an extra ten." She gives a nod, ending her explanation.

Sid uncrosses her arms and gives Xavier an evil grin before turning her attention to the twins.

"If I can get him to say the F word more than once, do you get thirty for each time it's said?"

"Don't—" Xavier begins.

"Yes," the girls answer in unison, nodding their heads.

"If I get him to say it, will you split the money?" Sid wiggles her brows.

Both girls' eyes widen in excitement before nodding enthusiastically.

"Now, wait a damn minute," Xavier interrupts.

"Hah, you cussed. Pay up." Sid points at him, her finger only a couple inches from his chest.

"'Damn' doesn't count unless it's followed by something else." He smirks.

With a pout, Sid sighs, wrinkles her nose, and crosses her arms over her chest.

Xavier's eyes drop to where she's put her large chest on display.

"Nice shirt. I could go for a jug of milk."

Sid's mouth drops open. Her eyes narrow just a bit, but I swear I see the corner of her mouth twitch with humor.

"Okay, as fun as this exchange is," Red pushes between the two of them, "Sid, please take this over to that table. We'll go through it there."

She immediately turns her full attention to Red, taking the portfolio from him.

"Of course," she states, now ignoring Xavier and walking away.

"Just so we're clear," Xavier recaptures Sid's attention, "I'll have you screaming my name some day soon." Straightening to his full height, arms over his chest, feet parted, he's the picture of self-assured.

"Only in horror." She shrugs, giving a small frown before taking a seat at the table near the stage.

"I don't know what the hell that was, but can you please not piss off my possible photographer?" Red shakes his head, clapping Xavier on the shoulder.

"That, my friend, is what I call foreplay." Xavier grins at the back of Sid's head.

Taking that as my cue, I escape backstage to prepare for rehearsal.

A day after the Xavier and Sid experience and on the bus ride back from the recording studio, I start to doze against the bus window. Sleeping with Sid on the pullout bed is becoming less comfortable with each passing night. She's used to a regular bed, so her tossing and turning makes the night restless for us both. The chime of my cell interrupts my in-transit nap.

Unknown Number: You should know he's doing well and going to rehab.

A mixture of unease and comfort swirl through me. Unease from a stranger providing me information Jackson might not want me to have, and comfort knowing he has people to help him. Closing my eyes, I tilt my head back to the window, feeling more relaxed than I should—especially with my next stop being the social services office to talk to my caseworker about outstanding items.

"Good morning, Miss Campbell." The receptionist is always kind and has seen a lot of me lately.

"Good morning." I prepare to sit, but my caseworker appears.

"You can come on back," she states with a smile.

The smile makes me think things with Sean and my financial situation are starting to improve. I follow her down the familiar beige hallway and into her small office. Thick folders rest on bookshelves, are stacked on tables, and clutter her desk. She picks a stack up out of the extra chair in the room.

"Please, have a seat."

Sitting, I place my bag on my lap and twist the strap.

She settles behind her desk, flips open the thick manila file folder, and rests her hands on the papers within.

"I have good news and not so good news."

Every muscle in my body tenses and I swallow the lump in my throat.

"The good news is the guardianship papers are processing." She gives a kind, reassuring smile.

I relax a little.

"It will go through the review process for a few weeks, but it didn't get an initial rejection, which is a very good thing." She nods and then sighs. "As for your housing, I'm afraid you will have about a month and a half to find a new place or you will have to pay the full lease price. Lucas will retain medical insurance until you can move him over to another plan. The food and cash benefits will cease after this month."

I exhale loudly and rub my forehead.

"There's no way I would pay the full amount for one of those places," she adds, causing me to look at her. "Don't get me wrong," she continues, "they are well kept, but they really hike up the price once it goes into a public lease."

I nod in understanding.

"I'm looking, but haven't been able to make anything really happen yet."

"Good. Do you have any questions?"

"What about Sean's benefits? Are they affected by my financial change?"

"No. He will still receive his benefits. You are simply being instated as his legal guardian to make decisions such as medical and school. He is still based on his grandmother's income. However, should she pass away, he could be placed into foster care if a more permanent arrangement isn't established for him."

I nod.

"Any other questions?"

Giving a shake of my head, I answer, "No."

"Okay, well, I just need you to sign these documents." She places a few forms and confirmation of information in front of me.

Upon completion, I sit back and take a deep breath.

"I know it seems daunting now, but, Liza, I've known you for years. You'll be fine." When she closes the manila folder, a feeling of closure comes over me.

"I think you're right." I meet her eyes and smile.

Jackson

"What the fuck could I possibly do with a cell phone?" The edginess has every muscle aching and sweat dampening my hairline. *Stupid fucking withdrawals.*

"It's policy, Mr. Shaw." My newest nurse, Joe, stands at the nurse's station. With a look of annoyance on his face, he points to the *Rules to Live By* sign on the wall near the front desk.

I scared away two nurses before they brought in Joe last night. He's bigger than Elliott and as strong as a damn ox. I'm only on my second day and he's already got me under his damn thumb.

"It's not like I can fit an iPhone up my goddamn nose," I growl, turning back to my room.

"You need to be on your way to therapy." Joe ignores my tantrum.

"I don't need goddamn—"

"Wow." The voice makes me spin on my heels, causing me to get dizzy and sway. "Are you sure you and Christopher aren't blood?"

A smile parts my lips. My family sent reinforcements. Dr. J, Chris' psychiatrist, the only shrink Chris would open up to about his past, stands next to the nurse's station. "Finally, you came to spring me from this place!" I throw my arms in the air.

"Uh, no." He crushes my elation.

"What do you mean 'no'?" Dropping my arms, I slowly walk toward him.

"I'm here to collect you for therapy." Without another word of explanation, he waves for me to follow him.

"What? You take care of Chris."

He's Chris' shrink, helping him deal with his shit as well as putting up with Chris' need to be a constant pain in his ass. I mean, he practically toured with us.

I catch up with him, but he doesn't elaborate until we are inside a small, light blue room used for individual counseling.

"Take a seat, Jackson." He's suddenly all business.

I don't sit.

"What the fuck is going on?"

"Jackson, your family asked me to counsel you for the rest of your detox so we can continue sessions after your release." He sits down in a black chair at a small, round table.

"I don't need a shrink," I argue.

I sit across from him and spread my legs wide so I don't bang my knees on the pole under the table.

"I'm going to provide support during your recovery, that's all." He settles back in the chair, tenting his hands in front of his mouth.

"This isn't like Chris. I got carried away with partying. I don't need—"

"Someone to discuss the feelings that drove you to the drugs and alcohol?" His brows raise.

"It was just an escape. Once it's out of my system, I'll be fine." I press back into the chair, crossing my arms over my chest.

"Yes, well, I've been assigned the task of creating your recovery plan."

I open my mouth to argue, but he lifts a hand, silencing me.

"Whether you like it or not, you will have an ongoing plan. The first thing you need to understand is that you are an addict." Dr. J leans forward, his elbows on the table.

"I'm not an addict. I just...I..."

"There's nothing wrong with admitting you're an addict." He shrugs.

"Nothing wrong with being an addict? Doc, you may not be doing this right." I curl up the right side of my mouth.

"Nice attempt, but Chris is much better with the witty taunts."

My could-have-been smile drops from my lips.

"I didn't say being an addict is okay. I said there's nothing wrong with admitting you are one, and Jackson," he eyes me sharply, "you are an addict. You took the drugs for fun and then they became a necessity during daily life."

"I just got carried away and—"

"Lift your hand," Dr. J cuts me off. "Do it."

Unfolding my arms, I put one hand up between us. The tremors in my hands are noticeable to the naked eye. There's no hiding my jonesing.

"That right there is your body fighting the effects of not having a foreign substance in your system. Your body craves the drug, the euphoric feeling." Dr. J reaches out and takes my hand.

"Jack, you have permanent liver damage because of how far it went. There's a chance you will have kidney problems in the future."

I drop my head and take a deep breath.

"What's the plan?" My question is my resignation.

"You'll finish the detox week. At the end, I'll consult with your doctors and nurses, and we will decide if you can leave the facility."

"Then?" I press, finally meeting his eyes again.

Releasing my hand, he sits back once more.

"You will meet an AA sponsor this week. If you are comfortable with them, then you will regularly connect with them to check in and for support. We'll find local AA meetings you can attend to support your sobriety goal."

"So, what the fuck are you for?" I grin. "Are you just trying to make Chris jealous?"

Rolling his eyes, he explains his role.

"I'll be doing some sessions with you to discuss the pressures you face. And, perhaps, it's to make Chris a bit jealous." He shrugs, keeping a straight face. "Let's take a selfie together and send it to him." He cocks his head before a wide grin spreads across his face.

Our laughter fills the small room.

Walking Dr. J back up to the front, I notice a satisfied look on Joe's face and flip him off.

"You still got your therapy session, didn't you?" He pushes his bottom lip out in a fake pout.

"I don't like you," I inform in a bored tone.

"Good." He nods. "Just remember, I've worked here for six years and I'm not going anywhere. In order to avoid me, you will need to stay out of here."

A familiar voice interrupts before I can take my edgy-withdrawing-addict attitude out on Joe.

"Jackson?" Nicholas sounds both sad and stern. I'm not sure

how he pulls that off.

Turning to face him, I'm shocked by how tired and aged he looks. This isn't the Nic I know.

"What's wrong?" My feet carry me until there's only a foot between us. "Is it Mom?"

He looks up and shakes his head.

"She's okay. I just came to check in on you so she would rest this afternoon. She's been worrying herself about you all night."

Guilt assaults me and by the hard look on his face, I'm sure that's his intention.

Walking by him, I say, "Tell her I'm fine and doing what I agreed to do."

I enter my private room and sit on the bed.

Nicholas follows, closing the door behind him.

"I never thought I'd be here with you." Deep lines mar his forehead. "I wasn't prepared to do this..." he motions around the clinically clean room, "with you."

I open my mouth, but he puts a hand up, silencing me.

"I know I'm not your biological father, Jackson, but I can't hold back my disappointment." He closes his eyes and presses this thumb and pointer finger into the lids.

"Yeah, well, you disappointed me, too."

My response brings his eyes back to me.

"You didn't think about telling me my mother has cancer. That MY mother has a disease that destroys lives like a tornado." The venom in my voice surprises me.

"I respected your mother, MY wife's wishes." Nic steps closer to me.

Resting my elbows on my knees, I focus on a dark green fleck in the mint green tile at my feet.

"I know you're angry. But when she finally opened up and told me what was going on, the only way I could help her was by doing as she wished. Do you understand how helpless I feel?"

Bringing my glare from the fleck to his face, I answer, "No, Nic, I don't, because no one told me."

I push to my feet and Nicholas raises his head to keep his

eyes on mine.

"I could've helped," I say, pointing to my chest. "I would've been the person you could lean on, but you didn't give me that chance."

"You didn't give me that chance either, Jackson." He closes his eyes, inhales, and blows the breath out. "I know I'm not your real father, but—"

"Not my real father?" I choke out the question. His words both anger and sadden me.

"Yes, I understand I'm not." His arms cross over his chest like he needs something to hold on to. "But I wish you would've come to me. I would've listened. You aren't the only one who knows how deep heartache can go."

"How can you say that?" My body goes lax, my anger washed away by his words.

His eyes meet mine, confusion on his face.

"*You* are my father, Nicholas." All expression leaves his face at my words. "No one else has been there for me, raised me. You did that when you didn't have to."

Nic drops his arms and visibly swallows.

"I thought you understood. *You* are Dad."

The watery look in his eyes puts me in motion. Stepping forward, I reach out and pull his chest to mine, embracing him.

"It's hard to stay strong for her." The unfamiliar waver in his voice causes an ache in my chest. This is Nic—confident, strong, decisive Nicholas Shaw. He doesn't falter.

But he's human, an internal voice reminds me. I hold him tighter.

"We'll do it together."

"You just get better first." He pulls out of my arms, returning to the Nicholas I've always known. "She needs that from you."

My response is a quick nod.

Three days have passed since the emotional confrontation with Nicholas. Today, I'm surrounded by too many guests. And if Nurse Joe's scowl is any indication, he's not happy about the rule breaking.

"Is this her?" Elliott turns up the next online contestant's submission.

Her voice induces the same reaction. My body warms and my cock stirs to life. Licking my bottom lip, I nod.

"Fuck me. I'm going to need to talk to Red about reservations." Elliott sits back in his chair, closing his eyes and listening. "Do they all sing this well?" His fingers tap out the beat on his massive bicep.

"The real question is, do they get naked?" Kat asks without looking up from the magazine she's flipping through while seated on the window sill. "If so, I'll need to be added to the reservation."

"Now you're into women?" Jimmy asks, slouched in one of the uncomfortable chairs.

"Maybe I've always been into women. Ever think of that?" She finally looks up from the magazine.

"Ever been into Serena?" Elliott's face displays genuine perverse curiosity.

"Will you guys shut the fuck up?" I snarl, taking the laptop from Elliott. "I can't hear shit."

Still not allowed access to my cell phone or computer, Elliott was kind enough to smuggle his inside. Having hidden it in the acoustic guitar case I've been given permission to have, along with my black lyric book.

"Well, look who just can't stay away from a rehab or psych ward." Elliott grins widely as Chris enters the room.

"Asshole," Chris greets him.

"Captain Emo." Elliott salutes.

Chris turns his scowl on me.

"What's wrong?" I close the laptop, silencing my snake charmer.

"You're gonna want to open that back up." Chris motions to

the laptop as he approaches the bed.

I lift it open just in time for Chris to turn the computer toward him. He starts typing and when he turns it back around, nausea assaults me.

"When—?"

"An hour ago," he answers before I can finish asking.

"What the fuck?" Elliott's voice comes from over my shoulder.

"Who is that?" Kat asks, leaning forward.

She starts scrolling through picture after picture of Liza and me going into the hotel, Liza coming out of the hotel, and a fucking video of her leaving my room. The images are blurred and grainy. It would be hard to identify her, *if* you didn't know who she is.

"This shit is fucking viral." Jimmy drops his phone in my lap.

The images are all over the entertainment websites, being used as teasers for upcoming 'news' shows.

"I need my phone." I clench my fists.

"You can't—"

"I need to call her, to prepare her. I need to talk to Una," I growl, focusing on Christopher.

He shakes his head.

"Una is already on this, but..."

"But what?" I scream. "Una was supposed to be on this shit. She said she had Kristy under control."

"You think it's her?" Kat asks.

"Who the fuck else?" I start to pace. "I need my phone. Her number is on it."

"It could be any fucker looking to make some cash," Jimmy argues.

"You heard what that bitch said before she stormed out of the hotel room," Elliott counters.

"I need my—"

Chris' phone chimes, cutting me off. He answers, looks at me, and holds out the phone.

"It's Una. She needs to talk to you."

I snatch the phone from his hand. "What the hell, Una? You

said you had this," I snap.

"Jackson, I know you're pissed, but I can't trace it back to Kristy."

"You know she—"

"Yeah, I do, but we've got a bigger problem."

"What?"

"Your drug use is getting more attention and rumors are flying around saying the girl in the pictures is a stripper you were getting high with at a club. They're also claiming they have clearer photos showing her with bruises and a swollen lip," she finishes with an exhausted sigh.

"What the fuck! That's a goddamn lie," I growl.

"Jack, I've got an anonymous message threatening to expose Liza and implicate you in some serious drug and abuse related shit. This isn't good. I know you want to immediately act on it, but I need you to take a breath and let me work this out."

I inhale deep, swallowing the roar threatening to escape.

"You better work it out right fucking quick."

Ending the call, I toss the phone onto the small table in the room.

"One of you needs to get to her."

"To who? Kristy?" An evil gleam flashes in Kat's eyes

I shake my head, even though I like how she's thinking.

"No. I need you to get to Liza. This is my fault and I need to fix it."

Chapter Fifteen

Liza

"No one can tell it's you," Sid reassures, dropping my cell to the counter between us.

"Then why would someone purposely send it to me?" I snatch the phone off the table and scroll through the grainy pictures sent by an unknown number. They also felt the need to include the word "whore" along with the website link.

Sid growls, "Damn it, Liza. Whoever released the pictures sent it, or someone involved. Nowhere on any of the websites does it say your name." She sweeps her hand over my laptop, my tablet, and our cell phones. "If they released your name or found out who you were, trust me, they would post it everywhere."

Realization smacks into me. It had to be that bitch.

"Kristy," I groan out her name, closing my eyes.

"You think that skank did this?" Sid slides my laptop in front of her and starts tapping on the screen.

"Yes. No. I don't know." I rub my tear swollen eyes before refocusing on my cousin. "Who else would do it?"

"Maybe it's not about you." Sid doesn't look up from computer. "It could just be about profiting off Jackson's drug scandal."

"Great." Rolling my eyes, I walk around the counter and slip onto the stool next to her. "That makes me feel so much better."

On a tired sigh, I ask, "What are you doing?"

"Tracing the phone number." She shrugs.

"Please don't do something that will get my laptop confiscated." And then, for good measure, I add, "Again."

She looks up and flails her arms into the air. "Once. It happened once." She holds her pointer finger up in my face. "You're never going to let me live it down, are you?"

"Sid, the FBI took my eleventh grade English essay and computer," I remind, trying not to smile. As scary as it was at the time, the memory of three agents arriving and the look on Aunt Char and Uncle Mark's face is funny now. Though, it wasn't funny when they showed up again, much later in high school.

"I replaced your essay," she blurts before turning back to the computer. "And I bought you a new laptop," she concludes on a mumble.

Covering my face with my hands, I lean forward, elbows on the counter.

"This isn't going to be the end of this," I moan.

"You don't know that." She tries sounding positive, but I can hear the lack of surety in her voice.

Later that night, I receive another unknown text.

Unknown Number: He's sorry about the photos and worried about you. He's trying to fix it.

Tired of unknown numbers, I hit reply to finally find out who this is. But before I can type a letter, I lose my nerve, afraid to scare off my one link to Jackson.

I'm a pathetic loser.

"You realize you're on the live show, right?" Sid greets me from my seat in the dressing room.

"Voting doesn't close until midnight." I shoo her from the chair at my dressing table.

Sighing, I sit, exhausted. Between sleeping next to Sid, the stress from the show, my current life changes, and dreaming about Jackson, my brain and body are close to a complete shutdown. Letting my body sag, I take three deep breaths.

"It doesn't matter," Sid continues. "There's no way anyone

can knock you out of the top twenty."

A rush of nerves spikes my energy level. Straightening and turning, I look at Sid.

"What?"

She sits in Bethany's chair, flipping her tablet around for me to view.

"You're number five, my darling cousin." She grins, wiggling her brows. "Even with an hour to go, no one can knock you out of the top twenty now."

"How did...? I was at..." A lump of nervousness clogs my throat.

"Your numbers jumped over the past hour." She turns the tablet back to her.

"I'm going to the live show," I whisper.

"You're going to the live show," Sid confirms, grinning.

Our eyes lock for a second before we burst into squeals.

"Oh my God, I knew you would dominate!" Sid claps.

"Did you make it?" Bethany stumbles into the room, trying to walk and remove a platform heel.

Sid slips from her chair and moves over to the worn loveseat.

"She's top five and there are only minutes left before voting closes."

Bethany drops into her chair and lets the heel fall to the floor.

"Oh. My. God!" she screams, grabbing my hands and squeezing them in hers. "Are you excited?" She drops my hands and continues before I'm able to respond. "Of course you are. Why wouldn't you be? Did you tell Red?" She fires off the questions while touching up her makeup.

Pulling pins from my hair to change over for the last performance, I respond, "More nervous, I think. No, I haven't been able to tell Red yet, besides it's not final."

With a shrug, I roll the sides of my hair and pin them back, sticking tall feathers into the knot I created. Leaning toward my mirror, I grab my lip brush and touch up the bright pink lip stain.

"It might as well be official," Sid scoffs.

"Ten minutes," Jennifer yells through our door.

"Okay," Bethany and I yell in unison.

"I should've gotten the taxi like I wanted to," Sid growls from the bus seat. "It always smells like hooker armpits this late at night." She wrinkles her nose.

"And how would you know what a hooker's armpit smells like?" I raise one brow.

In a flash, she grabs my arm and leans into my pit.

"That's gross," I laugh, pulling my arm away.

"Well, now I know, don't I?"

"Bitch," I say on a giggle.

Ignoring the insult, Sid launches right into her favorite topic of the night.

"What song are you going to sing for the show?"

Shrugging, I tilt my head back and forth.

"Not sure yet."

I drop my head onto the back of the seat and close my eyes. Jackson's face flashes behind my lids as my brain rushes through the current state of my life. A pang in my chest joins in at the moment.

"You would totally win if you wore the pink corset with the black stripes."

"I don't think that would go over very well with the show producers," I respond, amusement in my voice.

"Liza?"

"Yeah?"

"You aren't really excited about this, are you?"

Taking a deep breath, I lick my dry lips.

"I'm just nervous."

"Liar." She knows me too well.

Lifting my head, I turn to look at her. Our eyes meet.

"I am a bit nervous, that's not a lie, but it's more than that." I shift my gaze to watch the dark city pass by through the bus window. "I don't know if this is something I want anymore."

The warmth of her hand on my arm draws my attention.

"You've wanted this for forever. What's changed?"

With a humorless laugh, I give her the most honest answer I can. "Me, Sid. I've changed."

Our eyes meet again and we sit in comfortable silence. With a quick nod and a small smile, she turns to look out the window.

"I think you should sing something sweet, but sad." Sid doesn't turn around to me when she finally speaks.

I nod, even though she's not looking.

Two days later, an assistant producer for Hidden Talent calls to confirm my qualification for the live show. Papers arrive by courier an hour after the call, who waits for me to review and sign the documents so he can return them the same day.

Signing my name on the bottom line was bittersweet. All the years I wanted this very thing—to be noticed, discovered. Now...I'm not sure what I want anymore.

During club rehearsal, Red is more than thrilled I made it to the live round. He's pretty sure this will be great publicity for the club. Though, he's not happy I have to miss Friday night's performance. And again, he's expressed his concern over me leaving once fame takes hold, but his genuine belief in me is touching. It makes the thought of having to walk away from the club even harder to stomach.

The bus arrives at my stop and I step off onto the sidewalk, ready to just be home and in bed. Tonight's rehearsal combined with my nervousness about tomorrow's first stage rehearsal for Hidden Talent has me completely exhausted.

"No," Kelvin barks at Sid.

"Come on," Sid whines. "We all have to match."

"Match what?" I set my bag down and close the apartment door.

"She wants to wear matching shirts for the show." Kel rolls his eyes, answering my question.

"And what's so bad about—?"

"Oh, it's not the shirts. It's the bedazzling she wants on them." Looking away from me, Kel narrows his eyes on Sid. "I'm not wearing t-shirts that say 'Liza's Bunch' in rhinestones."

"But it will look better when the light hits them, especially for the cameras," Sid informs.

"I don't care. I'm not wearing rhinestones. Pick another design." Kel walks out of the room and down the hall to show the finality of his statement.

"Fine," Sid barely agrees.

I know that little glint in her eye all too well.

"What are you planning?"

She shrugs.

"He said no rhinestones, but he didn't say anything about glitter." With a large grin, she turns to the open laptop and taps away on the keys. The grin never leaves her face.

Too tired to attempt to sway her, I walk into the kitchen. Grabbing a wine glass, I fill it to the rim before taking a seat on the couch.

"I ordered pizza," Sid says to the computer.

"We just ate pizza the other night," I remind.

"So." She shrugs. "Pizza can be eaten at least three times a week. In fact, if you're a college student, it can be eaten twice a day, every day."

Shaking my head, I take a long drink from the glass and put my feet up.

While Lucas and Sean get ready for bed, Kel helps me clean up from dinner. Sid ordered pizza alright. Three different pies, cheesy bread, cinnamon sticks, and a family size salad. The kitchen looks like a Dominos explosion.

"Liza, come here." Sid's urgent tone draws my attention away from dishes.

"What?"

"Don't what me," she almost yells. "Come here. Hurry!"

Grabbing a dish towel, I enter the living room, drying my hands.

"What's going...?" Her finger pointed to the computer screen answers my question.

"That's Jackson," Kel announces over my shoulder.

"Shh." Sid waves her hand in the air and turns the volume up with the other.

Jackson sits at a table with microphones. A very attractive woman in business attire sits on his right, and his mother on his left.

Swallowing a lump in my throat, I read the banner scrolling below the live feed and freeze.

Jackson Shaw addresses his latest drug scandal.

Sid reaches up and pulls me to sit next to her on the couch. Kel follows, squeezing between me and the armrest.

Clearing her throat, the attractive woman leans toward the mic. Below her, the screen flashes the name Una Nobil, VP Nobil Records.

"Mr. Shaw would like to take this opportunity to address some current rumors and set the record straight. We will take questions at the end of the statement. Please be respectful and polite." Sitting back in her chair, she glances at Jackson and give a small nod.

Rolling his head on his neck, he sits forward. When he looks into the camera, every muscle in my body tenses. His dark blue eyes cause the familiar tremors of desire and lust. I take deep breaths, trying to calm my libido.

"First, I'd like to thank my family and friends for supporting me during this time in my life. I would also like to thank the outpour of support from the fans. I love you all." He grins into the camera and my thigh muscles clench. *Dear God, this isn't the time to get turned on.*

"Now, I'd like to address my prior relationship. The matter is private and out of respect for Kristyna and myself, I'd like to keep it that way. As everyone knows, when a relationship ends, people get emotional. Some choose to handle their emotions one way, while I choose to keep them private."

He reaches out and grabs a water bottle on the table, taking a quick drink before returning his attention to the audience.

"I can assure everyone I was a single man when I arrived in California."

Was? Is he with someone now? Back with Kristy?

He takes his mother's hand, entwines their fingers, and lays them on the table.

"My current medical situation is the result of drugs. I'm not going to try to make it sound pretty. I've dealt with my personal stresses in a way that's led to permanent liver damage, the risk of kidney problems, a nice stint in rehab, and who the hell knows what else the doctors will find. I'm at the end of my detox treatment and I'm lucky to have the means for an extensive team of support to help me get back to a better place."

I inhale sharply and Sid grabs for my hand. The realization of how close to death he'd truly been makes my chest ache.

"However, I need to thank a very, very special person for helping me during my darkest time." His eyes grow intense and my heart beat pounds in my ears.

"I'm forever indebted to you, snake charmer. I plan to thank you wholeheartedly."

My hitching breath gets caught in my throat and I cough. I'm coughing on air for Lord's sake.

"You okay?" Sid asks.

I nod.

"Good. Now, be quiet. I'm pretty sure he's talking about you." She turns back to the screen, and mutters, "We're totally discussing this snake charmer thing, too."

Jackson continues speaking into the camera.

"I want to apologize for disappointing my family, my friends, and the fans. Being the cliché of a rock star isn't the type of person I want to be. I hope you'll give me the chance to make it up to you."

Sitting back into his seat, he brings his mother's hand to his lips. She grins, pride radiating from her.

"Mr. Shaw will take a few questions," Una says, straightening in her seat.

His name is called out until he nods to someone in the crowd and the camera turns to them.

"Jackson, can you tell us what led you to drugs?"

Rubbing the back of his head, he leans forward.

"I'm afraid I was tempted in some convincing ways to partake, and, unfortunately, it became an addiction. Stress and circumstances led to bad decision making."

"Is it because of your breakup with Laney?" a reporter asks before being selected.

His face darkens for a moment before he shakes it off.

"No." His voice is assertive and final.

The crowd begins to chant his name once more before he nods to a small woman.

"Can you elaborate on the friend who helped you? Is it the same person in the pictures that have surfaced online?"

I squeeze Sid's hand tighter, praying he won't say my name, but it's Una who takes control of the question.

"Out of respect to the parties involved, we have no comment at this time. We aren't here to make them a headline."

"Okay." The small reporter nods. "Can you at least explain your statement that you *were* single?"

Jackson looks a bit confused by the question.

"Are you referring to me being single when I came to California?"

She nods. "Yes. You said, and I quote, 'I can assure everyone I was a single man when I arrived in California', which insinuates you are no longer a free man. Can you elaborate?"

His mouth forms an 'O' and I see the wheels turning before a mischievous expression paints his features.

"I'm not a free man," he confirms.

"So, you're involved with someone new? You aren't single?" she presses.

It's hard to breathe, to swallow, to process why this affects me so much.

Releasing his mother's hand, he leans his elbows on the table.

"I said I'm not a free man and if I think about it, I suppose I'm involved, but I can't make that decision for her." His smile is lopsided, teasing.

The reporter grins. "I guess we aren't going to get a straight answer."

He laughs, but says nothing more.

"Will there be legal charges for the illegal substances?" a round man asks, pushing up to the front.

"All the details have been handed over to the police," Una answers smoothly. "They are reviewing the information to see if or what measures need to be taken." She places a hand on Jackson's forearm. "I can assure you, Mr. Shaw is not trying to sweep this matter under the rug. He is taking full responsibility for his actions and working very hard to mend things."

The reporters all try to speak at once, but Una stands from her seat.

"We appreciate you all taking the time to see us this afternoon, but we must be going. Mr. Shaw has prior obligations." She nods to the crowd.

Leaning forward, Jackson looks up at Una and licks his lips before speaking.

"Thank you for being politically correct, Una." He turns to face the reporters. "I have my first AA meeting to attend in thirty minutes and don't want to be late. Thank you, everyone, for coming out to listen to me."

He stands and is genuinely caught off guard when a few of the reporters start clapping. With a hesitant grin, he gives a wave before the camera cuts to a local entertainment reporter.

"There you have it. Jackson Shaw has confirmed and denied a couple of the allegations. We wish him all the best and commend his honesty about seeking sobriety. Now, we go to—"

Sid closes the laptop, turning her attention to me.

"Snake charmer?" Her brow raises.

I shrug. "I don't know."

"Yeah right." Her eyes narrow.

"I really don't. It may not even be me he's—"

"Yeah right." This time, it's Kel.

Whipping my head around, I purse my lips at him.

"Don't you have dishes to finish drying?"

He chuckles but leaves the couch toward the kitchen.

"Well, regardless, he's not finished with you, *snake charmer*." Sid's voice holds too much amusement for my liking, but I can't say my body isn't burning and my heart isn't banging in my chest.

Chapter Sixteen
Jackson

"So, this is it?" I ask Dr. J while looking out the tinted window at the small, brick building.

"This is it," he responds, and then adds, "It's not the place that makes the difference. It's the people, the message, and how you participate."

"Yeah," I breathe out the word.

I exit the car with Dr. J right on my heels and we enter a set of steel double doors.

"You gonna make sure I stay in my seat?" I tease.

"No, Jackson. The meetings are private and for you, not me." He stops just outside a single metal door at the end of a beige hallway.

With a deep breath, I reach for the door handle.

"I'm proud of you Jackson," Dr. J says to my back.

Surprisingly, his words mean enough to warm me.

"Thanks, Doc," I respond without looking back.

Inside, a group of people mull about. Some stand, chatting in groups, others near a table with snacks and drinks, and a few sit silently, looking through their phones.

"Jackson?" A baritone voice comes from my left.

Turning, the short, thin man is not what I expect to find.

"You *are* Jackson Shaw, correct?"

Facing each other, I nod my confirmation.

He reaches out a hand, expecting mine. I hesitate. Years of fans and being approached making me cautious.

"I'm Greg. Greg Martin?" His hand still lingers between us.

"The sponsor." I nod, taking his offered hand.

"Yes." He smiles. "I was pretty certain it was you,

since...well, you are Jackson Shaw."

"I guess I'm easy to identify."

Releasing his hand, I look around the room once more. Most of the eyes are on Greg and me.

"Yeah, most of them will know you, too."

I sigh. "It's to be expected."

"You can rest assured everything here is private." His serious tone draws my attention to his face.

"Thanks." My response is awkward. I've been exploited so many times over the years; it comes with the celebrity status.

"I'm serious." His face is frozen in stern sincerity. "You need to be comfortable enough to share your story and ask questions. While most will know who you are, it will stay inside these walls."

"What happens in AA stays in AA?" I ask with a grin.

He smiles. "Should be a t-shirt."

"If you make them, I want two," I say, holding up two fingers.

"Let's get started."

"What's first?"

He looks at the silver watch on his wrist.

"We have ten minutes before the meeting officially starts, so I'd like to run through a couple things about the program and being your sponsor."

"Okay," I relax my stance, putting my hands in my pockets, "hit me."

"First, you'll have people introducing themselves, stating their addictions, their stories, and so on. It stays private and we don't judge. We support everyone. Even if they've had a transgression."

I nod and he continues.

"Second, if you are comfortable enough today, you are welcome to contribute or you can just watch. Third, if you choose to accept my sponsorship, I'll expect weekly check-in calls. You can call more than that, but I at least need a weekly update of how you are doing. I want you to be honest, too. Brutally honest."

"All the dirty details?"

He gives one short nod.

"I can do that."

"Good." He takes a deep breath. "Do you have a girlfriend, boyfriend, significant other?"

I narrow my eyes.

He puts his hands up, palms out toward me.

"I only ask because we suggest you don't start any new relationships during the first year. If you're already in a relationship, then we suggest your partner get involved in a support group as well."

"My girlfriend has to come to meetings, too?" My body tenses. I fold my arms across my chest, raising one brow.

"We suggest a support group for spouses, not require it, but we find it helps them to have somewhere to go to talk about their struggles of being with an addict."

I drop my brow, relax the tension from my shoulders, and swallow. *A fucking year. There is no way I can stay away or leave her alone for a year. Not when every part of me screams out for her.*

"My relationship is new, but it's not going anywhere."

"New relationships are a challenge, Jackson. You need to make sure this is the right time to proceed." His eyes are soft, understanding.

I shake my head and drop my arms.

"I don't know if it's right, but I'm not walking away." My statement leaves no room for argument.

Instead of pressing further, he concedes with a nod. Side stepping to a small table by the door, he returns with pamphlets in hand.

"These are for you to read over. Learn the steps and rules of the program." He hands over three more. "These are for your girlfriend. There's information about support meetings for family and spouses, along with some general FAQs."

Taking the flyers, I slip them into my back pocket.

"How does this work when I'm not around for this particular meeting?"

"Good question. You can find a meeting in almost any town.

Given your resources, I'm sure someone can find a local meeting. All I ask is that you let me know about the meetings."

"So you can keep track of my attendance?"

The sound of people moving takes my attention from Greg. He touches my arm and motions for me to walk toward the group, each of them claiming a metal chair in a circle of seats.

"I won't lie. It's a way for me to know you are doing weekly meetings and adhering to your sobriety goals so I can be an effective sponsor." He motions for me to take a seat.

"Makes sense. Thanks."

The metal chair is cold and uncomfortable, but surprisingly, the meeting isn't. By the time the fourth person has contributed, I feel connected to this group like I never imagined.

"This week marks my seventh month of sobriety," Adam, the current speaker, announces.

Praise and congrats rings through the group, but Adam's face stays somber.

"It also marks the third anniversary of my partner's death." He drops his head, pressing the fingers and thumb of one hand to his eyes. "I was supposed to be watching the back door during a domestic violence call, but I was too shaky and distracted. I hadn't been able to shoot up for a few hours and needed my fix. When the shot fired, the first place my thoughts went were to my stash back in the patrol car." His body begins to shake, voice breaking. The person next to him places an arm on his shoulder. "It was my fault." He sucks in a breath, straightens, and gives a humorless laugh. "You'd think losing my partner of eight years would be enough for me to realize I had a problem, but it wasn't. I buried myself deeper in heroin and anything else I could get my hands on. I lost my job, friends, and some of my family even gave up on me."

His tale, his journey, is like a knife between my ribs. The warmth of embarrassment creeps up my neck. Adam and the others have lost so much more and been through hells I could never fathom. I feel like an asshole for sitting here with my pathetic story.

"Jackson?"

I jerk my head up, my eyes locking with the meeting leader,

Dave.

"Would you like to contribute?"

I open my mouth and close it. Taking a deep breath, I grow a pair and speak.

"I feel like an asshole with the pitiful excuses for my addiction."

"Start from the beginning," Dave encourages.

"Hello, my name's Jackson, and I'm a drug addict."

"Hi, Jackson" and "welcome" ring out from the group.

I share the story of my first taste of cocaine in the back of a limo and all the gory details that follow. I'm used to vultures circling my secrets for a hit of their own addiction—gossip. But this group is different. They listen to every word, nodding and understanding. There's no judging and in the end, I feel lighter.

The group bows their heads and does a prayer I'm not familiar with, so I listen as they pray. When they finish, Dave stands at the center of the circle.

"Before we go, I want to acknowledge a couple people." He turns to Adam. "Adam, thank you for sharing today. I know it's hard. Let's celebrate your sobriety. Congratulations on seven months." He holds out a small key tag.

The group claps as Adam hesitantly takes the tag.

When Dave's eyes land on me, I sit up straighter.

"Jackson, thank you for joining and sharing during your first meeting. I also want to commend you on your sobriety." He holds out a white key tag.

Reaching forward, I take the tag and read the gold print: *24 Hours of Sobriety.*

"Thanks," I whisper.

The key tag is cheap, but worth so much. I clasp it in my fist, fighting back tears.

Dave addresses one other person in the room before closing the meeting.

A few people approach me, asking for an autograph and asking about the band. These are questions I'm used to and answer with ease. Greg and I exchange cell numbers and with a large thank you, I leave him to linger with the rest of the group.

Upon exiting the room, Dr. J stands from a row of metal chairs against the wall. I expect him to ask me about the meeting, but he remains quiet, walking with me to the building's doors and into the waiting car. We pull from the curb and ride in silence until we reach our destination.

"Are you comfortable with the meetings?"

"Yeah."

The limo door opens.

"Good."

Nodding, I exit the car and come face-to-face with Sam. He steps back, allowing me a clear path to the entrance of the hotel—the hotel I hope to be out of in a couple days if Julia and Una come through. Dr. J slips out of the car, following me inside.

"I thought I'd be waking your ass up." Christopher barges into the bedroom of my hotel suite.

"Nah, couldn't sleep." I drop my pencil onto my notebook and lay my guitar on the bed. "What's up?"

Shrugging, he sits on the edge of the bed.

"How're you doing?" He focuses on the notebook and not me.

"Fine." I keep my answer short, but relish in the discomfort he obviously feels.

Reaching into his back pocket, he pulls out some paper and unfolds it.

"I've been playing around with this."

I take the paper he's offering and look over the words.

Intoxicated by your mouth,
You fascinate me.
I want to taste the red of your
lips.

"This is my—"

"Yeah, I know," he interrupts. "It really works with some of the music I've been working on."

I look over the arrangement he's put together from what I wrote. Words inspired by Liza cover the page while my brother's musical genius has composed lyrical gold.

"It's good." I smile and nod.

"This is her, isn't it?"

Looking up from the paper, I lock onto his sharp blue eyes. No words are necessary to confirm his suspicion. Chris nods and looks away.

"You need to tell her." His voice is soft, but frank. "Don't let her go until she knows."

"I don't plan on letting her go," I say, my voice just above a whisper.

He gives one firm nod. "Good, 'cause when you feel that," he gives the paper in my hand a pointed look before meeting my eyes once more, "it changes everything."

"I know," I breathe out the words.

"I was afraid she was just a rebound, a distraction you didn't need."

I open my mouth to protest, but he puts one hand up, stopping me.

"Stop," he clips out. "I know, I was wrong. Kristy was definitely all of those things, but this girl..." he gives his head a shake, "she's your angel, your Mia."

I grin. "She's my snake charmer."

"I don't think I want to know what you fucking mean by

that." His grin matches mine.

"Probably not, unless you want to talk about my dick." Placing my arms behind my head, I lean my head back against the wall.

"You're the dick." Chris chuckles. "Now, tell me you're good with writing the song."

"I'm good."

"Thank fucking God. I've got so many things I want to do with this." He snatches the paper from my lap, stands from the bed, and begins pacing. "I want to taste the red of your lips," he reads, and then looks up at me. "That's fucking sexy as hell and completely relatable."

"She wears red lipstick," I confess, dropping my arms and picking up my guitar.

"Hungering to wear the fragrance of your skin?" He raises one brow.

"She smells like sin, and what can I say? I like to sin." I strum the guitar.

"Yeah, she's definitely your Mia." Chris grins wide, turning back to the paper and reading lines out loud.

Three hours later, we have the first draft of our latest song, *Intoxicated*, and some ideas for another two playing around in our heads.

"Jack..." Julia stops abruptly at the sight of Chris. "Sorry, I didn't know you—"

The panic on her face concerns me. *Mom.*

"What is it?" I place my guitar on the bed and stand in a pair of black basketball shorts. Her eyes focus on where they ride low on my hips and continue to roam over my half-naked body before giving herself a shake.

"Information has gotten out about Liza." Her eyes fill with concern. "Here." She holds out her iPad.

It takes four long strides before I can reach out and take the tablet from her hand. As I scan the popular entertainment website, I feel Christopher's presence on my left.

The site has pictures of Liza plastered all over it: from the hotel footage, personal photos, and another of her with Lucas and Kel.

My muscles tense, heart races, and my mouth is suddenly dry.

"What the hell?" Chris asks from beside me.

"Someone gave them her name and enough information for them to go on. I don't know what all they got on their own or if it all came from a source," Julia rushes out, causing my head to spin.

"Get Una on the fucking phone," I growl, scrolling through the online article claiming Liza is a prostitute working under the guise of a stripper, a single mother in L.A. ghetto housing, and, the worst, her son is a product of child molestation.

"She's already—"

"Now, Julia." I toss the iPad onto the bed. "Fucking now!"

She freezes in fear. I march to the bedside table and pick up my phone. Tapping her contact, it barely rings once.

"I'm working on it, Jackson," Una answers.

"I want Kristy," I growl into the phone.

"So do I," she answers. "But we don't have any solid proof. I've got people tracking down the cause of the leak, but the reporter won't give up the source."

"It's not a fucking leak, Una." I begin to pace. "They're fucking lies. She's not a whore!"

"I didn't mean to imply she is what they are saying, but we have to—"

"Did you see what they are saying about her son? He's just a fucking kid." All of my energy drains and I sit down on the bed. Running my free hand through my hair, I sigh.

"I'm sorry, Jackson." Una's words are sincere. "We'll get this figured out, but you need to stay away."

"How the hell can you expect me to—?"

"Because if you show up, the media will crush you both. You will only make it worse for them."

"Fuck," I breathe out, realizing she's right.

"Julia's getting the apartment secured for you today," Una

informs. "Work with her to get it set up and I'll work on getting Liza and her family moved into the hotel suite."

"No, get her into the apartment," I demand.

"But... Fine," Una concedes. "Work out the apartment details with Julia. I'm going to work on this shit storm." She disconnects.

I drop my phone to the floor and fight every instinct I have to rush to Liza.

"You got an apartment?" Chris' question tears me away from my thoughts.

"Yeah." I rub my face, leaving my hands over my eyes.

"What do you need me to do?" Julia asks from the spot where I left her.

"We have an apartment to finalize and furnish today." Dropping my hands, I look at her.

She nods, moving into action. Grabbing her iPad, her fingers fly over the screen.

"It's going to affect the show," Chris states.

"Christ," I groan, flinging back onto the bed. "I didn't fucking think about the damn show. It's a *family program*," I emphasize. "This is my fault, Chris."

"She didn't have to come to your hotel with you," he argues.

I push up, leaning back on my elbows. "Fuck you."

"I'm not being a dick..." he pauses, "this time. I'm just saying, she made a choice and crazy shit has happened. You can't take all the blame."

"Oh, I don't. I blame that fucking bitch."

"Kristy?" Chris sneers her name.

"I know, I know." I push back up to sitting. "You told me she was trouble."

"I am always right," he adds.

"Dick."

"Yeah, pretty much." He shrugs. "Go shower and get dressed. I'm going to make some calls."

"You're calling in the cavalry, aren't you?" I ask, walking to the bathroom.

"Why do this alone when you have all of us?" With a wink, he puts his cell to his ear. "Baby, I need you," he says with a grin on his face. "Fuck, don't say shit like that when I can't get my hands on—"

I close the bathroom door just in time to cut off their conversation.

Liza

Having just finished stage rehearsal for the show and not expecting to see three assistant producers waiting for me, I stop short.

"Miss Campbell, Mr. Thorne would like to speak with you privately." The woman in the middle speaks.

"Mr. Thorne?" I choke out the question. *Why would the show's producer want to speak with me directly?*

"Yes," the man on the right answers.

"Is there a problem?" I swallow my nerves.

"He will tell you everything once—"

"Liza!" Sid calls, rushing toward me.

A security guard puts an arm around her waist.

"Let me go, you steroid ridden jackass!" She hits his arm, but turns her attention back to me. "Liza, it's Lucas!"

Something snaps inside me and I rush to Sid. Voices call out from behind me, but I can't hear them. My temples pulse, breathing labors, stomach cramps, and every muscle in my body is tense.

"What happened?" I push the guard's arm from her waist and grip her upper arms.

"I'll show you on the way. Let's go." Grabbing my arm, she pulls me down the hall and out to an awaiting taxi.

Inside the car, I turn to her.

"Sid, please," I beg for answers.

She shoves her phone in my face.

I swallow down the bile rising at the words written on the website.

Sid pulls the phone away. I take deep breaths, trying to calm myself.

They know who I am. They think I'm a whore.

"Then, there's this." Sid pushes the phone into my hands.

Lucas and Sean's faces flash in the video as the reporters call out to Lucas and surround him, separating him from Sean.

"Lucas, did you know about your mom?"

"Lucas, do you need help getting away from your home?"

"Who's your father? Do you know him?"

"I'm going to be sick." I cover my mouth.

"Drive faster," Sid orders the driver.

Kel breaks onto the screen, pushing through the crowd, and picks Lucas up.

"Kelvin, are you and your sister in a romantic relationship?" a report calls out, shoving a camera in his face.

Kel rears back, balls his fist, and punches the guy. Though holding Lucas is an obstacle, he still gets a clear hit and the guy's camera flies to the ground.

"You'll pay for that!" the asshole calls out.

"You deserved it," another reporter yells, stepping up and helping Kel get Lucas out of the crowd. The screen goes dark.

"Oh my God. What am I going to do?"

Sid takes her phone and replaces it with her hands.

"Lucas is fine. He's in the apartment, but those jerks are still outside."

I roll down the window and let the cool air hit my face. Inhaling deep, Sid squeezes my hands.

"It's going to be okay. We'll get out of town if we have to," she assures.

"The show," I groan. "That's why they were waiting and wanted to talk."

"You think they're going to kick you off?" Sid asks, anger in her tone.

"Probably," I laugh humorlessly.

Minutes feel like hours, but we finally arrive at my apartment where the media sharks are indeed surrounding the entrance.

Sid pays the driver and we slip from the car.

"Liza, look here?"

"Is it true Jackson paid you?"

"Does Jackson like rough sex?"

They are relentless, but I push by each of them.

"Get back!" Sid screams, shocking a couple of them still.

This gets us through the last of them and into the building. I take the stairs two at a time and burst into my home.

"Lucas?" I gasp.

"Mom?" He jumps up from the couch and rushes into my arms.

"I'm so sorry," I say to his head.

"I'm okay." He squeezes.

"We're going to go visit Aunt Char and Uncle Marc to get away from—"

"What?" He pulls away, looking up at me. "What about the show?"

"Forget the show, Lucas. I need to get you away from this chaos." I cup his face.

"No." He pushes my hand away. "I know it's all lies. Don't let their lies win."

"It's not that easy." I drop my bag to the floor and take a deep breath.

"Yes, it is."

My phone rings, but I ignore it.

"No, it's not. They will probably release me from the show because of this anyway." I place my hand on his shoulder.

"Tell them they're lying. They can't remove you from the show without proof," he insists, and for a brief moment, I wish I was this naïve once again.

My phone rings again and this time, Lucas grabs it.

"See? It's the show."

Before I can stop him, he taps the screen and answers.

"It's the show."

That it isn't some media hound allows momentary relief, but then knowing this is the call where I'm going to be kicked off the show before it starts sets my nerves off.

I take a deep breath and answer.

"Hello?"

"Liza Campbell?"

"Yes."

"This is Ms. Smythe. I'm one of the assistant producers for Hidden Talent."

"I'm sure you're calling about the current story in the media. I assure you it's not true," I defend before she's able to judge me.

"Yes, well, while we are a family show, we do not have facts regarding this...development. The first live show is tomorrow evening. You will perform, but we will be investigating the allegations. I wanted to personally call you and let you know so you aren't surprised upon your arrival."

"I understand." I swallow.

"Good. We'll see you tomorrow." She disconnects before I can respond.

"See, you are still on the show." Lucas' face lights up. "They have to prove this crap is truth and we know it's not."

"I'm not going." The words aren't easy to say, but getting Lucas away is the smartest thing.

"You have to." His face drops with disappointment. "Don't let them win. This is what you've always wanted."

"Lucas—"

"No, mom," he snaps. "This is your dream and you would be living it if you didn't have me."

My head buzzes from his words and chest restricts, as if all the air has been sucked from the room. Dropping to my knees, I wrap my arms around my little boy.

"Oh, baby," I finally choke out. "No."

I squeeze him one last time before pulling back. Taking his face in my hands, our tear-filled eyes meet.

Chapter Seventeen
Liza

Lucas' smile is the only thing that gets me through the group of photographers and reporters. Thankfully, their numbers are down, but there are still twenty too many.

"I can't believe the bastards are following us." Kel looks out the rear window.

Sid snorts from the front seat. "Of course they are. They want to be the first to get whatever story they can."

I drop my head against the back of the seat.

"It's okay, mom." Lucas takes my right hand and squeezes.

"They're a bunch of jerks," Sean grumbles, leaning his head on my left shoulder.

Freeing my hand, I wrap them both under my arms.

"I'm sorry you guys have to go through all this." I kiss Lucas' head before turning to Sean's.

"If they don't leave you alone, I'm gonna kick them in the balls," Sean mumbles.

The car falls silent for a moment before Sid starts laughing and the rest of us do, too. Even the driver chuckles.

Luckily, the theater has a gated rear entrance only authorized persons can enter. My gratitude dissipates when just inside the building, I have to say goodbye to my family.

"Here." Sid holds out the small flash drive.

"You finished it?" I ask, excitement and nerves battling inside my stomach.

"Stop worrying," she orders.

"I'm not—"

"Yes, you are, and you don't need to. You can do this. You're the strongest person I know, Eliza." Sid leans in and kisses my cheek before a show assistant leads them in the opposite direction.

Once they round a corner, I comply with the assistant's request to follow him.

"I need to speak with the band, staging manager, and lighting—"

"You're needed backstage to meet with producers and then in the green room for quick interviews with reporters." He motions for me to climb a few steps leading to a dark gray door.

"Fine, but I need to change my song for tonight."

"That's not possible." The assistant finally looks at me.

"Make it possible. I need to do this."

A look of confusion crosses his face, and then irritation.

"It's for my son." I hold up the flash drive.

His face softens. "Okay, but we have to be quick."

He opens the gray door and looks back and forth before hurrying us toward the stage. We find the band in a small makeshift studio working on a song with one of the other contestants.

The music director looks up from his piano.

"We aren't done here yet." The irritation in his voice is evident.

"She wants to change her song," the assistant states, pointing accusingly at me.

The director drops his head, sighs heavily, and leans forward to rest his arms over the shiny lacquered finish of the piano. Folding his hands together, he raises his head and gives me an annoyed look.

"Look, this is kind of zero hour. A song change is going to be a lot of work."

The other contestant snorts loudly before adding, "It's not like it will help you anyway."

All eyes turn to the young, tan-skinned girl.

"What? Everyone knows the show is only using you for first-night ratings. That's why you perform last tonight. After that, I'm sure you will be given your walking papers."

"They put her on last for ratings?" a backup vocalist scoffs.

The contestant shrugs. "No one has said it directly, but come on, why else would they put a singing prostitute on stage last? They want the ratings her scandal is going to bring."

"I'm not a prostitute," I growl, growing angrier every time the girl opens her mouth.

"Whatever," she says, drawing out the word.

"Look, you clearly don't know anything about burlesque or cabaret, especially since you're barely out of high school. There is a difference between selling myself for sex and performing on stage in a style that some of the greatest female singers have done in the past."

The girl opens her mouth, but I continue.

"And the fact that my personal affairs are being publicized doesn't give you the right to assume one damn thing about me. If your privacy were invaded, I bet you wouldn't look so sweet and innocent, would you? In fact, I'm sure I could get some easy information from that other contestant..." I turn to the assistant. "The guy with the long, dark hair and neck tattoo, what's his name? Ya know, the one with a pregnant girlfriend back home?"

"You don't know what you're talking about!" the girl screams, yanking her headphones off her head.

"Neither do you, so try to remember that," I snap at the little bitch before turning back to the music director. "I am changing my song for my son."

"Let the girl change her song, Ray," the backup vocalist says, joining my plea.

He shakes his head and grins. "Fine, let's see what you got."

"We aren't done going over—"

"Wait outside for a minute," Ray instructs. "After I speak with her real quick, we'll get back to you. Alright?"

She stands rod straight for a moment before stomping out of the room while complaining under her breath.

"So, what song are you doing?" He motions for me to step closer.

I do, handing him the sheets of music. "*Nightingale*."

"Demi Lovato?" He raises a brow.

I nod.

"Okay, let's run through the keys real quick. I'll try to get you in here before the show tonight, but I can't make any promises. Understand?"

"Yes, and thank you."

When we finally reach the originally planned destination, we're stopped short by three men and two women in suits.

"Miss Campbell, we've been waiting for you." I immediately recognize Gideon Thorne, judge and Bel Suono Studios producer.

"Yes, I'm sorry about that. I needed to speak with the directors to make some changes for tonight." I fail to sound as strong and sure as I'd intended.

"Changes?" He raises one dark, perfectly arched brow over his piercing blue eye.

"Um, Miss Campbell decided to change her performance song and—"

"You changed without speaking to us first?" A woman in a dark gray suit steps forward, exasperation on her face.

"It's my performance," I snap.

She opens her mouth, but Mr. Thorne puts a hand up, stopping her.

"We need to make sure you understand the allegations are still under investigation. This is a family show and we need to maintain a moral responsibility. So..." He drifts off at the end.

"So, if you find out I have prostitution in my past then I suddenly don't get enough votes to keep me on the show, right?"

The right corner of his mouth twitches, but he remains serious when he nods.

"Yes, I'm afraid so."

"Understood," I state firmly. "Can I go now? I have a show to prepare for."

"We'll talk more after the show, when Mr. and Mrs. Mackey are available to speak with you."

All my confidence shrivels into a ball of anxiety. The

Mackeys, who own and operate Bel Suono Studio and Mack Productions, two major forces in the music industry and by whom the winner will be contracted, want to speak with me personally. *Oh my God.*

A ragged breath leaves my body, making my panic obvious. Mr. Thorne spares me a pitying smile before excusing himself and his team from the room.

"Are you okay, Miss Campbell?" the assistant asks.

"Just give me a moment." I prop myself against a wall and breathe deeply.

The crew flits about in the darkness, preparing each contestant before they go out to face the crowd. Knowing this will most likely be my one and only performance on this show doesn't help my nerves. Even though I'm used to performing on stage, this crowd is in the thousands and the mentors' feedback is a toss-up.

I wipe my sweaty hands on the long, black, lace dress, my nerves ratcheting higher and higher.

"You're up." A crew member appears on my left and instructs me toward the darkened stage.

With a deep breath, I walk to my mark. The mic stand is right where I asked and the lights are so dim, I can see part of the audience.

Well, I didn't think that out very well, did I? My Lord, there are so many—

The show's host breaks me from my thoughts, welcoming the TV viewing audience back from a break and begins to introduce my performance.

Shaking out my hands and arms, I breathe deep and exhale a couple of times before he finishes. My name is the cue.

The stage lights barely raise and a soft spotlight finds me alone on the darkened stage. The large screen behind me casts a glow against my back.

"For you, Lucas. You are everything," I whisper into the mic. The music begins and tears already threaten, but I swallow the emotion.

I start the song, knowing the first picture on the screen behind me is of the day I brought Lucas home from the hospital and a slideshow of his life will follow. I want everyone to know the truth; that my son is a regular boy and has led a typical boy's life. They can take their rumors and choke on them.

The spotlight makes it impossible to see the audience or their reactions, so I focus on one spot. Picturing the boy who will forever be the main man in my life, I sing for him.

The red lights on the cameras moving around me demand my attention, but I can't focus on them. I pull the mic from the stand and reach my arm out to the light bathing me. A feeling of love, peace, and satisfaction sweep over me. When I hit the arc in the song, I know what I want isn't this gimmick—this reality karaoke show.

Not caring about the audience, mentors, or all the judgmental assholes backstage, I lose myself, unleashing my emotions. Tears fill my eyes as I sing to my son, giving all of me to the moment. Me, Eliza Campbell, not Miz Liz.

"'Cause, baby, you're my sanity. You bring me peace. Sing me to sleep," I belt, feeling the words through my entire body. I finish the song, one arm extended over my head, the other clutching the mic to the rapid rise and fall of my chest.

The crowd erupts, breaking me from my personal awakening.

I wipe away a stray tear and blink at the intrusion of the stage lights glowing brighter, until I see Jackson at the edge of the stage. He lifts Lucas onto the edge and Lucas says something to Jackson before setting his eyes on me.

His smile lights his face and he charges toward me. The love and happiness I feel in that moment spill over my cheeks. He enters my open arms, wrapping his around my waist.

"I love you so much!" he says, his voice muffled by my dress.

"I love you, too, baby." I kiss the top of his head.

Pulling back, he looks up and I cup his face with my free hand.

"You don't have to stay on this show. I know I wanted you to, but they don't deserve you." He buries into me again, not realizing his words were heard by every person watching.

Jackson

After assisting Lucas onto the stage, he rushes to his mother—their embrace for the world to see and a verbal exchange the world hears.

His declaration makes me grin. Instead of returning to my front row seat, I head backstage. She may have finished singing, but my charmer has already called out to my body; a request I'm eager to respond to.

Even from backstage, I hear the mentors provide exemplary feedback and joke about my absence. Gemma even throws in something about having that something everyone wishes they had and I catch her wink from a prompter set up behind the curtains.

I'll have to ask her about that later.

Liza exits the stage with Lucas tight against her side. With her focus solely on him, she doesn't see me until there's only a foot between us. And, fuck me, her dress is better up close. The cutouts have a skin tone lining, giving the illusion she's only wearing lace. My palms itch, wanting to peel away the dress and hear her sing out my name.

Her head raises, focusing on my chest before lifting higher to my face. Surprise widens her eyes before they shift to my left.

As I twist around, the clapping begins. Contestants, stage crew, and more familiar faces like Chris, Mia, Jimmy, Kat, Red, Bethany, Xavier, Sid, Sean, and Kel. Turning back to Liza, I clap with them.

Sid brushes by me, wrapping her arms around Liza.

"I am so proud of you!" she squeals. "You made that stage your bitch!"

"Thank you for doing the slideshow." Liza's arms flex, tightening the embrace.

Sid waves her off as Kel moves in to steal her into his arms.

"She's amazing," Mia says, her voice coming from my left.

I nod. "Yeah, she is."

"She's only talking about her voice." Chris chuckles.

"I'm not." I give him a side glance, catching his grin.

"Miss Campbell?" Everyone turns to the sweet voice of a young woman in a suit dress.

"Yeah," Liza sighs out, like she knows what's coming next.

"I've been asked to bring you to Chloe." Her body turns sideways, an indication to follow her.

"Chloe?" Liza asks, stepping forward.

"Mrs. Mackey." The assistant gives a genuine smile and leads Liza away.

Being a nosey bastard, I follow close behind, feeling the others at my back.

"Please wait..." She fades off, taking in the sight of everyone.

Liza turns around to see the entourage she wasn't aware of and her mouth drops open.

"If you could all please take a seat, they're in a meeting right now and will arrive in just a moment." She motions to the chairs and couches around the room.

"What are they meeting about?" I ask before she makes her quick exit.

"I'm afraid I don't have the details of the meeting." Her politically correct response is rehearsed, but I don't press further.

"I know what they're meeting about," Liza states.

She crosses the room and takes a seat, relaxing back into the cushions.

My first instinct is to pull her out of the chair and hold her tightly against me. Taking a deep breath, I ball my hands and root myself to stay where I stand.

"But it's all rumors," Kel states, sitting on the couch across from her.

She shrugs. "It doesn't matter, and honestly, I don't really care."

"They don't deserve to have you on the show." Lucas crosses his arms over his chest. He sits on the arm of Liza's chair with Sean quietly taking a place on the other arm, her personal security detail.

"Are you okay?" The question is strained from my internal fight to allow her space.

Her eyes meet mine and she visibly swallows.

"Yeah." She nods, her response tense.

Our eyes remain trained on one another. The room fades away and our breathing syncs, chests rising and falling faster and faster. Praying I have just a tiny amount of the same effect she has on me, I lick my lips. Her mouth parts and warm satisfaction courses through my veins.

About to beckon for her, wanting her to come to me, I'm interrupted by the sound of the door.

"Una?" I ask, confused.

She looks around the full room before greeting us. "Hello, everyone."

Her eyes land on Liza and she smiles.

"You, my dear, are amazingly talented." She steps closer and puts her hand out. "How about I formally introduce myself? I'm Una Nobil."

Liza pushes up from the chair and takes her hand.

"Liza Campbell." She blushes and furrows her brow. "But you already know that."

Allowing myself to move, I step around Una to stand by Liza.

"I've been speaking with Mrs. Mackey in regards to your, uh...situation." She offers a genuine smile.

"Why are you speaking on Liza's behalf?" I ask, knowing Una is kind, but she's also a label representative.

"Because you asked me to take care of things," she quips with a tilt of her head.

I raise one brow. She smiles.

"And because she's ridiculously talented," Una finishes with an unapologetic shrug.

"Yes, she is."

The new voice draws everyone's attention.

A tall, extremely attractive brunette walks around Una and offers her hand to Liza.

"I'm Chloe Mackey, Co-President of Bel Suono and Mackey Productions. I apologize for my husband's absence. Unfortunately, he had a pressing business matter to attend."

Liza's hand noticeably shakes as she takes the offering.

Chloe quickly clasps Liza's hands in both of hers, a look of compassion softening her expression.

"Miss Campbell, our sponsors, along with Bel Suono and Mackey Productions, are very sorry for this situation falling on you. All parties mentioned are in agreement that the rumors are falsehoods against you."

Next to me, I feel more than see Liza slightly relax.

"But..." Chloe continues.

"But...I'm still being asked to leave the show?" Liza finishes in a soft voice.

A look of pity crosses Chloe's face.

"I'm afraid the contract you signed is very particular about relationships with show executives, which includes mentors."

Guilt and tension tighten every part of my body as a throb forms between my temples.

With the recent scandal and my addiction going public, you'd think they would've permanently added Chris, but the announcement of Liza's exit from the show has already resulted in a drop of ratings. And Chris refuses to do more than sit in for a couple weeks. Truth is, without my scandalized ass, they're betting they would lose more publicity.

"She had no idea he was on the show," Kel argues, standing from the couch.

"And he had no clue she was a contestant," Chris states in his familiar I-dare-you-to-argue tone.

Chloe nods. "Yes, I know, and I can't say I agree with this

decision. However, the point has been made about fairness to the other contestants. I'm sorry, but we will need you to exit the competition."

Liza sighs loudly.

"This is—"

Liza's burst of laughter cuts off Kel's next protest and garners surprised looks from everyone. She grips my arm, using me to stay upright while holding her stomach with the other.

"I'm sorry," she says around laughs, "it's the stress." She fights between hilarity and gasps for air.

"Miss Campbell?" Chloe requests Liza's attention once more.

While she's calmed herself some, she's still fighting a battle with her "stress".

"Yes?" she chokes out.

"Bel Suono is very interested in discussing a deal with you. Though this didn't work out, I'd like to set up a meeting to discuss your career."

"Get in line," Una snorts, giving Chloe a teasing look. "You aren't the only one."

Chloe grins. "It's been some time since I've gone head-to-head with you."

"It will be like old times." Una smiles.

"Hold up." Red moves into the small circle and stands in front of Liza. "Liza, don't agree to anything. Not until they provide offers and terms in writing. Then we'll review them and you can decide what you want to do."

His rush to help her doesn't surprise me. Red's always been a good guy, regardless of his man-whore ways.

"But, Red—" Liza begins.

"I won't let anyone take advantage of you." He shakes his head. "We haven't worked together long, but you're a good girl and I won't let this industry eat you up. You've been through enough." His eyes drift to me before returning to her.

"Red..." She removes her hand from my arm to place it on his chest.

A primal need to remove her hand, wanting it back on me,

slides through my body in an angry, tormented heat.

"I don't want to leave the club," she finishes. "I know where I belong and where I wanna be."

Red's face falls clear of emotion just before a large grin takes over.

"Sweetheart, if these two," he thumbs over his shoulder to Una and Chloe, "have brains half as impressive as their asses, they'll make it work the way you want."

"Excuse me?" Gideon Thorne steps forward from the group of suits who followed Chloe in the room. "I think you should apologize to Mrs. Mackey."

Una and Chloe burst into laughter.

"Calm down, Gideon." Chloe waves him off. "It's nice to know I've still got it."

"Well played, Red," Una adds on a giggle.

"Miss Campbell, we'll be in touch." Chloe smiles, nods, and exits with the suits in tow.

Chapter Eighteen
Jackson

As soon as the door closes on the show execs, I take Liza's arm and pull her to face me.

"I'm sorry." I cup her face.

She visibly swallows and parts her lips. I want to devour her mouth.

"This shit's my fault, but I'm going to try to make it right."

My eyes search her soft baby blues, the battles of a million emotions warring within them. I clench my jaw, fighting the urge to ask what they are. *Does she hate me? Or, is she, like me, craving the taste of our mouths mixing and the feel of our skin touching?*

She places a hand over my heart, the heat from her touch branding my skin.

With a slight shake of her head, she blinks, and says, "It's not your fault."

"Yeah, it is. I brought Kristy into your life. The bitch is going to pay for all this bullshit." My anger seeps into my words.

"Jackson," Una sighs, "don't do anything rash. We don't have anything on her to shut her up or—"

"What kind of something do you need?" Sid asks from where she sits on the couch.

"Proof she released the information to start," Una states. "But no reporter is going to release their source."

"True." Sid stands and walks closer to Una. "But, and this is just hypothetical of course..."

"Of course," Una responds hesitantly.

"What if I happen to know someone with some itty bitty hacker-like skills who may be able to get something on her or get lucky and find out she's the source? Would you be *okay* with them getting involved?"

"Sid," Liza warns, turning to face her cousin.

I grip her hips and dig my fingers into the lace, bringing our bodies together.

"Shh..." Sid hushes Liza.

"We already had the one FBI conversation. Do we have to go over the other?" Liza pleads.

The FBI?

"I just wanted to see if I could do it. Besides, *that* was a bogus investigation. They had no proof," Sid answers in a blur of words before turning a sickeningly sweet smile on Una.

"Do what exactly?" Xavier asks, leaning against the wall and rubbing his bearded face, clearly eyeing her curves with apt appreciation.

"I'd tell you, but I have no idea what you are referring to." Sid looks completely clueless.

"You're kind of scary," Xavier states, a half-grin on his face. "It's a little hot." He gives a slight shrug.

She blinks at him before turning back to Una.

"So, about that," she brings her fingers up and air quotes, "'friend of mine'?"

"What would this friend need?"

"Access to a secured internet connection, a couple gadgets, and immunity should legal authorities get involved." She grins sweetly once more.

Una stares at Sid, contemplating. With a sigh, she nods.

"Kacey?" Una barks and her newest junior assistant hurries to her side. "Get Miss Campbell—"

"Sid," she corrects. "No need to be formal."

"Okay," she breathes the word. "Please, get Sid whatever she needs."

"Of course," Kacey responds, reminding me of a puppy with her eager nod and the obvious need for approval.

Kacey turns to Sid. "What can I get you?"

Grinning, Sid steps forward and snakes her arm around Kacey's, walking them both away from the crowd.

"We should talk where there are less...ears." Her lips purse. "But first, any ideas how to get your hands on her cell phone?"

"Th-that's stealing," Kacey stutters.

"I'm just kidding." Sid pats her arm, and under her breath, adds, "Unless you can get it."

"I might be able to help " Kat counters up to Sid and Kacey as they exit the room.

"Do you have any idea what you've just done?" Liza asks Una.

"No, and for the sake of future legal action, I think it's for the best." Una crosses her arms over her chest and turns her attention back to Liza and me.

"Did you discuss the apartment?" She raises her brows.

"No. Haven't really had a moment with the show bullshit and possible organized felony going on back here." I'm sure to give my best are-you-fucking-serious-right-now look.

"What happened to my apartment?" Liza takes a step forward, gets caught on my arm, and twists her neck to look up at me.

"Nothing," I say in a soft voice, trying to calm the panic on her face.

"Aside from the fucking media trap sitting on her front door," Jimmy adds.

"Thanks," I say, my sarcasm thick and eyes narrowed.

He shrugs, unapologetic.

"He's right," Una confirms in a gentler tone.

"I know," Liza responds. "They've been there for two days now, but the numbers had thinned out this morning."

"Yes, that was before tonight's show and the producer's decision. When this goes public, they are going to be even more ruthless," Una explains.

"But—"

"And we aren't sure what else Kristy has up her sleeve. If she's the one—"

"It's her," I snap.

Una puts her hands up, palms out.

"I'd like for you to consider staying somewhere else until things die down." She drops her hands.

"Where are we supposed to go?" Liza asks, her body tensing against mine.

"I have an apartment," I answer before Una.

Liza turns in my arms, her chest almost pressed to mine. Her confusion is written in the frown lines on her face.

"You have an apartment? Here?"

Cupping her head, I use my thumb to smooth the lines between her brows.

"It's a three bedroom suite above the W in Hollywood. I just got it."

"We'll be fine at home." She shakes her head.

"What about Lucas?" I know it's a cheap shot, but I need her safe from the impending craziness. On a more selfish note, I want her with me. "They will surround him and harass him on his way to and from school."

Fear flashes in her eyes and she bites her lip. It's almost enough to make me feel guilty. Almost.

"School will be out soon." Her protest is weak.

"The W has security gates, cameras, guards, and I can arrange a car to drive Lucas and Sean to school with minimal harassment. It would only be, what? A thirty, maybe forty, minute ride?"

"But Kel—"

"Can also have a driver for school and work," I add before she can argue.

"Three rooms won't be enough for all of us." She tries to pull out of my arms.

"I had twin beds put in one room for the boys. Kel can have the other room. And I've had the media room arranged with a bed for Sid." I sweep her jaw with my thumb.

Her mouth pops open. She doesn't speak, simply licks her lips and closes her mouth tight.

Fuck, I want to suck the lipstick from her mouth.

"Sid and I already bunk together," Liza nods, focusing on my shoulder, "so I guess it would work."

I slide my fingers from her neck into the hair behind her ear and tilt her head, coercing her to meet my eyes. Leaning down, I bring my face so close, I can feel the heat of her breaths on my lips.

"You think you'll sleep with Sid?" I whisper.

"Yes." Her response is too breathy to match the slight narrowing of her eyes.

It's fucking adorable. She thinks she can resist us. The way we gravitate toward each other, feed off the other's energy.

"Okay." Fighting back a smile, I give a one shoulder shrug.

Her hands press to my chest and push. Straightening to my full height, I allow the space. When my hand slips from her hip, I don't like it. I cross my arms over my chest to stop myself from pulling her back into my arms.

"I'll need to get some things from my place." She turns to Una.

"We really need to get you and the boys to the penthouse—"

"Penthouse?" Lucas squeaks.

"Yes." Una looks between him and Sean. "As Jackson stated, his condo is at the W in Hollywood."

"Are you okay with this, Lucas? We can go home. You just say the word." Liza moves to her son, kneeling the best she can in her dress.

"No." He shakes his head. "I want to go to the penthouse." He sends a large smile my way. "Can I bring my Xbox?"

"Of course." I nod. "We'll have someone grab it for you."

"I can get our things," Liza says, trying to stand.

"It's best if we have someone else collect the things you'll need. I'll go make the arrangements for cars. Hopefully, we can get out of here with little notice."

"Good luck with that," Jimmy snorts, shaking his head.

"Thanks, Jimmy, you just volunteered to help." Una's tone doesn't leave him much room to argue.

Grumbling, he pushes up from a chair and follows Una out of the room.

Liza covers her face with her hands and exhales loudly.

"I'm so going to regret this." She drops her hands and looks right at me.

I lick the metal hoop in my lip, smiling when she shivers and looks away.

Eliza

I don't have to open my eyes to feel him watching me. The only time his eyes haven't been on me was when I found the privacy to change out of the dress provided by the studio. And now I'm in the back of a dark limo, wearing the clothes I arrived in, with a man who draws me to him like a moth to a flame sitting across the way, and two boys vibrating with excitement. Keeping my head back against the seat and eyes closed, I try to make sense of everything.

My performance was supposed to be a polite *fuck you* and I guess I succeeded. I never expected to draw out crazed reporters, but dear God, I have. Nearly one hundred reporters and cameramen had to be waiting just outside the performer's exit. Thankfully, Una arranged an alternate exit route through a large garage, putting us into cars parked inside and out of the public eye. Before we shot off, she assured me our things would be delivered tonight.

"Liza?"

I open my eyes for him, like he has some power over me. *Who am I kidding? He has a power—a key that unlocks me, leaving me open and bare.*

"Yeah?" I breathe the word.

Leaning forward, he puts his elbows on his knees and places his palms on my thighs.

Damn his long arms and warm hands! Tingles travel across my skin, focusing their attention between my legs, which twitch to open for him. I tense my muscles to keep them shut. His fingers flex.

"I meant it when I said I'm sorry." His eyes search mine as they did before.

"I know." I want to reassure him with a smile, but I'm exhausted, my nerves are raw, and he's too close.

Our eyes lock and he drags his tongue over the ring on his lip. A breath catches in my throat. Christ, I want to suck the moisture from his flesh, dip my tongue into his mouth, and demand its submission.

"We're here!" Sean's shout breaks the moment.

Jackson sits back into his own seat and I squeeze my legs together tighter.

I need to get my body on the same page as my brain. *No sex,* I silently demand as the car comes to a stop inside a parking garage.

The limo door opens and Lucas and Sean shoot out in a flash of khakis and polo shirts.

Sliding to the open door, I slip out of the car and pause. The boys stand next to Julia at silver elevator doors. Taking a deep breath, I prepare to move.

His large, warm hands settle firmly on my hips. I stiffen when his legs stretch out on either side of me. When he stands, he allows the front of his body to slide over my ass and back until the length of him is flush against me. I melt, leaning against him, absorbing his heat and inhaling his scent—leather and sandalwood.

The warmth of his breath on my neck should cause alarm. Instead, I loll my head to the side, allowing him access. The feel of his teeth sends a spasm through my body. I fist the denim covering his thighs and he lightly sucks at my skin, turning the spasm into a pulsating firestorm.

A throat clears and I jump, putting half a foot between Jackson and me. Turning, I catch Jackson glaring at the driver.

"There's a car coming, sir." The driver nods toward approaching headlights. "It may be the other limo, but I'm not sure."

"Alright," Jackson says coldy.

His hand comes out, snagging the waist of my jeans and pulling me against his side. "Let's go." He guides us to the elevator.

Oh God! Craning my neck, I look around the parking garage. Lucas and Sean are nowhere to be found.

"Where's—?"

"Julia took them up," he answers before I finish.

Closing my eyes, I exhale sharply, pissed at myself. *Jesus, I'm a horrible mom. So caught up in—*

"Stop." His voice cuts through my thoughts as the elevator door opens.

"I'm not doing—"

He walks us onto the elevator.

"It's all over your face. Lucas and Sean are fine. You saw they were with Julia."

He presses a button with his free hand.

Unsettled by his ability to read me and by how easy it is to just be with him, I stay silently pressed against his side until the elevator reaches the penthouse. With his hand on my lower back, he directs me into a foyer with dark wood floors.

Jackson's presence at my back spurs me to keep walking. Following the dark wood slats, I reach a large open living space with an oversized taupe, U-shaped couch and a large flat-screen TV on the wall. To the left of the area is a bar and the right has a wall of windows leading to a balcony.

"One of the rooms is back there past the kitchen."

I follow where Jackson points to a door at the far end of large, open dining and kitchen spaces. The dining table seats twelve, the kitchen bar six. Swallowing hard, I simply nod.

"The other rooms are this way." He thumbs over his shoulder.

Walking around him, I follow the dark floors down a long hallway.

"Closet on the right, half-bath on your left. The next door on the right is the master bedroom." He pauses, but I don't give him the reaction he's waiting for. Instead, I keep walking.

"Another bedroom is on your left. That's where the twin

beds are for Lucas and Sean."

As if summoned by their name, the boys emerge from a room at the end of the hallway.

"This place is amazing!" Sean shouts.

"There are two balconies and they have a rooftop pool." Lucas grins. "Please, can we go swimming?"

"You don't have swim trunks." I brush stray blond hairs from his forehead.

"With your permission, I'll have some sent up." Julia walks out of the same room.

I can't fight the scowl forming on my face. Her eyes drop to the floor in submission.

"If you would rather them not—"

"It has nothing to do with swimming," I keep my tone even, "and you know it."

Her wide eyes meet mine and I raise a brow in challenge.

She totally gets that this isn't about swimming. It has everything to do with her stupidity in dealing with Jackson. I'm surprised he's allowed her to continue working for him.

Tears form in her eyes. She opens her mouth, but closes it and only nods.

"Come on, Mom," Lucas begs.

"Yeah, Miss Campbell, please?" Sean pleads.

"Yeah, Mom," Jackson teases, "let them swim."

Twisting, I find him half grinning.

"Fine," I sigh, turning back to the boys. "You have an hour. Then you come back and get showers. Hopefully our stuff is here by then."

I doubt they hear the part about showering because they cheer loudly and high five one another before hugging me.

"If you'll follow me, I'll take you two up and have someone meet us with shorts." Julia moves to walk around me.

"Are you sure you can handle them?" I can't keep the snark out of my voice.

She pauses and looks me in the eyes.

"I promise, they'll be fine."

I nod and she has the boys follow her.

"What the fuck was that about?" Jackson's question is a mixture of amusement and concern.

"Nothing." I shrug, turn, and try to walk by him, but his arm shoots out, stopping me.

"Not so fast."

He places both hands on the wall, fencing me between his arms. Turning, my back meets the wall.

"Tell me." He leans his face close to mine.

"It's nothing." I cross my arms over my chest, a useless barrier between us.

"Did she do or say something to you?" His eyes narrow.

Is he really this dumb? Doesn't he realize what could've happened to him because of her decision?

"You're serious, aren't you?" I drop my arms.

Confusion furrows his brow.

"Her decisions...that night..."

"The night I overdosed?" He drops his arms, crossing them over his chest.

I nod.

"Because they brought me back to the hotel instead of the hospital?" His eyes search my face.

Thinking about that night, my throat clogs with emotion and my vision blurs.

Clasping the sides of my face and tilting my head, his lips crash into mine. I fist his t-shirt, pulling him closer.

He slips his hands from my face, tracing the shape of my body. Releasing my mouth, he reaches down, grasps behind my thighs, and lifts me, pinning me to the wall. I wrap my arms around his neck; it's my turn to claim his mouth.

Breaking the kiss, I gasp for much-needed breaths. His forehead presses to mine.

"You're pissed at her 'cause of me?" His question is labored.

"I just think she's stupid and almost made the situation worse."

He grins, squeezing my ass.

"You're pissed at her 'cause you care about me." It's not a question this time.

I stiffen and change the subject.

"Did you buy this place?" I ask, trying to get back on my feet.

This is stupid. He's so new to sobriety and I'm sure there's a rule about relationships, even if they are purely physical.

"Leasing it." He reinforces his hold with another squeeze. "Stop squirming."

"Why?" I ask, pressing against his chest.

"Why what?"

Rolling my eyes, I stop squirming and purse my lips. "Why are you leasing the penthouse? The hotel kick you out?" I taunt.

He smiles wide.

"Just testing the idea and location." He presses his body further into mine. "I've found a pretty good reason to stick around." He holds my eyes.

"Liza," Sid calls.

I push at Jackson's chest, but he doesn't release me. Instead, he lifts his head and looks down the hall.

Sid finds us and grins. "Maybe I should just..." She points over her shoulder and starts to turn around.

"No!" I push harder at an immoveable Jackson. "We were just..." I don't know how to finish.

"Getting your freak on?" Sid humps the air, her tongue sticking out.

Jackson's laughter vibrates against my chest.

"No," I deny.

"Bow chica, bow wow!" she sings, swinging her hips.

"Will you stop?" I try not to laugh. "Jackson, put me down," I demand, going for a more annoyed tone with him.

He studies me for a brief moment, places a kiss to my lips, and releases me.

On my own two feet again, I sway—just a bit—as I walk away. Passing Sid, I wrap my arm in hers, dragging her out of the hallway and away from sex on stilts.

Chapter Nineteen

Eliza

"Tell me again why you aren't climbing Mt. Jackson while the boys are distracted by video games?" Sid pulls another shirt from Lucas' bag.

Looking around at the bags and boxes, I start to think they brought everything we own.

"You know why." I hang the shirt in one of the many walk-in closets.

"Oh, yeah, cause of his sobriety, your guardianship status, blah, blah, blah." She digs into the bag, pulling more clothes out.

"Blah, blah, blah?" I place a hand on one hip and raise a brow.

"Yep." She continues on to the next bag of clothes, not bothering to look up.

"I can't just..." My words fall away, unsure how to explain.

"You just can't what?" Sid finally looks up, meeting my eyes. "Can't let go of your neatly scheduled day-to-day and live for once?"

"I'd hardly call my day-to-day neat." I purse my lips, wrapping my arms around my middle.

She growls, plopping down onto one of the twin beds. "Liza, in the past ten years, the only semi-spontaneous, totally crazy thing you've done is move across the country with a baby."

"Excuse me?" My voice raises an octave. "I just performed on a stage in front of thousands of people."

"Kel and Lucas entered you into the contest. You don't get to take credit." She lies back on the bed, her arms behind her head.

"I spent the night with Jackson," I say in a whisper.

She's already shaking her head. "He came to you."

Sighing heavily, she sits up, crisscrossing her legs.

"You deal. That's your thing."

"I deal?" I sit down at the end of the bed.

"Yeah, you run your day—school, house tasks and errands, soccer, dinner, work. When things come to you—Hidden Talent and your night with Jackson, for example—you deal with them because they happen to you." Leaning forward, she takes my hand. "I love you and who you are. I just want to see you live."

"When did you become the advice giver in this relationship?" I ask.

"I don't know, but I don't think I like it." She purses her lips. "So, take my advice so we can get back to you lecturing me about my bad choices in men."

"I don't lecture," I defend. "Though, you do choose guys who don't deserve you."

"They don't need to deserve me." She grins. "I just need him to be good with his mouth and know how to swivel his hips in just the right way..."

"Paul." It's not a question, it's a confirmation.

Her mouth forms an 'O' shape before she says, "That's a low blow."

Guilt riddles me and I slouch.

"I'm sorry. I shouldn't have brought him up." Paul is a touchy subject and I know I shouldn't have mentioned him. I just hate how much power he holds over Sid. He always has and I pray for the day when he no longer does.

"It's okay." She shrugs, but I know, deep down, I hurt her. I also know she won't talk about it anymore. Her defenses are up and there's no crashing through that barrier.

"You think I need to live?" I redirect back to our original topic.

The familiar tingle starts at the bridge of my nose and tears pool in the corners of my eyes.

"Yeah." She nods. "You adult way too much."

A tear escapes along with a laugh, breaking the tension.

"Come on." She pats my leg. "We have your entire

apartment to fit into this one."

"I know, right?" I wipe away the tear, sniff, and get back to work.

An hour later, most of the necessities are put away. Kel's in the converted media room behind the kitchen, the boys in the middle room, and Sid and I have taken the room at the far end of the hall. And now, we sit around the open living space, eating pizza and wings.

"I don't ever want to leave this couch." Sid snuggles into the spot where she's stretched out, her empty plate resting on her stomach.

"It is pretty great," Kel agrees, standing from next to her and grabbing the plate from her belly.

"Thanks, handsome," Sid mumbles, eyes closed.

"Want me to take yours, too?" Kel motions to the plate in my lap.

I hand it to him. "Thanks."

"You want me to help with those two?" Kel returns from the kitchen moments later.

My eyes move to where both Sean and Lucas lie sprawled out on oversized bean bag chairs.

"Yeah," I sigh, trying to figure out which one will weigh less.

"They could just sleep there," Jackson says, stretching his long, prone body. He's lying in almost the same position as Sid, just on the other side of the couch, closest to me. Close enough that I often felt his fingers in my hair.

"I don't know." I scoot to the edge of the cushion.

"He has a point." Kel leans over the couch, his hands pressed into the back.

"I guess." I furrow my brow, not sure why I think this matters so much.

"Well, if we aren't moving them, I'm going to bed." Kel leans forward further and kisses the top of my head. "Night."

"Good night," I say, turning and watching him disappear behind the door at the far end of the kitchen.

"Sid," I call, but all I get is a soft snore. "Sid," I say a bit louder.

"What?" she grumbles.

"I'm going to bed." I stand, keeping my eyes on her and not Jackson.

"'Kay," she sighs, turning onto her side, giving me her back.

Realizing she isn't planning on moving, I kiss Lucas' head and turn toward the hallway. With a quick good night to Jackson, I walk a bit too hastily from the room.

The bed is too soft. I toss. It's too warm. I turn.

"Why am I so hot?" I growl low into the empty room.

I kick off the covers and push up to sit on the edge of the bed. Pulling the hair tie from my wrist, I twist and secure my hair on top of my head.

With a frustrated sigh, I look at the large window doors and accept my inability to fall asleep. I walk to the balcony door and slide it open, stepping out into the night. The air is warm, but not stifling.

There's a comfortable breeze swirling around the penthouse, cooling the skin my sleep shorts and tank top leave exposed. Inhaling deep, I lean against the railing, gaze up at the stars, and exhale. The sky is clear and feels so close. My hand twitches on the railing, wanting to reach out and touch.

Is Sid right? Am I so day-to-day I've forgotten to live my life? I mean, I have to take care of Lucas and Kel, and now Sean. They have school and sports, I have a job and need to have meals ready to keep on track for the… I drop my head and sigh. *Crap! Maybe I've*

SADIE GRUBOR

gotten a bit neurotic.

The heat of his body surrounds me before he says, "You're too beautiful to look so defeated." His whisper is close to my ear, each word caressing my skin.

"I'm just thinking," I whisper in response.

Escaped strands of hair are swept aside and his lips press against my exposed neck.

"I like your hair up," he states against my skin.

Squeezing my eyes shut tight, I hurdle my nerves, and ask, "What is this?"

He stills. "You mean us?"

Feeling warm and flush from embarrassment for asking, I can only nod.

Jackson moves and the breeze blows away the heat of him. I instantly miss it.

His long fingers trail down my arm until they find my hand. Lacing our fingers together, he pulls me away from the railing and around a small privacy wall. When I see the door to his room on the other side, I stop.

"Relax." He looks over his shoulder—his bare shoulder.

In fact, his torso is completely naked, every inky swirl, line, and jagged edge on display. Swallowing my nerves, I continue to follow him, taking in every inch of him. From his back to the black waist of his red boxer briefs, the colorful patterns decorating his legs all the way to his bare toes.

Thinking back to our night together, I try to recall whether his penis is the only place he's not tattooed. He stops inside his room, bringing me out of the memories of his naked body, and drops my hand.

His eyes search my face, making me self-conscious. I look away and see photos on top of his dresser. The weight of his stare follows my move to the pictures.

The first image is a gorgeous woman with a small boy at her side.

"Me and my mom," he explains. "Nicholas took the picture."

Looking back over my shoulder, I give a small smile.

"Sorry. I shouldn't just go through your things." I put the picture down.

"It's okay." He shrugs, coming over and picking up the photos.

I step back, letting him collect the photos.

"Come here," he says, motioning for me to follow him to the bed.

Taking a seat, he pats the mattress next to him.

Hesitantly, I sit down, arms holding my stomach to keep the butterflies from escaping through my belly button.

Why am I so damn nervous? I've seen him naked, had sex with him, and bathed him in an ice bath for God's sake.

"This was the first time I met Nicholas." Jackson holds up the photo. "He scared me."

"Why?" I move my eyes from the picture to his face, taking in his profile. The long, lean lines of his face. The graceful way his neck curves.

He shrugs. "I didn't know him and wasn't used to a man being around." His eyes meet mine. "As far back as I can remember, it was always just me and mom. Sort of like you and Luke."

"Luke?" I raise one brow and fight a smile.

"Lucas is nice, baby, but Luke is manlier." He grins. "We had a conversation during video games."

"Oh, really?" The smile wins, spreading over my lips.

Dropping the picture, his hand cups my face, tracing my smile with his thumb.

"I totally get the expression 'the face that launched a thousand ships'." His face comes close.

"What?" I breathe, my eyes staring at his mouth as it inches closer and closer.

"You're my Helen of Troy. The face I would launch a full-scale attack to possess." The intensity with which he says this makes me inhale sharply.

His lips are so close, I can taste his breaths.

"Your sobriety?" I whisper, pulling back a bit.

In a fluid motion, he twists. The pictures slipping to the floor

SADIE GRUBOR

catch my attention for a split moment before he lays me back on the bed. With his body over mine, he holds his weight on his forearms.

My breathing increases, my chest rising and falling like my nipples are reaching out for his touch.

"You are my sobriety."

His mouth comes to mine, his lips pressing gently, lovingly, making their mark.

I wrap my arms around his shoulders, one hand sliding into his hair.

A gasp escapes when he moves his lips over my cheek, my chin, and down my neck, his tongue touching and tasting my skin.

His body shifts and he slides one hand over my shoulder, collarbone, and cups one breast. My entire body sighs at the contact, and when his knee presses between my legs, I open without hesitation.

Jackson crawls down my body, pushing my tank top over my head and kissing every inch of bare skin along the way. The tip of his tongue touches my right nipple and a jolt of need shoots through me. I fist his hair, holding him to my breast. He takes me into his mouth and sucks just hard enough to make me tense while his free hand rolls my other nipple between his inked fingers.

I force my eyes open and glance down. The contrast of his decorated skin next to my pale white, his mouth sucking on my sensitive flesh, and him looking up at me from under his lashes, pulls a moan from the deepest part of me. I lift my hips, but only achieve a press against his stomach.

"Why are you so tall?" I whine, still pressing my hips against him, wanting the feel of his hard length against me.

The vibration of his laugh makes me moan once more before he continues his decent.

With his legs taking his weight, he fists the side of my shorts and looks up at me, waiting for permission.

My muscles clench in anticipation and I lift my hips.

Pressing his lips against my bare stomach, he pulls the shorts down my legs. He stands at the end of the bed, taking my shorts over my feet. Throwing them to the floor, his hands grip the waist of his boxer briefs and shove them down.

I allow my eyes to travel over all of him and bite my lip. His lean swimmer's build towers over me.

He turns and walks to the dresser. Propping up on my elbows, I watch his muscles flex, making the images on his skin look like they're dancing. Even the flex of his ass is like a moving painting.

Jackson catches me staring and smiles, returning to the end of the bed with condoms in his hand. My eyes drop to his hard cock jutting out.

Yep, inked everywhere but there.

The dim light of the bedroom catches on his piercing as he slips the condom over his length. I can feel his eyes on me, but can't look away from his hands. I spread my legs, slide one hand down my body, and touch myself for him.

"Fuck, there you are, my little charmer," he growls.

Kneeling on the bed, his hands press against the inside of my thighs, opening me further for his viewing pleasure. He licks his bottom lip and I drop my head back.

"Spread yourself." His command brings my head up.

With my first and middle finger, I part my wet lips.

He inches forward, still on his knees, and lines up with my entrance.

"Put me inside you." His words are strained, struggling to keep composure.

Gripping him with my wet fingers, I guide him in slowly. The way he fills me, stretches me, and the rub of the piercing sends a direct pulse to my clit. I pull my hand back and he grabs my wrist, thrusting my fingers into his mouth and sucking to the same rhythm he thrusts his hips.

"Oh, God," I cry out, already feeling my body climb toward release.

Jackson releases my fingers and pushes my hand between us.

"Feel us, Liza," he commands, leaning forward.

Keeping his weight on one bent elbow, our joined hands feel his smooth hard shaft slide out and in, out and in, covered in my arousal.

His bowed body moves in rapid succession, pushing me closer to the edge of bliss.

Burying his head against my neck, he asks, "Can you feel me?"

"Yes," I pant, nodding.

"Do you feel how we fit?"

"Yes," I groan.

His words, the slick feel of his cock against my fingers, knowing the wetness is from my pussy, builds my impending release into a burning coil.

"Do you still question what we are?" he asks, accentuating his question by licking my collarbone.

For a moment, my desire wanes. *Sex? Is he saying we're just fucking?*

"Liza?" Concern fills his expression and he stills inside me. "Where'd you go?"

My eyes find his and I shake my head, looking away.

"Fuck," he growls, removing his hand from between us and grabbing my chin.

I smell the mixture of us on his fingers and struggle not to let tears form.

"No, baby. That's not what I meant." His hand slips over my cheek until his fingers dig into the hair behind my ear. He drops his head to my chest, pressing a kiss between my breasts.

Taking a deep breath, I will away my tears.

"It's fine." I try to look away, but he won't allow me. His face comes close and he presses his lips to mine for just a moment.

"I thought you felt it," he whispers against my mouth. "This connection."

He presses his lips to mine once more before lowering his head to my chest again.

"How we fit." A kiss is planted between my breasts. "That you understand the way you make me feel." His hips pull back, just a bit. "I guess I thought you might feel the same."

His sigh warms my skin.

"I didn't mean for you to think this is just fucking," he growls low, bringing his face back to mine. "If that's what I wanted, Liza, I could go anywhere."

The anger in his voice startles me, but the fear and insecurity residing in his eyes quells my fear.

He's...scared, so vulnerable. He's putting a piece of himself out there...for me. Taking my family into his home in an attempt to protect us from the media. This man is reaching for something, and I think it's me.

Cupping his face in my hands, I bring it to mine. Taking his mouth in a slow, but claiming kiss, I shift my hips. He pushes back into me, growing harder, and stokes the low burn back into flames with slow, possessing thrusts.

His body presses entirely onto mine, our kiss deepening. He pulls my hands from his face and stretches my arms over my head, lacing our fingers. The thrusts increase and I break the kiss to catch my breath.

"This is us, Liza. Entwined, feeling, fitting together," he moans against my cheek. "Do you feel me now?"

"Yes, Jackson." I lift my knees higher against his sides.

Hearing his name, he increases his pace. The sound of his hips slapping against the back of my thighs fill my ears. Orgasmic bliss rolls through me with a scorching vibration. His mouth covers mine, catching the guttural moan escaping my lips.

The drive of his hips comes harder, faster. My body jerks beneath his determination to possess.

Breaking away from his mouth, I turn my head and gasp for air. He pants against my cheek, the wetness of his lips dampening my skin. His fingers tighten on mine, pressing the back of my hands deeper into the mattress. I squeeze back.

Driving harder, his mouth opens around my jaw. The graze of his teeth and tongue against my skin causes my clit to throb in tribute to my recent orgasm.

"Jackson," I practically sing his name.

"That's it." He pumps once, twice, and locks his body against mine, grinding.

His mouth releases my jaw, kissing over my cheek until he reaches my mouth. Our bodies still locked together, he frees my hands and rolls, taking me with him.

Long, inked fingers trail over my back and cup my ass, grinding me down before slapping my ass cheek. Squealing, I pull away from the kiss and stare at him in surprise. He shrugs, grinning.

He grabs my hips, causing me to squeak again, and moves me onto the bed before he rolls off and walks to the bathroom. I watch the way his tattoos move with his fluid movements.

Breathing deep and exhaling, I lie on my stomach and grab my clothes from the floor, revealing the forgotten photos. I bunch my shorts and tank in one hand, collecting the photographs with my free hand.

The picture of Jackson and his mother is on top. Even in the dim light, I can make out the vulnerability on little Jackson's face. The same exposed look I saw on Jackson, the man, tonight.

The shift of the bed jostles me and I almost drop the pictures. He cages me under his body, his stomach muscles tensing against my ass. The long length of his arms settling on each side of me.

"You don't need these." His hand snakes over my shoulder.

I tense, thinking he's going to take the pictures out of my hand, but he grabs my clothes and flings them to the other side of the room. He settles against me, the warmth of his mouth pressing to my shoulder. A shiver runs down my spine and I feel him smile.

Slipping the top photo to the back of the pile, I study the two boys. One is clearly Jackson. A guitar strapped on him, he's grinning and giving devil horns. The other boy sits behind a piano, hunched and scowling.

"He looks so sad," I whisper.

"Christopher was never really in a right place until he found Mia." His response is nonchalant as he tugs on the hair that had fallen loose. "Can you pull your hair back up?"

"Huh?" I heard what he said, but the request confuses me.

"Your hair. Can you pull it back up?" he requests.

"Oh. Yeah."

I set the pictures on the floor and bend my head over the edge of the bed. Pulling out the hair tie, I collect my hair, twist, and secure the sloppy bun.

"Much better." He kisses the back of my neck.

Picking the photos up once more, I flip to the next photo.

"That's the day we signed with Nobil," Jackson says, describing the image of The Forgotten and two older men standing in front of a wall of gold and platinum records.

"Your hair's really grown out," I say after seeing the super cropped bleached style he typically wears.

"Yeah," he responds against my shoulder. "I've been thinking of letting the bleached part grow out."

"Is your hair naturally brown?" I flip through more pictures, finding mostly his mother.

"Same as Mom's."

His warmth and weight disappears. I twist, curious to see what he's doing.

"Come here." He lies back on the pillows, putting his hand out to me.

Keeping the pictures in my hand, I push up and go to him. When I'm in reach, he pulls me into his side. Settling me in the crook of his arm, he takes the pictures out of my hand and spends the next twenty minutes narrating the small parts and moments of his life in a slideshow.

Jackson

Even at this ungodly hour, when the sun hasn't fully risen, the warmth of her back against my chest and the softness of her ass pressed into me is something I want to feel every morning. I'm fucking spooning and it feels like goddamn home. I tighten my arm and pull us closer. She mumbles something I can't make out, but doesn't wake.

Nuzzling her neck, I inhale. Smelling *me* on her skin is the hottest fucking perfume this woman could ever wear. And underneath that lies the rawest essence of her—a fragrance impossible to describe. If warmth, soft, and heaven have a smell, she's every one of them. And it's mixed with me. *All. Fucking. Over. Her.*

My dick hardens, every growing inch gliding along the smooth skin at the back of her thigh. Reflexively, my hips press forward, my balls tightening.

Sliding my hand over her stomach and between her thighs, I slip one finger through her lips. One swirl around her clit and she moan softly. Second swirl, her ass pushes back into me. My cock jumps, smacking against her leg.

I slip one finger inside, finding her so wet and ready, even in sleep. My name falls from her lips in a part growl, part sigh.

I pull my finger out and grip the inside of her thigh, my slick fingers sliding on her skin. Lifting her leg onto mine, my fingers dig into her flesh. I position and plunge deep.

Her body arches, giving me ease of access. Releasing her leg, I palm my way over her hip, stomach, until I can cup her breast.

"Oh, God," she moans, placing her hand over mine.

Bending my knee a bit more pushes her legs open wider. I can get deeper, go harder.

"Fuck, Jackson," she whimpers, meeting my thrusts. "Harder. Fuck me harder," she demands.

And I lose my fucking shit.

Tightening my hold on her tit, my pelvis slams against her ass. My balls tighten and tingle. My dick throbs in anticipation of the release, a burn at the base of my spine growing, wanting to break free and consume my body in flames.

Liza's hand leaves mine, sliding down until she touches between her legs. Lifting my head from her neck, I watch her circle and rub her clit.

"Come on, baby. Get yourself there," I groan, watching her

fingers increase in speed.

The sight is too much. I look away, burying my face in her neck once more, hoping I can hold off from coming too soon.

Shifting my hips, I thrust and grind.

"Yes," she calls, her fingertips brushing against my cock. "Yes, I—" The cry of her release cuts her off.

Moving my hand from her breast, I push her legs closed and pump fast and hard to release.

"Fuck," I growl against her neck, grazing my teeth over the skin where it meets her shoulder.

Breathing heavily, I wrap her in my arms and hold tight.

Liza squirms, pulling on my too-tight grip.

"Sorry," I whisper, easing my hold.

She doesn't say a word, just lays her arm over mine. Entwining our fingers, we hold hands against her chest as she falls back to sleep. The beat of her heart is a bassline etched in my soul.

Giving her a light squeeze, I take a deep breath. Exhaling, I've never felt so right. Where I should be fucking scared of letting this woman in, it feels like nothing I've experienced. Not with anyone. *Fucking Chris is right. This is my one, my Mia.*

Entering the kitchen on a mission for coffee, I stop and take in the set up at the kitchen bar. Sid sits with her back to me, headphones covering her ears. Two large screens in front of her, along with a mini laptop, two cell phones, a keyboard, three black boxes, and a slew of wires. Random numbers and images flash across one screen while another shows what looks like audio software.

Shuffling into the kitchen, I go straight for the dark, delicious ambrosia. Lifting the sleek pot to my nose, I inhale and drop my head back in a silent prayer to the coffee gods.

"You're welcome." Sid's voice startles me. Not because I

forgot she was there, just because I didn't expect her to speak.

I turn around, coffee still in hand, and she looks me over, unabashedly. I suddenly feel like I should've thrown on a shirt with the black basketball shorts.

The headphones now around her neck, she takes her hands from the keyboard and crosses them over her chest. When her eyes make it back up to my face, she raises her brow.

"What exactly should I be thanking you for?" I ask, reaching toward the counter on my left and picking up a mug.

She uncrosses her arms and removes the headphones completely.

"If I hadn't stayed on the couch till the wee hours of the morning, my cousin wouldn't be naked and in your bed right now." Elbows to the table, she puts her chin in one hand. "She *is* naked, right? Please tell me she's naked and preferably covered in love bites with aches in all the right places."

Unsure how to respond to that, I busy myself by returning the coffee pot back inside the machine. Since I take my coffee black, I'm out of further distractions.

"Do your tattoos cover your entire body?"

Her question brings me back to face her.

"Yes." I step around the kitchen island and stand on the other side of the bar. "And thank you." Sipping the coffee, I close my eyes, reveling the flavor.

"You should be thankful, 'cause my neglected lady parts aren't seeing any action in this deal." She clears her throat and continues. "I have two questions," she states, continuing before I can object. "Did she come to you or you to her?"

For a moment, I'm not sure this is information I should share. The look on Sid's face tells me there is no damn way she will be ignored. Setting the mug on the counter, I lean onto my hands and level my eyes on the interrogating brunette.

"We sort of met on the balcony." I study her face upon my response.

She sighs, rolling her eyes. Then, in an exaggerated move, she throws herself back on the stool.

"You went to her," she groans.

"I didn't say—"

"Look," she cuts me off, "I know my cousin, probably better than anyone else."

"And?" I press.

Hell, the more I learn about Liza, the fucking hotter. Maybe this is a sneaky way to get the information, but I'll be damned if she'll be walking out my fucking door. At least...not without her hand in mine.

"And the woman you know isn't the girl I grew up with." She shrugs.

Grasping my mug in one hand, I raise my brow in question and take another sip.

"The girl I grew up with was carefree and crazy." Sid grins, her eyes getting a far off look. Shaking her head, she continues. "You don't get pregnant at fifteen without a bit of a rebellious streak."

Slipping from the stool, she rounds the breakfast bar and goes to the coffee maker. She pours herself a mug and adds sugar and milk before returning to her seat.

"And the woman in my bed?" I coax her to go on.

Eyeing me thoroughly, she blows over her mug, sips, and sets it down in front of her. Elbows on the counter again, she narrows her eyes.

"The woman in there plans just about every second of her life. Having Lucas and coming out here, her dream was stripped away. At least, that's what she believes." She takes another drink.

"You want the rebellious girl back?" I question, uncertain where she's going.

She shakes her head. "No, Jackson. I want Liza. That's not her." She thumbs over her shoulder.

"I'm not saying I don't understand, but if she's happy with how things are why—"

Sid snorts. "She's not happy. Liza is merely surviving."

She leans her body further forward, and instinctually, I lean in, too.

"Haven't you seen the difference when she performs? I mean, with the way you watch her, you have to have seen it."

I straighten. She's absolutely fucking right. Liza comes alive under a spotlight, in front of a crowd. What I saw on stage yesterday evening...that was Liza, my fucking snake charmer.

"I see you get it." She grins over her mug. "I think you help bring it out in her."

She tilts her head.

"Is that so?"

"Yeah." She nods. "But if you fucking hurt her again, don't think for one second I won't ruin you. You heard some of my past last night. I've never been arrested or caught, so don't press your luck." The gleam in her eye and the wicked sneer on her face surprises me, but it's the 'hurt her again' part that feels like a knife in my chest.

This girl is fucking scary.

"Warning received."

Her face goes neutral and she takes a deep breath. After exhaling, she nods, settling back on the stool, completely relaxed.

Really goddamn scary.

"Alright, now that we got that straight, question number two."

"Shoot." I half-grin, putting my mug to my lips and take a larger drink now that it's cooled.

"Do you have ink in your pen, Jackson?" Her eyes drop to my waist.

The coffee goes down the wrong pipe and I spit what remains onto the counter.

I gasp for air, coughing so hard my chest aches. Sid sits, smiling and sipping at her coffee.

"I'll take that as a solid yes." She sets her mug onto the counter, picks up the headphones, and puts them back over her ears.

I stumble to the sink, spitting and coughing. Looking back once in her direction, she's completely engrossed in her screens.

A heavy hand slaps my back.

"You okay, man?" Kel asks from behind me.

"I," cough, "think so." My eyes stay on Sid.

Kel takes stock of my face and then looks at Sid.

"Ah," he says, nodding and smiling, "I see. Sid threaten you?"

I shift my eyes to him, keeping my mouth shut. Maybe I shouldn't discuss anything with her family at all.

"By the look on your face, she totally did." Kel pulls open the fridge door and bends down, pulling out a white jug. "She's totally serious, too."

It's not a threat, not from Kel. He's just confirming what I already know.

"But she means well," he adds, patting my shoulder.

"She's fucking scary," I whisper. Keeping my eyes on her, I make sure she doesn't read my lips or some crazy shit like that.

Kel shrugs, snagging an apple from a bowl on the kitchen island.

"Yeah, but it's cool as hell to hear about the stuff she can do with a computer." He grins, leaning against the island and taking a bite of the red fruit. Around his mouthful, he continues, "Like, right now, she's working on that Kristy girl. I wouldn't want to be her. She messed with the wrong person."

"Liza?" I ask, though I already know the answer.

"They're more like sisters than cousins."

I nod, understanding.

"Is there only fruit to eat?" Luke's sleepy voice pulls my attention from Sid.

"Hey, Luke. I'm not sure." Turning, I open the kitchen cabinets, finding them completely stocked. *Score!* "Who want's pancakes?" I pull out a box of mix and grin.

Chapter Twenty

Eliza

I roll to my back, stretching my limbs. Pleasant aches throb in different locations of my body. Propping up on my elbows, I look around the sunlit room.

The bedding is all over the floor, except for the sheet tangled around me. The balcony door is wide open, but I can still smell sex lingering in the room. Dropping back, I cover my eyes with my palms.

What the hell am I doing?

I kick the sheet off my body and stand. Feeling a damn stickiness between my legs, my fingers instinctively reach down. Bringing my hand up, I sigh.

Damn it. Did the condom break?

Then, last night's round two flashes into mind.

Shit. No condom. Well, that's just fucking great.

Wrapping the sheet around my body, I walk to the balcony door, silently calculating when I had my last period.

A week and a half, give or take.

Entering my temporary room, I see the bed has been slept in and groan internally.

I'm going to be interrogated.

A long time ago, I learned it's best to just tell her everything and get it over with. Because eventually, you would tell her—she'd make sure of it. Like back in eighth grade, when I wouldn't spill who gave me a 'secret' love note. Sid spent our lunch period walking to each guy, pointing down at them and screaming across the cafeteria if he was the guy. If I didn't love her so much and know everything she did was never in malice, I may be serving a life sentence right now for murder.

Dropping the sheet, I grab denim capris, two layering tank tops, and underclothes on my way to the bathroom.

After washing away the evidence of last night, I dry off and dress. I comb my hair and dig in my cosmetic bag for my anti-frizz serum. Untangled and scrunched, the waves start to form. I pull a hair tie off the end of my brush and clip it around my wrist. Examining my face in the mirror, I grab my face lotion, which also helps fight acne—the stage makeup is starting to do a number on my skin. I mentally make a note to arrange an appointment with the dermatologist and a spa.

I walk down the hall with bare feet, my steps silent, though the noise from the kitchen would've masked any noise I could've made. Rounding a corner, I freeze next to the dining room table.

Sid sits in an electronics haven, Kel's taking cups out of a cabinet, and Jackson stands at the stove, shirtless, flipping a pancake. Lucas and Sean stand on either side of him, fists full of something I can't make out.

"Okay, drop them in," Jackson instructs.

The boys bring a fist over the pan and drop chocolate chips. Jackson flips the pancakes.

"Grab the plate," he orders. The boys rush to get a platter of stacked pancakes and he moves the now-done food onto the plate with the others.

"Morning, sis," Kel calls out, bringing cups to the dining room table. "Breakfast is almost done." His head nods toward the stove.

Looking back at Jackson, his eyes meet mine. A smile spreads across his face.

"Morning, babe." He licks something off his thumb, causing my pulse to race.

"Good morning," I say, my words just above a whisper.

The kitchen scene shakes me. I don't hate it—not at all. I like it too much. Nerves assault my stomach.

"Mom," Lucas comes toward me, a dish of butter in his hand, "Jack's making pancakes." He slips the plate onto the table next to me and wraps his arms around my waist.

I place my hands on his head and snuggle close to him.

"He let us help." Sean carries a bottle of syrup and forks, a super large grin on his face.

"Well..." I swallow the emotion, "that's awesome."

Lucas pulls back, smiling up at me.

"Sit down. I'll get you a plate."

We release each other and I sit, watching my son. I'm not sure if it's confidence or just excitement, but there's something new about him. When he goes to get plates, he grins wide and adoringly at Jackson, who winks at him.

My stomach flips, worry tampering any appetite I had. I shouldn't have come here. He can't get used to this...this life. This isn't our life. It's a temporary illusion to what some people have— not us. Jackson may like having sex with me and enjoy my family, but I don't think he's looking to stick around with a mother of two, and Kel makes three.

"Get out of your head," Sid says, pulling me back to the present.

"I'm not awake yet." I shake my head, looking at the plate Lucas puts in front of me.

"Yeah, okay." She sits in the chair across the table from me. "So, how was your night? Was the bed comfortable?" She smirks.

My eyes widen.

"It was fine," I say through clenched teeth.

"Only fine?" Jackson pulls out the chair next to me. "Well, looks like I'll have to fix that, won't I?"

Grinning, he pulls in close to the table.

"That's not—"

Before I can finish, he grips under my chair and pulls. Our thighs practically share a seat. My head snaps to Lucas. He's forking three pancakes onto the plate in front of him. The grin he wears overjoys me. *He's so happy.*

I lean into Jackson, and whisper, "Thank you."

Straightening, I grab my glass and the jug of orange juice in reach.

"For?" Jackson leans close to my side, his hand coming to my thigh.

I swallow down the not-appropriate-for-breakfast feelings he inspires and pour a half-glass before looking at him.

"He looks so happy," I answer, keeping my eyes on Lucas.

"They're both good kids." His hand leaves my thigh and he turns his attention to the table. "Let's eat."

Yeah, he's happy now, but when this all ends, it will crush him.

Stomach full of chocolate chip pancakes, the boys lounge on the couch watching some annoying cartoon. Kel loads the last plate in the stainless steel dishwasher before excusing himself for a shower. Sid sits at her geek station, eyes shifting and fingers dancing across her keyboard.

Wanting to check in with my caseworker regarding Sean's case, I lean against the kitchen island, my cell to my ear. I leave a message and exhale heavily. Setting my phone on the counter, I pick up the coffee Jackson poured before going to shower. Knowing I need to have a talk with him about last night and this morning, I rub my forehead, not looking forward to the conversation.

"This bitch is cray cray." Sid's outburst draws me away from thinking about the lack of condom use and my son's attachment to Jackson.

"What?" I walk around the island and stand across from Sid. I put my hand up about six inches from the back of the monitors. "These things are putting out some heat."

"Yeah, they've been running since five this morning." She shrugs and taps the keys before pointing to the screen. "She must have no idea how to clear her phone."

Sid snorts, shaking her head.

"Her phone?" I choke on the question. "You stole her phone?" My voice raises, drawing Lucas and Sean's attention.

"Nooooo." Sid puts on her innocent face.

"So, you don't have her phone?" I cross my arms over my chest, raising one brow accusingly.

"I didn't say that." She grins. "I said *I* didn't steal it," she clarifies.

"Then how—?"

"Did you know Kat has really fast hands?"

"Kat?"

"Hushed Mentality Kat." Sid gives me a duh look.

"She stole the phone?" I ask in a breath.

Sid stops typing and turns, meeting my eyes.

"Kristy left her phone on a table at a club last night and Kat happened to find it for her." She smiles sweet and guilty. "Una's going to let her know it was found."

I open my mouth, but Sid continues.

"Once, I finish…" she teeters her head back and forth, "checking to make sure it wasn't damaged."

Keeping a straight face, she looks back to her screens.

Bringing my elbows down on the counter, I bury my face.

"Oh my God," I groan. "You're going to jail and I don't have bail money."

"Who's going to jail?" Jackson enters the room in full freshly-showered swagger.

"Me." Sid raises her hand.

"The FBI?" he asks, rounding the kitchen bar.

Coming up behind me, he places his hands on the counter, caging me against it.

"I don't think she has that kind of influence." Sid doesn't look up from the screen when she answers. "But, she definitely has an active social life." She turns her head toward us. "In her vagina."

"Sounds about right," Jackson mumbles into the side of my head.

I stiffen. *Great, I've slept with a guy who fucked a whore—repeatedly.*

I open my mouth to tell him we need to talk, but Sid goes on about Kristy.

"She has a video on here of you," she says, her focus over my shoulder on Jackson.

"The stuff that leaked?" He moves closer to me.

"Uh, no." Sid looks like she expects some sort of explanation.

"That's the past," Jackson states with a touch of menace in his voice.

His arms come around me and squeeze.

"It better be." She uses her first and middle finger, pointing to her eyes, and then to him.

"Anyhow, she may not have anything to prove she's the source of the leak, *but* she's got shit on here that wouldn't exactly keep her sweet girl model facade. She also has stuff on a few other people who would be less than thrilled to know it's right at her fingertips." Sid turns a broad grin on us.

It's her huntress look—her prey is in sight and she's ready to pounce. As much as I dislike this woman, hate the fact that she unleashed chaos on my son without a second thought, that look in Sid's eye makes me fear for her. Just for a moment.

"Like what?" Jackson releases me, moving around the bar for a better view of the screens.

"Like this." Sid clicks a couple keys and a slideshow of pictures begin.

Kristy partying with different celebrities isn't a big deal, but the married ones snorting a line off her bare breast is another thing. Then there are the selfies with known drug dealers.

"And this," Sid says as the photos conclude. Another tap on the keyboard and a video pops up.

"Is that..?" I gasp, watching one of Hollywood's most sought after leading men making out in a dark corner with another man. "I didn't know he's gay."

"I'm pretty sure he doesn't want anyone to know." Jackson's voice is flat, his expression stoic. "That bitch would out him the minute she found a way for it to benefit her."

"Then, there's this." Sid clicks and brings up another video.

This time, it's Kristy having sex with three men. One heavily tattooed body catches my attention and nausea threatens until the guy's face comes into focus. *Not Jackson.*

"Who the fuck is videoing?" Jackson leans closer to the

screen, disgust on his face.

"Wait for it." Sid sits back, crossing her arms over her chest.

Kristy releases a dick from her mouth, smiles at the camera, and reaches out her hand. The image shakes for a minute until someone places the phone on a stable surface.

A bare ass fills the screen, the person walking toward the bed. When the woman drops to the bed, Jackson stiffens.

"Shut the fuck up." He twists his neck to look at Sid. "Is that—?"

"Yep. It's Felicia Ferrah, the notorious Hollywood Madame." Sid smiles. "Oh, it gets better." She half talks, half laughs.

Felicia joins the group and I look away, unable to watch any longer.

"Can we fast forward?" Jackson asks.

"What? Why?" Sid loves her porn.

I sigh loudly.

"Okay," she grumbles, tapping a key. "Here it is."

The video resumes at normal speed just in time to see Kristy passed out on the bed and a now-dressed man hand a stack of cash over to Felicia.

"Did he just pay her?" I ask on a gasp. "Kristy sold herself to—"

Sid's head is already shaking. "This video was sent to her from another IP address. I don't think she knew the deal was going down and fifty bucks says I trace that IP address to Felicia." She shrugs. "But now we have it and can do with it what we will."

"Send it to the media vultures. Post it online," Jackson growls.

"Wait!" I protest.

Both of their heads turn to me.

"I know she's done some bad shit, but come on."

Sid gives me an are-you-fucking-crazy look. Jackson's eyes narrow.

"Fuck her," he snaps.

My eyes shift to Lucas and Sean. They are still staring at the TV, so I don't think they heard everything. Jackson follows my gaze.

"Sorry," he says softly. "She deserves whatever happens to her."

"Yeah, she deserves karma kicking her in the butt." I nod, agreeing. "I don't think we need to post something like this. She was being used."

"She used me." He points to his chest. "Then she used you to get to me." His finger turns to me.

"This makes us just like her." I wrap my arms around my middle and squeeze. "I'm not like her."

"Damn it," Sid grumbles. "No, you aren't like her. Why do you have to make sense?" She gives me a half-smile.

"Then walk away, 'cause I'm doing it." Jackson's voice is hard, ruthless.

"Fine." A cold edge seeps into my one word response.

Turning on my heels, I start to walk away, pausing only to say one last thing. "You aren't the man I thought you were."

In my temporary bedroom, I find my bag and start packing things I need.

"What are you doing?" His voice startles me.

I spin, grabbing my chest.

"You scared me."

"What's this?" He steps into the room, his presence filling the space.

"I'm packing stuff I need." Turning back to my task, I place my makeup kit inside.

"You aren't leaving." His hand fists the bag at the open zipper.

"What's wrong with you?" I tug on the bag.

"So, you're just going to walk out because we don't agree on something?" He yanks the bag away, causing my body to jolt.

Surprised by his action, I right myself and take a step away.

"I guess you aren't the woman I thought you were," he snaps, tossing the bag to the center of the bed.

My shock contorts into burning anger.

"You're such an ass," I state through clenched teeth.

"Who's the one running?" He steps closer. "What's wrong? This," he motions between us, "doesn't fit in your careful plans and schedule?"

The barb cuts deep, causing a lump to form in my throat.

"I don't know why I thought you would be different than the rest."

Tears fill my eyes.

"You want to pack your shit? Go ahead." Curling his lip, he turns and sits roughly on the bed.

Then, it all clicks.

He thinks I'm packing everything. That I'm leaving him.

"Jackson?" I say, my voice softer.

"What?" he snaps.

I take a deep breath and close the distance between us, putting my hand on his face. He pulls away from my touch and I drop my hand, clenching it at my side instead.

"It's my work bag. The bag I take to the club."

His head jerks up, confusion and guilt lining his face.

"For the club?" His brow furrows.

"I take it with me to carry my make-up, clothes, and some of my personal costumes."

"Fuck," he sighs.

Snaking his long arm around my waist, he pulls me to him, his face pressing into my stomach. Lifting his face, he looks up at me.

"I'm so sorry, Liza." Worry creases his eyes. "I keep fucking up and overreacting." He presses his forehead against me.

"Maybe we should just end this now before someone gets hurt," I whisper, the words making my chest ache.

His arms tighten around me and he shakes his head.

"You didn't feel me last night," he says, laughing humorlessly.

Setting me away from him, he stands from the bed.

I raise my head, meeting his eyes.

"Last night...I felt you, but we can't stay naked in bed all the time." Fighting the urge to reach out and touch him, I clench my fists at my sides.

"That's what you think I mean?" He steps forward, causing me to take steps back. "You think I mean physically feel me?" He shakes his head, laughing without humor again.

Grabbing my hand, he puts it to his chest.

"Do you feel that?" His eyes are as intense as his question

"Yes," I whisper.

"This," he pats my hand on his chest, over his heart, "this is for you."

He moves us until my back is against the wall.

"You own it."

I shake my head.

"Yes, you do, Liza."

"No. You hardly know me. Aside from sex," I add before he can make some smooth remark.

He smiles.

"You just blew up, thinking I was leaving. That doesn't scream healthy," I add.

His smile fades and he nods.

"I'm sorry." He releases my hand, but I leave it on his chest. "I came back here to say you were right and I wasn't going to send out that video. But I saw you packing things and I thought, after last night, you were just walking away from me."

"This is so much more complicated than walking away from last night."

His eyes search mine.

"It doesn't have to be." There's a plea in his voice that tugs at me.

"Lucas is getting attached to you." My chin wobbles and nose tingles.

"Good." His hand cups my face. "'Cause I like that kid."

Closing my eyes, I take a deep breath and lay it all out there.

"Jackson, it'll crush him when you leave."

"When I leave? When?" His thumb caresses my cheek. "Why does it have to be when?"

Everything rises to the surface in a hysterical girl moment.

"Because I'm a single mother of basically three boys, I take my clothes off for a living, and live my life with government assistance. You don't have any idea what you're getting, and when you do, you won't stick around."

Opening my eyes, a tear escapes, rolling over my cheek.

He blinks once, twice, and then laughs.

"It's not funny." I sniff.

"Oh, Charmer, it's fucking hilarious." He presses his body flush against mine, tilting my head up to him. "First, I'm not an idiot. I know with you comes three boys and a scary ass cousin who's like a sister to you. But newsflash, Liza, Kel's a man. And Luke and Sean are the coolest little dudes I've ever met. Second, I know what you do for a living and it's equally hot, mesmerizing, and amazing. So just get that shit out of your head right now. I met you in that club and sure as fuck don't deserve you if I demanded you quit. Baby, I don't give any fucks about the role you play on stage. Want to know why?"

His words put too much hope inside me. I swallow the emotions clogging my throat, but my nerves win out. I shake my head.

"No, I don't want to know."

He grins.

"Yes, you do." His mouth presses to my forehead before saying, "It's because your mine and your ass will be in my bed after the show. In fact, your ass will be mine in your dressing room, backseat of a car, elevators, hotel rooms, and any damn where else I can get in you."

"Oh," I squeak.

"Yeah, 'oh'."

His mouth slants over mine, pressing me into the wall. Breaking the kiss, I push at his chest until he straightens.

"We need to talk about last night," I say between pants of breath.

"What about it?" His free hand comes up and cups the other side of my face.

"You didn't use a condom," I announce, my words a broken

whisper.

His brow furrows just before his eyes widen.

"Shit. I'm sorry." His hands drop and he backs away. "I swear, I didn't do that shit on purpose."

Closing my eyes, I gather my courage, and say, "You've slept with Kristy."

"We used condoms. She was paranoid about pregnancy," he explains, rubbing the back of his neck.

"And the...the others?" I choke on the question.

"Condoms." The guilt and embarrassment are noticeable in his answer. "But I'll get tested. Anything you want."

I nod and drop the next bomb.

"I'm not on birth control," I rush out, my eyes still closed. "It was only once, so I doubt that it...that I could be pregnant, but you should know."

His hands grab the sides of my face again.

"Look at me. Please. Look. At. Me," he begs.

Slowly, I open my eyes.

The second his eyes find mine, he says, "I'm an asshole and didn't think. I'm sorry."

I nod, unable to speak without spilling tears of emotional exhaustion.

"Liza, honestly, I didn't do it on purpose."

Gripping his wrists, I nod. "S'okay."

"No, it's not." He presses his forehead to mine. "I'm always apologizing to you."

"Well, you fuck up a lot," I say, trying for humor.

It works. He plants his hands on the wall beside my head and starts chuckling, which grows into a full belly laugh. A smile breaks across my face and I start laughing, too.

After both of us calm and catch our breath, we stare at one another for a long moment. Jackson breaks the silence.

"You know I'm okay if you're pregnant, right?" His eyes don't leave mine.

The doorbell chimes through the penthouse.

This place has a doorbell?

I open my mouth to respond, but he continues. "I do have one condition."

"Condition?"

"You'll have to marry me." He shrugs.

"What?" I choke out.

"Hey, Jackson?" Sid's voice carries down the hall. "There are some people here for you."

Ignoring Sid's announcement, he continues.

"My mom didn't raise me to have a baby momma." He grins. "I'm afraid you're going to have to marry me or my death is on your conscience."

I shake my head. "You're joking."

"Guess we'll find out."

He places a quick kiss on my mouth before turning and walking out of the room.

"No, we won't!" I shout.

Bag finally packed, I carry it down the hall. Multiple voices grow louder the closer I come to the living space.

Dropping my things to the floor near the door, I continue forward and take in a room full of people. Both The Forgotten and Hushed Mentality fill the open space.

Christopher Mason sits on the couch with Mia Ryder in his lap and my son sits in a beanbag in front of them, gazing adoringly at her.

Oh, dear Lord. Could he be more obvious?

On the far end of the sofa, Jimmy Thompson sits on the edge, elbows on his knees. A very pregnant Serena lounges on the other side of Chris. She has at least three throw pillows around her and still looks uncomfortable. And then, to my surprise, Laney Trimball, Jackson's ex, sits on Serena's left.

Looking toward the kitchen, Kat Conway sits on a stool next to Sid and Kel, viewing the screens. I can only hope Sid isn't showing the homemade cell porn to my brother. And Jackson stands in the kitchen with a heavily muscled Elliott Brockman.

Elliott notices me first.

"There she is!"

I take a small step back as Elliott stalks toward me.

Christ, he's way bigger in person. Especially when he's charging toward you.

His large, muscled arm comes around my shoulders, guiding me to the couch.

"Girl, you shut that fucking show down!" he howls.

"What?" I laugh, his enthusiasm contagious.

"The website and voting lines blew up." Making an explosion sound, he raises his fist and flips his fingers out like his hand just blew up.

"Fat lot of good that does me." I continue to laugh.

"Doesn't matter." He shakes his head, stopping us in the middle of the room. "It was goddamn epic," he says with reverence, hugging me.

I stiffen.

"Quit molesting her." Jackson pulls him off.

"Christ," Elliott rolls his eyes, walking toward the sofa and pushing his large body between Serena and Laney.

"Hey," Laney squeals, scooting away before he smashes her into the couch.

He ignores her and puts an arm around Serena.

"He's going to be as bad as emo boy," Elliott finishes, pointing to Chris with his other hand.

"Shut the hell up," Chris retorts.

Mia smacks his leg, nodding toward Lucas and Sean.

Jackson wraps his arms around my waist.

I stiffen again, forcing myself not to look at Laney's reaction.

"Ignore the ape," he says before pressing his lips to my temple.

Guiding us to an open spot on the couch, I can't help but glance at Laney.

A smile adorns her delicate face, and I swear she seems jubilant. She catches my gaze and her smile grows larger, her eyes softer. She's pleased for Jackson.

I return the smile and allow Jackson to settle us onto the

sofa. He situates me against his side, spreading his arms out over the back.

"So, what are we doing tonight?" Elliott asks, looking at the group around the room.

"We could go to dinner?" Laney's suggestion sounds more like a question.

"Food is always good. Huh, baby?" Elliott leans into Serena and rubs her belly.

"It better not be some Sushi place." Serena narrows her eyes on Laney.

"I didn't even say a place," Laney defends.

"I've got a meeting this afternoon and then I'm going to Lux."

Twisting my neck, I look up at Jackson.

"You're coming to the club tonight?"

His arm slips off the back of the couch and around me.

"Of course." His brow furrows. "Why wouldn't I?"

Shrugging, I answer, "I just didn't know you were coming."

"I want to do that!" Elliott points at Jackson. "Can we go, too?" He turns pleading eyes on his wife.

"Do you need permission from your mommy?" Jimmy teases, sticking his bottom lip out.

Elliott grins wide at Jimmy. "Hey, if she'll breastfeed me, I'll call her mommy."

"You're sick," Jimmy laughs.

Serena drops her head back on the cushion and groans.

"Sick?" Elliott snorts. "Have you seen the size of these bad boys?"

His hand almost makes it to her breast, but Serena's head snaps up and she snatches his wrist.

"I will cut off your favorite body part before you can reach my boob," she threatens.

My boys burst into laughter, throwing themselves back on the bean bags. I bite my lip, trying not to giggle. Jackson's chest vibrates with his silent laugh.

"You never let me touch them anymore." Elliott sits back,

crossing his arms over his chest, pouting.

Everyone trying not to lose it, erupts into full fits of hilarity.

"How are you?" Bethany asks, grabbing me into a hug before I can even set my bag on the floor.

"I'm okay." I return the embrace with one arm. "It wasn't easy getting in here tonight."

She pulls away, but keeps her hands on my biceps.

"Yeah, they've been waiting all day for you to show up." She rolls her eyes. "They stopped just about everyone who came in through the front doors. Red won't send them away since it's free publicity." She gives an apologetic shrug.

"It's fine, but I'm keeping my fingers crossed for someone else to draw their scandal-obsessed attention. There has to be some affair going public soon, right?" I give her a hopeful glance.

She doesn't say anything else about the cameras or gossip writers blocking the entrance to Lux. Instead, she looks down my body and back up to my face.

"You look good." She nods her approval. "Jackson does a body good, I guess." Her brows wiggle over her eyes.

"Shut up," I laugh. She grins, releasing my arms.

I drop my bag to the floor and sit down to take out my things. Once my make-up, hair things, and paper towels are set up, I push out of my chair to peruse the costume rack.

"What costumes are needed tonight?"

"You don't honestly think you're working the kick-line," Red's voice startles me, "do you?" Walking straight to Bethany, he plants a quick kiss on the top of her head to avoid messing up her make-up.

"I don't know the set." I furrow my brow. "I'm sure I can improvise in the background."

Red shakes his head, settling into the worn couch like it's a throne.

"No fucking way, Liza. The crowd is going to be clamoring—and they're clamoring for you." He points a thick finger at me.

I rub my forehead, suddenly not so sure I want to face the masses tonight.

"Don't even try it," Red's order brings my attention back to him. "You aren't a quitter. I saw what you did on that show."

"I'm no longer on the show," I say with a sigh. "And, to be honest, I was walking away regardless."

Red just shrugs.

"Doesn't matter. You went out there and showed them all what I've caught a glimpse of every time I watch you perform." Pushing up from the loveseat, he closes the distance, leaving two feet between us. "You've been Miz Liz and now you've performed as Eliza Campbell."

He clasps my shoulder with one large hand.

"Now, it's time to show them Liza." Red drops his hand away. "Girl, you have so much awesome inside you. It's the reason you're my damn headliner."

Taking a deep breath, I will away the tears threatening to drown my eyes and straighten my spine.

"What's the set?"

A smile breaks the seriousness lining his face.

"That's my girl." Red nudges my arm with his fist.

Bethany squeals, clapping in her seat.

I spend the next hour letting Bethany and Nikki do my hair and make-up while I read lyrics and listen to recordings through headphones.

Chapter Twenty-One
Jackson

"You sure you don't want to join us?" I ask Dr. J one more time.

He nods, grinning. "Perhaps another time."

"Your loss." My cheeks ache from smiling.

"It's good to see you again," Dr. J says, turning serious.

"You just saw me a couple weeks ago." I furrow my brow.

He shakes his head.

"No, that wasn't you." He lifts his chin toward me. "This is you."

I rub the back of my head, feeling heat crawl up my neck.

"Don't fall for his sappy bullshit." Chris barges into the room.

"Sure, Christopher, come right in," Dr. J deadpans.

"I know I'm still your favorite." Chris settles into the chair where I sat talking with Dr. J moments before. Putting his hands behind his head, he forces a large, sarcastic smile. "Quit trying to make me jealous through Jack."

"And why would I want to make you jealous?" Dr. J inquires.

Oh, here we fucking go.

Chris scoffs, dropping his arms. "Why wouldn't you want to? Obviously you feel like you aren't getting the attention you deserve from me." Sitting up straight, he tilts his head, his expression turning serious. "Do you have abandonment issues, Dr. J?"

Groaning, I turn for the door.

"I'll wait out here."

"This won't take long," Chris assures. "Dr. J just needs to get a couple things off his chest and then I can get back to my regularly scheduled program."

"God, help me," Dr. J sighs. "Why do I put myself through

this?"

"Because you want me," is the last thing I hear before closing the sitting room door of the hotel suit Doc is utilizing today.

While I wait for Chris, I go through emails and messages on my phone. Julia sent an updated schedule for Hidden Talent. Curling my lip, I almost wish they would've removed me from the show. Reminding myself it's good for the band, I save the updates to my calendar and confirm with Julia.

Thirty minutes later, my emails aren't even halfway resolved. For a moment, I consider making Julia take care of them, then my mind drifts to Liza's dominating alpha female behavior with the girl.

Fuck. It was so hot.

The door opens and Chris exits, a scowl marring his face.

"What the hell's wrong with you?" I stand, slipping my phone into my pocket.

"Nothing," he growls, stomping out of the hotel suite.

"Well, alright then," I say to the empty room, following after the moody fucker.

On the elevator, Chris stays silent.

"Either drop the attitude or tell me what the hell is going on," I say impatiently.

"The doc doesn't approve of my wedding planning," he grumbles like a little kid.

Jesus, how does Mia put up with his ass?

"I didn't know you guys started planning," I say, keeping my tone light, hoping to improve the atmosphere.

The elevator pings its arrival and the doors slide open to the parking garage. A sleek black car waits.

"We didn't." He steps off the elevator and walks toward the car.

A driver slips out, coming around and opening the door.

"Wait, you just said—"

"Mia wants to wait. Said too much is going on and we need to let things settle down." He waves off the statement and slips into the car.

Crawling in behind him, I press for more information. "And?"

He gives me an incredulous look.

"And, that's bullshit! Our daughter needs her parents married," he barks. "So, I put a deposit down on a private island."

"Without talking to Mia about it?" I really, really try to give him my best are-you-fucking-insane look.

"She loves the beach." He throws his arms up. "I'll tell her about it and then we can just get this shit moving along as it should." He crosses his arms over his chest.

"Did you pick the date without her, too?"

"Of course not," he scoffs. "She can pick a date within the week I've reserved the island."

"How very thoughtful of you." I suck on my lip ring to prevent myself from laughing.

"I know." He nods, putting his head back on the seat.

RIP Christopher Mason. You are so fucking dead.

After watching Hush rehearse on the theater stage for their Hidden Talent appearance, we spent some time chatting with Gemma, Big Kam, and Zarek. With the tension between Gemma and Zarek still at level nuclear, I tried my best to keep them separated. And she wouldn't elaborate further on the reason.

Noticing the time, I stand to go.

"I'm going to get over to the club," I announce.

"I thought we all were going?" Elliott looks around the room.

"Seriously? You're all coming?" I knew Elliott was on board, but that didn't mean everyone else was.

"What club?" Big Kam raises his brow.

"Lux Hedonica," I explain.

"Oh, shit, that's where your girl performs, right?"

"Yeah." I can't keep the smile off my face.

My girl. That's right, my fucking girl.

"Damn, boy, I'm so down." Kam rubs his hands together.

"Raise hands if you're going," Elliott states, raising his hand.

"We aren't in fucking school." Chris rolls his eyes before

turning to Mia. "You wanna go?"

She nods. "I've never seen a burlesque show and this sounds pretty epic."

Looks like everyone is going. I pull out my phone and place a call to Red, hoping he has room for all of us.

The club is surrounded by cameras and reporters, as expected. The minute we step out of the cars, the lights flash and questions start.

"Jackson, are you here to see Liza?"

"Mia, when's your wedding?"

And before Serena climbs out of the car. "Elliott, does Serena know you're out watching girls strip?"

"I made him come," she announces after Ell helps her from the car.

The crowd roars with laughter, snapping picture after picture.

"Laney, are you trying to get Jackson back?"

The question makes my step falter. I look back over my shoulder for her answer.

All she does is grin, and say, "I'm here to watch Liza perform."

At that moment, things click together in my chest like I just figured out the jigsaw puzzle of life. Things are good, very good. And this is so fucking right, it's scary.

Inside the club, the guys and girls have the same reaction I had the first time I entered the place.

Red meets us by the bar, Sid sitting on a barstool next to him.

"Look at you little fuckers," Red boasts, pulling Chris and Elliott each under an arm.

"Who you calling little?" Elliott flexes.

"It's a good start." He returns a flex, out-muscling Ell.

"You have to be using steroids, old man," he taunts.

Red laughs, shaking his head.

"It's good to have you guys here."

Keeping an arm over Chris, he guides us to the back wall of VIP booths.

"Holy shit!" Xavier exclaims, sliding out of the booth.

"Xave," Chris greets.

Xavier brushes by him, sidling up to Mia

"I've been dying to meet you in person." He takes her hand and kisses the back just before putting the tip of his tongue to her knuckle.

"That's not funny, fucker." Chris takes Mia's hand out of Xavier's.

The two of them go back and forth while Red seats everyone in the large VIP booth and a table he's set up in front of it.

As Sid passes me, I grab her arm.

She looks back at me in confusion.

"Who's with the boys?"

The confusion melts away into a smile of approval.

"You'll do after all," she says, winking, before answering my question. "Kel and Julia are with them at your place."

"Hey, scary lady." Xavier slides up behind Sid.

She twists and looks up at him.

"And I know you...how?" She takes a drink from the bottle in her hand.

He grins wide. "Admit it, you haven't been able to stop thinking about me."

"Oh, ginger beard man, I see you've started a strict regimen of erectile dysfunction meds."

Xavier's mouth drops open in surprise.

"'Cause you're a bigger dick than the last time."

Squeezing by him, Xave stands with a dumbfounded look on his face.

His eyes snap to mine, and he grins.

"I might be in love, brother." He looks back at Sid and then back to me. "I'm at least going to experience that attitude naked." Spinning on his heels, he follows after her.

Shaking my head, I find a seat and prepare for my girl to

own the stage.

Everyone in a seat and drinks served, we settle into casual conversation.

"So, what should we expect tonight?" Big Kam asks, his excitement filled eyes on Red.

"Miz Bette will be the first on stage to warm things up. Then you will all get to see Miz Liz make my stage her bitch." His grin is full of as much pride as my chest currently holds.

The lights dim and the spotlight floods Bethany. The black and white pinstripe corset and micro skirt contrasts against her pale white skin and bright red hair. The matching hat on her head shadows her face until she raises it to the white light and sings her opening verse.

"I was five and he was six." Her voice caresses the words.

At "bang, bang", she gives the crowd her back and shakes a large red bow.

The backup dancers appear, gliding around her in slow, sensual movements. Bethany makes her way to the end of the stage, sits, and uses her thumb and finger to imitate a gun while removing piece after piece of clothing.

She's gorgeous and amazing, but I chew the inside of my lip in anticipation for Liza.

Bethany finishes her sensual performance of Nancy Sinatra's *Bang Bang*, and the stage goes dark. The crowd applauds.

Next, a dark-haired woman in a pinup swimsuit and hula hoops struts to the catwalk and performs a bump and grind in one of the most creative hula hoop performances I've ever seen. When she finishes, she steps off the stage, weaving through the crowd.

In a sudden burst, lights fill the stage, revealing three red doorways with silver glitter beads hanging in them. The strands sway from either vents or fans, and then the beat kicks in. A backlight shines behind her, revealing Liza's silhouette in the center door. The beat kicks in and her voice—sexy, gravelly, and seductive—fills the room. Two dancers fill the doorways on either side of her dressed in tuxedo styled lingerie.

Pushing the beads aside, she steps center stage, wrapped in white silk, the material knotted at her right side. Her hair's curled on top of her head, loose ringlets framing her face. This time, there are no gloves, stockings, or shoes. Her bare feet move across the black floor like she's walking on air.

She purrs the line, "I'll be your pussycat, licking your milk," and my cock stands to attention. The invisible lust she wraps around me tightens—the familiar call of my snake charmer.

Strutting on stage, she swivels her hips. Stopping to bump and grind when the beat kicks in, she charms and ensnares the audience when she interacts with them. At the end of the catwalk, she turns, wraps her arms around her body, and gyrates, all while singing, "Seduce me, nibble, and bite."

The fingers of her left hand untie one knot and the material falls away from her chest, leaving her in only a silky skirt barely covering her ass.

Keeping an arm over her breasts, she struts back to the doorway, disappearing behind the beads.

A couple people inch to the edge of their seats, wanting to follow her.

Let one of those fuckers try.

The beat kicks again and she slaps dangling beads open with one hand. Wrapping a thick group of them around her chest, she sings. She drops the beads, her silver glitter cat-shaped pasties on display before she pulls back, vanishing with the end of the song.

The audience roars, clapping and whistling.

The lights return to their normal dim. And without looking, I reach out, grab my bottle of water, and gulp. Closing my eyes, I will my body to calm the fuck down. Someone may need to strap me to the booth.

Fuck, that wasn't water.

"Fuck me," Kat exclaims, getting my attention. "She's like a different fucking person up there." Her wide eyes lock on mine. "My nipples are hard." Kat cups her boobs.

"Are you sure?" Elliott asks. "I should check."

He reaches across Serena, the grin falling into to a frown

when she doesn't react.

"Babe? You okay?" His hands go to her stomach instead of Kat's chest.

"Do you think Miz Liz is into pregnant women?" Serena ignores Elliott and looks at me.

"What?" Elliott chokes on the question.

"I would do her in a second." She looks to her husband, unapologetic. "I would do her so hard, regardless of our marriage."

Laney spits her drink on the table. Mia and Chris burst into laughter.

"We're out of here." Elliott slips out of the booth, pulling Serena with him.

I catch Serena looking back at Mia, grinning.

"Tell your girl I said thank you." Elliott points at me.

"For what?" I laugh the question.

"'Cause it's been weeks, and I'm so getting laid tonight."

Serena starts laughing at his confession.

Wrapping his arm around his wife, Ell's hand drops to her ass, guiding her to the exit.

"Cheers." Xavier lifts his drink to the departing couple.

"Seriously, my nipples are hard," Kat reminds everyone. "Jack, is she into girls?" She waggles her brows.

"No," I state as the sound of music fills the room.

A drumming begins, followed by chimes. Dancers move in synchronized movements to the stage, each of them in leopard tops and fringed panties. The back curtain parts, revealing Liza in a harem girl outfit.

"Trust in me," she sings and the dancers stop.

Liza continues singing and the dancers kneel to the floor in levels while two others help Liza descend their backs like they are steps. Her bare feet hit the stage and she flows toward the edge, going into the crowd. The dancers follow like they're in a trance

Welcome to my fucking life.

"Shut your mouth," she purrs, using her fingers to lift one guy's chin. "And trust in me." Her hand slips over his shoulders and she's on to the next person. This time, it's a woman.

"You said she isn't into women," Kat accuses in a hush.

Dancers flow around her, pulling at scarves dangling from her waist and a hoop around her neck.

Ignoring Kat, I watch Liza stride toward our table.

Her eyes meet mine and she curls her lip, moving toward me.

The dancers continue to pull away material until she stands in a barely there, diamond studded bra top and thong.

My throat goes dry, making it difficult to swallow, and my dick throbs uncomfortably, wanting to follow her and maybe just fuck her in front of the crowd.

That will show all the fuckers staring at her bare ass thinking they can have her.

Reaching the table, Liza walks right by to the hidden stairs behind me. In the booth, I turn to follow her movements. She twists her body back and around, putting her face in mine. Winking, she straightens and continues leading her followers up the stairs and behind the mirror on the wall.

"Damn, this place deserves respect." Big Kam claps Red on the shoulder after the lights come back to normal.

"I'm hoping it gets some soon." Red lifts his beer bottle and drinks.

"You've got mine and you got some talent in this joint." Kam settles back in his chair. "I mean, Liza's a given, but, damn, that redhead is tight."

"Thank you." Red gives a sly smile.

Knowing about his relationship with Bethany, I'm sure that's the reason behind the look.

"I think you'll enjoy Madame J and Lady Nikle. They're up next." Red nods to the stage.

"You plan on doing guest performances?" Big Kam asks.

"I've actually done one." Red's eyes move to me for a moment. "But, I'd like to do more. You know, to draw people in."

Kam nods, looking deep in contemplation for a moment before he says, "If you can get me on stage with Liza, I'd be down for a spot."

"We'll talk." Red raises his beer.

"I wanna do it," Mia says, leaning her upper body onto the table.

"The hell you do," Chris protests.

Rolling her eyes, she keeps looking at Red. "I don't know anything about burlesque, but I'm open to whatever."

"It's more a cabaret-slash-burlesque kind of thing," Red clarifies.

Mia opens her mouth, but Chris breaks back into the conversation.

"The only thing you're open for is me." Chris sets his glass down, making it clack against the table.

Mia finally gives him her attention. On a sigh, she says, "Do you always have to be an asshole?"

Shrugging, he nods, answering, "You already know this."

"And yet, I still put up with you," Mia says, sitting back into the booth.

Chris puts his arms around her, pulling her into his side. "You fucking love me." He presses his lips to her temple.

My chest aches with want and I crane my neck, looking for Liza.

"She is amazing," Gemma says, obstructing my search with her appearance.

Squeezing into the booth, she forces me to scoot over to accommodate her.

"Do you think she and the redhead would be interested in auditioning with my stage director?" Her large eyes are filled with as much hope as her question.

Shrugging, I say, "I can ask her, but I'm not sure what she wants to do."

The statement is true, and the fact that I don't know what she wants to do, bothers me. I glance back at Chris, who still holds Mia captive.

Am I being like him? I haven't asked Liza once what she wants. Closing my eyes, I rub my forehead. *Damn it, I am being like Christopher. Fuck.*

"Are you okay?" Gemma's hand lays on my forearm.

"No," I groan, throwing my body against the back of the booth. Lifting my hand from my head, I motion to Chris. "I'm acting like the douche sitting across from me."

After the show when most of the crowd is gone, Sid leads the way backstage. She, Xavier, and I the only ones, besides Red, left from our group.

"You're not gonna act like your brother, are you?" Red asks, keeping pace with my strides.

"Meaning?" I round a small table.

"Meaning, you aren't going to rush the stage and carry her off because she's half-naked." His brow raises, anticipating my response.

Grinning, I shake my head.

"Nah. I'm a proud man, watching her perform."

"Good, cause I don't want to ban your ass."

"You'd ban me?" I fake shock.

We reach the curtain camouflaging the door to the back.

"Damn straight."

Sid pulls back the sheath of red velvet, grabbing the door handle. Xavier stands close to her back, holding the curtain open.

"Can I get some space, Gandalf the Red?" she asks, obviously annoyed.

"I'm just being helpful," Xavier responds innocently, but he could definitely help without riding her back.

"Mmhmm." She pulls open the door, putting force into it, landing an elbow in his rib.

Xavier gasps from the pain.

"Damn, woman. I'm all for rough, but at least ask my safe word first."

Growling, she slips through the door.

Xavier stands, holding the door open, giving us a large, goofy grin.

"You're a masochist." Red shakes his head, passing through the door.

"Maybe a little." He shrugs.

"You're a brave man," I say, patting his shoulder before ducking into the next room.

"Not really," Xavier says, closing the door behind him. "You guys are just a bunch of pussies. And speaking of pussy, where's my little hellcat?"

He cranes his neck, finding Sid talking to some performers.

"Excuse me," he says, moving in her direction.

At the private dressing room door, Red knocks. Calling through the door, he asks, "All the goodies covered?"

The door swings open to Bethany standing in a pink kimono.

"Like you wouldn't come in either way." She smirks.

"If it were just you, yes." Red grins back, grabbing her hips and backing her into the room.

The moment I enter, Liza turns from her mirror—one fake eyelash still on, curly blonde extensions hanging from the corner of her vanity, and a pile of make-up covered face wipes in front of her.

"Hey," I greet, taking the chair next to her.

"Hi." She blushes.

Looking away, she removes the remaining false lash and scrubs at her face. I watch the way she moves the cloth around her eyes, nose, mouth, neck.

And...I'm hard. Christ, is there anything she does that doesn't turn me on?

"You're making me self-conscious."

Her words pull me out of my lustful thoughts.

"Why?"

"Because you're staring." Twisting in her chair, she drops the used wipe onto the pile. "I warned you."

Furrowing my brow, I ask, "Warned me 'bout what?"

"That I don't look like Miz Liz outside of this place."

She turns away again, hiding behind her hair.

Grasping the bottom of her chair, I pull her toward me.

"Jackson," she yelps, holding the sides for balance.

Taking her face between my palms, I kiss her hard and push her chair back in its place.

"Hurry and finish, so we can get home."

Her eyes wide in surprise, she nods

"And so we can save Xavier from an early death."

Keeping her eyes on the reflection, she asks, "Death?"

"Yeah." I nod. "Death by Sidrome."

"Sid..?" She stops and bursts into a fit of laughter. "Oh, shit," she pants, "I'm going to have to tell her that one."

"Don't you dare." I straighten in my chair.

"Why not?"

She collects the wipes, throwing them all in a trashcan between the vanities.

"Because she scares me," I answer honestly.

It makes her laugh harder.

"Don't worry," she pats my leg, smiling, "I'll protect you. Besides, she'll love the nickname."

I snatch her hand from my thigh, bring it to my lips, and kiss.

"Let's get out of here."

Nodding, she quickens her clean up routine.

Before we leave the dressing room, Red mentions Big Kam's interest in performing to Liza. He also mentions what Gemma said to me about auditioning. I hadn't even realized he'd been listening to the conversation.

Liza looks both nervous and surprised. Red tells her to just think about it and they'll talk later. Then he tells us goodnight and kicks us out of the dressing room.

"They're going to have sex in the room where I get dressed," Liza groans.

"Probably," I agree, placing my hand on her lower back.

"I need to add disinfecting wipes to my bag," she sighs.

"Where's Sid?" I ask, scanning the open backstage space.

"I don't..." She pauses and then stiffens. "What did you do?"

SADIE GRUBOR

Snapping my eyes to Liza, I follow her gaze.

Sid gives a big smile and releases the doorknob she holds, rushing toward us.

"Talk later, walk now," she rambles, rushing by us.

Looking back to Liza, her worried eyes meet mine.

All she says is, "Run, run now," before bolting after her cousin.

Hurrying to keep up with them, a muffled crash comes from behind. Not looking back, I pick up my pace.

326

Chapter Twenty-Two
Liza

Entering the apartment, I'm still pissed at Sid.

"You can't stay mad at me," she says in a sing-song voice. "You never could."

Brushing by me, she goes straight to her geek station.

"This time I will." It sounds pouty and I know it, but I don't care. "But, maybe I'll forgive you if you tell me what exactly you did."

"I didn't *do* anything," she says, her response too quick and innocent.

"I don't believe you." I'm going for mean, but it sounds shrill. *Damn it*

"I don't want to know," Jackson says, walking to the couch.

He pulls off his t-shirt, leaving him in only a wife beater and black pants, before sitting on the sofa.

"Good idea," Sid says to her monitor.

"Um, Miss Campbell?"

Julia appears next to me, a look of nervousness on her face. *Good.*

"Yes?" It's hard not to give her a bitch face.

"I just wanted to let you know Luke and Sean ate pizza, went swimming, played video games for only an hour, and were in bed by ten. So, they should be well rested for their soccer game tomorrow."

Fuck, the soccer game. It's their last game for the year and I forgot.

"Are you okay? Did I do something wrong?" Julia's eyes widen with worry.

I shake my head and swallow my pride.

"No. I'm okay. The game slipped my mind."

Taking a deep breath, I exhale and tamper down my bitch mode.

"Thank you for taking care of them tonight."

"It's no problem at all," Julia assures. "Is there something I can do to help with tomorrow?"

"No, but thank you." Smiling small, I nod and begin to walk away.

"I'm sorry," she blurts.

I turn on my heel.

"For what?" I ask, furrowing my brow.

"That I didn't listen to you and do the right thing."

Crossing my arms over my chest, I nod slowly. I feel both Jackson and Sid's eyes on me, waiting for my reaction.

"The one you need to apologize to is over there." I thumb over my shoulder toward Jackson. "He's the one who could've died."

Rounding and looking at Jackson, I say, "I'm going to shower and then bed."

I heft my bag on my shoulder and step into the hallway.

"As long as you make sure you're climbing into the right bed," Jackson calls after me.

Sid's giggle follows.

Rejuvenated by a long shower, I dig through dresser drawers. Slipping into a pair of cotton shorts and a tank top, I bend back down to get clothes for tomorrow.

"The pajamas are futile," Jackson says.

Looking over my shoulder, I watch him breeze in from the balcony door. His attention is on my ass, but under the weight of my stare, his eyes find mine. Knowing he's busted ogling, he grins.

Stepping close, his hands come to my hips and I straighten.

"What are you doing?" he asks, glancing over my shoulder into the open drawer of simple cotton underwear.

Reaching out, he lifts one pair in front of us, the white cotton dangling from his long finger.

I snag the underwear out of his hand, and say, "I wear thongs made of glitter and itchy lace panties at work. All under stage lights that feel like heat lamps. I prefer comfort at home."

His chest vibrates against my back. On a laugh, he says, "I didn't say anything."

Before I can reply, he continues, "In fact, I don't care what underwear you prefer." He puts his arms around my waist, his hands on my stomach, and pulls me to him. "If we're alone, they aren't staying on long anyway."

In a rare bold moment, I respond, "Good, since half the time I'm not wearing any at all."

I push the drawer closed and his arms tighten around my middle.

"Commando." It's not a question. "Right now?" His hands slip low.

"I prefer not to sleep with them on."

"Funny, we share the same preference," he quips, bending and lifting me into his arms bridal style.

"What are you doing?" I squeal, gripping his shoulders.

Striding out to the balcony, he carries me to his dimly lit room.

"Just making sure you climb into the right bed."

He lays me on the bed, grabs my shorts, and pulls them off. I fist the bedding so I don't slip down the mattress.

Tossing the light gray shorts to the floor, he says, "And that's because I want you to be comfortable."

Jackson pulls his wife beater over his head and tosses it to meet my shorts on the floor. He shoves his black pants and boxer briefs down before kneeling on the bed and crawling over me.

Glancing at the side table, I find the clock.

2:49 a.m.

"I have to be up early tomorrow," I remind.

His fingers slip under the hem of my light purple tank and strip it over my head.

Pressing a quick kiss to my nose, he tosses the shirt and settles in on my left.

"I know."

Draping one arm over my stomach and folding the other under his head, he snuggles in tight.

"Shh, I'm trying to sleep," he finishes, nestling his face into my damp hair.

Unable to hold it back, I laugh. He joins.

After a minute or so, he rolls to his back, pulling me with him. I cuddle into the crook of his right arm, place my hand on his bare chest, crook my leg over his, and close my eyes.

"I do want to ask you something."

I reopen my eyes at his words.

"What?" I ask, shifting my head to look at his face.

Exhaling loudly, he begins.

"I realized something tonight."

Every muscle in my body stills.

"I've been a little obsessive about some things and I don't want you to feel forced into anything." He tilts his head down and looks at me. "What do you want, Liza?"

His eyes search mine, worry lining their edges.

"I agree. You've been...a bit controlling."

The muscles under my hand tense. I rub his chest, trying to soothe him.

"But I could leave, if I really wanted to." The truth sends a flush over my body.

His arm tightens around me.

"Tell me what you want?" he asks again.

Draping my arm over his stomach, I snuggle into his side. It's an attempt to get closer, but also hide my face.

"I want Lucas to be happy and safe, Sean's custody to be finalized, for Kel to go to college, and Sid to stay out of federal prison." I say the last with a smile.

His chest moves in silent laughter.

"After tonight, I'm not sure she's capable of evading conviction."

Jackson's lips press against the top of my head and he wraps both of his warm arms around me.

"And..." I continue with my list of wants, "as crazy as this may sound, I think I want you."

His arms tighten.

"Fuck, Liza, I want you so much."

Gripping under my arms, he pulls me up until we are chest to chest. My legs fall on each side of his body and I curl my foot under him. Jackson's hands slip down my back until he cups my ass, our faces only inches apart.

"Stay here with me," he whispers.

Dropping my eyes to his mouth, I answer, "It's too fast."

He licks his bottom lip before responding, "Yeah, it's fast, but it's right."

I pull my eyes from his lips and meet his gaze.

"And you know it is." He squeezes my butt.

"This place is too much and Lucas' school is—"

"It doesn't have to be here. I'll have Julia research places. It can be a house if you want. And how about we let Lucas, Sean, and Kel decide, for themselves, where we live?"

"It's only been a few weeks, Jackson," I sigh, laying my head on his chest. "This is a lot to decide."

"Then just think about it. We'll stay here for another week and see how things play out. I know you've got shit going on with Sean and we'll take of it. I'll make sure everything's cool on that end. Don't worry about it, yeah?"

His thumbs rub circles against the bare skin of my ass, causing goose bumps to appear.

"Okay," I answer quietly.

"Okay," he mimics, bringing his arms back around to embrace me.

The morning is a blur of soccer uniforms, missing shin guards—which Julia miraculously gets a replacement pair this early in the day—and Jackson.

After last night's talk, he's been completely relaxed and playful—teasing Lucas about brushing his teeth so girls will want to kiss him, which earned him a look of disgust. That is, until Jack mentioned Mia prefers clean white teeth. Then the boy couldn't scrub his mouth fast enough. Jackson also spent almost thirty quiet moments with my brother. Too busy with the boys' breakfast and getting ready, I wasn't able to find out what their conversation was about. I only know it ended with Jackson patting a hand on Kel's shoulder. Sid didn't emerge until we were heading out the door.

The ride to the soccer field is longer than usual, given our new location, but not one media person is on the radar. Until we reach the field.

"How did they know about his game?" Sid asks, peering out the tinted window of the car.

"The website," I groan.

"Website?" Jackson asks, brow furrowing in confusion.

"The soccer association has a website and the teams' schedules are listed on there." I rub my face, taking a deep breath to calm.

"Are they going to film the game?" Lucas asks, sounding a little too excited about it.

The car stops in the parking lot near the fields. The driver exits the car and opens the rear door.

"Let me out first," Jackson orders, pulling Lucas away from the door.

Slipping from the car, the gossip hounds start right in with the questions. I can only hope they don't say something I'd rather my boys not hear.

"Okay," Jackson calls above the crowd. "I know you all want pictures and answers, but this is a soccer game with families and minors. I'll chat with you for a minute if you can keep from disturbing the kids' games."

"Where's Liza?" a man calls out.

"Is she with you? Are you together now?" another person

asks.

Taking a deep breath, I crawl over Sid's lap and climb out of the car. The camera shutters click in rapid succession.

"I'm right here," I greet, lifting a hand to give a small wave.

Jackson's arm comes around my shoulders in a protective fashion.

"If I give you all five minutes, I need you to respect my terms. Alright?"

Heads nod and vocal confirmations hiss.

Leaning down in the open door, I catch Sid's eyes.

"Can you get the boys to the field so they can warm up?"

"Of course," she says, scooting to the doorway and climbing out.

Behind her Lucas, Sean, and Kel file out of the car.

"Keep the cameras off the boys." Jackson's hand covers a lens pointed in the boys' direction.

The cameraman nods sheepishly, turning the camera back to our united front.

"Are you two a couple?" a young, dark-skinned man asks.

"Isn't that a violation of your twelve steps?" A petite blonde woman pushes by the man.

"Liza?"

My eyes snap to a round man.

"Did you know Jackson was with Kristy when you started seeing him?"

My lips part on a gasp and eyes widen in surprise.

"I wasn't with Kristy when I met Liza," Jackson growls. "That was over before I came to L.A.."

He pulls me tighter to his side.

"Yes, we're a couple, and, no, I'm not violating one of the steps."

Jackson pulls out a key tag and holds it up for the reporters. They snap photos of him holding the tag stating his sobriety. I wrap my arms around his waist.

"What do you have to say about the abuse rumors?"

Jackson tenses and I act.

"If you're referring to me, then they are entirely false," I state.

"How do you feel about being kicked off the show due to your relationship with Jackson?" The petite blonde slings her question.

"The show really wasn't for me, but I wish the contestants well."

I smile and the cameras click.

"Do you have any comment about the article Cheyenne Post released online this morning?" Another journalist steps forward.

"I...I don't know about an article," I stutter, swallowing hard.

What the hell is being said now?

"She states in the article she expects big things from a woman with the caliber of talent you hold and she's disappointed in the narrow-minded suits running the show."

The man shoves his recorder closer toward me.

"Cheyenne Post said that?" Jackson asks in disbelief.

The man nods emphatically.

"I thank her for the kind words," is the only response I can think to give.

Almost ten minutes later, we walk away from the group of reporters. I keep looking over my shoulder.

"They aren't following," I whisper.

"Good," Jackson replies.

"I didn't think they would actually do it."

"Do what?" He guides me toward Sid and Kel.

"Listen to you." I step up on the bleachers and settle next to Sid.

"It only happens occasionally." Going up one bleacher higher, Jackson sits behind me and stretches his long legs on either side of my body.

Sid puts her arm on his knee and leans.

"Thanks," she says, keeping her eyes on the field of practicing players, "these metal things hurt my ass."

Jackson doesn't pull his leg away or push her off. Instead, he pulls me back into his body, perfectly at ease and ready to cheer on

Sean and Lucas.

For the first time in my life, I understand epic romance movie moments. My heart thuds, my chest feels so full—almost too full—and every inch of my skin tingles with a pleasant burn.

After the game and awards, we lounge around the penthouse living space. Sean and Lucas sit in the oversized bean bag chairs they've claimed, playing a racing game on the TV. Kel lies stomach down, head toward the end of the couch cushion. He watches the boys play their game, dozing off and on. Jackson slouches against the curve of the sofa, one leg stretched along the cushions and the other bent at the knee with his foot on the floor. Lying between his legs, on my side, head resting on his thigh, I'm still amazed by the length of his body.

Having been talking off and on with Una regarding the videos and information she's found so far, Sid makes her way over and plops onto the couch.

"Una's going to be calling you," she says, getting situated against the overstuffed cushions.

"Why couldn't she just tell you?" Jackson asks, his head back and eyes closed.

"Dunno," Sid answers, but her interest is already on the video game. "I've got next winner."

Lucas and Sean groan in unison.

"Sid, you'll be on for the rest of the night," Sean whines.

"So?" She shrugs.

"So, we want to play together, too."

"Well, your mother should've bought more than two controllers," she snips.

The vibration from Jackson's phone travels through the couch before it rings.

"It's probably Una," Sid says, distracted. "Lucas, you missed the nitro launch."

Jackson shifts, trying to get his phone from his back pocket. I attempt to move out of his way, but his free hand presses my head back to his thigh.

Reaching his phone, he answers, "Yeah?"

"Wait, it's not my—"

Lifting my head, I watch Jackson roll his eyes. Pulling his phone from his ear, he presses it to his chest.

"Where's your phone?" he asks.

Reaching over the edge of the couch, I pull my phone from my bag and hand it to him.

Putting his own phone back to his ear, he says, "Shut up for two seconds," before reading off a phone number.

"Why are you giving out my number?" Sid questions with an edge to her tone.

He ignores her and continues talking to the person on the other end of his call.

"Well, it's your own damn fault," he lectures, tossing my phone to the empty cushion next to him. "No, but I'll definitely ask Red for the photos." He disconnects, dropping the phone next to mine.

Sid's phone vibrates across the counter next to her geek station.

She turns and looks at the phone like it might bite her.

"That will be Xave." Jackson winks. "Good luck with that, he's known for his revenge schemes. You can ask Chris about them."

"You bastard," she hisses. "Why would you give that overgrown ginger-jack my number?"

"Because I'm not your receptionist. You two handle your shit. I've got my own to worry about," he says, giving her a pointed look before putting his head back on the couch.

The phone vibrates again, but Sid ignores it.

"Looks like I'll be changing my number," she grumbles.

"What did you do?" Kel asks from his prone position.

She shrugs. "Nothing."

"Bullshit," Jackson snorts.

"What did she do?" I ask this time.

"He was in that closet last night." He rubs his eyes.

Whipping my head back to Sid, eyes wide, I find a small grin on her face.

"You didn't?"

She shrugs again.

Kel chuckles.

"He had it coming," she defends. "Did he," she points at Jackson, "tell you how his buddy was up my ass all night talking about how pretty and sexy he thinks I am?" she scoffs like it's impossible for someone to believe that very thing.

"Sid," I warn, shifting my eyes to the boys, but a part of me aches for her. Nothing and no one can get it through her head that she *is* pretty and sexy. I've tried so many times.

Her mouth drops open. "He just said bullshit." She stabs a finger at Jackson.

"Good point," I nod, "you both need to watch your mouths."

"Will do, baby." Jackson's fingers find my hair.

Sid sighs when her phone vibrates again and pushes up from the couch.

"I guess I should just get this over with."

She marches away and disappears with her phone.

"Good luck, Sid," Kel calls after her, earning him a middle finger salute.

He laughs.

"What else did she do?"

Jackson's laughter shakes me before he answers with, "She teased him into the closet, shoved him inside, handcuffed him to the hanger pole," he pauses to laugh harder, "and then," he gasps, "then she pushed a bra into his mouth."

My and Kel's laughter joins his.

"Whew," Jackson blows out a breath. "We literally walked out just after she did it all. Red has pictures."

"I'm not going to even lie. It totally sounds like something she would do." Propping up on my elbow, I glance up to his smiling face. "Actually, he's lucky she didn't take his pants first."

He raises one brow, questioningly.

Shaking my head, I lie down in his lap.

"You don't want to know, man." Kel turns back to the TV.

The next morning doesn't go as smoothly as I'd like, but it being the first time for the school routine, I suppose it could've gone worse. Kel rides in the car driving the boys to school so I have peace of mind.

I arrange the dirty dishes in a dishwashing machine so clean, I almost feel sorry for filling it with food covered plates and cups.

"You know a cleaning lady comes in right?"

Looking up from the dishwasher, I find Jackson leaning against the fridge. His arms crossed over his naked chest, he looks like he's posing for a magazine.

"It's weird having someone clean up after us." I look around the kitchen. "I feel like I should clean before she comes to clean."

Laughing, he shakes his head.

"'Cause that's not crazy," he teases, pushing off the stainless steel appliance and stalking toward me.

Backing up a step for every one he takes, my butt hits the counter.

"What?" I furrow my brow.

"Una called this morning," he confesses, placing his hands to the counter on either side of me.

"And?" I press.

"Kristy will be back in L.A. at the end of the week."

He lifts a hand to my hair, twirling a strand around one long finger, studying his actions.

"She's agreed to meet me at the hotel." His eyes move to mine. "Una has her thinking I want to talk."

"Well, you do."

"Yeah, but not the way she's thinking." He grins.

"Ah," I say, nodding, finally catching his meaning.

Great. I'm sure the skank will come wearing nothing but a smile.

"Chris texted right after the call, telling me he would be there, which means all of the guys will probably follow. Probably the girls, too."

"Okay." I nod.

Emotions ranging from hate and anger, to fear and anxiousness war inside me.

"Will you be there?" he asks, licking his pierced lip.

If I see her, I'm afraid I'll beat the shit out of her.

"If you want me—"

"Of course I want you there," he interrupts in a raised voice. I flinch.

"Sorry," he softens. "You know I want you around, right?"

His eyes search mine.

"I think so."

"You need to know so," he states. "Do you want to be there?" he asks.

Nodding, I answer, "Yes."

But think, *it will take all my strength not to break her face.*

"Okay, then you'll be there."

Releasing my hair, he cups my face.

"Are you okay around the bands?"

"You mean Laney?"

"Partially," he inclines his head, "but I want you to be comfortable with them all."

"They've been nothing but nice." I shrug. "But I don't really know them yet."

"And Laney?" he presses.

"She seems really happy for you."

He runs his thumb over my cheek.

"That surprises you."

"Honestly, I didn't expect anything. I didn't plan on standing in your penthouse kitchen this morning."

A grin splits his face.

"But you are." Keeping the smile, he sticks his tongue through his teeth.

"Yeah, I am." I beam up at him.

"You stay'n in my kitchen?" he asks, his face moving closer.

"I thought we are seeing how things go?"

I press my hands to his chest, sliding my arms up to his shoulders.

"I'll just take that as a yes."

He dips his head and I knot the hair at the back of his head in my fingers, taking his mouth with mine.

Palming my ass, he lifts me onto the kitchen island and moves between my spread legs.

"People prepare food on that surface," Sid yawns the words.

Groaning, Jackson lifts his head, narrowing his eyes on her.

"Don't give me that look," Sid scolds. "This is public domain. Go play grope-and-poke in your bedroom."

She pulls open the fridge, taking out the jug of orange juice. Closing the door, she levels a look at Jackson and holds his stare.

"Cockblock," he taunts.

She stops, tilts her head, and looks contemplative before she says, "Hundreds of thousands of sperm and *you* were the fastest?"

I stiffen, immediately reminded of the no condom incident. *My period can't come soon enough.*

They silently standoff for another minute before Jackson turns his attention back to me.

"I also have Julia contacting my lawyer today," he says in a casual tone.

"For what?"

"About Sean," he answers in the same cool tone.

"Explain, please."

I push on his chest, putting some space between us. He steps back, leaning against the counter behind him.

"I told you not to worry about the caseworker." He shrugs. "My lawyers will contact the caseworker and his grandmother to get your guardianship solidified. Then he'll be able to feel secure about being here."

The fact that he makes it about Sean feeling secure melts my insides.

"You know that shit affects him, right?" He raises his pierced brow.

"He told you that?" I slip from the counter onto my feet.

"No, not directly, but he's made comments to Luke about appreciating the mom he has and how his house will never be anything like this." He motions to the open space.

I cover my mouth to hold in my gasp.

"We're gonna get things handled before this week is over. So, don't plan on your caseworker returning your call. At least, not until my lawyers are done filing motions or petitions, or whatever the fuck they do." He waves a hand in the air.

"Well, well," Sid says, walking between us, a bowl of cereal in her hands, "you're good sperm after all."

Chapter Twenty-Three
Jackson

Five days. The mornings filled with school routines and—my favorite—afternoons in bed with my snake charmer. It's been five amazing days. It's also only been five goddamn days and she already has the head of security for the W in my penthouse foyer.

Liza stands to the side, scowling at a smirking Sid.

She's pissed, but I know part of the problem is the upcoming meeting with Kristy. Liza won't say it, but I see the flames light in her eyes when the psycho bitch is discussed.

"I promise it won't happen again," I assure, closing the door on the departing manager.

"Why?" Liza growls.

"'Cause it was way too easy," she says, shrugging and turning a pointed look on me. "And if I can hack their firewalls and change the network settings, you really need to rethink how safe you feel in this place."

"You changed the hotel's Wi-Fi to *Free Porn – click me long time,*" Liza blames.

Sid snorts, "Yeah." She grins, proud of her accomplishment.

"It's not funny," Liza cries, covering her face with a hand.

"It kind of is," I say, still not happy, but able to admit the humor.

Dropping her hand, she glares at me. "Not helping."

"Come on," Sid draws. "It's only Wi-Fi. It's not like I gave everyone free room service or reversed room charges."

"You could do that?" I ask, intrigued.

She gives a sly smile, and says, "Maybe."

My phone vibrates in my back pocket, ending my opportunity to ask more about her hacking capabilities.

"I can't take you anywhere." Liza throws her hands up, striding away from Sid and down the hallway.

"Liza," she calls after her cousin, following.

"Hello."

"Mr. Shaw, this is Susan, Mr. Lawrence Preston's legal aid."

"What can I do for you?" I ask my lawyer's assistant

"I'm just calling to update you in regards to Gertrude Johnson and the minor Sean Johnson."

"And?" I press, walking into the kitchen to reclaim the drink I poured before the Wi-Fi incident.

"The guardianship papers will need Miss Campbell's signature. They are being brought over now for her to sign. Just return them to him and he'll bring them back to us this afternoon."

"When will they be final?" I lift my juice to my mouth and gulp.

"They should be filed with the state by the end of the week. We'll send your copies as soon as they come available."

"So, they should be here in two days?"

"Yes, sir."

I visualize the girl nodding.

"I also wanted to let you know, Mrs. Johnson, the boy's grandmother, will not be returning to their previous home. It looks like she will have to go into an assisted living home. You may want to let Miss Campbell know so she can coordinate the retrieval of Sean's things."

"Do you know where Mrs. Johnson is being sent?"

"No, sir. I'm afraid I don't."

"Okay, thanks. Tell Lawrence to call me when he's free. I may need him for something else shortly."

"I'll let him know."

"Thanks."

Disconnecting with Susan, I walk to the couch and call Julia.

"Yes, sir?"

"Don't start with that sir shit again," I admonish, settling onto the sofa.

"I don't feel right using your name," she laments.

"Julia—"

"She's right," Julia hiccups. "I'm so sorry for the choices I made that night."

"I get why you did it. Liza doesn't understand the dirty side of working with public figures."

"But she's still right."

Sighing, I rub the back of my head.

"Yeah, Julia, she is," I confess.

"I'm sorry." She sniffs.

"I know you are, and, if you want to make it up to me, I need you to add something else to your list of tasks."

She sniffs once more, takes an audible breath, and says, "Of course. What can I do for you?"

"I need you to research assisted living homes in the same area you're looking for homes. Sean's grandmother is going to need a place to go and I'd like her to stay close to him."

"You are so amazing." Liza's voice surprises me, making me twist to look over the back of the couch.

"I'll start this afternoon," is Julia's reply.

"Great, thanks."

I disconnect, watching Liza come around the couch. When she reaches me, she sits on my lap, wrapping her arms around my neck.

"You don't have to do all this," she says, furrowing her brow.

Brushing away strands of hair from her face, I say, "I know, but it matters to you, which means it matters to me. Also, his grandmother is the closest Sean's got to a mother. He needs her."

She burrows against my chest, warming my skin and heating my blood. Encircling her in my arms, we sit this way for a while.

Fuck, this girl twists my insides.

Friday arrives and the Bel-Air hotel feels foreign to me now.

Like my time here was so long ago, when, in fact, it's only been a few weeks. From where I'm sitting in one of the beige seats, I glance at the chair across from the couch—the same chair Liza and I began our first night of debauchery in. A smile comes to my face and I tighten my hand on the thigh she has propped on the arm of my seat.

"What the hell are you smiling at?" Elliott asks, sitting in said chair. He puts his hands over his t-shirt covered chest. "Quit checking me out. I'm a married man."

"There's something wrong with you," Jimmy says.

"If you're referring to my awesome manly physique, there's nothing wrong." Elliott rubs over his chest. "I can't help it if he wants me."

"You finally get laid by your wife and you think you're a sex god," Kat says from her spot on the couch next to Jimmy.

He scoffs, "I've always been a god."

"Enough," Chris exclaims, pushing off the wall, starting to pace. "When the hell is this bitch going to show up?"

"She's not exactly known for being on time," I answer, bored with this already.

"No, she's known for being God's gift to runway," Sid adds, causing everyone to look at her. She shrugs. "I could make her famous for other things."

The evil glint in her eye matches my own malicious desire to post that sex video to every website imaginable.

"She's on her way up." Una steps out of the bedroom, slipping her phone in her pocket. "We should clear out this area."

"Why?" Chris stops pacing, crossing his arms over his chest.

"So she doesn't go running out the door when she sees everyone in here," Una explains.

"Screw that," he snaps. "Julia, you answer the door, excuse yourself when she comes in, and close the door behind you. I block the door as soon as you're out. This shit ends and he does it with us at his back."

Always the asshole, he raises a brow, challenging Una.

His out of character caring, in his own asshole-like way,

doesn't go unnoticed by Una. Her lips thin to hide her smile and she gives a nod.

When the knock comes at the door, Julia hurries to pull it open.

"Hello, I'll just get out of your way." She motions Kristy in and closes the door behind her.

Chris moves in a blur, pressing his back to the door.

Kristy stops in her stilettos. Taking in the group, the smile she wore disappears. Her eyes flit from Elliott to Jimmy, Kat, Una, Chris, Mia, and Sid, finally settling on Liza sitting at my side.

"Well, this is unpleasantly unexpected," she says, her voice heavy with sarcasm. "I thought you wanted to be alone, Jackson?" She bats her eyelashes.

"You're going to cease providing source material to the media," Una demands.

Kristy rolls her perfectly made up eyes. "Didn't we already have this conversation? I don't repeat myself."

"No, you fuck three guys at a time," Sid mutters.

"What did you say?" Kristy sneers, twisting her head in her direction.

Sid opens her mouth.

"Eyes on me, Kristy," I order, preventing Sid from launching into all the dirty details.

Her eyes come to mine, fire still blazing in them.

"I know you're the one spreading shit and providing whatever pictures you can get your hands on." Reaching out to the table, I pick up the bedazzled cell phone. "Whether it's from your own phone," I lift it for her to see, "or someone else's."

"How did you get my phone?" Stalking forward, she rips it from my hand. "You stole it?" she accuses. "I'll have you arrested."

"Oh, no, that would be me." Kat raises her hand, a large smile on her face. "But, I didn't steal it. I happened to find it on the floor of a club. I grabbed it so it wouldn't fall into the wrong hands." Kat's face is a mask of sweetness.

"Like mine," Sid adds, smirking.

Kristy, trying to ignore Sid, sees right through Kat's act.

Seething, she turns back to me. Her mouth twisted in fury, she parts her lips to breathe fire.

"You'll pay for this and everything else, you pathetic asshole," she threatens.

Standing, I tower over her.

"You," my voice rises, "will stop this bullshit or every dirty thing we found on your phone will find its way to certain people."

Our eyes bore into each other, neither one wanting to back down.

"That means," Sid steps up next to me, "a particular celebrity will find out you have a video of him and his lover. And if he happens to believe you're trying to blackmail him, well..." Sid lets the sentence fall off and shrugs.

"You fat fucking—"

"And perhaps YouTube needs a new celebrity sex tape!" Sid claps her hands together, smiling. "Could you imagine the number of hits my channel could get?" She looks wistful.

Kristy's face falls, her body going still as a gush of air puffs out of her.

"Let me just tell you," Sid drops the smile and steps into Kristy's personal space, "You are no Kardashian. I don't think you'll skyrocket to fame on that one." Her eyes rake over Kristy's body. "You don't have the ass or tits for it, so I suggest you do as Jackson asks or I'll crotch kick your boney ass."

Liza grasps Sid's arm, pulling her away from a shell-shocked Kristy.

The room falls silent, aside from Kristy's heavy breathing. Her mouth pops open and closes, then opens again to say, "You wouldn't?" Her watery eyes come back to mine.

My silence widens her eyes. Stepping forward, her hands come to my chest, fisting my t-shirt. "You can't. I didn't...it wasn't..." she sobs.

Gripping her wrists, I pull her off of me and step back. Reaching back, I take Liza's arm and haul her to my side, wrapping my arm around her back.

"You mean like you tried with her." I nod to Liza.

A large tear spills over Kristy's cheek.

"And with me," I add, pointing to my chest. "You're a fucking piece of work, you know that?" I sneer.

Her shoulders shake and another sob escapes her mouth. More tears flow, causing her mascara to run.

"If it were up to me, that shit would've been viral four days ago. You can thank Liza for that not happening."

Her eyes move to Liza and then back to me.

"What do you want?" she whispers.

"You know what I want. Leave us the fuck alone," I growl.

"And you'll give me the video?" Kristy's eyes gleam with hope.

I shake my head.

"I don't trust you. I'm not giving anything back."

"How do I know you won't use it anyway?" she whimpers.

"Because I'm not like you, Kristy," I growl. "I won't use any of it, as long as you stay away."

Sniffing, she uses the back of her hand to wipe away her tears.

"Fine," she agrees through clenched teeth. "But—"

"But nothing," Liza interrupts, her words containing the strong suggestion of reproach. "Just end it before I stop feeling sorry for you and give my cousin the green light to go live. Your modeling career may end, but at least you'll have porn to look forward to."

"Jackson, you should teach your home wrecking whore to be quiet," Kristy quips.

I flex my fingers into the flesh of Liza's hip.

"I'm sorry," Liza puts her hand to her chest. "Whose home did I wreck?"

Kristy opens her mouth, but Liza doesn't allow her to speak.

"You were out of the picture before I met Jackson. You weren't even on his mind when he took me back to his hotel. And if you think my cousin is a scary threat, you come at me or my son again and you will regret every moment. I sure as fuck can assure you it will be much, much worse than crotch kicking your boney ass."

Christ, she's hot. Do not bend her over the chair in front of everyone.

Kristy clamps her mouth shut and straightens her spine. The fight visibly dies from her body.

"Fine," she says, defeated.

"Good," Liza says on a sigh, giving a nod.

Gripping her phone in her fist, she holds her head up and walks to the door.

Chris doesn't move.

"Excuse me," she bites out.

Chris doesn't move.

"I said, excuse me," she whines. "What else do you want from me?"

Snorting, Chris finally steps out of her way, shaking his head and allowing Kristy to leave the hotel room.

Exhaling loudly, Liza falls back into the chair behind us.

"That was fun," Kat says, smiling wide.

"I've missed our little get-togethers." Elliott fakes a sniffle as his phone rings. Pulling the device from his pocket, he answers, "Yo, baby, yo—"

He jumps from the chair.

"I'm on my way." All humor gone, Elliott rushes to the door and out.

"What the fuck?" Jimmy asks.

"Serena's in labor," Mia blurts, her eyes on her phone.

Her fingers working on the screen, she strides to the hotel room door. Chris has it open before she reaches and follows her out.

"Hey, wait!" Kat calls after them.

"I'm texting everyone the hospital she's going to," Mia shouts, the door closing behind them.

Multiple pings go off in unison as everyone files out of the room.

Liza

In the back of a car taking us to Cedars-Sinai Hospital, Jackson holds me close to him. With his arm draped over my shoulder, I'm blissfully happy. Maybe too content, because all this good has to go wrong at some point, right?

Taking a deep breath, I exhale the nervousness dulling my ease.

The chime of my phone surprises me. Jackson's hand slips down my back, pulling it from my pocket and handing it to me.

Taking it from his hand, I look at the screen and see another text from the unknown number.

Good job with the whore.

"Why is Chris texting you?" he asks.

My eyes widen. *Chris is the one who's been texting me updates?*

Jackson turns my hand so he can see better and reads the message. He chuckles, giving me a squeeze.

"He's right about one thing," Jackson says, releasing my hand.

"What's that?" I choke out, still surprised by Chris being my unknown source of information.

"She's a whore," he says with disdain. "But you did more than a good job."

"I didn't do anything." I put the phone back in my pocket.

He grips my chin, pulling my face to his. Dipping down, he says, "It's fucking hot when you defend me," against my lips.

I inch closer to kiss him, but he won't allow it. Determination setting in, I stare at his evading mouth.

"Like with Julia," he groans low, "I'm hard thinking about you getting fired up."

"Unless you're making this a threesome, you need to control your pheromones," Sid says, interrupting our lusty moment.

Jackson drops his head to the back of the seat.

"You are like the queen of derailing dick," he says in exasperation.

Without missing a beat, Sid quips, "Undefeated champion, five years running."

Shaking his head, he chuckles.

At the hospital, we're the only ones in the waiting room, which works well since there are so many of us. Chris sits in the corner of the room with Mia on his lap. Kat and Sid sit across from Jackson and me, looking through magazines. Laney sits adjacent to them, leaning with her head on Jimmy's shoulder.

After thirty minutes, a young boy rushes in.

"Where's my baby?" He looks around.

Jackson's mother and Nicholas Shaw follow, Nicholas holding a gorgeous little girl in his arms.

"Daddy," she squeals. Stretching her arms out to Chris, she clenches and unclenches her fists in excitement.

Mia slips off his lap, allowing Chris up. He goes straight to her.

"Hey, princess," he coos, taking her from Nicholas. "Come sit with me and mommy."

The little girl's eyes flicker to me before landing on Jackson.

"Jack," she squeals.

"Hey, baby girl," he calls out, grinning.

"Jack," she calls again, smacking her dad's shoulder.

Rolling his eyes, Chris puts her down on her little feet. She wobbles and then finds the right pace to bring her to Jackson.

Jackson puts his arms out, lifting her against his chest.

"You been a good girl?" he asks, tickling her sides.

She giggles, burying her face in his neck.

The precious moment is almost enough to make me hope my period doesn't come.

"Where's my baby?" the little boy asks again, turning to

Gwen and Nicholas.

"The baby isn't here yet." Gwen tousles his hair before collapsing in a seat.

"Come here, Ry," Laney calls the little boy over to her.

Jackson stiffens, catching the tired look on Gwen's face.

Nicholas quickly takes the seat next to her.

Standing out of his seat, he hands the little girl over to Mia's waiting arms.

Chris and Jackson move at the same time to Gwen's side; Chris taking the seat on the other side of her and Jackson squatting in front of her.

They speak in intensely hushed tones before Gwen smiles at each of them and shakes her head.

"She's started some medicine in preparation for surgery," Mia says, taking Jackson's seat.

"She looks so tired," I whisper. "Beautiful, but tired."

Mia nods. "I hate it. Gwen's usually so vibrant and full of life."

The little girl smacks my arm.

"Maggie," Mia scolds.

"It's okay." I smile. "How old is she?"

"Almost two." Mia bounces her with a knee.

Maggie giggles.

"She's gorgeous."

"Thanks." Mia looks up from Maggie to me. "She looks like her daddy."

"I think I see a bit of her mom in her, too." I grin.

"I'm a dad!" Elliott's booming announcement startles everyone.

"You're my dad," Ry says, furrowing his brow.

All eyes study Elliott and Ry's interaction. Elliott lock's eyes on the boy and grins manically. Squatting down, he opens his arms.

"Damn straight, little man," he confirms, and the boy runs into his arms. "I'm a dad for a second time is what I meant."

I furrow my brow, not sure what's going on.

"Ryan is Serena's son," Kat whispers.

"Elliott just adopted him," Laney adds.

I nod, now understanding the dynamic.

"My baby's here?" Ryan asks with a smile.

"You're a big brother, dude. Want to come meet your sister?"

"A girl?" Kat, Mia, and Laney all ask in unison.

If possible, Elliott's grin grows larger.

"Yep. Zoey Mae Brockman came screaming into the world ten minutes ago." He bounces Ryan in his arms. "Mom wants you, little man."

"My baby's here!" Ryan cheers. "We did it!"

"Come on." Elliott motions to us all.

"I'm pretty sure there's a limit on visitors," Laney says, but still stands to follow.

"I don't give a shit," he exclaims. "Come meet my daughter."

Striding out of the room, he carries Ryan down the hall. The rest of them follow, except me.

I stay seated, pulling out my phone. Shooting a text to Kel, I let him know where we are and that I'll be back soon. Sid sits next to me, bumping my shoulder with hers.

"Hey. I can get a cab back to the penthouse," she offers, nodding to my phone.

"We can go together." I slide the phone back in my pocket. "I'm just giving Jackson a minute before I take off."

Sid rolls her eyes.

"What?" I ask.

"You think he's going to let you—"

"Liza?"

Twisting in the chair, I find Jackson poised in the doorway with his brow furrowed.

"Yeah?"

"You coming?"

He lifts a hand toward me.

I shake my head.

"Go ahead. I'm going back to the penthouse. The boys will

be back from school soon." I wave him to go on.

His furrow deepens.

"Well, now you did it," Sid mumbles.

"You want to leave?" he asks, an edge I don't like in his tone.

"It's a family thing," I explain. "I don't want to intrude."

His brow unfurrows, but he doesn't move.

"I can wait for you if you want?" I offer.

"I'm just going to catch a cab," Sid says, slipping out of the room.

"What did I do now?" I ask, my shoulders drooping.

He shakes his head.

"You didn't do anything." He runs his fingers through his hair. "I want you to come with me, but I understand why you're uncomfortable. It just took me a minute."

Lifting from the chair, I close the distance between us, putting my hand on his chest. I raise onto my toes and fist his shirt, pulling him down so I can kiss him. Our tongues slip into the other's mouth, tangling and fighting for dominance.

Breaking the kiss, I drop back to the flat of my feet.

"I'll wait here for you," I say, releasing his shirt and smoothing the wrinkled material. "Take your time."

"I'll be right back," he assures, walking backward out of the room.

Back at the penthouse, Kel sits at the dining table with the boys doing homework.

"Hey," he greets, looking up from some brochures.

I walk toward them and kiss Lucas on the top of his head.

"What are those?" I ask Kel before kissing Sean's head.

"Nothing."

He pushes them into a pile, but I catch the words on one.

"Are those college brochures?" I know my question sounds

way too excited, but I can't control myself.

"I'm just looking at them," he rushes to explain. "Don't get worked up."

Biting my lip, I breathe through my nose, trying to calm the thrill coursing through my veins.

"I won't." I fail at sounding casual.

"I told you she'd act like this," Kel says to Jackson.

I twist to see Jackson give a one shoulder shrug before saying, "Is it really such a bad thing?"

"No," Kel sighs.

"You did this?" I ask Jackson.

"Your brother did it," he responds, flipping through the mail on the counter. "It was his decision to make."

"Can we have pizza?" Lucas asks, looking up from his homework.

"Again? We eat pizza all the time." I purse my lips.

"Chinese?" Sean suggests.

"You know how to win me over." I ruffle Sean's hair.

"We should go out to eat," Jackson announces, lifting a large manila envelope in the air.

"What's that?" Lucas asks.

Jackson rips open the end, pulls out a stack of papers, flips through them, and then presents one page with a seal on it.

"This makes Sean an official member of the Campbell/Shaw household."

All eyes turn to Sean, who drops his pencil and visibly swallows.

"Those papers mean I can stay?" he asks, a bit of sadness in his voice.

Pulling out a chair, I sit next to him and nod.

"Yes."

"What about Grandma?" Tears form in his eyes.

Jackson comes to his side, offering him the paper. He takes it.

"Sean," Jackson starts, "listen, your grandma isn't going to be able to take care of you anymore. She's gotta stay in a place where people can help take care of her."

"The hospital?" Sean asks, looking up from the paper.

"For now," Jackson answers. "But we're looking for a safe place for her to move into where you can visit her anytime you want."

Sean's eyes brighten a little, the guilt he must have felt dissolving a smidge.

"Really?" Hope returns to his face.

"Really," I respond. "We'll make sure she's in a place close to where we live."

Sean launches out of his chair and into my arms. The force scoots my chair back an inch.

"I've dreamed about a mom like you," he says, throat clogged with tears. "I love Grandma, but she's not a mom, ya know?"

Unable to fight my tears, I let them fall and nod. "I know."

"Time to celebrate!" Lucas exclaims, pushing his chair back and hugging his best friend. "We're like real brothers now."

More tears streak my cheeks and Jackson wipes them away.

Jesus, this man twists my insides.

"You stay'n in my kitchen?" Jackson asks, his eyes burning with desire.

I nod. "I'm staying in your kitchen."

His knees come to the floor in front of me before his lips press to mine.

"Gross." Lucas fakes a gag.

Jackson pulls away, one hand cupping my face.

"You won't think so in about five years, my man."

"No way, not me," he argues.

"What about Mia?" Sean sings her name and makes kissing noises before rushing away from Lucas.

"Shut up." He chases after him. "You'll pay for that."

"You sure you're ready for that?" I ask, motioning to the boys with my head.

"Baby, I don't think you realize this just yet, so I'm going to help you out," he says, leaning in closer. "I wasn't ready for you when you stepped on stage at Lux. I wasn't ready to feel more at home and relaxed in your tiny ass apartment than I do in my Seattle house. And I sure as hell wasn't ready for this crazy little family you come with, but..." his mouth comes so close to mine, I feel his breath, "even when it was the last fucking thing I wanted a few months ago, I'm damn ready to make you fall for me the way I'm falling for you, snake charmer."

Oh. My. God. Falling for me?

For a moment, I swear my heart completely stops. And the ensuing heavy thud is an acceptance. The acceptance of a new dream—a dream I would never dared believe was possible.

Our mouths meet and our tongues dance seductively, but the kiss ends too soon.

"Now, let's feed the natives and get them to bed so I can feast on something more delicious."

His eyes roam over my body and I shiver.

"You don't have to make me," I whisper.

The right side of his lip curls.

"Good to fucking know, baby."

Things may be fast, may be too good, but we can handle whatever comes. The truth is I can fall in love with this man. I'm on my way there now.

Epilogue
Jackson

1 ½ Months later...

"Thank Christ tomorrow tonight is the end of this damn show," I exclaim, entering the master bedroom.

It took Julia two weeks to find multiple listings in L.A. and less than two days for me to convince Liza on a three bedroom condo in Brentwood. She fell in love with the wood laminate flooring, which the boys couldn't destroy as quickly as real hardwood, designer stone work, carved sinks, and Viking appliances. The look on her face gave away her excitement and appreciation for the place. The price tag on the place, however, nearly gave her a panic attack.

The $1.8 million was actually an excellent deal on the ready-to-move-in, partially furnished home. It took some convincing and perspective by comparing the cost to the Seattle house. I hadn't purchased the Seattle house alone, of course, but I *did* buy out the rest of the band as they moved on with their lives. And it had been on the market during my time with Laney, but now I'm glad to have it as a place to go when I need to be in Seattle.

And, I suppose, Sean's grandmother being transferred to an assisted living home only a ten-minute walk away and the private school Luke and Sean will attend next year swayed Liza.

Besides, the Brentwood condo at Las Ventanas is a gated community and has fifteen-foot ceilings. Come on, how many places have ceilings high enough I can't touch them or have to duck through a fucking arch to get into the next room. Not to mention the wall-length shower with a built-in tile bench. Definitely an excellent feature when my girl is lucky to top off at five-foot-six barefoot in said shower. Christening the shower is definitely the newest addition to my highlight reel.

"How did rehearsal go with your brother?" Liza steps from the bathroom, twisting her hair on top of her head.

"Good," I answer, hopping onto the bed.

Placing my hands behind my head, I watch her secure the messy bun on her way to the walk-in closet.

"I have more good news."

She reappears with the worn bag she won't let me replace and the new garment bag I bought a week ago.

"You're skipping the photo shoot to spend the night naked with me?" I grin.

Tilting her head, she smiles.

"No, I'm not pregnant." Her smile grows.

A part of me feels the loss of the possibility. It's a part of me I hadn't realized was so ready for a baby with Liza.

Watching my grin fade away, her brow furrows. "You aren't happy about this."

It's not a question.

Inhaling deeply, I take one hand from behind my head and reach out to her. I exhale when she moves without hesitation.

Pulling her onto the bed next to me, I kiss her cheek.

"Jackson?" The trepidation in her question makes me feel like shit.

"It's all good, baby."

Placing my fingers under her chin, I lift her face to mine.

"I think I got a bit too used to the idea of being a dad."

Her eyes widen as a flurry of different emotions fly across her face.

"I'm sorry," she chokes.

"Hey, don't be sorry."

I touch my lips to hers briefly and pull away.

"It's definitely for the best."

Smiling, I move my hand to the side of her face and circle her cheek with my thumb.

"We need time to be just you and me," I say, but then

continue, "and Luke, Sean, and—"

"I get it," she laughs.

Pressing my lips back to hers, I roll so she's beneath me.

"We should celebrate," I pant against her mouth, licking her bottom lip.

"Um…no," she quickly responds. "I just told you I'm not pregnant."

She pushes on my chest to stop my tongue's assault.

"That means I just started my period."

"I don't care." I shrug. "We can take this to the shower."

"You and the damn shower," she giggles, shaking her head. "I swear, it's the only reason you bought this place."

"We bought this place," I correct.

Growing more serious, I capture her eyes with mine. "I'm not gonna have this discussion again. It's all of ours. You got that?"

She nods, swallowing.

"I need to hear you say you got it, Liza."

"I've got it, Jackson," she whispers, biting her lip.

"Good." I give a nod and then dip my face close. "Now, back to naked celebrating."

"You're incorrigible," she says with an exaggerated sigh.

"Does that mean horny?" I purse my lips.

She smacks my chest and laughs.

"Come on, it's summer!" Luke begs Liza.

She's tough as shit. I would've given in three pleases ago.

"You have until midnight, Lucas." Liza crosses her arms over her chest.

It does wonders putting them on display. *She can't be serious about no sex during her period. This isn't fucking medieval times. People fuck through this shit all the time.*

"You're ruining everything," Luke growls. "Blaze and Colton

are going to think I'm a baby."

"Their mom and I already spoke. She laid the rules down for them as well," Liza says through clenched teeth.

"Great," Luke snaps, throwing his hands in the air. "Now they've told everyone else about my *bedtime*."

Liza rolls her eyes, turning away from him to address Julia.

"Video games off by midnight. I don't care if they watch a movie, but it's lights out and down for the night."

"Understood," Julia responds, agreeing to the terms.

Luke growls again, stomping up the stairs.

Liza and Julia aren't best friends by any stretch of the imagination, but she's worked overtime to prove herself to Liza. The atonement was enough for Liza not to say anything when I decided to hire Julia full-time as a personal assistant. In fact, she agrees Julia is great at her job. Her job doesn't typically include watching the boys, but tonight Kel is helping Sid with her equipment for the photo shoot. We also haven't had time to talk about a sitter/nanny situation further than mentioning the thought.

Luke's door slams shut—hard.

Liza fists her hands in frustration.

"I've got this," I blurt. Putting my hands out, I push off the couch in the living room and walk to the stairs.

"You don't have—"

"It's cool."

I slap her ass on my way by her and she squeals.

"You'll just owe me later."

"I could just go beat him myself," she replies.

Giving her a look that feigns horror, I put my hand on my chest, and say, "You will not beat my favorite kid."

Smiling, she shakes her head and turns back to Julia. I finish the climb.

"Open up," I command in a casual tone, knocking on the wooden door.

The door creeps open, Sean standing there with his brow furrowed.

Sean's been so thankful and appreciative, but the darn kid is almost terrified to show any unhappiness or emotion. No matter what we say, he just swallows it down. I'm afraid one day he's going to explode.

I should mention having him talk to Dr. J. Note to self: talk to Liza about it.

Luke lies on his top bunk. He pulls the pillow off his face and sighs when he looks at me.

"So, she sent you to yell at me?" There's a bit of fear in his eyes.

Sitting on the wooden desk in their room, I cross my arms over my chest.

"When have I ever yelled at you?" I ask.

"Never," he mumbles, sitting up and dangling his legs off the edge.

Sean quietly sits on his bottom bunk.

"Exactly," I state. "So, I get you're pissed."

His eyes rise from the floor to my face.

"I was a kid too and it sucks to have a curfew or bedtime, but she's the mom." I shrug.

"I know," he grumbles.

"What time are the twins...what's their names?" I ask, forgetting the two boys Luke and Sean met after we moved in.

"Blaze and Colton," Sean answers.

"Thank you. So, what time are Blaze and Colton coming over?"

Uncrossing my arms, I plant my hands on the desk on either side of me.

"In an hour," Luke mumbles.

Glancing at the Star Wars clock on the wall, I note the time and look back at Luke.

"Luke, my man," I draw, "that's going to be like six hours of video games. You really getting pissed about that?"

"It's embarrassing, Jack," Luke cries, throwing himself back on the bed.

"I feel ya," I concede, "but I also think six hours of video games and then movies to go to sleep is a pretty kick ass deal."

I shift my focus to Sean. Pushing away from the desk, I walk over and crouch in front of him.

"What do you think? You embarrassed?"

Sean's eyes widen and he gives a quick shake of his head.

"So, you think it's a fair deal?"

He nods.

I sigh and push off the desk.

"Sean, buddy, tell me what's on your mind."

His eyes shift to Luke's feet dangling next to him and back to my face.

"Come on, you have to think something," I press.

"He thinks I'm being a jerk to Mom," Luke sighs, still thrown back on the bed.

My eyes don't leave Sean.

"That so?"

Sean starts to nod.

"Use your words, dude."

The look I give stops his nodding.

"I...I think six hours is cool," he whispers.

"But?" I press further, feeling something's unsaid.

"But..." he pauses, taking a breath, "it's embarrassing that she called their mom."

"Hah!" I exclaim, causing Sean to jump. "I knew you could do it."

Giving him an easy punch to the arm, he matches my grin with one of his own.

Straightening to my full height, I step back from the bunk beds.

"I agree, calling their mom was kind of shitty. I'll talk to your mom about it, but remember, that doesn't mean anything will change. She's the boss, my boys."

They nod, half smiling.

"Do me a favor, Luke, and apologize to your mom for the attitude. Okay?"

Our eyes meet and for a moment, he looks thoughtful.

"Good talk. I'll let myself out." Pointing to the door, I spin.

"Hey, Jack?" Luke's call turns me back around.

"Yeah, man?"

"I don't know much about dads, but I think you make a pretty good one," Luke states, and Sean nods.

The air leaves my body, an ache forms like I'm taking double punches to my chest, and all I can do is walk out of the room. I close the door and press my back against the wall, breathing deeply.

He just cracked open my chest, grabbed my heart, and took it. The little fucker stole my heart just like his mother.

Finally able to move again, I stride down the stairs and find Liza at the kitchen bar going through her bag.

"Have you seen my—?"

I grab and spin her around, lifting and planting her ass on the bar.

"What's wrong?" she asks, worry lining her face. "Did Lucas—?"

Putting my hand over her mouth, I take a deep breath, collect my thoughts, and launch everything at her.

"You know those boys are my favorite little fuckers."

She pulls at my hand. I know it's to protest the way I call them little fuckers, but that will have to wait.

"Let me finish," I bark, causing her to still and drop her hands.

Releasing her mouth, I press my palms on the counter on either side of her and push between her legs.

"They just twisted me inside out like a fucking girl losing her virginity on prom night."

She opens her mouth, but the look I give silences her.

"I didn't ask to love you, but I do. I didn't ask for a premade family, but I got one. I didn't plan to feel like this."

Fear flashes in her eyes and tears start to pool.

Shaking my head, I continue, "Don't. You're reading me wrong, baby."

Palming each side of her head, I hold her face inches from mine.

"I thought I knew love, knew I'd found the one before, but I didn't know shit."

Emotion bubbles up and out of me in a harsh laugh.

"I fucking love you, those two boys, your crazy ass cousin, and...well, I'm cool with your brother. Declaring love for him would be fucking creepy as hell, but you get what I'm say'n."

Tears spill from her wide eyes and I wipe them away with my thumbs.

"I fucking love it, Liza. Every goddamn thing about you and all this, I love it."

Leaning forward, I crush my lips to hers in a bruising kiss. Her hands capture my wrists and hold.

Pulling back, I smile down at her.

"And you may not be pregnant now, but you can guaran-fucking-tee it won't take me long to correct that shit."

Her look of surprise morphs to shock, and she asks, "What the hell happened?"

"A fucking revelation, baby."

Liza

Lux Hedonica is home. Even with the new signage to compliment the remodeled front of the building, the inside is still where I belong. The updated furniture only compliments the vintage wall mirrors and bar. Red treats the place like it's his baby, which I completely respect and appreciate. The man may look like he belongs on a tour bus bouncing unwanted guests, but he has a mind for business. And having not been on tour for years, since the end of Corrosive Velocity, he's put his know-how into multiple thriving businesses.

So, three weeks ago, when the contract offers came in from Nobil and Bel Suono Studios, I felt confident with Red reviewing the papers and discussing them with me. After input from Jackson, I formally asked Red to manage my career.

Red's been supportive, brutally honest, and clear about our working arrangement being parallel to the club. He sets up my appearance at the club as if I'm a featured guest so I am free to arrange something else should it arrive. And his suggestion to go with Nobil's deal allows me and Red the freedom to choose most performance venues and appearances, while agreeing to give them exclusive rights to any recorded and live music.

The deal is perfect since I don't have any intentions of becoming a pop singer or doing huge tours like The Forgotten and Hush. Though, I do have a clause requiring me to record with some of their artists, Nobil is listed as my recording label, and I've also agreed to a five venue burlesque tour. The studio time and tour is currently being figured out logistically to allow time for me to work on the creative end of the live show. This means I'll need to record the music in the show for retail sales.

"It's about time!" Sid exclaims when we reach the sitting area of the club.

The tables and chairs stacked off to the far side allow room for different photo shoot sets.

"Damn!" Jackson exclaims, glancing around the room.

"These look great." I take in the scenes.

The large gilded mirror above the VIP booth is draped in red velvet, overflowing into the black leather booth. The table is gone, leaving the opportunity for full body photos. The stage is arranged with a clear bathtub, and pink satin drapes from the ceiling with black and white bows accenting areas. The tub is empty, but a large bubble machine sits just in front. The shimmery white chaise lounge we occasionally use onstage is surrounded by dangling pearls and diamond strands with a white fur rug beneath. The baby grand piano is polished and draped in metallic gold. A plain white background is set up just in front of the bar, and last is a raised platform covered in red satin with a red and white striped background set up behind it.

"Because I'm awesome," Sid boasts, giving me a wink.

"Yes, you are." I nod.

"Go get dressed," she orders. "The costumes are set up and numbered in order."

"Yes, ma'am," I salute.

Turning to Jackson, I push up to my tiptoes for a kiss. He leans down, cupping my ass and squeezing.

"Get a room," Sid teases.

Jackson's head snaps in her direction, a large grin on his face.

"Oh, I can take this to the dressing room if you want?"

"No," Sid cries. "Then I'll never get the pictures."

"See ya in a bit." I pat his chest and disappear backstage to get dressed.

"I have no idea how to put this on." The voice is new, but I know it's Mia.

Entering the changing room, Bethany is fully costumed in a leopard print corset dress. She's leaning over and attaching a garter to Mia's fishnet stocking.

"There you go." She straightens and examines her work.

"Thank you so much," Mia sighs in appreciation. "I don't know how you guys do this all the time."

She places her hands on her black leather corset, rubbing her stomach. The black, leather boy shorts hug her ass perfectly and her legs are complimented by the knee-high gladiator boots.

"You get used to it," I say, dropping my bag on my chair.

A large grin spreads across her face and she slips a black, cat-ear headband on her head.

"Hey," she greets, opening her arms and engulfing me in them.

"I didn't know you were doing the photo shoot." I return the hug. "I thought Chris didn't—"

She pulls back, dropping her arms.

"Yeah, Chris likes to think he's in charge of everything." There's a hint of rebellion in her voice. "Anyway, I figure this is a good compromise. I won't perform live, but I will be a part of the calendar Red is putting together." She moves with a grace that makes me jealous and sits in Bethany's chair. "Besides, he can't argue when he finds out it's for charity." She gives an evil smile.

"You go, girl." Gemma Harper enters the room.

"Red recruited you, too?" Mia asks.

"Yep." She smiles, flipping her neon red curled hair over her shoulder.

She looks around the room and her brow furrows.

"The rest of the band isn't participating?"

"Laney and Kat are in another room." Mia tilts her head toward what used to be a storage room until Red remodeled backstage to provide more private dressing areas.

"Cool," Gemma says to Mia before turning to me. "And you," she starts, walking toward me, "when are you going to come to New York and read for my director? He's dying to add a burlesque inspired steampunk character to the show."

"I believe Red is trying to work it out," I explain. "It's just been a bit…"

"Overwhelming?" Mia offers.

"Yes," I sigh out the word, and drop into my chair.

She nods, understanding written on her face.

"Chris and Jack aren't exactly the same, but they both go balls-to-the-wall when they desire something," she says. "When they work on a song, I won't enter the room for fear of losing a limb."

I laugh.

"Oh my God!" Gemma exclaims, slipping out of her sailor inspired dress. "I remember recording with them. I thought their brotherhood and the band was over, but in the end, they just nod and fist bump."

"That's part of it," I say, shrugging. "The rest is just the career stuff. If I didn't have Jackson and Red, I'd be in a moving truck bound for Pennsylvania."

Gemma holds an emerald green bra-top to her chest with one hand and clasps my shoulder with her left.

"It will take some getting used to, but I'm confident you'll handle it well."

"Thanks." I give a small smile and start slipping off my street clothes.

"My boobs look amazing!" Kat bursts into the room, wearing the circus ringleader costume: shiny, black, second-skin pants, a red brocade corset with gold tassels, thigh-high black boots, and a miniature black and red top hat on her head.

"Let me feel," Mila says, pushing out of the chair and grabbing Kat's boobs.

"Pretty fucking awesome, right?" Kat puffs out her chest.

"Damn, they are pushed up to perfection, aren't they?" Mia taps the curve bulging from the top. "Serena could play a sick beat on them."

"I'm never taking this off." Kat walks over to the loveseat and plops down.

"Yeah, right. One hot, dirty boy and you'll lose the duds in a blink." Laney leans against the doorway dressed in a silver flapper inspired corset. The color compliments her fair skin and light pink hair. The metallic silver stilettos add a couple inches to her tiny frame.

"Where are my models?" Sid yells backstage.

Barging into the room, she looks each of us over, one by one.

"Kat, your tits look awesome. Mia, I may grab your ass. This is fair warning. Laney, you are too fucking cute. I think I want to take you home as a pet."

Laney blinks at Sid as the rest laugh.

"Come on, Hush, we've got to get this shindig started." With a wave of her hand, she motions for them to head out to the scenes.

Mia stops long enough to present her ass to Sid and true to her word, she clasps with both hands.

"Chris is a lucky fucking man," Sid states before following a laughing Mia.

"This is going to be one crazy ass day, isn't it?" Gemma asks, still staring at the door.

"Yep," Bethany and I say in unison.

In a crystal chandelier dress with a white satin corset beneath, my hair pulled up on my head with white feathers, and clear, glass-inspired heels, I walk out for the photo shoot.

"No fucking way, Mia," Chris shouts.

She stands on the gilded mirror stage with her arms over her chest.

"It's for a charity calendar. Stop being—"

"Stop being what?" he interrupts. "Stop not wanting you to be half-naked for millions to see?" He shakes his head violently and then points to the floor. "Get the fuck down and go change."

Dropping her arms to her sides, she fists her wrist-length fishnet-gloved hands.

"Private Island, Chris," she says through clenched teeth.

His body stills.

"You reserved an entire island without fucking asking what I wanted," she continues grinding the words through her teeth.

"Baby," his voice softens.

"Don't baby me," she barks. "You didn't ask about a half-million dollar island, so I don't have to ask about a charity calendar."

Half a million dollars for an island? Did he buy the damn thing?

"I hope you got a receipt to return that shit," Sid mumbles, but shuts up when Chris cuts a glare her way.

"The opportunity presented itself," Chris explains. "It will be the perfect way to keep reporters out of our wedding."

"And you couldn't bother to ask me about it?" Her brow raises.

"Okay, so maybe I could've, but you aren't interested in planning the wedding," he accuses.

Bad move.

Mia's face contorts in anger, but before she can unleash, Sid interrupts.

"I'm just gonna move on to Kat for now. I'll be back," she informs, putting up a finger and pointing to where Kat sits, waiting in front of the red and white striped scene.

"No," Mia blurts. "I'm ready." She nods to Sid and then

glares at Chris.

"Get out of the way, Christopher."

He opens his mouth.

"Christopher Tobias Mason, I swear to God, if you don't walk away right now, not only will there be no sex until we're married, but I'll insist we live separately."

Chris snaps his mouth shut, but flames burn in his eyes.

Grumbling inaudibly, he storms off to lick his wounds in a chair next to Jackson, Red, and...Xavier, I think. It's Xavier who claps Chris on his back, which earns him a glower.

"Damn, girl," Sid whistles and begins the shoot.

While Sid does her thing, I walk over to where the guys are watching.

"Liza, your cousin is a girl after my own heart." Red grins.

"She can be pretty amazing." I return the smile.

"And fucking insane," Xavier mumbles.

I fight not to laugh when I remember the picture Jackson showed me of Xavier in the closet tied up.

"Where's Kel?" I look around for my brother.

"I've got him looking over inventory." Red motions over his shoulder with a thumb. "Your brother is a damn wizard with that shit. I've been trying to get Todd, the head bartender, up to speed on it, but he just can't get it. Your brother stepped right in to help me out and he's rocking it."

"Really?" I ask, the warmth of pride filling my chest.

"Red's almost convinced him to go to Business College," Jackson adds, pulling me to him and sitting me on his knee.

"Seriously?" I ask Red, eyes wide with hope.

"Told him he needs to go to school and I'll hire him to help manage this place." Red shrugs.

"He's only eighteen."

Red nods. "I know. I talked to him. He can help out around here and learn, but won't be official until he has a degree. He won't be serving, so he doesn't have to be twenty-one."

Slipping off Jackson's knee, I wrap my arms around Red's shoulders and squeeze.

"Thank you." I fight off the tears.

"No problem," he says, giving me a one arm hug and pat on my back.

"Okay, he gets it." Jackson grabs my hips, pulling me back onto his lap. "Red was also just telling us about an idea he has for a benefit concert," Jackson says.

"When?" I ask Red.

Sighing, he rubs his large hand over his cropped hair.

"Not sure. It will take at least a year to plan and it's a lot to take on right now."

"Because of my stuff," I say.

"Partly, yeah." He nods.

"Red, you don't have to—"

He puts a big hand in my face, shutting me up.

"I chose to be your manager, Liza. I know the business and you're good business."

He levels a look at me, daring an argument. I keep my mouth shut.

"I'd like to plan it for next year around the anniversary of Ethan's death," Red says, eyes shifting to Xavier.

He stiffens and slowly looks at Red.

"What are you up to?" Xavier's brow furrows.

"I'd like to have Corrosive Velocity play for the benefit," he admits.

"Without a fucking lead singer?" Xavier snaps.

Red shrugs, and says, "I was thinking of asking Chris or Mia to stand in as the front man."

"You're out of your mind if you think Corbin will go for any of this."

"If we present a united front, I think we could get him to step up for a cancer benefit."

Jackson stills and his thigh muscle tightens beneath me.

"We'd probably play the benefit," Chris offers quietly. "I'd have to talk to the guys first, but..." he lets the words die off and completely ignores the topic of singing for Corrosive Velocity.

"Liza," Sid calls, getting my and the rest of the table's

attention. "You're up."

She leans forward to pick up a lens from her bag and catches Xavier staring. Slowly, she raises her middle finger, kisses the tip, and blows. Xavier growls.

"Damn it, she's soooo my kind of crazy."

Red chuckles.

I climb off Jackson's lap and follow Sid to the piano set.

"We're starting here and then you can change for the next set." Sid directs my body in front of the piano, ass facing her camera angle.

"How many of the scenes are we doing?" I ask.

"You are doing all of them." She lies on the floor, focuses her lens, and snaps up at me. "Then Red can decide what he wants to use on the calendar and other shit like your website."

"I have a website?" I ask.

"Don't make that face." She cringes. "It won't photo well."

Schooling my features, I pose for her shot.

"Yes, you have a website." She clicks the camera and climbs from the floor. "You're welcome."

"Sid?" I ask through a perfectly practiced lip curl and eye fucking.

"Yes, my dear." She brings the camera close to my face and snaps.

"I want to hire you."

"For what?" She lowers the camera.

"Well, Jackson has Julia to help him and me, but you can do the website and such. You can obviously still do the other stuff, I just want to be one of your clients."

"You really trust me to help you with stuff?" Her head tilts.

"I trust you with my life, Sidra."

Her nose wrinkles at her full name.

"I trust you with my son."

She smiles and wraps her arms around me, pulling back quickly.

"Holy shit, those crystals are hard as fuck," she states, rubbing her boobs. "They tried to take out the girls."

Shaking my head, I giggle.

It's bittersweet to sit front row at the Hidden Talent finale. And, if I'm honest, I wouldn't be here tonight if Jackson and Chris weren't performing. Their set has been kept a secret, only being mentioned as a surprise performance in the commercials leading up to the show. Jackson won't tell me what they're doing.

The reporters went crazy when Jackson and I entered the building. Over the past weeks, we've established an understanding with most of them. We give the reporters and cameramen ten minutes or so and most will back off. Of course, it doesn't always work and not all of the paparazzi actually follow through, but it does lessen the numbers.

Big Kam is the first to take me away from Jackson, talking about wanting to feature me on a track he's working on. Jackson steals me back, telling Kam to speak to Red.

Tonight, the mentor chairs are gone. They've been given the first few rows for themselves and their guests. Chris and Mia sit on Jackson's right with me on his left. Jimmy, Kat, Laney, Xavier, Sid, and Kel sit a row behind us.

Hushed Mentality is the second act to take the stage and bring the audience to their feet. Xavier fills in on drums since Serena is home with the new baby. Jimmy even steps out from the side and joins Laney. The performance makes me a bit more jealous of Mia. The girl can sing, play guitar, and bare her soul in beautifully constructed lyrics. And the look of pride on Chris' face makes my stomach warm. The raw love in his eyes is the stuff little girls dream about.

Next up is one of the finalists. In fact, it's the sweet bubblegum snob who called me a prostitute. It's taking a lot of effort not to stand up and out sing this little bitch during her performance. It's petty and arrogant, but I know I could do it.

Instead, I take satisfaction knowing she had to follow Mia Ryder's performance.

"I've gotta go back," Jackson whispers.

I smile and nod. He and Chris make their way around the side of the stage into darkness. Anticipation brings pterodactyl size butterflies to life in my stomach.

"It will be great," Mia whispers, slipping into Jackson's empty seat.

"Do you know what they're doing?" I ask in a hush.

She shakes her head. "Chris only said Jackson needed to do this," she says, and glances over her shoulder.

I follow her gaze and find Jimmy.

"The fact that he's not going back has me really curious," she states, her face turning back to me with a large grin.

The stage darkens and a spotlight lands on the host of the show up on a balcony.

"Tonight, we have a special performance by two members of The Forgotten. They will be giving you a peek into their newest unreleased song," he announces with a grin.

The crowd screams.

"In a stripped down performance, I give you, Christopher Mason and Jackson Shaw."

With a wave of his hand, the backdrop of the stage turns blue. A soft spotlight lands on Christopher behind a grand piano and microphone. The piano is slanted so he faces the crowd at an angle. Another illuminates Jackson sitting next to him on a stool, holding his guitar on his lap. A mic stand stretches from the floor toward Jackson's mouth.

The once roaring crowd falls silent.

Jackson starts a slow rhythm, leading everyone along his journey, higher and higher, until Chris comes in with the piano. He strokes keys, licks his lips, and hums into the mic. And then, Jackson's voice fills the room, starting off the song.

"Your presence consumes me.
Taunts me without a single touch.

I'm freed by your beauty,
Making my tainted chambers beat once more."

Chris joins with him on the chorus.

"Intoxicated by your mouth,
You fascinate.
I want to taste the red of your lips.
Intoxicate me."

And then it's back to Jackson.

"Slipping under layers of betrayal,
Desire burrows beneath my flesh.
I crave the torture of your existence,
Hungering to wear the fragrance of your skin."

They continue to alternate between the two.

"Intoxicated by your charms,
You taunt.
I want to taste the words you speak.
Intoxicate me.

Eyes see through the illusion,
Piercing the darkest parts of my soul.
Fear of a four letter word disintegrates,
Replaced with a need for devotion.

Intoxicated by your kiss,
You haunt.
I want to taste the air you breathe.
Intoxicate me.

My shadowed heart is unworthy,
But I'll own your love.

I sacrifice what remains of my soul,
Staking yours with my claim.

Intoxicated by you.
Devoted to your taste.
I will savor your submission.
Intoxicate me."

Chris carries the last note to a place Jackson can't. The stage dims back down and the crowd erupts so loudly, my first reflex is to cover my ears. Then, I see him.

Jackson strides to the end of the stage, focused on our seats. There's no way he can see me with the spotlight on his face, but he knows where to find me.

"Go to him," Sid orders, shoving at my back.

"That was for you, Liza," Laney adds. "Go to him," she yells on a laugh.

He leaps down from the stage, a spotlight finding and following his every move. Mia grabs my arm and pulls. I finally move, meeting Jackson halfway between the seats and stage.

Jackson slides his hands up the sides of my neck and holds my head. Thumbs under my jaw, he tilts my head and leans in close.

"I fucking love you, Eliza."

His words dampen my lips and underwear.

"I love you, Jackson," I respond.

"Say it again," he says against my lips.

"I love you."

Our lips meet in a mutually hungry kiss as the cheer of the crowd fades away around us.

END

Coming Soon...

Stellar Collision (a Falling Stars novella)

Christopher Mason is done waiting. He's going to get his ring and last name on Mia Ryder if it causes him the loss of his balls.

Chris and Mia share a home, daughter, and life. Both of them know its forever, but someone has a secret and is tired of the waiting game. A destination wedding, immediate family and a week on a private island is any girl's dream, right? Christopher Mason is hoping and praying it is – for both he and his balls sake.

It's the moment you've been waiting for, the wedding of the year.

Tentative Release – Fall 2015

Snare (a Falling Stars novel) Book 3

When two explosive personalities collide, it can only end in disaster.

Xavier Stone, former drummer to one of the greatest rock bands, Corrosive Velocity, finds himself a full-time dad, fearing the loss of the mother of his children, and possibly losing what's left of his band mates for good.

Sidra Campbell is loud, crazy-funny, brutally honest, and curvy. She came to L.A. to support her cousin Liza, but she's also running from the vicious cycle she left behind in Pennsylvania. To everyone else, she appears confident and happy, but they're always the ones hiding the deepest pain.

When two explosive personalities collide, one runs and the other snares.

Tentative Release – Winter 2015

Other Books by Sadie Grubor

Falling Stars Series

Falling Stars
Stellar Evolution (a Falling Stars novella)
Hidden in the Stars (a Falling Stars novel) book 2
Stellar Collision (a Falling Stars novella) coming soon...
Snare (a Falling Stars novel) book 3 coming soon...

Modern Arrangements Trilogy

Save the Date
Here Comes the Bride
Happily Ever Addendum
Terms and Conditions

Stand Alones:

Live-In-Position

All Grown Up

VEGAS follows you home

About the Author

To keep up to date on upcoming releases, sneak peeks, cover reveals, and inspirational music & images you can find Sadie Grubor on Facebook, Twitter, Goodreads, and her website.

Amazon Author Page: Sadie Grubor
Facebook: www.facebook.com/authorsadiegrubor
Goodreads: Sadie Grubor
Website: www.sadiegrubor.com
Twitter: https://twitter.com/SadieGrubor

You can also find me on Authorgraph.

About the Editor

It has been my pleasure to work with Monica, and I look forward to working with her in the future. She already knows all the crazy I have planned for her.

THANK YOU MONICA!!!

This is where you can find her, but she's really, really, really, really, really, busy, so she can't…. OKAY, perhaps I'm being a bit selfish. I'll still be pouty about it, just saying!

Monica Black – Freelance Editor
www.facebook.com/wordnerdediting
www.wordnerdediting.com

Sneak Peek:

Guided Love by Tracie Redmond: Chapter One

Sam

I never realized how much crap one person accumulates. I mean, seriously, I am standing in my tiny apartment surrounded by fifty boxes full of crap. I absolutely hate moving, not that I have moved that much. Only once, really, and that was to attend college four years ago. Yet, now that I have graduated, I am ready to start my life.

"You have so much stuff, Sam. Where the hell did it all come from?" my friend Gabby yells, as she is trying to rummage through my closet. I know what she is doing, she was supposed to help me pack and label but she hasn't moved from that closet and she keeps pulling clothes out telling me that I don't have to take them. Yep, her pile is growing and she hasn't packed one box yet.

"Gabby, get your ass out of my closet and start taping some boxes for me. I have to have all of this packed and loaded in the next two days." I hear her sigh, but I also hear the tape and movement of boxes. Thank goodness.

"I don't know why you're moving across the country, Sam; you didn't even land a permanent job in Philadelphia yet. Why not just stay here in the beautiful state of California? You're not even going to know anyone on the East Coast."

"I'm moving to be closer to Camaron, you know that, and I do have a job at Camaron's shop."

"Yeah, as the bookkeeper. Come on, Sam, you didn't bust your ass to go through four years of college to move across country to be a freaking bookkeeper!"

Gabby is getting emotional, I can hear it in her voice. She has been my friend for the last four years. She truly is a sweet soul and I know she doesn't want me to move, but this has always been the plan.

Camaron and I have been friends since elementary school. I met him the first day of second grade. Some mean girls were picking on me, pulling my hair and throwing dirt at me and

Camaron came to my rescue. A big fourth grader coming in and protecting me. From that day on, my loyalty and heart belonged to Camaron Willis. During recess, he would go up behind the slides and pull out a tablet and draw. I didn't think he would want a second grader hanging around, but he always let me stay. We would be "friends forever," he would say, and we have from that day on.

Even when we started high school and we found ourselves in two different cliques, nothing broke us. I became the "nerd" and Camaron became the "freak." I joined the math club and the debate team, while Camaron dyed his blonde hair black and started to pierce and tattoo his body. Looking at us you would think we had nothing in common, but looks could be deceiving. No one could understand the weird connection that we have, saying everything to each other with just one look. When I was a sophomore and Cam a senior, we made our plan. He was going to graduate that year and get his Associates Degree in art at the local community college, while I continued school. Then I would go to college and get a degree in journalism. We would move to the city and he would open his own studio and I would become a famous author. When I graduated, I chose not to attend the local university, and went two hours away to USC.

That was a big change since Camaron and I never spent time apart. It was different, being all alone and having to meet new people; yet, the bond Cam and I have, didn't diminish. We talked multiple times a day and saw each other whenever I was able to head home on weekends. It wasn't that lonely, especially when I finally became friends with Gabby. While I was away, Camaron actually did an apprenticeship at a local tattoo parlor. He shadowed Rags the owner and learned the art of tattooing. He was determined to be the best, his dream of opening a studio, turned into opening a tattoo parlor. He is an incredible artist and became one of the best tattoo artists in our area.

Yet, he wanted bigger and better and staying here in California, was not in the cards. I remember the day he broke the news to me. He drove down and surprised me that morning. I knew something was up because it was Saturday and there is no way Camaron would be up and visiting me before ten. When I opened the door I knew, by looking at his face, that something was wrong.

"Hey, Cam, are pigs flying? What's going on? Why are you here before ten am?"

He rolled his eyes at me. "I wanted to see my anchor, I've missed you," he said before giving a slight pause. "We need to talk."

Yeah, something was up. He was using his nickname for me: his Anchor—that's— what he calls me. I am the "only constant in his life" he says. He never opens up to anyone——no one has gotten through the walls he built, except me.

"Okay, Camaron, what's up? You have me nervous here."

We walked into my apartment. I notice he truly looks like he is going to be sick, as he is pacing back and forth, just mumbling.

"Camaron Willis! You better tell me what the hell is going on before I come over there and kick your ass."

"Yeah, as if you kick my ass. I would love to see that," he says. "Wouldn't want you to chip a nail or get a hair out of place in your perfect bun, Sam," he smirked. "Okay, sit down, I want to talk to you and I need to say this as fast as possible."

My heart stopped. What could be this important? It's a girl. He found someone and now he is here telling me that he is getting married or worse he is having a baby—he is having a baby with someone else. Ugh, why didn't I ever tell him! Why didn't I ever let him know that he owns my heart and soul? Dear goodness, I think I am going to be sick!

"So, what, did you find the love of your life and now you're having a baby and getting married?"

Oh my, I can't believe I just asked that. What is wrong with me?

"Sam, you are hysterical, aren't you. Come, sit down, please. You know I'm never getting married and you are the only woman in my life that counts. You're my anchor, babe."

Thank goodness he laughs at my reaction. I sit down and look at him—he still looks nervous.

"Okay, Sam, there has been a small change to our plans. Remember we said that we were moving to the city after you graduate, and live our dreams?"

"Yeah, I remember."

"That's still the plan, but the city and time frame has changed."

"What do you mean the time frame and what city are we going to?"

"Well, that's the thing. Instead of moving to San Diego, when you graduate, you'll be moving to Philadelphia, with me. I'm moving there . . . today."

"What! What the hell, Camaron? What do you mean you're moving to Philadelphia? Like, Philadelphia on the East Coast? TODAY! I don't understand what you're saying!"

My heart is breaking here. I can't stop the tears that are falling from my eyes. It's not a girl and it's not a baby, it is much worse-- Camaron is leaving me. I look up at him and he looks mad.

"How could you leave me, Camaron?"

"Leave you? I am following my dream here, Sam. How could you even ask me to stay? You are my best friend, the one person who always said I should be happy. 'Find your happiness, Camaron'!

And now, now that I have this huge opportunity to go and open a shop with Rags' nephew, you are asking me why I'm leaving you? Sam, I'm not leaving you. I'm always going to be there, just like when you left to come here. We'll still talk on the phone. And when you graduate, you will come and be with me. We will live our dreams, Sam, we ll have it all."

"I know you're right and I know that I can't ask you not to go, but freaking Philadelphia, Pennsylvania? Seriously, Camaron, that is across the country!"

Available Now at Barnes and Noble and Amazon

Tracie Redmond: Author Biography

I was born and raised in Northeastern, Pennsylvania where I still live today with my husband and three beautiful children. Like everyone, I have had my ups and downs and have seen my life take a complete change. Previously, I was a working mom putting in 60 hours a week as a Financial Advisor but with the sudden loss of my mom who was my best friend I found myself giving up the suits and meetings for jeans and snack time. I have always had the passion for reading and found an escape through the words of all the talented authors I have read. My passion allowed me the opportunity to blog and to get a wonderful insight into the indie world. I have enormous pride and stay true to the characters and their stories as they reveal themselves to me. I am so excited to have this opportunity to share my stories and hope you love them as much as I do.

Made in the USA
Las Vegas, NV
05 April 2025

20571622R00212